They

"Don't worry, boy," the old man added reassuringly, *"they* won't bother us."

The younger man nodded respectfully, but in his heart, he didn't believe his father. *They* were beyond the old man's control. You might as well promise to keep away a dust storm. All five men clamored into the giant "king cab" of the fire truck. It was a beautiful machine, bright green and chrome with all manner of hoses and fixtures attached to it. It was four-wheel-drive, and could carry 2,000 gallons of water or fire retardant spray over nearly any surface. Iverson was very proud of Hualapai's lone fire truck. It was one of his jobs to maintain it, and this he did meticulously. He changed its oil and other fluids out every three months whether the truck had been taken out or not. He kept its chrome polished to a lustrous shine, and had vacuumed and scrubbed its interior so thoroughly that the seats showed no sign of the rugged treatment they'd received over the years. He was obsessive about it, and so good at it that he had received a county citation in recognition of the work he'd done. He kept it framed in his living room above the flat screen TV he used for his Xbox.

The men turned on the lights, fired up the siren, and barreled out of the stationhouse as fast as they could. They smiled nervously at one another as they drove southwest out of town toward Highway 447. A few moments later, they swung left off the comforting paved highway to become the vanguard of fast-moving cloud of dust as they bounced down a barely maintained gravel road into the heart of the Smoke Creek Desert.

Iverson sunk down into his seat, not bothering to look out of the windows at the desolate landscape they were passing through. To an outsider it looked just like the surface of the Black Rock Desert: but not to him. The Black Rock was home. The Smoke Creek was another kind of place entirely, a big, empty stretch of dead that formed a kind of "Bermuda Triangle" between Susanville, Hualapai, and the Paiute town of Sutcliff. Locals from all three towns generally avoided it, and even some smarter city people knew not to drive through it. It had its... people... but there was only one inhabitant of Smoke Creek that Iverson knew and liked. Wolfman Walker. He was too smart to ever have a fire at his place, so that obviously wasn't where they were headed.

An Unforgiving Land Reloaded

Tales of Horror from the Black Rock Desert

by Jason S. Walters

a BlackWyrm book
Louisville, Kentucky

AN UNFORGIVING LAND, RELOADED
Frightening Stories & Opinionated Essays from the Black Rock Desert

By Jason S. Walters
Copyright © by BlackWyrm Games

All rights reserved, including the right to reproduce this book, or portion thereof, in any form. Written permission must be secured from the publisher to use or reproduce any part of this book, except for brief quotations in critical reviews or articles.

The characters in this novel are fictitious. Any resemblance to actual persons living or dead is purely coincidental.

A BlackWyrm Book
BlackWyrm Publishing
10307 Chimney Ridge Ct, Louisville, KY 40299

ISBN: 978-1-61318-141-6
Cover design by Dave Mattingly
Edited by Carol Darnell

First edition: July 2010
Second edition: August 2013

Originally publicized as *The Hualapai Cycle* and published as *An Unforgiving Land* in 2010. New edition includes the story *Crucified Coyote* and a variety of essays that were not included in the first edition.

ABOUT JASON S. WALTERS

For *The Vast White*

"I was extremely impressed with [the Vast White] – it's funny, extremely well written, highly original, and has some really terrific innovations." — John O'Neill, *Black Gate*

"Jason Walters has a bloodhound's nose for story, a jeweler's eye for detail and a healthy appreciation of the joys of history, both true and certainly-should-be-true." — Darren Watts, *Millennium City*

"Jason Walters's work never fails to impress and intrigue me. With a voice that mixes intelligence, humor, wisdom, insight into the human condition, and gleefully barbed observations about life, he's a desert-bred cross between Hunter S. Thompson and Chris Rock who's thankfully chosen to set his sights on genre fiction rather than reporting or comedy. I'm already looking forward to his next book." — Steven S. Long, *Dark Champions*

"Sometimes the cover says it all. Desert setting. Mythological creatures. Warriors battling to the death. An overemphasis on the female anatomy. The Vast White is one for the guys." — *Tribute Books Reviews*

For *An Unforgiving Land*

"These are horror stories. But what makes them unusual and evocative is that the horrors rise right out of the rocks and sand and flora and fauna of the desert. A Judas horse, trained to help men bring in herds of mustangs, realizes it's turning its own kind into dog food — and rebels. Hunters encounter a cat that is ... well, just a little bigger and wilder than all the rest. A lonely old lady invites a pack of coyotes to do a deed that she herself cannot. Even the meth cookers are a little crazier, a little more violent, and quite a lot stranger in this bleak land. But if you've spent time in the desert you'll almost believe these things could be real." — Claire Wolfe, *www.backwoodshome.com*

"A tribute to the people of Gerlach." — *Reno Gazette Journal*

"This collection of horrific short stories from Nevada's Black Rock Desert will give you nightmares for years to come." — Dave Mattingly, *The Algernon Files*

"This book may need a warning label: a possible side effect is that your mind will become altered." — Marge Fulton, *All Roads Lead to Hazard* and *The Holler*

"The skillful structure of the stories is matched by Walter's wordcraft. He evokes the danger and beauty of the Black Rock environment in spare terms that, over time, allow the reader to get to know the place." — *RobotViking*

"In the introduction of *An Unforgiving* Land Jason explains the the book is a love story to his home and the Black Rock Desert. That is really what this is in a horrific and twisted sort of way. The tales meander to different peoples, places, and events giving the reader a bitter taste of this desolate place." — *Kingbeast's Lair*

"Eight well written but dark and stark tales of life in and around Hualapai on the Black Rock Desert." — *Alternative Worlds*

"I frickin' loved reading *An Unforgiving Land*. Like many, my introduction to the Black Rock Desert was through Burning Man. But over the years as the newness of Burning Man has waned, the call to the desert has waxed. There is something deeply American, rugged, mysterious, independent – something Cowboy that comes out in me when I visit this place. In *An Unforgiving Land* the author trapped into this resonance and took me there from the cozy confines of my Seattle condo. If, like me, you feel the call of this haunting place – with or without Burning Man – do yourself a favor and buy this book. You won't be disappointed!" — Peter Adkinson, *GenCon*

"Jason Walters' tales are violent, lustful, and more than anything else, compelling. The sex demon of Burning Man is, alone, worthy of iconic stature. At once obvious and unthinkable, she-who-cannot-be-denied is one of the great creations of contemporary literature. The stories of wacko cowboys, tattooed postmodern crazies and supernatural fauna at first appear unrelated, but they build to a narrative of place – and end-of-the-road, out-of-chances, desperate kind of place that is both the real Northwestern Nevada and a state of mind. You will never see the West the same way again. You will never hear the wind rustling in sagebrush without reaching for your gun, even though you know the shots will not save you. When you read Walters, you enter a parallel universe that leaves you creepily unsure of your own, forever." — Donald Asher, author and lecturer

For *Posthegemony: Terra Nomenklatura*

"Mr. Walters's dystopian Utopia is a great example of how to create a plausible, convincing society. It's frighteningly realistic because one can easily imagine such a world coming to pass." — James Cambias, *Terran Empire*

"I really think Jason has something special with Posthegemony." — *Kingbeast's Lair*

Introduction

Gerlach, Nevada isn't much like San Francisco, California. Of course, Gerlach isn't much like anywhere. A tiny, isolated community nestled into the vast Black Rock Desert some 130 miles north of Reno; it is as remote from civilization as some of the outer Bahamas. Moreover, like all such isolated places, it exists in a dimension uniquely its own. To fall in love with such a place is to be doomed by a longing few understand. It slowly changes you, until you're incompatible with the life you once knew. The more time you spend in the Black Rock, the more you long to vanish into its desolate depths, and to wander its wild valleys and uninhabited mountains toward the distant horizon. You learn to savor the emptiness of the place, and to enjoy the privacy that is promised by that emptiness. The Black Rock becomes ever more real even as your own life becomes illusory: something to be endured rather than enjoyed. Eventually, the siren's song of the desert becomes so unbearable that there is no choice but to abandon that life for its barren embrace.

Like most San Franciscans, I first became aware of Gerlach and the Black Rock Desert because of the Burning Man Festival: that awesome, awful, hard-to-describe gala of 50,000 punk rockers and pyromaniacs that happens every Labor Day weekend. Unlike most San Franciscans, I became more interested in the area itself than the festival that takes place there. It's vast, open spaces and hard-bitten, independent people spoke to me in a way that San Francisco's jostling crowds never could. The more I came to know this unique land and its equally unique inhabitants, the more I came to admire them both. Eventually, I ceased resisting the desire to become part of that place, and moved there for good.

To most people the mythology of the Black Rock Desert is the mythology of Burning Man: orgasms, ecstasy, and things that explode in the night. Indeed, Burning Man is part of the mythology of the Black Rock Desert. However, it is only one part. Northwestern Nevada has its own indigenous, organically grown myths and legends that can be traced back thousands of years to when the first family of proto-Paiute Indians wandered over the Sierras, cut around the Granite Mountains, turned to one another, and said: "Wow - this looks like *Hell*! Let's live here!" Since then settlers and prospectors, cowboys and shopkeepers, railroad men and road workers, hippies, hunters, survivalists, and artists have all lent a hand in growing its peculiar culture. It is an exotic, hothouse flower, doomed to wilt if forced into close contact with the outside world that it eternally seeks to avoid.

There have been several fine volumes written about the history, geography, and people of rural northwestern Nevada. This book isn't one of them. The imaginary community of Hualapai envisioned in its pages isn't Gerlach. It's similar, but not the same. From the front porch of my battered doublewide, I can look down upon what used to be the town of Hualapai. Nothing is left of it now but a ramshackle, unpainted building in the middle of Burning Man's work ranch. Yet in the universe imagined in this collection of stories that town survived and thrived rather than being abandoned when the mines ran dry. Because it survived, the real towns Gerlach and Empire never needed to exist. Reality in this invented universe took a different fork in the road of time and then, being mischievous, took several more for good measure.

The world of *An Unforgiving Land* isn't our world. Its geography, roads, and rules are all slightly different. It exists close to this reality, but not in it. Strange, horrifying, and impossible things happen in that place. They are not things that have happened in ours, but they are close. The largest mountain lion killed in the history of the Black Rock Desert was indeed named Fat Albert. The BLM does herd up mustangs using a Judas Horse. The local people do have their own camp at the Burning Man Festival. Heavily armed speed freaks do inhabit the Smoke Creek Desert, as does a very decent man who prefers to live alone with his wolves. That too is true.

This book is my tribute to the people of Gerlach. While purely fictional, the heroes and protagonists of *An Unforgiving Land* - Hippie, the PH, Iverson, the Scarred Girl, Uncle Hank, and the Guerrero family - contain bits and pieces of real people from that area. Heroic, sturdy, individualistic men and women who need nothing from the outside world save to be left alone by it. It is my love poem to a people that I fear will pass from the pages of history uncelebrated. A truly egalitarian culture one can join by merely surviving in the place from which it sprung. Its characters, though in many ways flawed, behave in the heroic, larger-than-life manner that I know my friends and neighbors would behave if confronted with giant mountain lions, carnivorous horses, or voracious desert gods. Even in a pretend universe, their beloved desert rewards strength of character and self-reliance, while punishing weakness and ignorance.

In conclusion, this collection of short stories is one writer's attempt to take a snapshot of some of what is best, most noble, and human about a group of Americans that are the most American of us all. If I were a different sort of writer, I would have crafted a different sort of book; but I am a writer of fantasy, so this is the best tribute I can give. It is my portrait of a way of life that may yet vanish, consumed by the insatiable hungers of an urban America that demands more and more from its wild places and rural provinces. In the time I've lived in the Black Rock Desert, Sempra Energy, a 12 billion dollar S&P 500 company, attempted to build the largest coal powered plant in America's history right in her heart. Meanwhile, Sonterra Development, a powerful collaboration between developers and agribusiness, is attempting to gain permission to pump the vast majority of the region's water south to Reno's ever-growing bedroom communities. Local people working in conjunction with environmental, hunting, and other groups have thus far thwarted these schemes, but it is uncertain how much longer any wild place in the West can hold out against an indifferent, urbane America whose appetites only increase and nature becomes more callous as it changes and grows.

That is far more horrifying than any monster you will find in this book.

Table of Contents

Story: Desert Dawgs...1
Essay: Evil Eight: The Secret Language of Slasher Films............23
Story: Phat Albert 32
Essay: The Three Periods of Survivalist Literature......................54
Story: Judas Horse 61
Essay: The Coals, Waiting To Become Ashes 74
Story: Big Momma..79
Essay: Roadside Crosses 107
Story: Tweaker Creek 110
Essay: Unloved Dogs. Unloved Children. Unloved Old Men and Women..133
Story: Crippled Stray 135
Essay: Out Here In The Freezing Fog 155
Story: Mexican Cowboy..157
Essay: Ironic Antipathy: The Relationship Between Gerlach Locals and the BLM 186
Story: Crucified Coyote 189
Essay: Geppetto's Bench 198
Story: Guerrero's War..203
Essay: The Angel and the Saint...271

Dedication: For the people of Gerlach and Empire, who stood by my daughter when others would have turned away.

Desert Dawgs

>Here's how to survive:
>Watch as everyone around you dies.
>Scream until your eyes work.
>They will work when you pick up a weapon.
>They will work when something changes.
>Maybe the Native Americans are just like you.
>Maybe money, your Father, is the great tyrant.
>Pick up a weapon and gain sight.
>You will fight back or die.
>You will fight back.
>You will become a girl who is a boy.
>—Daphne Gottlieb, *Final Girl II: The Frame*

If the desert is like God – vast and unknowable, with a logic that only prophets and madmen can understand – then the Black Rock Desert is a dead god. The remnant of a long deceased inland sea, it stretches lifelessly across northern Nevada like the corpse of every dream the settlers dragged west. A flat, unbroken wasteland of baked clay surrounded on all sides by uninhabited mountain ranges, it's also the annual site of the massive drug, sex, and pyromania festival known as The Burning Man. The rest of the year the Playa ("the Beach" in Spanish) and its surrounding mountains keep their secrets to themselves.

Because of this annual festival, the Black Rock has erotic connotations to many San Franciscans. Even by the jaded standards of that pleasure-and-pain-seeking culture, it is a place of almost mythical extremes: orgasms and sunburns, acid highs and hangovers, hot springs and blowing sand. This is probably why Jamie got wet seconds after Chris turned his Scion off Highway 35 and headed out into the dust.

Cars always made her horny. She figured it had something to do with the things they symbolized: independence, wealth, status, and stuff like that. She also liked the comfort they provided. Compared to the leathery old cowboy that had just given them directions, inside of the car she was an astronaut traveling through dusty space: in her environment, but not of it. Even if she wasn't that impressed with Chris' ride (the little purple Scion looked like a giant matchbox car to her), the fact that he was willing to trash it going off road to please her was a big turn on.

Jamie's top and sports bra were off before her poor befuddled boy even knew what was happening. She had his zipper open and was going down on him before his body had a chance to respond. Moments later the little van swerved crazily in the desert, changing directions like a ball bouncing around a pool table. When she was certain he was ready, Jamie pulled her miniskirt up and straddled him, cutting off his view entirely.

Chris mashed down on the accelerator as he entered her. He kept it down for the most incredible two minutes of his life.

"What the hell," he thought as he climaxed into her, "it's not like there's anything to hit out here."

Hippie shoveled gravel. It wasn't that he enjoyed shoveling gravel. Hell, who does; especially in summer? Unfortunately, one of the hydraulic lines on his skid steer was busted, and it would take two whole tanks of gas and the better part of a day to go to Fernley for another one. That was a whole lot of drinking money and time gone for the dubious privilege of going into the outside world. So, he shoveled.

It had been a bad year for brush fires. The eastern side of the Sierras had been one big inferno for the last two weeks. Lightning strikes had set off dozens of smaller blazes in the hills outside of Reno. The nearest one was over sixty miles away, but his sensitive nose could still smell the smoke.

Graveling the firebreaks around his trailer-and-Quonset-hut compound was scant protection against a serious desert wildfire, but it was his only protection. The Hualapai volunteer fire department was a half-hour drive from his spread; too far away to save him if the worst happened. He didn't trust the Bureau of Land Management's firefighters to come at all. Not for him.

So, he shoveled.

He was raking roadbed evenly along the side of a singlewide when one of those goofy-looking new minivans pulled into his driveway. He squinted at it. "A Scion, maybe?" he thought to himself, "Who makes that, anyway? Toyota?"

The burgundy box gingerly picked its way three hundred yards up his rutted, river rock covered driveway until it finally came to rest in a cloud of dust about a dozen feet from him. Its doors opened, disgorging a young, pale pair of what looked like Californians. They were good-looking, in the way that people from places like Los Angeles and San Francisco are good-looking, anyhow. If you took away the piercings and most of the tattoos, one of them looked a lot like a girl Hippie has dated back in the '70s.

"Can I help you folks?" he asked.

"Yes sir." The boy with the pompadour was polite at least. "Could you point us in the direction of the road that leads to Soldier Meadows? We must have missed it."

"You've been coming down 35 east or west?"

"East." Yeah. That would figure. Californians.

"Well," Hippie scratched his salt-and-pepper stubble and glanced at the girl. Could his old girlfriend have had a daughter? "There are a couple of ways you could go. Best way is to drive about five mile that way and hang a left onto the gravel road. There's a sign."

He pointed helpfully.

"It'll be a bit hard on that rig of yours, but it's the easiest way to get out there if you're not from around here. It's about 50 miles, so take a few hours and take it slow."

"We were hoping to take the road that leads out onto the Playa. Is that in the same direction?"

"Oh," he hesitated, and then shook his gray ponytail. "You don't want to take your nice new car out there. You'll never get all of the playa dust out – even getting it detailed won't help – and it's always possible that a new wallow has opened up along the road somewhere."

The young man looked at him blankly.

"The Playa is geothermally active," Hippie explained. "Hot water bubbles to the surface and turns the ground into something like clay. New wallows open up all the time and people get stuck in 'em miles from any help. They can be hard to spot at a distance. If you're not from around here, you probably won't see one until it's too late."

"Take the 50-mile road. It's slow and it'll play hell on your suspension, but it's safe."

The kid smiled. It was a cocky smile; the kind found on young men who had never yet caught the whiff of death.

"No worry there, sir. Our car has GPS and a digital compass. We can't get lost."

Hippie nodded, but not in agreement.

"Well, most places that's true, yeah. But 'bout a million years ago a bit meteor hit over there at the base of King Lear." He pointed to a sheer mountain just visible in the distance. "It sprayed magnetic iron all over the place out there. Compasses don't work worth a damn, and even after all these years its plays hell on everything from cell phones to satellite radio."

The kid just smiled at him.

"Crater's still there," he added rather weakly. They weren't going to listen to him.

"Please, sir." The girl spoke for the first time. "We've heard that it's beautiful out on the Playa floor. We may never come out this way again, and we'd really like to see it at least once."

He signed inwardly. She was lying. The girl looked like a Burner – a person that went to Burning Man – which means that she'd been out here before; though probably not as far out as Soldier Meadows. It was a nice place. He was envious that the young couple had the money to spend the night at the combination dude ranch/bed and breakfast. Why couldn't they just take the 50-mile road to Solider Meadows? Why didn't the young ever listed to the old? He could already tell that they weren't going to take his advice.

"Well," he knew that he sounded reluctant, "if you're fixed on going out there, go down to 12 Mile and get onto the desert there. Drive in about a quarter mile, and then turn left. That'd be north."

The young couple nodded in unison. They weren't really paying attention. He sighed again inwardly.

"Pay close attention. Things can get real confusing out there. Now, you'll find some jeep tracks that you can follow. You're going to drive about 20 mile down that road before you come to a wooden pole that's been driven into the playa floor. That's your marker. Turn left again, and then toward the Calicos – that's that range over there."

He pointed.

"You should hit an obvious gravel road 'bout two miles later. That'll take you all the way to Soldier Meadows. Now, you're rig's gadgets are going to start acting funny 'bout 10 mile out. So stick to my directions."

"There are other poles and other tracks out there, but don't take 'em," he added a bit hastily. "They don't lead anywhere good."

"Does anyone live out there, sir?"

It stung him a little that the pretty girl called his sir, but only a little. He was old enough to be her father, after all.

"Nope," he paused for a moment. "Well, only some old desert rats that won't bother anybody who doesn't bother them. You won't run into them. Still, this is a big country. No way that the sheriff in Hualapai can keep track of everything goes on out here. Three-point-five million acres of beautiful nothing: it was outlaw country back in the day, and in many ways, it still is. So be smart and follow my directions *carefully,* all right?"

They nodded politely. The young kid with the pompadour thanked him profusely, and the pretty girl favored him with a smile that could have melted solid rock. Then they clamored back into their ridiculous little rig and drove away. Hippie thought about things for a while as he watched their car turn off his spread and speed its way down 35. Then he set down his shovel, walked over to his truck, and made sure that he had at least half a tank of gas.

"Well," she thought when it was all over, "that was certainly impressive. Usually they stop. Or at least they slow down." Chris was the first man actually to speed up when she did something like that. Still topless, she flopped back into her seat and luxuriated in the cool comfort of the air conditioning. Chris still had a startled, somewhat amazed look on his face.

He should, she thought.

They zoomed along, each wrapped in their own peculiar afterglow as they shot randomly across the vast, white flat that is the Black Rock Desert. It was then that Chris noticed something was wrong.

"Hell," he thought, "that old boy was right." The electronic compass mounted above his head to the right was going crazy, spewing out directions in a completely random manner. East. North. South. West. East. East. East. South. West. North. He reached down and turned on his Global Positioning System, or GPS. The screen came on, wavered for a moment as if hesitating, and then displayed the warning, "No Signal. Location Unknown."

Chris whistled, and then motioned to Jamie. He pointed first at the GPS, then up at the compass. She looked at them but didn't really understand. It was too alien, too far out of her experience. As far as she knew, electronic devices didn't just stop functioning. Sure, if you dropped them then maybe they'd break – or maybe if you didn't put batteries in them or something – but they didn't just stop working for no reason.

"Yeah," Chris externalized, "it looks like what that old boy told us is true. These black rocks you see every once and a while out here on the floor must be magnetized iron – just like he said. It's screwing up all of the car's electronics. We're lucky it drives at all."

She shivered at that thought.

Chris glanced about, really *looking* at where he was for the first time in five or ten minutes. He was on a vast plane surrounded on all sides by towering mountain ranges, most of them nothing more than lifeless black stone. Here and there small, brown tornadoes of dust zoomed about – exclamation points indicating nothing. He knew that the old cowboy had told him to stay on the far side of the Calicos. The problem was that he didn't know precisely which of the mountain ranges the Calicos were. They all looked pretty much alike to him. He picked the one he thought was the most likely candidate, turned his car, and began driving in that direction. Before too long he found a pair of jeep tracks in the desert.

Well, that's a good sign, he thought. *How many jeep tracks could there be out here, anyhow?*

It seemed to lead in the direction of the mountain range he thought were the Calicos; or, more specifically, in between them and another mountain range. He figured that was probably good enough.

The two drove along in silence for a few minutes: Chris basking in the afterglow of a truly memorable sexual experience, Jamie enjoying the feeling of sweat cooling and drying on her naked breasts as the air-conditioning blew over them. Before too long they came to a pole.

"Good," said Chris. "It looks like we didn't get lost after all." As instructed, he turned left, and within a few miles came to a gravel road that led off into a saddle between the two ranges.

The Playa floor had been flat and smooth: pleasant to drive on, actually. Kind of like a giant ocean of asphalt. The gravel road was nothing like that. Shockingly, it was poorly maintained, filled with ruts, sandpits, and large irregular rocks that didn't look much like roadbed to Chris. It mercilessly pounded and scraped at the bottom of his Scion, causing him to wince every time he heard its oil pan scratch against the surface of a large rock. Jamie looked equally alarmed.

"You think they would work harder at maintaining this road," she said. "I mean the people up at Soldier Meadows make their living off of tourists coming and spending the night, right?"

Chris shrugged.

"Well, yeah; but I think most of the people that come out here are probably driving, you know, big trucks and that sort of thing. Four wheel drive stuff."

"Well, I guess...," said Jamie with a squeak as the car bottomed out again. She had picked Soldier Meadows on a lark just to see if Chris would pay for it and take her out there. She selected it because it was the remotest Bed and Breakfast she could find that was still technically one-day's drive from San Francisco. Now she was starting to regret not picking that erotically themed B&B down on Highway One just west of San Luis Obispo. But those theme hotels never made her feel the way that the desert – *this* desert – made her feel. Or, even the way that sleazier, low-rent hotels made her feel, for that matter. Chris really wasn't a sleazy hotel kind of guy, and that was one reason why she liked him. She's always thought him a little too bland, a little too controlling for her tastes. The fact that he'd leadfooted the car while screwing her... now *that* showed some real promise. There was definitely more going on inside of him than she knew about, and she looked forward to seeing what that might be.

Then, with a simple jolting bounce and a final terrifying scrape of metal upon rock, the surface of the road improved dramatically. Chris sped up, and they started shooting through a narrow strait formed between two sheer cliffs with something approaching reasonable speed.

In Mother's defense she'd never really had to worry about cars all that much. The only ones she had encountered were large, slow, and loud, gingerly picking their way across the landscape like rusty scorpions in search of dinner. Too sluggish to be of any danger, they also generally contained people that gave her tasty snacks. No, it never occurred to her to worry about cars.

Earlier that day she had decided to get the hell away from her children and go out hunting. They were mostly grown up, anyhow, and didn't need her around as much as they used to. It was nice to get away. Plus, if she managed to capture a rabbit or a ground squirrel, she could have it all to herself. She paused at a stand of grease brush, tested the air with her nose, and then ambled over between the prickles to where a fresh pile of coyote scat lay. She gobbled it up. Delicious. Coyotes didn't have particularly efficient digestive systems; their scat is basically pure meat. Delectable! She always learned something new every time she ate some.

No, she didn't know this guy.

A few minutes later, she paused to gobble up a horny toad. Easy prey; they were all over the place out here. Not a lot of nutrition found in them, though, and they weren't that tasty. She could live off horny toads – hell, everyone had done it – but if you had to, that meant that times were lean indeed.

Mother saw the narrows down below and smiled to herself. They were good for hunting. There was a little hot spring down there you could drink out of (it wasn't *that* hot), and it drew in all sorts of good game. She'd have to keep her eyes open for mountain lions but, unless times were hard, they tended to avoid anything as big as Mother.

She could catch a rabbit while she was down there. It wasn't like there weren't plenty of them around. Then she'd have herself a nice drink, drag the rabbit off into the shade of the cliffs, munch on it for a while, and then maybe settle down for a nap. If she timed it right, she could get up around dusk and go home at a time when the desert is as cool and clear and as close to paradise as anything could ever be.

It was right then that she saw the rabbit. It was a big one, with tall, proud ears, and that dopey look she liked in her rabbits. There's no time to think when chasing rabbits – you just have to act – so she immediately took off after it, hoping to grab it and break its neck within moments. The big old buck rabbit was smarter than she thought, though. Within a second of her coming after it, the rabbit tore off into the canyon below at a pace that would have been respectable in the biggest, fastest coyote. Undeterred, she shot after it.

Chris knew that he should really drive more slowly. The land they were traveling through now was beautiful in its own stark, sandy way. Sheer cliffs covered in painted rock towered above them on either side. Tiny pools of steaming water bubbled forth from the ground here and there. Most importantly, there was lots of shade. It was a fine place to get out and spend an afternoon; or, at the very least, to drive slowly through and admire from the comfort of his car. But, he was being driven by his instincts now, and those instincts told him two things: 1) get out of this unfamiliar environment to somewhere safe and 2) get his new girlfriend somewhere private where he could fuck her for more than two minutes at a time. The thought that he ought to be going slower didn't really occur to him until the huge, brown figure shot in front of him and he hit it going over 50 miles an hour.

He felt the impact through his body. First though the front of his car, and then he felt a series of sickening crunches as the low-slung Scion bounced repeatedly over something. Jamie screamed. He fought for control as the small car slid precariously this way and that, finally skidding to a grinding halt against one of the cliff faces that towered above them.

Chris sat there in shock for a moment, and then snapped to his senses. Jamie looked about wild-eyed.

"What happened?"

"I dunno. We hit something." he replied, and reached around the grab the emergency pack he kept in his back seat. "Come on. Let's find out what it is and see if we can help."

The passenger side door was pressed up against the rock wall, so Jamie followed Chris out of the driver's side. He quickly glanced at the front of his car. The grill was caved in, but it didn't seem to be leaking anything, so he thought that there probably wasn't any mechanical damage. He slung the courier bag over his shoulder, filled with various driving supplies, and ran back to where an enormous lump of brown fur lay sprawled in the middle of the road.

Immediately Chris realized two things. It was as if the shock of the accident had cleared his mind and caused him to focus sharply for the first time in an hour or two. The first was that they hadn't been on a road. It wasn't a road at all. It was a dry riverbed. They'd been driving up a dried riverbed, he realized with considerable alarm.

The second was that right in front of him laid the largest dog he had ever seen in his entire life. He'd never seen an Irish wolfhound – or, if he had, he hadn't known that he had – but he imagined that this must have been a bit bigger than that. The impact with the car had crushed it. Bits of broken rib protruded out of a chest that still heaved limply up and down. The force of the accident had crushed both of its back legs.

As they ran up to it, the beast turned its enormous oversized head and regarded them with intelligent blue eyes.

"Is there anything we can do for it?" asked Jamie.

Chris shook his head dumbly. He looked down. The animal had a collar on it; a crude one made out of studded brown rawhide. Carefully etched into it was a single word: Mother.

"Shit!" said Chris. He began looking around the canyon in panic.

"What? What is it?" asked Jamie.

Chris lived in the city, but he hadn't been born there.

"The farmers and ranchers that live out in places like this," he replied, terror creeping into his voice, "they take their dogs real seriously. Real serious – they're like family."

He looked deep into her eyes.

"We just killed a member of someone's family."

Jamie shook her head, not really understanding.

"But, but it was an accident!" she stammered. "The dog just ran out in front of us."

"It won't matter," he replied, shaking his head. "Come on; let's get the hell out of here!"

He grabbed her wrist, turned, and began running toward the car. It was then that Mother began to howl. It was a weak, forlorn, strangled, hopeless thing – but it was a howl nonetheless.

Tyson had been born in west Oakland. The child of a crack whore and a nameless father, he'd been sent to the worst school system in the country. The fact that he could read and write was a miracle he thanked no one for but himself. One-by-one he'd watched his childhood friends succumb to the evils of that place: drug addiction, prison, and death. However, Tyson had not succumbed.

There's lots of time to think about your life when you live out in the desert and, like everyone else out there, Tyson had done a lot of that. He'd concluded that one thing and one thing alone had saved him from the fate of his childhood friends. It was love – pure love. Not screwing, but love. Tyson loved dogs. From the time he was old enough to walk, he'd spent more time with the neighborhood strays than he had with other children. Moreover, the affection was fully returned. He had a natural affinity for them, and they for him.

By the time he was twelve Tyson was raising fighting dogs in a squalid abandoned building near where his mother lived. He'd fed them using choice bits and pieces scavenged from the trashcans of nice restaurants along Broadway Street. He cared for them, nurtured them, and bred them. He read the greats: Mendel, Morgan, and Crick. By the time he was fourteen, he was good at it. By the time he was sixteen, he was making money at it. Lots of money.

Tyson never had any serious moral qualms about raising dogs for fighting the way people said he should have. The dogs that he raised *liked* to fight. Dogs like to do the things that they are bred and born to do. They're pure and sharp, like swords or knives, not all dulled down by doubt and hypocrisy like human beings. Tyson was very good at sharpening those knives, at shaping them for specific purposes to reach specific goals.

By the time he was twenty, Tyson had made enough money to buy a house. He bought a rundown, ramshackle old Victorian not too far from where he was born and raised. He left it looking ramshackle and rundown too – on the outside. Inside he converted the ground floor to a giant kennel, and lived upstairs above it on the second floor. He left the backyard as an exercise area for his dogs. He was careful about things. His house never smelled bad. It was never dirty. The dogs never went out unless he was with them.

By then he wasn't just breeding fighting dogs. He was doing his own experiments. He could *feel* his dogs wanting to become something. Evolution hadn't finished its work, hadn't brought them along to the point where he felt they ought to be. He just needed more raw materials to make that happen. Tyson wasn't educated or sophisticated. He didn't have a lot of experience dealing with different sorts of people, either. He was large and black and spoke with an accent typical of someone raised in the poorest parts of Oakland. But he knew the language of dogs and, when he stuck to that, he did all right.

Tyson began taking fieldtrips out to places like Nevada, Oregon, and Idaho, trusting the care of his animals to automatic feeding machines that he bought through catalogues. He began meeting people that were very different from him in appearance and upbringing, but who at their core were the same. Like swords. Like knives. Narrowly focused. Leathery old men and women that lived on hilltops out in deserts or deep in forests, breeding and raising their dogs with single-minded devotion. From them he got sperm samples – coyote and wolf, hyena and dingo. He learned more tricks too. Like how to make his animals smarter, stronger, and faster.

Realizing that at some point he was going to have to get land somewhere more quiet and private, Tyson bought 40 acres from another dog breeder way, way up in the Jackson Mountains of northern Nevada. Far away from thieves, prying eyes, or interference of any kind. It was a quiet, private deal. Money changed hands, documents were signed, but nothing was every publicly recorded. This is why he didn't lose it six months later, after two teenage burglars broke into his Oakland home while he wasn't there and were mauled to death by his beloved dogs.

Charged with second degree homicide, criminal negligence, and (rather ridiculously, as far as he was concerned) with animal cruelty, Tyson was arrested, tried, convicted, and put into the California state prison system for eight years. It was grotesquely unfair and he knew it. Couldn't the jury see that his dogs were just defending their home? They were just doing what they were raised to do. It was their job for Christ's sake. But the Oakland DA and the press were on a crusade against pit bulls, dogfights, and most especially those who raised pit bulls for dogfights. Tyson became a casualty of that war. He had the last laugh, though. Shortly after being arrested, he posted bail, beat the SPCA back to his house, threw open his cages, and released his dogs – every last one of them – out into the streets of Oakland. He knew they could survive and stay free. They were smart; smarter than most people he knew, and certainly smarter than the idiots who worked at Animal Control.

As he let his beloved pets out of their cages, Tyson had a rushed, whispered conversation with each dog, explaining what had happened and when he would be back. They added more years to sentence for that, of course. He would do all eight years now without probation. But he didn't care. He took only one item into the system with him. One single item that the guards scratched their heads about, but in the end didn't confiscate. It was a small tin whistle on a necklace. For eight long, brutal years, he clung to that necklace, a symbol of what he once was – and what he might be again. He never spoke a word of explanation about it to anyone while he was inside.

When they finally – reluctantly – let him out, he returned to where his house – now the site of a complex of bright red and yellow stucco condominiums – used to be. He placed that whistle to his lips and blew it long, hard, and *silently*.

They came.

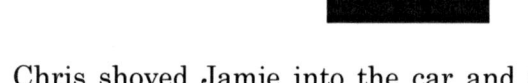

Chris shoved Jamie into the car and threw his pack into the back seat. He slammed it into reverse; scraping the small car along the rock wall with such force that it threw sparks in every direction at once. Mother's long, warbling howl cut through his skull. He could feel it vibrating down in his bowels, down in his scrotum, down in his soul. He had no idea how far the narrow, winding canyon he had been driven up continued or even where it led. So he continued in reverse, carefully backing around the wounded animal. As quickly as possible, his head turned and his left arm around his shivering girlfriend, he began backing rapidly down the dried riverbed. If he could make it down to the Playa, he could head straight for the small town of Hualapai and safety.

His mind was a whirl of terror: terror of the unknown and unseen owner of that animal. That beast. That horror. Anyone who could own something like that and, in the throes of affection or God knows what else, name it "Mother" was not someone that Chris ever wanted to meet. He could taste the anxiety and fear in his mouth. The terror was like a grey blanket of fuzz covering his mind, keeping him from thinking about anything except escape.

Tyson was sitting on his rickety front porch, carefully annotating some genealogy records in his cramped, intense script when he heard Mother's long, mournful scream come over the ridge. He sprang to his feet, ran inside, and grabbed his rifle from the rack above the door where he kept it. It was a Marlin .22 LR semi-auto that held 12 shots in a fixed tube magazine below its barrel. He had traded two very good border collie/dawg hybrid puppies to one of his neighbors for it, and he was wickedly good with it. He had to be. Tyson lived on the same diet as his beloved dawgs did: rabbit, ground squirrel, mice, crow, snake, the odd poached pronghorn or deer. There were a couple of indigenous root plants that were also edible. He used those for fiber.

Tyson traded puppies to all of the outlying desert dwellers for those few needs he couldn't supply himself: ammunition, spices, cans of propane, and a little gasoline. He lived without electricity, bathing in a hot spring that lay on his property and drinking from a stream that poured down off a nearby rock face. One of the side benefits of his breeding project – or his Project, as he liked to call it – was that he could crossbreed various "pure" breeds with his dawgs to produce hybrid versions that were smarter and better at their jobs than anything that anyone had seen before. His hybrid border collies and hybrid basset hounds were especially popular in these parts for herding and guarding, respectively.

Though he lived up here alone with his pack, Tyson wasn't lonely. After the sexual horror that was prison, he didn't want really want to be around women – or a men, for that matter. He didn't want a P.O. Box and he didn't much care about the Internet. He didn't like television. He had an old VCR and, on those rare occasions that neighbors came to visit him, they would bring him dog movies purchased from the 99-cent bins at Wal-Mart. He liked Old Yeller, Where the Red Fern Grows, and old episodes of Lassie the best.

They knew that his interests were narrow. Like a sword. Like a knife.

Once every six months or so Opal Jim or one the Guerreros brought him a whole bunch of dog magazines picked up from pet food stores. He liked those. He kept up a written correspondence with half a dozen or so friends he knew around the world. Men and women interested in the same sorts of things he was. Opal Jim, a crazy miner who lived a few mountain ranges over, had an Internet satellite connection and maintained his correspondence for him. He printed things out and brought them around every few months so that Tyson could respond.

His Project had had many successes. They were lying round the ranch or were out hunting even as he slung the rifle over his shoulder and put the dog whistle to his lips. Mother was the author of many of those successes. She was biologically the mother of over half of the dogs in his pack. Spiritually and emotionally, she was the alpha female to his alpha male; they were as close to a wife and lover as Tyson would ever have in his life.

And he knew it.

He blew his whistle and the pack, or at least those who were already at the ranch, formed around him. A moment later, they were all running to the top of the ridge nearby, her pitiful screams lashing them forward with its urgent insistency. As they crested the top of the ridge, Tyson saw two things: the crumpled, howling body of Mother and a tiny, delicate looking car desperately backing its way down the old gravel riverbed that had, over the course of millions of years, cut a channel straight through the solid rock of the canyon.

Without even thinking, he turned, aimed his rifle down at the car, and shot all 12 rounds straight into it. Trailing dust and smoke, the small car spun about crazily to slam hood-first into the canyon wall before it, and then was still.

When Tyson reached Mother, she'd stopped howling, lying dazed, desperate, and close to death in a pool of her own blood. Her guts had been spilled out by the impact of the car. Her ribs were protruding out of her chest and her back legs were broken. It was a miracle that she had been able to howl at all, let alone live this long. All around him, her pack made pitiful whining noises and hung their heads in sorrow. Tyson wept. Not for very long – he was unaccustomed to such things – and when he was done, he placed his large hands over her eyes, spoke a few words comfortingly into her ears, and then quickly broke Mother's neck, putting her out of her misery.

Tyson turned his angry, bloodshot eyes down at the crumpled wreck of the Scion.

"U gonna pay," he rasped out, unaccustomed to speaking. "U gonna pay dearly."

Jamie awoke draped over a deployed airbag, the crumpled remains of the Scion smashed in around her. She was covered in blood, glass, and bits of plastic. Without thinking, she shoved the passenger side door open and tumbled out into the sand. It was hot, and the sun beat mercilessly upon her naked torso. She looked down at herself in alarm. Although nothing seemed to be broken, her body was a mess of cuts, slashes, and abrasions. Her left breast was a mess. Its nipple was missing, and something had gone through the top and exploded out of the bottom. She was dripping blood everywhere.

Then, with the full horror of the situation dawning upon her, she looked into the car's broken side view mirror and realized that her life had changed forever. Jamie's face, a face so beautiful that it had been her meal ticket since she was a child, a face that had gotten her minor jobs as a model and allowed her turn major tricks as a call girl, was ruined. Her nose was broken and her cheeks had been slashed by chunks of flying glass.

She was a horror.

Yet she felt oddly calm. The shock of the situation was so extreme and so total that, rather than getting upset, she took careful stock of what was going on. She knew that if she didn't do something quickly she would bleed to death. She reached behind the Scion's broken seats and deployed airbags to where Chris' emergency bag lay on the back seat.

She didn't actually know what was in it, and was relieved to find a huge wad of bandages, disinfectant, and various other items. Choking back a scream, she carefully poured the entire bottle of disinfectant over her wounds, taking special care to pour it into the soft flesh were her nipple was missing. Then she carefully bandaged up her chest, warily wrapping an entire roll of bandages around herself like some kind of primitive sports bra. Then, using a pair of tweezers, she slowly and cautiously pulled shards of glass out of her face. When she was finished with that, she took a second set of gauze and wrapped it around her face, bandaging herself up like a mummy.

When Jamie was done, she looked into the mirror and realized that she looked like some kind of monster or mutant from an old black and white horror film. However, she wasn't bleeding anymore, and probably wouldn't die in the next few minutes, in any case. She looked back into the courier bag. There were some bottled waters. She took one and drank it immediately. There were some energy bars, a pair of binoculars, and a couple of road flares. She slung it over her back then walked around to the driver's side of the car.

Jamie couldn't remember what had happened exactly. First, they were speeding backward down the canyon road. Then there was a sound like hail hitting the car, Chris lost control, and everything went black. Chris was gone. The driver's side door was open, but his seat was empty. She looked down at the ground below and among the bits of broken glass and twisted plastic she saw a single pair of very large footprints, a *lot* of small footprints, and what looked like drops of blood. All three lead away to some sandy hills that tapered steeply into a wash in the cliffs above her.

Jamie steeled herself. She would have to go after him, but she was terrified. She remembered what Chris had said about the sort of people who lived out here. She felt like running. She felt like screaming. She felt like falling on the ground and weeping. Jamie didn't do any of these things. She didn't know why she didn't. It was as if some different person had taken over her body. Some separate personality that she had never had a clue lurked inside of her skin along with her "self."

She was halfway up the wash when Chris began to scream. It was a high-pitched, pitiful, and frightening thing that got louder and louder as she scrambled on her hands and knees toward the top of the ridge. There were words mixed in with the screaming. He was begging someone. She grew desperate as his screaming grew louder. She slipped and began to slide down the side of the wash, scrambling to gain traction as she flailed her hands and feet about. Calming herself, she dug her heels into the loose gravel, pressed her palms flat against the ground, and began to scuttle quickly toward the top.

Chris stopped screaming.

She reached the top of the ridge and looked down the other side. Beneath her lay a small valley that had been completely hidden from sight by the steep walls of the narrow canyon she and Chris had been driving up. It was a picturesque location. Even in her current state, she could see how beautiful it was. A small stream tumbled down some rocks on the far side opposite from her. Down below a hot pool vented a reeking stream of smoke into the air. In the center of the valley lay a small cluster of bleached wooden buildings, their planks gapped and twisted from decades in the sun. There was a flurry of animated movement in front of one of the buildings, but she was too far away to make out any details. Rummaging through the pack, she removed the binoculars, put them to her eyes, and examined the scene far below her.

A man stood at the center of dozens of huge, brown, bizarre looking dogs much like the one they had hit on the road down below. He was large and black, with grey dreadlocks that hung limply down to his shoulders. He wore a sleeveless trench coat made of some rough leather material that allowed his massive, bare arms to protrude from either side. Next to him what was left of Chris hung upside-down from a rusting metal A-frame. One of his legs had been cut off with a hacksaw and he had been disemboweled. His intestines hung downward like streamers from his limp body. As she watched, the black man hacked off Chris' manhood with a giant knife and casually threw it to his dogs. They immediately began fighting over it.

The man took his knife, sliced off a chunk from her lover's inner thigh, and then slowly turned to look up at her. He snarled, revealing a mouth filled with yellow, sharpened teeth. Then he popped the chunk in and chewed methodically.

For a brief moment, they locked eyes: hers wide, blue, and frightened, his brown and bloodshot and angry. Then she threw the binoculars to one side, leaped over the opposite side of the ridge, and began sliding on her back down toward the road below.

■

Filled with the redness of anger, Tyson had forgotten about the passenger. If he hadn't noticed the glint of her binoculars, he might never have remembered her. He'd been consumed by wrath and rage as he carried the unconscious form of the driver back to his kennel. In fact, he'd planned on torturing the boy for days, first using the sorts of things he'd learned in prison, then cutting bits off of him inch by inch and feeding it to the dawgs as he watched, still alive.

Tyson wasn't a cruel man at heart. He'd simply been angry beyond all measure. When the boy started to scream, plead, and beg, the wrath had gone out of him, and he quickly slit the boy's throat. But he also wasn't one to let anything go to waste. When the boy finally ceased jerking, he began quartering him like a deer, tossing treats to his pack as he went along, as he would have with a buck, a pronghorn, or a bobcat. Man is just another animal, after all.

He probably never would have eaten any himself (well, maybe in a stew), but when he saw the passenger staring down at him from the top of the ridge the rage came back, and with it the desire to hurt. His cannibalism was an impulse. Nevertheless, he couldn't very well let her get away now, could he? She'd undo everything he had ever worked toward.

"Cujo! Blood!" he shouted at two of his biggest males while pointing up the ridge, "Get her! Kill her! Then bring her back here."

The two massive mastiffs looked at him quizzically with their blue eyes, then turned and bolted off into the salt brush.

Jamie hit the gravel with a thump, taking the shock with her knees. She wanted to throw up. She wanted to cry. She wanted to piss in her jeans. She felt like doing all three of these things at once. In short, she was freaked out; but somehow, using a strength that she had never even imagined she might have, she managed to push all of these emotions down and lock them away gibbering and screaming somewhere at the bottom of her stomach. She had to get the hell out of there. She knew that very clearly. It resonated through her body like vibrations through a tuning fork. She had to get the hell out of there *right now*.

She ran. She ran past the wreck of the car. It was obviously totaled. There was no way she was going to drive it out of there. If she were going to escape, she would have to do it on foot. She wasn't sure why she was holding it together as well as she was. Jamie had never been a strong person, and she knew it. It was almost as if the shock – the incredible horror of what happened and what she had witnessed – had awakened some deeper, more primal self she'd never known existed. Jamie had always been soft and interested in pleasure. She was lazy too, and more than willing to use her extraordinary beauty to keep from having to work very hard at anything. Yet, rather than feeling shock and self-pity at the ruin of her beauty, she felt somehow liberated. It was as if a dragging chain had been unshackled from around her legs.

She'd been changed, altered – and not just physically. Jamie wanted to do things. She wanted to live. She wanted people to look at her with respect for her accomplishments, not just with lust for her beauty (not that there was much chance of that anymore). As she ran down the dry, dusty riverbed, looking as much within as without, she found that she would like to be a man's wife. She would like to raise his children. She felt with a twinge of sadness that bordered on nausea that she might have enjoyed being Chris' wife and having Chris' children. It occurred to her then that she had gotten him killed. If it hadn't been for this awful misadventure, he'd be home right now, back in San Francisco working in his office on Market Street and daydreaming about spending the evening carousing in the Haight-Asbury District with his friends.

She ran faster and realized that she was trying to run away from herself.

The courier bag pounded painfully on her back, and she knew that she was getting sunburned. She would have to stop soon and drink the other bottle of water that was in it. But she couldn't stop. She wanted to keep running. She wanted to run down this riverbed, past the pole that marked its beginning, out into the vast white desert where nothing lived. She wanted to feel the dust passing through her, pounding into her, purifying her. She wanted to feel it clot in her wounds and congeal in her sweat.

It was then that she heard a howl. Looking up and behind, she saw two of the large, mutated dogs bound over the top of the ridge and slide down the gravelly face of the cliff straight toward her.

Cujo and Blood smelled the female long before they saw her. They could smell her blood and her sweat, and they were hungry. They were always hungry. They had been bred to be hungry...*always*. It was one of the traits that allowed them to grow so big. They both figured that the strange biped female had something to do with the death of Mother, though what precisely the connection was they had no idea. Were it not for Mother's death – and for Tyson's orders – they may have chosen to leave her alone. They knew that humans, even female ones, were large and dangerous. Canines, even ones as big as desert dawgs, aren't apex predators. They had no illusions about being on the very top of the food chain: *near* the top, yes, but not *at* the top. In the Black Rock Desert, that was where men, mountain lions, and other less pleasant, little known things dwelled.

Like revenge, and the master's orders. And there was the hunger; always, the hunger. They plowed down the hill toward her as fast as their legs could carry them.

Jamie knew that she couldn't outrun the huge coyotes, or whatever they were. She wasn't stupid enough even to try. But she wasn't ready to die and, even if she were ready to die, she definitely wasn't ready to be eaten alive. She looked desperately about for a weapon, but there wasn't as much as a branch or a rock big enough to be used as one. Then she remembered the road flares that Chris had left in his courier bag. Yanking them out and taking one in each hand, she ran between two large boulders that had a roughly man-sized space in between them, using the rough surface of the rock to light them as she ran. Even in the blazing midday sun, the phosphorus burned and dripped from the ends of the long red sticks.

The creatures decided to approach her from either side of the opening between the boulders, but slid to a halt, alarmed and frightened by the sudden fire. They began advancing on her cautiously, their clever blue eyes never leaving the dripping fiery tips of the road flares as they looked for some opening, some way in so that they could fasten their jagged fangs upon her pale, tender flesh. She realized with a shock that she was going to have to take the offensive if she wanted to live. Given more than a few moments, they *would* find an opening. They *would* bring her down. They *would* tear her to pieces and eat her alive.

Without warning and without thinking, she struck downward at the one to her right, driving the flaming phosphorus directly into its large, wet nose. The beast howled – an oddly human sound – and flung itself to the ground, thrashing wildly about as it tried to bury its wounded muzzle in the dirt. Almost instantly, she spun about, striking with both flares at the clever blue eyes of the one to her left. It screamed like a mortally wounded infant and bound blindly away into the salt brush. In sudden violent frenzy, she turned once more to the wounded animal to her right, striking wildly at it repeatedly with the flares as it howled, burned, and thrashed about on the ground. She could smell its fear. She could smell its burning flesh and sizzling fur. She stabbed at it with the lit road flares until they broke off halfway down and the animal lay still and unmoving in the dust.

It was then that she glanced back up to the top of the ridge where she had stood just a few moments (or was it an eternity?) before. The dreadlocked man stared silently down at her, flanked by dozens of equally silent beasts that were spread along the ridge like spectators at a sports match. He glared at her, but this time she returned his glare with full force. Throwing the broken stubs of the road flares to one side, she raised her fist into the air and shook it at him in defiance. Then she turned and fled, bloody bandages trailing out behind her.

Jamie ran as if she'd never done anything but before. She'd never drunk, screwed, cursed, or cried this hard before. She wasn't even looking where she was going. She just ran, thankful for every moment that she could run, ignoring every pain that could make her stop running. The ground stopped being gravel and became sagebrush. Seemingly moments later, it became hard baked clay. Then she was out of the canyons and onto the Playa floor. She looked up. As if in answer to her prayer, as if it were summoned, she was suddenly enveloped in a massive cloud of blown brown dust.

It was a mixed blessing. Dust storms were common on the Playa in the summer. They reduce visibility to a few feet, which meant that Jamie could no longer tell which direction she was going in. It also meant that her scent was now being blown backward toward the man and his monsters. They couldn't see her, and odds were that they could barely smell her with all of the fine dust being in the air. She kept running, and heard eerie howls behind her as well as the shouts of a rough, masculine voice. She couldn't see them, and they couldn't see her. So she ran.

The sky became light yellow brown. The howling of the dawgs and the angry cries of the man grew ever closer. Then, somewhere nearby, came the sound of an engine.

Evil Eight: The Secret Language of Slasher Films

[First published in the collection *Butcher's Knives & Body Counts: Essays on the Formula, Frights, and Fun of the Slasher Film* in 2011. Published by Dark Scribe Press, and edited by the award-winning Vince Liaguno.]

Slasher films, as stylized and formalized as Japanese Kabuki, are a cornucopia of potent, terrible symbols filled with psychological power. Directors use these images against the audience like the bladed weapons that give the genre its name to provoke revulsion, excitement, terror, and anxiety: a mute, masked killer who is himself unkillable, a butcher's knife bursting through a human body, the physical isolation of rural America, the final girl rising above the terror and mediocrity of her friends to strike the maniac down. More than any axe, scythe, or saw, these images, in the hands of a skilled director, have a profound psychological effect on all who view them. In many respects, the slasher's great reliance on concrete, archetypical images of horror, slaughter, and terror can be seen as an artistic rejection of minimalist, existential psychological horror films like Taxi Driver or Memento, in which the viewer is left to puzzle his own meanings from the events on screen.

Like its antihero maniacs, the slasher film has things it wants to do to you, not the other way around.

Still, it is important to remember that the genesis behind the powerful images of slasher films was largely inadvertent. It's not as though directors like Wes Craven (The Hills Have Eyes, A Nightmare on Elm Street), John Carpenter (Halloween), and Tobe Hooper (Texas Chainsaw Massacre I & II) sat down with a copy of Jung's Man and His Symbols when they created their films (well, possibly Hooper did). They were young men out to make a fast buck on a limited budget, fledgling directors who dug deep down into their own twisted unconscious minds in search of things that scare the hell out of people. Building on traditions established by great directors like Alfred Hitchcock and Mario Bava — and constantly borrowing from one another — they created a potent library of symbols designed to haunt the nightmares of American teenagers.

However, inadvertent genius is by nature spontaneous and powerful, filled with repressed, horrible truths. Deep down in the basement of the slasher library flow a red river of metaphor: an 'Evil Eight' of scandalous subtext or eight critical lenses through which these films can be examined. Some of these concepts conflict with one another; others are complementary. Yet all can be used to reveal the secret language of the slasher film.

Family Values vs. Valued Family

One of the most fascinating subjects examined by slasher films is family conflict. To be more specific, films like The Hills Have Eyes, The Devil's Rejects, and The Texas Chainsaw Massacre depict conflicts within — and between — two families, one normal and the other... not so normal. In each case, a feral family of maniacs has been preying on travelers (or teenagers) unlucky enough to be caught passing through their territory. In two of the films — The Hills Have Eyes and The Texas Chainsaw Massacre — the maniacs are actually cannibals who survive largely off edible tourists. In both of these films, members of a normal family have the ill fortune to be set upon by the maniac family, which causes their surviving relatives to seek revenge, often in a sequel. Yet seeking vengeance robs the victims of their humanity, transforming them into monsters as bad — or even worse — as the ones they have set out to destroy. Faced with the murder of his wife and the abduction of his child, mellow 70's dude Doug kills a member of the rival coyote family at the bloody climax of The Hills Have Eyes (the cool, original one — not the remake). In the course of The Devil's Rejects, the initially noble Sheriff Quincy Wydell, played by tough guy William Forsythe, becomes a murderer, torturer, and predator of women, as his pursuit of the maniac Firefly family slowly drives him insane. In The Texas Chainsaw Massacre II, vengeful Texas Ranger Lefty Enright ends up in a vicious chainsaw duel with the maniac Leatherface, thereby completing the circle that began with the murder of his nephew and becoming a parody of the monster he set out to destroy. It's a quintessentially Nietzschean problem: if the teenager stares into the abyss long enough, the abyss stares back at the teenager.

During these films, numerous conflicts within the family also manifest. In The Hills Have Eyes, both maniac and normal sons struggle against the authority of their domineering fathers, while father-and-son murdering team Captain Spalding and Otis Driftwood similarly knock heads in The Devil's Rejects. His older brother's ghost torments Sheriff Wydell into madness, while Father Jupiter (in The Hills Have Eyes) is so proud of his mutant offspring that he brags about them to the burned corpse of rival father Bob Carter. Oddly, members of the hideous cannibal Sawyer family portrayed in The Texas Chainsaw Massacre movies seem fond of one another, despite their utter and bleak dysfunction as human beings.

Thus, the maniac family struggles against itself while also preying upon the normal family. Seemingly unified, it often comes apart when placed under extreme pressure. The normal family usually starts divided by petty rivalries, only coming together when placed under intense pressure to show unexpected backbone.

Well, its few surviving members do, in any case.

Rural Vs. Urban/Suburban

The conflict between maniac and teenager can also be seen as a manifestation of the ongoing clash between rural and urban (or suburban) cultures in America. Regardless of how one feels about his character and habits, the maniac can be seen as a crude, exaggerated embodiment of the frontiersman or backwoodsman. He lives a simple lifestyle that is close to the land (or, occasionally, under it), hunts regularly, is protective of his home, and is unafraid of administering frontier-style justice when he feels that it's required (which is often). He is also rather sedentary in his habits, antiauthoritarian (though tradition-bound), and, aside from his desires to kill the odd passing motorist, rather Spartan in his everyday life. In his institutional jumpsuit, filthy coveralls, or bloodstained circus clown suit, the maniac is also undeniably unstylish... at least by most reasonable definitions of the term.

The teenager, on the other hand, is a personification of the modern way of life. She is physically mobile (else she wouldn't be traveling), technologically reliant, accustomed to obeying authority figures (though perhaps not laws), and habituated to the creature comforts provided by present day society. Her lifestyle is affluent, so much so that she has difficulty functioning away from modern conveniences. It may even come as a total surprise to her that anyone lives without constant access to a hairdryer and 300 channels of cable television. She's attractive, with neatly groomed hair, manicured nails, and fashionable clothing.

Thus, like the extreme ends of rural and urban American society, the maniac and the teenager possess exaggerated Weltanschauungs that clash when placed in close proximity to one another. To be honest, the results are generally fatal — which is probably why the maniac generally sticks to his own rural environment, where he can dispense mayhem rather than receiving it.

Male vs. Female

The slasher film can also be thought of as a grotesque metaphor for the battle of the sexes. From this perspective, the maniac is a caricature of masculinity: tall to the point of gigantism, inhumanly physically powerful, robust to the point that he can survive multiple gunshot wounds, aggressive to the level of psychosis, and generally none-too-talkative. The strong silent type, but dialed so far up on the testosterone meter that he can't help running amok, sticking his phallic weapon into any warm body that seems suitable. In short, he is Western man as envisioned by a particularly bitter UC Berkeley professor of Women's Studies who really needs to get off the campus more often.

The teenager then becomes a cartoon embodiment of all that is stereotypically feminine: buxom and beautiful, unbelievably naïve, and helpless when confronted with danger. She is the perfect, voluptuous victim who is so helpless, in fact, that — in the face the maniac's advances — she either must flee or be reduced to helpless screaming. In short, she is Western woman as envisioned by an assistant editor at Maxim who really needs to spend less time at the strip joint.

From this angle, the maniac/teenager dynamic resembles that of an abusive husband tormenting his helpless spouse, who is seemingly psychologically incapable of leaving him (after all, nobody ever just leaves the spooky forest or sinister summer camp in a slasher film). Eventually, the wife actualizes her inner Amazon (the final girl) and is able to leave her husband by dissolving him in a giant vat of industrial acid, feeding him to a pond full of hungry alligators, or the like.

Individual vs. The Collective

By definition the maniac — and, by extension, his family — exists in a state of dynamic conflict with the majority of other people. Whether this is because he is a cannibal who preys upon them for sustenance, or because he adheres to a code of morality wildly different from theirs, he is starkly pitted against the hoi poloi. Thus, the slasher film can be thought of as a metaphor for the struggle between the individual and the collective, with the maniac as the personification of individualism. He's certainly independent (or at least his family is). He takes action according to his own ethical standards unrestricted by conventional authority (i.e. he kills people with an axe and nobody is able to stop him). To put it another way, he exists in a state of nature without any implied social contract, where his unknowingly evil actions produce a steady river of perfectly innocent murder and mayhem. A noble savage corrupted by the hands of others, the maniac cannot be judged too harshly for his sins for, as Rousseau would say, "Everything is good [left in] the hands of the Creator of Things; everything degenerates in the hands of man."

The teenager, on the other hand, is very much a creature of the collective. A great deal of her personal identity is derived from interaction with others — as is evidenced by the fact that she is not traveling alone — and she constantly looks to members of her group for guidance when confronted by unusual situations. Indeed, cut free from the gravity of her society, interactions with raw, uninhibited individualism (a maniac in a hockey mask with a chainsaw) reduce her to a state of near infantile uselessness. Thus, the conflict between the maniac and teenager can be thought of as metaphor for the conflict between the individual and the collective. In this reading of the slasher film, the final girl is a synthesis produced by the collision of two opposing forces: a conformist forced by the actions of an individualist to transcend the collective long enough to strike down individuality before returning once again to the comforting bosom of social homogeneity.

Natural Forces vs. Civilization

We live in a protected world. The majority of modern Americans are born, live, and die in the warm embrace of suburbia, gently cradled in the glowing arms of the power grid.

Our every need is served up on a plastic platter of convenience. We drift from our IKEA-furnished homes to our Staples-stocked offices to big-box mega-grocery stores without a single thought to how fragile our civilization is. Yet how thin the crown of industrial tinfoil looks upon our brows. In our time, crude, bloody nature has been murdered and replaced by the chromed god technology.

The truth hurts. Especially when it's wielding an axe.

Like most of the rest of us, the people who make Hollywood movies live in nice places with lots of great services: policemen, power grids, grocery stores, and carwashes to name but a few. To your average Tinsel Town screenwriter, places that lack these conveniences are as distant as Mars above and fantastic as Atlantis below: unthinkable, remote places where our chromed god has never penetrated — or, even worse, has been murdered by crude, bloody nature. Simply put, rural America frightens and horrifies urban and suburban Americans on a subconscious level. Services are nonexistent or unreliable. Law enforcement officers are few in number, disinterested, or simply absent. The local inhabitants are uncommunicative, unattractive, and interested in strange, grizzly things like taxidermy that their more urbane cousins find disturbing. Even more distressingly, many of the locals seem to possess moral and social "hang-ups" that they themselves long ago abandoned. Everywhere the urbanite looks the unconquered fist of nature is always close at hand, ready to punish the unwary for the crime of being ignorant.

In this reading of the slasher film, the urbanite's fear of natural forces has been articulated by Hollywood in the person of the maniac: a silent, masked, and often bizarrely clad figure that strikes down urbanites for sins they're scarcely aware they've committed. More like a puritanical, bloodthirsty superhero or pagan god than a traditional villain, he kills his victims with all the emotion of a lightning strike or a random mudslide. The terror of it is, he could probably be avoided or defeated... if one only possessed the knowledge to do so.

The Id vs. the Super-Ego

The world of the slasher film is a precarious one, especially for any locals caught in the crossfire between maniacs and teenagers. Nowhere is this better portrayed than the classic 80's horror film Pumpkinhead, where the local hill-folk — all too aware of the purpose and disposition of their indigenous supernatural maniac

— are forced to choose between assisting, ignoring, or actively opposing the teenagers desperately fleeing the creature's wrath. Thus, if the slasher film is viewed in Freudian terms as a symbolic conflict within the human mind (and, with all of its masks and severed heads, why wouldn't it be?), the locals function as a kind of ego, desperately mediating between the id (the maniacs) and the super-ego (the teenagers). They can be thought of as the mammalian "herd" consciousness attempting to strike compromises between an individual's animal and social needs.

The maniac is a creature of basic, almost reptilian desires. It kills victims, in some cases also eating them. Its personality is so basic, in fact, that it wears a mask as a symbolic representation of its lack of individual identity. Though it may possess supernatural strength, stealth, and toughness, its actual psychological composition is very simple. The maniac can therefore be seen as representing an out-of-control id bent on acting out its powerful but not terribly complex compulsions, mainly ramming its pointed phallic weapon into living things and/or consuming them (mating and eating).

Standing in its path are the teenagers, the living embodiment of cultural regulation, who would symbolically "castrate" the maniac by removing his weapon and "starve" it by denying the maniac his prey. Symbolically, the teenagers aren't very concerned with the individual's animal needs — but they care a great deal about the rules and regulations he has been raised to follow. To achieve this objective they must overcome the powerful id somehow, even if they have to compromise with it somewhat by temporarily transforming one of their own into a kind of "proxy" id in the form of the final girl.

Darwinism vs. Transcendentalism

The maniac is Darwinism in action, weeding out the weak and unadaptable from the strong and flexible with a single swing of his knife. In this reading of the slasher film, the maniac is an embodiment of the modern, dispassionate, and scientific concept of nature: an anonymous, silent, aloof, almost professional killing machine that lacks much of the personality of an old nature god like Thor or Pan. Inescapable and often inexplicable, the maniac performs its instinctive functions with a minimum of godly anthropomorphosis. Thus, the maniac becomes a physical manifestation of the archetypical essence of nature as conceptualized by modern science. He kills, therefore he is, and nothing more.

The teenager, on the other hand, is a child of God, utterly incapable of accepting the cold, cruel world of modern science. Even as the murderous events in the film unfold, she is unable to accept the destruction of beauty (her good-looking friends) by impersonal forces (the maniac). There simply must be a reason for everything that is happening and, assuming the teenager doesn't understand the reason for the killing when the film begins, she knows instinctively that uncovering it will bring the violence to an end (or at least a conclusion).

The purpose of a slasher film viewed through this lens is to examine the clash of Darwinism (or, if one prefers, realism) with a transcendent faith in the divine. Or, to put it another way, the maniac neither knows nor cares why he does what he does (he's a manifestation of nature), while the teenager attempts to assign reason and meaning to the terrible, often inexplicable events that are unfolding around her because the world is, after all, a good place ruled by a caring God in which things happen for a reason.

Ubermensch vs. Der Letzte Mensch

Finally, one could view the slasher film as a peculiarly Nietzschean contest between two opposing — and extreme — social forces attempting to confront the great specter of nothingness that has arisen from the death of God: a figure utterly removed from such films, though often mentioned. The maniac is an Ubermensch (literally "over-man"), an utter individualist confident enough to create and enforce his own values, strong enough to live without the solace of traditional morality, and utterly devoid of the stultifying effects of nihilism. As a member of the race of "homo superior," the maniac is the great hope of Western Civilization and a living embodiment of will to power: through the power of his own will (or satanic evil, take your pick), he has become superhumanly strong, is able to defy death, and can even consume other "wills" should he desire (well, he kills them with an axe). In essence, the maniac is an anti-superhero who lives by Nietzsche's maxim "In the face of a merciless Nature, let us be at one with our merciless nature!" Since God has died, the maniac takes his place.

The Ubermensch's great spiritual opponent is Der Letzte Mensch: the last man, or, in our case, the final girl in her chrysalis form as a teenager. The last man is a physical and spiritual coward interested only in his own comfort and security. The bane of Western Civilization, the last man is an apathetic creature without great passion or commitment outside of his own unexciting pleasures. The opposite response to the stultifying effects of nihilism from the Ubermensch, the last man takes no risks, feels no great enthusiasms, and goes meekly (or screaming) to the slaughter. This pretty well describes the teenager, who is incapable of resistance when confronted by a newly born god (the maniac) and is apathetic to the forces that created him. A creature of self-indulgence and mediocrity, it is essentially the teenager's fault that God died in the first place.

Thus, the dialectic of a slasher film involves its thesis (the teenagers) being exposed to its antithesis (the maniac), resulting in the synthesis of teenager and maniac that is the final girl. Empowered by her contact/empathy with her Ubermensch demigod, the final girl is at last able to destroy him, killing God once again, taking his place (often very literally), and completing the cycle of eternally recurring death-and-rebirth of the gods.

In conclusion, what makes the slasher film hated by many, yet loved by others, is its simple, potent symbolism. Slashers are personal movies in which characters — deliberately constructed to remind the viewers of them — are thrown into highly symbolic, supernatural situations from which there is no escape. Thus, it is all too easy for the viewer to imagine his or herself in the role of one of the film's victims or, even more disturbingly, as the maniac himself. Their suffering, fury, and confusion becomes our own, the emotional transmigration lubricated by a thick coat of dripping blood.

Through critical examination of the underlying themes of these movies, it is possible to learn a great deal about the human experience. Fear of the unknown, the terror of death, the lure of cruelty, human indifference, repressed sexuality, and anger at injustice, love of family and friends, a desire to understand the brutality that is nature: these are universal themes related to the human condition that can be found in slasher films. By learning about them, we learn about ourselves.

The Evil Eight: enlightenment courtesy of Leatherface.

Phat Albert

"There may be something more exciting than lion hunting, but I don't have her phone number anymore."
>— *Peter Capstick,* Death in the Long Grass

Sheriff Sal found the PH drinking in his kitchen. He hadn't invited him over, yet he wasn't surprised to find that he was there. He sat down wordlessly across from the big, white haired man and turned his bottle around to have a look at the label. Bookers. The Sheriff chewed his lower lip.

"This shit is about 300 proof," he said. The PH didn't answer. He just poured himself another double shot. The PH didn't drink.

The two men were a study in physical contrasts. The Sheriff was short and dark, with mournful brown eyes that seemed far too sensitive for a rural policeman. The PH was very tall, with white hair, pink skin, and bright blue eyes that gave away nothing. Spiritually, however, the two men were remarkably similar. They were creatures of the desert. Both were tough, taciturn, and soft-spoken, with a love of open spaces. Both thought nothing of killing, when it seemed necessary. It wasn't particularly hard for each man to guess what the other was thinking.

"So, do you want to tell me about it?" asked Sal as calmly as possible.

"No."

"Man," Sal said so softly it was almost inaudible, "you really don't have a choice."

The PH glared up at him as if through a bloodshot fog – which, the Sheriff reflected, was probably pretty much how things appeared to the older man now. He looked like that character from the Johnny Cash song where the guy gives his son a girl's name: big and mean and bent and old. He glared *hard* at Sal, then sagged a bit and looked away.

"You probably wouldn't believe if I told you," the PH muttered.

"Try me."

The older man stirred his bourbon with his finger for the moment.

"There are things out there in that desert that are better not talked about."

"I know. But not in this case." The Sheriff was firm. The PH sighed, downed his whiskey, and then leaned back in his chair, which creaked slightly under his weight. Then he leveled both bloodshot, unblinking barrels on Sal and began.

■

Barker had lived out in the high desert his entire life. Every kind of tough at one time, he looked like a shaft of barbed wire wrapped in beef jerky. Barker became a cowboy the moment his father could shove him into a saddle, until 50 years later when he'd contracted influenza. That had slowed him up a bit. Now he lived down in Hualapai, making the half-hour drive each day up to his isolated spread in the Granites where he kept a herd of horses.

He didn't ride that much anymore, but he still loved horses. Barker kept Western breeds mostly – Colorado Rangers, Appaloosa, Painted, and Indian – but there were a few Arabians mixed in as well. When he was a bit younger, he used to breed them professionally and strictly, but now he just let them mingle freely and enjoyed seeing what sort of random offspring they produced. He thought he was getting a bit soft in his old age.

Horses are tricky creatures. It takes years of experience to understand their body language, facial expressions, and behavior. Barker had been riding literally before he could walk. He knew horses better than he knew people. It didn't take him more than a couple of seconds after climbing stiffly out of his massive Ford F-350 on a Thursday morning to realize that something was terribly wrong.

The herd was upset. They had crowded up against one corner of the fence, and the wooden gate showed telltale signs of splintering where it had been kicked. Only force of habit prevented them from battering the corral down entirely. The moment his boots hit the mud they rolled their eyes at him, bobbing their heads up and down and whinnying loudly with terror. Barker reached under his truck's bench seat and drew out his lever-action Winchester. It was chambered for .45 Long Colt: an old-school cowboy round for an old-school cowboy. Forty-Five LC wasn't accurate past fifty yards, but Barker couldn't see worth a damn any farther than that – and never missed under it – so it suited him fine.

He threw open the backdoor of his crew cab. Dan and Ann spilled out in a flurry of fur and drool. They were hound hybrids: huge, droopy things the size of small ponies. He'd gotten them years before from a crazy mountain-man dog-breeder that lived up in the Jacksons for fifty bucks of canned goods and a few hundred rounds of .22 LR. Best deal he'd ever made. Dan and Ann were smart. Barker figured they had the brains of seven-year-olds. As loyal as your own children: which was a damn sight more than he could say for his actual children. He relied on the two of them more and more as he got older.

Barker reached down, grabbed his dogs by their collars, and looked directly into their brown, intelligent eyes.

"I want the two of you to go around that way," he pointed, "and have a good hard look around. You find anything, you howl. Understood?" They locked gazes with him for a brief instant, than shot off around the edge of the coral. Barker grunted. He was trying to reason with his dogs again, which meant he'd spent too much of his life alone in the high desert. Too much time alone in the Black Rock and your dogs become more than people, and people less than dogs. It was a sure symptom of desert rat madness, and he was most definitely a desert rat. Probably mad too, he thought with a chuckle.

Then he sighed, swung under the barbed wire fence that bordered his property with practiced ease, and hobbled off after his dogs. The horses emerged from the protection of their corral and crowded dangerously around him, nudging him and complaining with exaggerated motions of their mobile lips. He paused, dug some treats out of the pocket of his ragged Carhartt jacket, and tried to sooth a few of them with calm words. He fed them and stroked their long, bony faces, but the horses remained agitated. After a few moments, he continued walking across the field. They didn't follow.

When he was half way across, Dan and Ann bounded back to him, barking and leaping about nervously. He followed them to the far side of the field where the massive corpse of a stallion lay motionless in a great sticky pool of its own blood. It was Boss, one of his biggest and most spirited Arabians. Something had broken his neck, hurled the huge animal to the ground, and gutted him. Strings of intestines and bits of internal organs littered the ground in a crescent moon shape outward from his stomach. Most of Boss's back legs were missing, and one of his front legs had been ripped completely off.

Barker squatted stiffly, swatting away clouds of flies as he dipped his hand into the coagulated blood. Boss had been dead for about 12 hours. Whatever had killed him had come down to the ranch around twilight. No secret what it was, either. Barker cursed softly to himself, straightened, and walked back to his truck.

■

The Professional Hunter got the hell out of Zimbabwe while it was still Rhodesia. A veteran of the vicious Bush War, he didn't have to be a mathematician to know that the Rhodesians couldn't hold down the Indigenous with a population ratio of 22 to 1. Therefore, he deserted from the elite Selous Scouts, walked across the border into Zambia, and paid a brush pilot to fly him to Johannesburg where he caught a tramp freighter to Florida. The rest of his family didn't have his basic math skills, so they became dead. It was a lesson that hadn't been lost on him. The PH made of point of never being in the wrong place at the wrong time if he could help it.

Safely inside of the US, the PH found that he only had three skills: soldiering, farming, and hunting big game. He used the first to gain his American citizenship, spending four years at Fort Bragg training Special Forces in counterinsurgency techniques. Safely out of the military life for good, he decided that he liked hunting a lot more than he liked farming, and set himself up as a professional hunter. He was a deadly shot, with a natural affinity for firearms and the careful patience needed to stalk big game. His Boer accent didn't hurt, either. American's jumped at the chance to have their hunting expeditions led by the last of poor, dead Rhodesia's White Hunters (not that he personally liked or used the term). He led groups of puffing adventurers into the depths of Alaska in search of caribou, into the forests of Montana after big horn sheep, and into the mountains of California for brown bear. It paid well and was fun, so the PH saw no reason to interrupt his existence by giving a damn about much of anything else.

Yet there was one animal that the PH enjoyed hunting more than any other. He had killed plenty as a young man in Africa, but somehow going after them never got old. Here in North America, where his chosen quarry was smaller, smarter, and more elusive, he found the hunt even more intriguing. That was how he ended up living in the tiny, eccentric town of Hualapai high in the Black Rock Desert. It was where there were more of them than any other spot in the continental United States.

Lion. His home was a PETA member's nightmare of their stuffed corpses.

■

The PH was on his front porch chuckling his way through the bullshit-filled pages of Capstick's *Death in the Long Grass* when Barker's massive pickup slid to a halt in his gravel driveway, kicking up a magnificent plume of choking dust. Moments later the old man emerged angrily from the brown cloud, puffing furiously on a cigarette that the PH knew he shouldn't be smoking. Barker stomped up onto the porch, grabbed a rocking chair, and sat down across from the PH.

"You got a hunting party coming out here in the next couple days, right?" Barker spat out. He motioned with his Marlboro as if he were creating exclamation points out of smoke after each word.

"Sure." The PH answered levelly, intrigued by his neighbor's uncharacteristic agitation. The old man normally displayed about as much emotion as a stump. "I've got two guys coming out tomorrow from Reno. Figured on taking them out into the Limbos for a couple of days."

"Well, you can forget that shit. I know where the damn cats are." Barker explained how he found Boss's body. When he was done, the PH let out a long, sharp whistle.

"Yeah," the older man agreed. "I figure what we got here is a pair, or maybe even three, of young toms fresh out of the mountains. Probably all from the same litter. Or, maybe some of those bastard man-eaters the fucking Californians are always dumping over our border are working together. Anyhow, there's got to be more than one and they've got to be hungry if they're willing to take on a stallion."

The PH nodded in agreement. Sometimes in the spring adolescent mountain lions that didn't know any better would come down to the low country in search of an "easy" meal. Sheep, foals, calves, house pets, or even small children were their preferred prey – which meant that they didn't live very long. The California

Department of Game and Wildlife had made things worse in recent years by dumping any dangerous – meaning man-eating – cats they caught over the border into the "uninhabited" regions of northern Nevada. It was an unofficial, but well-known policy, that may have made liberal housewives in San Francisco and Los Angeles happy, but it made things a bit dicier in places like Hualapai.

Still, it was unusual for mountain lions to work together under such circumstances and the PH said so. Barker shrugged.

"No way that one cat – even a big tom – took down big old Boss on his own No sensible cat would even try. Too dangerous. So, I figure that we got two or three hungry teenagers that've been kicked to the curb by mamma-cat. They came as far down as my place looking for a foal or mare. Boss came out to challenge them, so they took him instead."

The PH agreed. It sounded like a pretty likely scenario.

"So you want me to take my guys up to your place and hunt them down? Not a problem. Can't say I don't thank you, Barker. You just saved me a lot of time and effort."

He grunted. "I liked that horse. Couldn't ride him anymore because of being all old and crippled up, but we were still friends. I want those bastard cats dead for it. If it makes you some money, than we're all better off."

He rose.

"I'm gonna get a cooler of beer and head back up to the ranch. If those fuckers show up before you do, I'll plug them myself. Otherwise, they're all yours. See you tomorrow."

The old man put out his cigarette in the PH's flowerbed, then turned and stomped back to his truck. A moment later, he was gone.

Like many older gun enthusiasts, the PH was a dedicated fan of old "Nitro Express" rifles from the turn of the last century. These were the ultra-powerful hunting weapons in their day, suitable for killing elephant and Cape buffalo. Named after the nitrocellulose and nitroglycerin worked into their smokeless powder, his particular favorites included .375 H&H Magnum, .416 Rigby, and .404 Jeffery. When he thought about Africa Rifle, he thought about one of these.

The PH also had a collection of custom weapons chambered for eccentric "wildcatted" cartridges that had been cooked up by some backyard American Frankenstein or the other: .585 Nyati, .577 Tyrannosaur, and .600 Overkill to name but a few. You didn't need that sort of cannon for cat hunting. So he went into his gun cabinet – so large that it could more accurately be thought of as a gun closet – and got out a hundred-year-old Krag-Jorgensen cambered for 6.5x55 Swedish. It was an old cartridge, but it had low recoil, superb penetration, and was inherently accurate He's put an excellent nine-power Zeiss scope on it, making it into what was in his opinion the ultimate cat-hunting rifle.

He patted the old weapon affectionately, and then walked back out to the living room where his two clients were waiting for them. They were a father and son: big, beefy men so close together in appearance that they could almost be brothers. Both were dressed in desert MARPAT camouflage, wore camelbacks, and carried bolt-action .22 magnum rifles that looked like toys in their large hands. In short, they were experienced, sensibly equipped hunters of the sort one expected to find in the rural West. They eyed his rifle curiously.

"You're right," he responded to their unasked question. "It's a bit big for hunting cat. I don't expect to use it. But the old Krag is an excellent 'what if' rifle, so let's bring it along, shall we?"

"A 'what if' rifle?" asked the younger hunter, genuine curiosity in his voice. His father chuckled.

"He means 'what if' you 'n' I are idiots and almost get ourselves killed by an angry tom."

"Or 'what if' a wounded cat turns on us," the PH replied tactfully, though in truth the older hunter was dead on. "It's rare, but it's been known to happen. We have to be especially careful since we know that there are two or more of them working together." He had phoned the older hunter yesterday, right after Barker had left, to apprise him of the situation. The hunter had quickly agreed to change their planed hunt from the Limbos over to the Granites. Both men seemed intrigued by the idea of taking down a couple of rogue cats, and were more than happy to help a local rancher in the process.

"It's rare for them to work together, isn't it?" asked the younger hunter. "I mean a big, male tom has a territory of what – 300 square miles?"

The PH nodded.

"Yes, that's right. It's rare. Cats – especially adult toms – are extremely territorial and don't work together. So, we're dealing with one of a few things here. Most likely, a couple of young toms have decided to throw in because food is scarce up in the mountains. Rare: but it could happen if they're littermates. Another possibility is that we have a female taking her almost-grown litter on a big hunting trip. Sort of like a final exam. It's the wrong time of year for that, but stranger things have happened around here."

"They don't normally go after horses, do they?" inquired the older hunter, "Especially not a full grown horse."

"No, it's too risky for them. One cracked rib because of a horse's hoof and a cat can't hunt. If it can't hunt, it's dead. So generally, attacks on horses only happen for three reasons. The first is because an adolescent tom is kicked out of the nest and goes looking for an 'easy' meal. They usually don't last too long before a rancher gets them. The second is because an old tom has lost its territory to a young one. It *has* to go looking for an easy meal. The third is because the cat is starving. I don't think that's too likely, though deer and pronghorn have been a little thin on the ground this year."

The three men walked out back to where the PH kept his kennel.

"Maybe it's a combination of two things?" asked the older hunter. "Say, a couple of starving young toms from the same litter? Maybe three even?"

The PH shrugged as he began opening the kennel doors. "Could be. Again, it's rare, but something killed old Barker's prize stallion, and it sure as hell wasn't a single 145 pound tom." He stepped back as his three redbone hounds – Marlow, Kurtz, and Leopold – came bounding out of captivity, frolicking about the men's legs and licking their hands enthusiastically. The PH patted Leopold's head affectionately.

"Load up," he commanded after a moment, and the three dogs shot off toward his Land Rover with howls of excitement. The older hunter chuckled appreciatively.

"Enjoy their work, do they?"

"They enjoy having work. As do I," the PH added with an appreciative nod.

The three men hooked up a trailer containing three beaten up quads to the Land Rover, piled in with the barking, excited dogs, and headed off toward the Granites.

One of the reasons that the PH had survived years of doing counter-insurgency operations against Black Nationalist guerrillas in the African bush is that he could *smell* when something was wrong. "Wrong" had a mildly poisonous scent – sort of like almonds – that he could detect instantly. It had kept him from stepping on a landmine or wandering into an ambush. He was reasonably certain that most people, given a certain amount of time and training, could probably smell "wrong" too. It was just that very few people who lived around "wrong" survived long enough to be any good at it.

Lucky them.

The PH got a big snoutful of "wrong" from the moment the three men pulled into the Barker ranch. To start with, the doors to Barker's Ford were wide open. The PH motioned to the two hunters.

"Load up your rifles, but stay in the car for a moment," he said a bit tersely. "Something's off-beam here; and I want to figure out what it is before I lead you into it."

The younger hunter looked at him sourly, but the older one simply nodded. He reached around and threw open the back door, allowing his redbones to spill out onto the dusty desert ground. He was unsurprised when they whimpered and hung around the car. The PH stepped outside. He chambered a round, nodded to his clients, and walked off toward the corral with his three hounds in tow.

It was empty. The gate had been thrown open, allowing the entire herd to escape and scatter. The PH thought he could see a couple of them grazing on a hillside a few miles away, but he couldn't be certain. Those might have been mustang. He bent down and had a hard look at the ground before the gate. There was no mistaking it: the horses had stampeded out of here all at once. It wasn't a good sign.

A few hundred yards away he could see several somethings lying on the ground. The PH was certain what they would turn out to be, so he turned around and walked back to the Land Rover.

"How much death have the two of you seen?" he asked calmly through the window.

"I was in Panama in '89." the older one answered. "Then in Desert Storm a couple of years later. The boy here has been hunting since he could walk. We've both seen our fair share."

The PH nodded. "All right then. Come on. I'd rather that there were more witnesses to this than just me."

The three men walked over to where the shapes lay upon the ground on the far side of Barker's field. One was the body of Boss, still lying where the old rancher had found it the day before. The second was an unidentifiable mass of blood, bone, and black fur that the PH figured was probably one – or possibly both – of Barker's dogs. He couldn't be certain. The final shape was the old rancher himself. What was left of him.

The older hunter turned pale but held steady. The younger one's eyes grew large, and he turned to vomit uncontrollably into a salt brush. It made a wet splashing sound as it hit the earth. The PH bent on one knee to examine his friend's corpse. It had been years since he'd had to do something like that, and he hadn't missed the experience very much. Something had torn the old cowboy apart. He was nothing but bloody tatters from the bellybutton down, with his guts pulled out below him like tentacles from a jellyfish. One of his arms had been completely bitten off above the elbow. Landmines did less damage to a man.

The PH had a good, long look at that bite mark and didn't like what he saw. A few feet away Barker's rifle lay discarded in the dust. He picked it up, swung down the lever, and checked the magazine. Unless the old cowboy had been carrying around an empty rifle, he'd fired every bullet before he'd been killed. The PH gingerly set the rifle down and began walking in slow, expanding circles around the corpse until he found what he was looking for. He whistled, set the Krag carefully down on the ground, and motioned for the two hunters. When they arrived, he silently pointed downward.

A large, healthy tom leaves distinctive four-toed tracks about the size of a dinner plate. The single paw print the PH was gesturing toward was roughly the size of a trashcan lid. The "toes" of the print were all wrong as well: non-symmetric and swollen, with distinctive marks at the end that suggested that the animal's claws weren't retractable. The PH pointed a short distance away to where several small pools of coagulated black blood lay. Cat blood. He grunted, as if he were having a conversation with himself, and then rose to face his clients.

"Phat Albert," he said, as if that explained everything.

"Huh?" asked the younger hunter, "What in the hell are you talking about? Cats don't ever grow to be that big."

The PH shook his head sadly. Again, he pointed at the track.

"I'd always thought that is was a bullshit legend," he said. "Kind of like those 'one that got away' stories fishermen tell each other. If I thought the story was real, I would have been off after him years ago. Guys would tell me that they had found entire buck deer or stallion way stuck up in big oak trees, the way mountain lions like to leave their prey to season as they rot. Or, they would tell me about tracks they found out in the mountains. Tracks like that one."

The older hunter looked incredulous. "How in the hell could it get that big?" The PH shrugged.

"Gigantism just happens in some mammals. Something goes wrong in the pituitary gland, and you grow to be two or even three times normal size. Remember Jumbo the Circus Elephant? He had it. Or that wrestler, Andre the Giant? Same deal. Maybe Phat Albert is just a freak of nature. Maybe it's because they used to mine uranium out here. Or it could be something else. The Paiute Indians never came out into the Black Rock if they could help it. Said it was haunted."

He shrugged again.

"According to hunters I've talked to, Phat Albert lives way up in a cave somewhere in the Granites. He sleeps most of the time, but once every month or two he comes down and grabs something big. Game *has* been a little scarce this year, so he must have been forced down to Barker's place to get a meal. First poor old Boss got in his way, then Barker and his dogs."

The PH sighed.

"Anyhow, I thought it was all bullshit until now."

Silently, the three men walked back to the Land Rover. The PH opened the Thule case he kept mounted to its roof, removed a tarp, and they walked back over to where Barker's body lay. He placed the empty rifle next to it, carefully covered it with the tarp, and then weighted it down with a half dozen large stones. Then he tossed the Land Rover's keys to the older hunter.

"What the hell are they for?" he asked.

"Take my car. Go back into Hualapai and tell the Sheriff what you've seen up here. He'll know what to do."

The PH glanced up at the mountains.

"Like hell I will." The older hunter was adamant. "You're not going after that damn monster alone. You need backup. The boy and I are expert shots. We'll pump a dozen rounds into that thing before it can twitch a whisker."

"Barker was an expert shot," the PH pointed out. "He got off somewhere between half-dozen and a dozen shots before it got to him. Those were .45 Long Colts, too – nice, big bullets with lots of kinetic energy behind them. Not like the spitballs you two are shooting. No way his dogs just stood there and let him die, either. Dan and Ann were as big as Irish Wolfhounds. They must have torn into Phat Albert with everything they had.

"And the bloody thing still walked away from it."

The younger hunter was looking a bit frightened, but his father continued.

"Twenty two magnums might be spitballs, but they're high velocity spitballs. We'll bleed him out through his exit wounds."

The PH started to shake his head, but the older hunter held up one hand.

"Look, this is the hunt of a lifetime right here. We'll probably never have enough time or money to go to Africa, but sure-as-shit here's an Africa sized lion right at our doorstep. It needs killing. Plus, I'll double your fee if you take us with you."

The PH paused. He *did* need the money... and the cat was already wounded in any case. Which made it more dangerous, but odds were good that they would track its spoor to a giant corpse. Backup couldn't hurt, either.

"All right," he said, more than a little hesitantly. "But the main goal here is to kill this damn monster, not get a good trophy. It's already shown it can take a bullet; let's give it its fill as soon as we get a chance. It's already killed one good man, and I'll be damned if I let it stay alive long enough to kill another."

It took a while for the PH to convince his dogs to pick up Fat Albert's trail. They were skittish and frightened, hanging back by the Land Rover as long as they could. Through a combination of coaxing and yelling, the men managed to convince Leopold, nominally the alpha male of the three, to pick up the trail. Once he did, however, the big hound's reluctance melted away, and the remaining two followed him – hesitantly at first, then with increasing enthusiasm as they picked up the wounded animal's scent.

The group formed a ragged line with Leopold taking the point and Marlow and Kurtz taking turns either following behind him or trailing back a little while nervously looking from one side to the other. The three men followed behind them on their quads with the older hunter taking up the front, the younger one behind him, and the PH taking up the rear. Slowly they began ascending a lower mountain known as the Banjo toward the forested saddle that joined it with the towering Granites above. They weren't a particularly quiet group, but that was all right. The PH wasn't counting on the element of surprise. The enormous cat was wounded – probably mortally – and wouldn't be looking for a fight. Ideally, the PH hoped to find him dead, or so close to dead as made no difference.

Still, you could never be sure. Not with something like *that*.

Following the head dog's lead, the group began ascending along the edge of one of the narrow "forests" that springs up along any stream that flows through a desert. When they reached the thin, muddy trickle of water that descended from the Granite's majestic heights, the dogs immediately plunged in, drinking greedily and taking a moment to wallow in the mud. The men turned off their quads and dismounted. They gathered up water from the stream in their hats and splashed it over their heads, enjoying the feeling of cold wetness flowing over their bodies as the temperature quickly ascended over the 80-degree mark, even though the sun had been up for less than an hour.

The younger hunter wandered over to stand underneath the shade of a massive tamarisk. At their elevation, the "forest" was only a half-dozen to a dozen trees wide at its broadest point. Farther up, however, where a saddle formed between the Banjo and the Granites, it widened to become a very real if very small forest. The grove they were in was like a tail leading down from a tadpole's body.

"Wow!" said the younger hunter, gazing out over the massive valley below, "It really is hard to imagine how beautiful it is up here from down there, huh?"

"Yes," replied the PH. "And almost no one ever comes up here to find out, either."

"So, what, nobody lives up here?"

The PH hesitated.

"No," he replied after a moment, "no one I'm aware of. This is all BLM – Bureau of Land Management – land. It belongs to the government. It's illegal to live up here, so nobody beside hunters and the odd, very eccentric backpacker ever comes up here."

"Wow!" the younger hunter once again commented. "It really is a lot nicer up here than you might think."

The PH laughed and put his fingers to his lips. "You're right. Don't tell anyone."

Refreshed and cooled down, the six resumed their climb. It didn't take the dogs very long to pick up the scent again. Here and there, the PH spotted congealing pools of blood.

"Good." He thought to himself. "He's still bleeding out."

The monstrous tom seemed to be skirting along the edge of the stream, probably pausing to drink and nurse its wounds as it went along. He imagined it was headed for its cave somewhere in the towering cliffs above. There was no way to know for certain. A healthy, youthful tom had a territory that ranged over 300 square miles. An older one might settle for a couple hundred. It was hard to say what kind of territory a freak of nature like Phat Albert might have.

Suddenly the PH smelled danger. Really, it was more of a reek than a smell. He cleared his throat and began to shout out a warning to the two men in front of him, when *it* happened. IT happened so fast that his voice caught in his throat. IT was also one of the few times in his life that the PH had been scared. Phat Albert flew out of a thick grove of Russian olive, aspen, and tamarisk. He was so large and powerful that his leap took him a full ten feet into the air. The creature was monstrous beyond anything the PH could ever have imagined. Its fur was black instead of the usual golden brown of a normal mountain lion. What looked like spines ran down the length of its back from the end of a ragged mane to where its tail began. The side that he could see was covered in dried and clotted blood from where Barker had shot the creature repeatedly with his rifle. The animal was at least 15 feet long and could have weighed as much as 300 pounds. Its teeth were a frightening, prehistoric mishmash of angles and points that jutted raggedly around its brutalized lips.

The worst part of the creature was its eyes, which glistened blood-red in the sunlight.

This primeval nightmare landed with one paw on top of Kurtz, pinning the animal to the ground with a yelp. Then it grabbed Leopold in its jaws and began shaking him like a terrier shakes a rat. The huge hound screamed, then died as its back broke with an audible snap. Marlow howled, then ran backwards in terror as the older hunter, still seated on his quad, snatched his rifle from its rack and began rapidly firing. The small bullets hit the side of animal with wet, smacking sounds. As the monster lion turned to lower its awful gaze down upon the desperately firing man, a single round ricochet off its massive atavistic skull.

It was then that the PH snapped out of it. He reached down calmly but quickly, grabbed his Krag, and chambered a round. In front of him, the younger hunter was panicking, trying to get off his quad and grab his rifle at the same time. With a single motion of his massive throat, Phat Albert hurled Leopold's lifeless corpse into the air behind him, then sprung at the older hunter. The PH fired while the grotesque thing was still in midair. He was arguably one of the best shots in Washoe County; a county filled with particularly good shots. The PH almost never missed.

Still, he couldn't be sure whether he hit it or not. If he had, the animal showed no sign of it. It plunged down on the older hunter with its two front paws, knocking him from his quad and sending his rifle spinning off into the brush. The man screamed as Phat Albert gathered him up in his mouth. The PH worked his bolt, chambered another round, and calmly aimed the Krag at the cat's left eye. It glowed with malignant, otherworldly hatred, causing him to hesitate for a fraction of a second. Unfortunately, all that the creature needed was that fraction. It turned and sprang back into the grove of trees with the older hunter shrieking and struggling in its mouth.

"Dad!" screamed the younger hunter. For a few moments the PH could hear the older man screaming somewhere out of sight. Then he couldn't hear him at all.

■

The young man was sobbing as the PH walked over to inspect the bodies of his two dogs. Leopold had been turned into a bag of bones and punctured organs. He was dead – but he died quickly. Kurtz was still alive, but only barely. Its front right leg had been crushed and its lungs caved in. The dog breathed in ragged gasps as blood poured from his nose. The PH put his hands over the animal's eyes, spoke a few quite, comforting words to it, and then put the barrel of his rifle to its head. He fired once, putting the grievously wounded animal out it its misery.

He then walked back down to the sobbing young man and struck him. Not too hard. Just once across the side of the face. The younger hunter looked at him uncomprehendingly, but stopped crying.

"Stop that," the PH demanded levelly. "We have to rescue your father. He might not be dead."

"Wha... whadda you mean?" the young hunter stammered. "You saw it. You saw what happened. You heard what happened!"

"Yes. It's still a lion though. Monster or not, it's still a lion and it will behave like a lion. If it's not hungry – and I'm not sure why it would be after what we saw down below – it may have just broke your father up a bit and stuffed him into a tree or a cave somewhere."

"He might still be alive," the PH paused. "And if he isn't, that damn thing still needs to be killed."

With a visible effort, the young man pulled himself together. He nodded. The PH walked back to his quad, turned it off, took his backpack off the rack, and then shouldered it. A moment later Marlow rejoined the two men. Redbones are normally brave, loyal, and tough; but the sheer ferocity Phat Albert's attack had driven the animal into humiliating retreat. Marlow had come back only reluctantly, but he had come back. In the PH's mind that was a more profound type of valor than not being afraid in the first place. He scratched the animal affectionately behind his ears, and then motioned for the younger hunter to gather his gear.

"I thought that Phat Albert would be half dead by the time we found him," he said. "I was wrong. Very wrong. For that I'm deeply sorry."

"But we will need to proceed on foot now." he continued. "That thing must have heard us coming from miles away and, obviously, lay in wait. You, the dog, and me: we can move quietly. Quickly too, if we hurry. It will still hear us coming, but not from as far away. Your dad hit it a bunch of times before it grabbed him and I'm pretty sure that I hit it too. There is no way it can keep going with that much lead in it."

He put his hand on the younger man's shoulder.

"We're going to find your dad, find that thing, and then we're going to kill it dead."

■

The three figures trudged up the side of the Banjo, each lost in his own dark thoughts. Marlow mourned for his two dead littermates, and wondered if he would have the courage to avenge them if given the chance. The young hunter mourned for his father, though that sorrow was tempered by the dim hope that he might still be alive. This only made it all the more terrible. The PH grieved the loss of his nerve. What in God's name made him hesitate to take that shot?

The day had started out hot, but that didn't mean it couldn't get hotter. By the time they reached the actual forest in the saddle between the two mountains, the temperature had risen to somewhere near 100 degrees. The three of them collapsed in the shade of a large birch, Marlow panting desperately in an attempt to cool off. The PH gave him a handful of water from his canteen, and then took a drink for himself.

"Hear that?" he murmured to the younger hunter.

"What? I don't hear anything." He whispered back.

"Exactly: there's not a sound coming out of this whole glen. Even the insects have buggered off somewhere else. That means he's either here, or he's been here recently."

The PH stood up and peered in to the densely packed trees.

"Come on," he motioned, "I don't think that he's here right now. Keep your eyes wide open, though, and try not to make a lot of noise."

The three of them rose and walked into the tangle of birch, oak, and aspen. It was cooler and dark inside of the little forest. The air smelled slightly of rot. Here and there, shards of light broke through the canopy of leaves above, casting shadows that scurried along the ground below. Desperate for a shot at the creature that had taken his father, the younger hunter nervously yanked his rifle at every tiny flicker of movement. Finally, Marlow barked once, sprinted to the base of a large oak tree, and began obsessively circling it. When the two men caught up the PH quieted him with a single, gentle touch to his muzzle, then peered up into the trees thick branches.

"Here," he handed the younger hunter his Krag, "I'm going to climb up and have a look. Might be that he stuck a buck up here, or it might be that your dad is up there. If you see anything that doesn't look like me or him coming down, shoot it with every bullet you have in your gun."

The PH vanished into the tree with a rustle of leaves. The younger hunter stood below, his expression a curious mixture of hope and grim resignation. Marlow danced nervously about, expelling the occasional quiet whine as he tried to look in every direction at once. The forest was deadly silent save for the occasional rustle of leaves above. Time got very strange for the younger hunter as his terror mixed with his hope. Could it be possible that his father was still alive? Could anything that encountered that terrible beast possible survive?

An eternity later, the PH descended from the tree and dropped athletically to the ground. A single glance to his face answered every one of the younger hunter's questions.

"It left his body up there, didn't it?" he almost whispered.

The PH nodded sharply.

"Best thing we can do is leave him up there for right now. The coyotes can't get at him that way." The older man shouldered his rifle and walked away without another word.

A little while later, they emerged from the forest at the base of an enormous granite cliff face. The PH pointed up toward the top.

"There's a bunch of caves up there at the summit. My guess is that..."

As if on cue, all three hunters turned to peer at a stand of greasewood about 200 yards away. Something large was moving inside of it, causing the tops of the plants to sway violently. With a snarl, the younger hunter brought up his rifle, aimed it at the movement, and pulled the trigger. At the last moment, the PH's left arm shot out, knocking the rifle's barrel out of alignment and causing the shot to go wild. The motion suddenly stopped.

The younger hunter turned angrily on the older man. "What in the hell did you do that for? I had him dead in my sights!"

The PH shook his head. "Wasn't him. Wrong size and wrong color. Probably a coyote or bobcat. It you were paying better attention you would have seen that. Plenty of creatures live out here that don't deserve to die because of what happened to your father."

The younger man only snarled in response.

The three of them began making their way up a narrow, winding path that took them around the edge of the cliff. The heat of the sun became disorienting, but the three hunters staggered on determinedly, once again lost in their own individual misery as they struggled along the steep path. The young hunter was awash with guilt over his father's death, and was angry with the PH for reasons he couldn't fully understand. The PH felt guilty over the death of his client, and was vaguely angry himself with the young hunter for not being more alert and competent. Marlow hungered for revenge against the monster that had murdered his brothers, but also wondered if the two humans he was traveling with knew what they were doing. As they staggered along, tripping over loose rocks and struggling around boulders under the blistering sun, even more doubt arose in his narrow canine mind.

Finally, the three struggled to the top of a ridge. Below them lay the magnificence of the Black Rock Desert: a lifeless moonscape of blowing sand, barren rock, and towering mountains punctuated by tiny oases of paradise. Behind them, a slate grey un-climbable cliff ascended up into the heavens. They edged gingerly upward along a ledge with Marlow at the point, stepping carefully around loose gravel and slippery granite as the desperate specter of falling rose to meet their sorrow, wrath, and terror of being eaten. At one point the younger hunter slipped, and was saved only by the steadying hand of the PH, which he shrugged off without a word of thanks.

At several points the PH found signs of Phat Albert: pools of black blood, paw prints the size of trashcan lids, and bits of hair. His stride seemed a little uneven, which brought a cruel smile to the hunter's face. He also found another set of tracks – smaller than the monster's, and not feline. Some sort of big male coyote, perhaps. It was hard to tell.

Finally, they reached a wider area where the ledge broadened out, allowing another ribbon-like "forest" to cling desperately to the side of the mountain. The PH sat down against a boulder, enjoying the minute amount of shade that it provided. Marlow collapsed at his feet panting desperately, and drank the last of his water. The grateful dog lapped it greedily down as the younger hunter paced impatiently in front of them.

"The caves are up that way," the PH pointed, "up past this glade. He'll go up there and try to sleep his injuries off."

The younger hunter glared angrily as the caves he could not yet see, and then chambered a round. The sharp, mechanical sound of the small bullet entering the rifle's action was like an exclamation point. It was then that the PH noticed how silent it was. It was then that he smelled almonds.

Everything began to happen in slow motion around him. Afterward he wasn't entirely sure if that was how he had really sensed it, or merely how his slightly damaged memories of the event had recorded it. He began to turn and rise to his feet as the huge, mutated mountain lion emerged from hiding onto a cliff a few dozen feet above him, its malignant eyes fastened upon him like the headlights of an oncoming semi-truck. The beast was covered in its own blood. It swayed unsteadily in the sunlight for a moment, then straightened its shoulders and released a roar that could have come directly through the gates of Hell.

The Krag felt impossibly heavy in the PH's hands as he brought it up and put the scope to his eye. Phat Albert leaped into the air, majestic and terrible as he reached out at the hunter with both of his forepaws. One of those malignant orbs bust into a shower of gore as the Krag barked, but the monster kept coming. The PH felt himself flung back against the boulder as his rifle flew from his hands. He felt pain explode in the back of his neck and head as he struck a rock. The PH sat down hard, stunned and unable to move but still wide-awake, a spectator in the horror that unfolded before him.

Phat Albert turned his maimed head so that his single functioning eye could glare at the hunter. He opened his mouth so that his victim could see the shark-like chaos of jagged teeth it contained. The PH understood: the lion wanted him to know the horrid, ripping death that awaited him. He was seasoning his prey with fear, with its terror of begin eaten alive. Then the crack-crack-crack of the younger hunter's .22 magnum opened up in the creature's side, causing him to scream and squirm away from the PH in pain. The younger hunter was screaming too, an unintelligible, primitive sound of rage as he ran directly at the lion, firing as he went. A howl joined the avenging son's scream as Marlow leaped from the PH's side to fasten his jaws onto Phat Albert's rear left leg.

The younger hunter fired his rifle until its hammer made clicking sounds as it struck against nothing in an empty chamber. Then his threw it at the monster that had killed his father, drew a long knife from his trousers, and leaped upon the creature, stabbing viciously at its neck. Phat Albert thrashed this way and that, desperately attempting to dislodge his attackers. As he watched, the creature bit off a piece of the young man's shoulder, then raked is claws against Marlow's side, exposing his ribs in a shower of blood. The two hunters refused to back off, biting and stabbing at their hated foe with a fervor that seemed monstrous even compared to the creature itself.

Then there was another howl.

The PH felt blood trickle down the back of his neck. Into the corner of his vision bounded one of Barker's hounds, he couldn't tell which one. He had been wrong, then. One of the huge beasts had survived the death of its master and mate. Like them, it had come, hunting for revenge high above the Black Rock. Now was its chance. For man or beast, monster or natural, vengeance when awoken became the primary motivator of all things. It was the director that stood behind the camera of their emotions, single-mindedly coordinating every one of their actions. Not love or faith or hunger or lust – but revenge. Sweeter than wine, stronger than the desire to survive.

Vengeance.

The enormous hound slammed into Phat Albert, sending all four of them sliding toward the edge of the cliff.

"No!" screamed the PH, but it was too late. Vengeance had taken every one of them in its unforgiving grip and would not let go, even as certain death loomed. The younger hunter craved it for his father, Marlow for his brothers, Barker's hound for his mate and master, and the PH for his wounded pride. Even Phat Albert wanted payback for all the horrors that nature and bullets had wrought upon his mutated body. Everybody wanted a bloody, red chunk of retribution, and nobody cared how much it cost when God came to collect his bill. Stabbing, screaming, biting, and cursing, all four of them tumbled over the cliff and out of sight.

■

"It was an hour before my legs started working again." The PH's voice sounded remote, almost disinterested. He stared down into his whisky glass as if trying to figure something out. "Everything still hurts like hell. Guess I must have struck my spine as well as my head. When I could get up, I worked my way down to the base of the mountain. It took me almost 'til sundown, but I found the boy's body and Marlow's carcass. Didn't find Barker's hound or Phat Albert, though. Maybe they fell down a crevasse or something."

He didn't sound very convinced.

"But you honestly think the monster is dead?" Sheriff Sal's large brown eyes bore down unrelentingly upon the PH in the way that cop's eyes always do. Searching, critical, distant. "You are 100 and ten percent sure that the damn thing died in the fall?"

The PH sighed, and then shook his head. "No. Until I've got its sorry ass hanging from the wall above my fireplace, I will never be certain."

The sheriff nodded. "You still got a bunch of those Africa rifles in your locker? That dinosaur gun or whatever it's called?"

The PH nodded.

"Right. I can cover up the deaths without lying. A big old tom got Barker, then the older guy, and the young one fell to his death while you two were hunting it down. That should keep those pencil pushers in Reno from getting their knickers in a twist. Now, I've still got a .50 Cal stuck up in the rafters of my office. Tomorrow morning you, my deputy, the game warden, and me are going up there armed with guns that would make Godzilla shit his britches. We're not coming back until this is finished."

The PH looked up at Sal, an unfathomable expression in his eyes.

"It's time to put this particular Black Rock nightmare to bed."

The Three Periods Of Survivalist Literature

[Posted to jasonswalters.blogspot.com on July 1, 2011.]

I don't believe I've ever read an article or a book analyzing survivalist fiction as a distinct sub-genre with its own literary qualities, artistic goals, and objective merits. Of course, it's easy to see why. The sort of people who enjoy performing that kind of abstract literary zoology tend to also be urbane, liberal academics, who either instinctively dislike the entire idea of the genre, or find the sorts of people who read and write such books to be so inherently repulsive as to be unmentionable. Hence, the lack of McFarland publications entitled things like "Preparedness Or Paranoia? A guide to the work of James Wesley Rawles" or "Boston T. Party: a guide to the fiction and non-fiction of Kenneth W. Royce."

There have of course been endless seminars, essays, and books on the post-apocalyptic genre. I even helped write some of them. However, "survivalism" doesn't seem to have received academic, or even extensive amateur, attention as its own unique endeavor. Therefore, since I am perhaps uniquely qualified to do so, I'll try to give the subject a least a cursory analysis, and hope that those of you reading this will add your own observations to mine.

Survivalist fiction as a genre can be reasonably broken up into three distinct periods: early (or "Atomic"), middle (or "Ecological"), and modern (or "Economic"). These designations are by no means definitive, though the periods do seem to build upon their predecessors, with ideas going in-and-out of style over time as with any other genre. Thus a reader is almost as likely to find survivalist fiction in which society has collapsed due to nuclear war during the Ecological period as he is during the Atomic period, while the during the Economic period he is less likely to encounter it as the Cold War slowly vanishes into the rear view mirror of history.

The initial Atomic period of the genre occurred during the 1950's and 60's. It produced such memorable works as Pat Frank's *Alas, Babylon* (sited as an inspiration by such later writers as Brin, Rawles, and Forstchen) and George R. Stewarts' excellent if downbeat *Earth Abides,* one of the first novels to interject ecological issues into the post-apocalyptic genre. It also lead to the creation of a whole lot of astoundingly awful cinema, with a few gems tossed in amongst the rubbish (Vincent Price's *The Last Man On Earth* and Harry Belafonte's *The World, The Flesh, and The Devil* come to mind).

While Nevil Shute's *On The Beach* falls into the same period and is certainly an excellent example of post-apocalyptic fiction, it doesn't qualify as part of survivalist canon, as its characters all accept the inevitable doom of the human race and commit suicide in various ways. This runs contrary to the basic theme of the genre: an advanced but corrupt inevitably society falls, forcing ordinary people to perform extraordinary feats of courage and ingenuity as they attempt to rebuild a new, often better world from the ashes of the old. Though the characters often face shocking hardships and tough ethical choices, the tone is generally upbeat. In the end, principled, intelligent, and civilized people win out over self-serving, shortsighted, and degenerate ones.

For these same reasons, several pre-Atomic period novels must be excluded from the genre of Survivalist literature, even though they would seem at first to merit inclusion with it. DeFoe's *Robinson Crusoe*, Johann David Wyss' *Swiss Family Robinson*, and Jack London's short story *To Build A Fire*, are all excellent examples of stories about survival (or in the case of London's story NOT surviving), but none take place after the destruction of the protagonists' entire society. In fact, in each case the protagonists are trying to stay alive so that they can return to a society they know to still exist, removing one of the core motivations of characters in Survivalist fiction: the driving urge to rebuild the world as a better place.

The second, Ecological period of survivalist literature took place during the 1970's and 80's. While the Atomic period generally relied upon nuclear devastation as its triggering event, this second wave of stories broadened its focus to include other, more abstract (and often magical) themes – though typically these include some sort of "mankind punished by nature for his transgressions" ecological theme. Some of this era's more memorable works include Niven and Pournelle's *Lucifer's Hammer,* John Christopher's *The Death of Grass* (Okay; it was written in 1956. They made it into a movie in 1970) Steven King's voluminous *The Stand,* and S.M. Stirling's quasi-magical *Dies The Fire.*

This period also saw the creation of many interesting (though not necessarily good) survivalist films and television shows. These include *The Road Warrior, Damnation Alley,* the American TV series Ark II, and the (much better) British series The Survivors.
Of course no discussion of Survivalist literature from this period is complete without mentioning David "I hate rural Americans" Brin's 1985 *The Postman.* To be very straightforward: I loathe this book. Not because it's badly written. Brin is, in fact, an excellent science fiction writer, and I am quite fond of some of his books (the Uplift series in particular). However, Brin uses the Postman to project his subconscious fears of rural Americans onto a wide screen (literally, since the book was turned into a crappy Kevin Costner film). In his mind, Survivalists somehow *cause* the apocalyptic event, though how this happened is never clearly explained. By being reactionary gun nuts, apparently. Civilization is only maintained by University of Oregon graduate students and, of course, that modern utopia known as California. Of course, it's the knuckle-dragging rural people from places like eastern Oregon who can't wait to swoop down barbarian-style on their more civilized urban cousins, who are (naturally) very able to take care of themselves in style after the apocalypse.

[Take a clue from Niven, Pournelle, Forstchen, Rawles, and (frankly) me David: it's definitely going to be the other way around. Bubba and Jose just don't do cannibal army.]

The Survivalist literature of the "modern" or Economic period reflects current economic concerns about hyperinflation, the instability of global markets, the unpredictable effects of information technology on human society, and a general sense of urban decay due to overabundance. As I mentioned in the last post, James Rawles *Patriots* is a good example of this type of type of novel, though possibly it isn't a good novel artistically speaking.

You can't really talk about survivalism in Modern America without mentioning James Wesley Rawles, the editor of www.SurvivalBlog.com. Rawles has a Bachelor of Arts degree from San Jose State University with minor degrees in military science, history, and military history. A former U.S. Army intelligence officer who held a Top Secret security clearance, he achieved the rank of Captain, attended the Army NBC defense officer's course, as well as Northern Warfare School at Fort Greeley, Alaska.

In other words: he's no Homer Simpson.

Rawles is very knowledgeable, very hardcore, and very Christian, and this comes through in his novel. His characters consider daily bible study to be an important part of the post-apocalyptic lifestyle, which makes a certain amount of sense. Who would you rather have watching your back in a firefight: a hardcore Evangelical Christian, or the guy who camped next to you at Burning Man? It's not a difficult question to answer.

Patriots plot goes something like this: a decade before America collapses due to hyperinflation, a group of students at the University of Chicago form a survivalist group. They are uniformly athletic, competent, and religious, though not homogeneously so. Rawles' protagonists include Catholics, Protestants, Mormons, and at least one Jew. Through hard work and constant investment, they purchase, stock, and fortify a small farm in rural Idaho. They also train constantly as a military unit and purchase identical matching equipment. Collectively this dozen or so men and women are known as The Group, and later as the Northwestern Militia.

When The Crunch (as the collapse in *Patriots* is called) happens, the various members of The Group make their way from Chicago to their compound in Idaho, where they work together to survive the collapse. As the novel progresses, they find themselves working with other militia groups to patrol and protect the Idaho countryside, first against looters and roving gangs of criminals, then eventually against a United Nations-sponsored totalitarian government determined to impose its will on a devastated America.

However, that's not really what the book is about.

In the tradition of Rand's *Atlas Shrugged* (a tradition Rawles alludes to several times in the book), Patriots is really non-fiction disguised as fiction to make it palatable to a larger audience. (Several online reviews have accurately described it as a "survival manual fairly neatly dressed as fiction.") Where Rand used her novel to outline her philosophical ideas, Rawles uses his to provide a staggering amount of survival information. I'm betting that much of the content of his non-fiction work *How To Survive The End Of The World As We Know It* has been packed into its substantial 384 pages.

In fact, I'm going to buy a copy and find out... which may be the whole point of *Patriots,* come to think of it.

The information in *Patriots* ranges from selecting proper clothing to long-term food preparation to creating homemade anti-tank weapons. Of course, gun info: lots and lots of lots of gun info, including proper maintenance, caliber size, modifications, manufacturer quality, and proper safety. In fact, there is so much information in *Patriots* that it interferes with Rawle's writing style. A character never takes careful aim and fires at a marauding biker. He "zeroed cautiously in on the target using a Zeiss Conquest 24-power scope mounted on his custom manufactured stainless-steel bolt action A-Square crafted in Chamberlain, South Dakota. It fired a wildcat 500-grain .470 Capstick cartridge designed to take down dangerous African game at distances of 200 yards or less."

Okay, I made that last bit up. Still, his writing style can be very distracting – though if you're interested in these sorts of things, it can also be very interesting.

Another fascinating aspect of Rawles' book is its focus on ethical behavior in post-apocalyptic situations. His heroes are devoutly, un-ironically religious. The pray regularly, hold bible studies, and try to apply their Judeo-Christian faiths to the situations they find themselves in, touching on some interesting questions that are seldom mentioned in the genre. Should you pray for the souls of rapists, murders, and other assorted scum-of-the-wasteland after you waste them? Is it vital to show charity in a survival situation? What is the ethical way of disposing of goods taken from looters in a situation where there is no law and order? What are the proper roles of marriage and sex under such circumstances?

These aren't problems that I'd considered before reading *Patriots,* and I think they are definitely worthy of consideration. Additionally, whether consciously or unconsciously, Rawles' work examines the role of Judeo-Christian faith in maintaining a coherent, principled society during periods of social disintegration. (Not an unreasonable proposition, given the Catholic Church's role in European society during the Dark Ages.) Because his characters are devout, they see themselves as part of a greater historical tradition, one that does not end or even greatly change when their society falls apart. To put it another way: a Christian or a Jew does not cease being a Christian or a Jew when their government collapses, and must behave accordingly even under the worst circumstances.

This seems like a Big Wisdom to me, and one I'm going to give some thought to.

However, religious questions aside, James Wesley Rawles and I aren't really the same kind of "prepper," or at least his characters and I aren't. His heroes are highly trained and affluent urbanites that had the foresight to prepare for worse case social scenarios. I think the rural, minimalist "post-apocalyptic" lifestyle is worth living in its own right, and that preparedness is simply a logical part of that lifestyle. Instead of spending countless hours and a small fortune getting ready to live that kind of life, it strikes me that his characters would have been better off living that life well before The Crunch happens, even if it made them poorer and a bit less prepared in advance. There is a certain rhythm to things, after all, and it's a lot less shocking to know that the power grid is gone when you haven't lived on it for years.

Unlike James Wesley Rawles, William R. Forstchen is unarguably an excellent writer, and while his 2009 novel *One Second After* isn't as packed to the gills with technical information as *Patriots,* it's quite a good novel. Based upon several years of intensive research and interviews, it examines what might happen in a "typical" American town in the wake of an attack on the United States with "electro-magnetic pulse" (EMP) weapons. It's set in a small college town in western North Carolina and is a cautionary tale of the collapse of social order in the wake of an EMP strike. The book was cited on the floor of Congress and before the House Armed Services Committee by Congressman Roscoe Bartlett, chair of the House Committee tasked to evaluate EMP weapons, as a realistic portrayal of the potential damage rendered by an EMP attack on the continental United States.

However, one of the interesting things about *One Second After* is its portrayal of the apocalyptic economic effects on the United States by an EMP. With communications, transportation, refrigeration, and manufacturing effectively eliminated, the country goes through a series of "die-offs" over the period of one year, leaving only about 20% of the population alive nationwide. (This is an average. Food-rich Iowa had the highest survival rate with a 50% die-off, while New York City and Florida had a 95% die-off from its fighting among the large populations, high elderly population, and so forth.)

What makes Forstchen's scenario even more horrifying is that a) no one is directly harmed by the atomic blasts that generate the EMPs, and b) The book contains a brief non-fiction afterword by United States Navy Captain William Sanders about EMP, which includes references to the reports of the United States EMP Commission. Chilling stuff!

We are far from done with the Economic period of Survival literature. Whether based (as I believe) on realistic fears about hyperinflation, or on imaginary, subconscious, and possibly even xenophobic terror of economic globalization, I expect that more and more books like *Patriots* and *One Second After* are in the offering. Let's just pray that they continue to be speculative fiction... and not autobiography or prophesy.

Judas Horse

> When God created the horse, he said to the magnificent creature: I have made thee as no other. All the treasures of earth shall lie between thy eyes. Thou shalt cast thy enemies between thy hooves, but thou shalt carry my friends upon thy back. Thy saddle shall be the seat of prayers to me. And thou fly without any wings, and conquer without any sword.
> — The Koran

The hills stretched out endlessly in every direction. In the distance, they ascended steeply to become dry, waterless mountains. The hills had been brown for so long that it was hard for the Judas Horse to remember when they hadn't been brown. He chewed distractedly at the dried grass and waited. The Judas Horse had spent a great deal of his life waiting. It was part of his job. It was part of what made him a Judas Horse.

He'd been trained so thoroughly that he didn't need a lot of human supervision. He could be counted on to wait somewhere very close to this spot, ready to play his role when the time came. He didn't like to think of himself as broken. Who did? He knew that his habits had been shaped by bit, spur, and corral more than anything else. Just as he had a hard time remembering when the prairie and mountains were green, he had a hard time remembering the time before he was a Judas Horse. He knew dimly that such a time had existed, but its memory was vague. He couldn't remember the details anymore.

The Judas Horse existed to betray his own kind, but any misgivings he may have once had about it were long since beaten out of him. Yet something like doubt nibbled around the edges of the Judas Horse's mind, as limited as it was and as shaped by the hand of man as it was. Left alone with his own thoughts, such as they were, as often as he was, he had been contemplating the same line of questioning that had intrigued many an ancient Greek philosopher; whom, had they known that a horse was capable of thinking about them, would have been even more intrigued. Namely, "What does it mean to be a horse?"

The Judas Horse knew that for most it meant a lifetime of subservience to men: herding cattle, carrying children, marching in parades, and the like. There was, however, that last wild remnant, those proud, feral few who were not mankind's clients or servants. Who lived for their own sake in the deserted, high places of the world. Was that what it really meant to be a horse? To be free and away from the influence of men? Or was that a dream, an illusion, a fading racial memory that he felt somewhere deep in his bones? One that he could smell but never taste?

The Judas Horse wondered about these things, even as he prepared to destroy them.

He could feel the herd through his hooves before he could see them. He felt their thunder like a chaotic vast heartbeat pounding along the valley floor. He flared his nostrils and looked up. In the distance, he could see a cloud of brown, choking dust with what looked like tiny black specks racing before it. Slowly both the cloud and the specks grew larger and larger, until he could start to make out details. Along the edge of the cloud were cowboys – men – on machines and horses. They drove the black specks between them like the sides of a funnel, forward toward the Judas Horse.

Only they weren't black specks anymore. They were mustang: wild horses. Magnificent, free horses. A bit smaller perhaps than the Judas Horse or the domesticated mounts that helped push them toward him. A little scrawnier, too. They were magnificent nonetheless.

Blinded by instinct and the fear of captivity, the mustang fled before the cowboys in a desperate, doomed attempt to outdistance their pursuers. The more they ran, the more exhausted they became, and thus the less able they were to outdistance their patient hunters. Like any contest between man and horse, the results were invariably the same: man got what he wanted, and horse has to do what he was told. It seemed to be the natural way of things.

The Judas Horse knew that he wasn't as smart as your average man was (though he suspected he was smarter than some). His limbs ended in hard, sharp hooves that couldn't be used to control, grasp, or manipulate machinery. He knew these two reasons were why men ruled, and their client species – horses, dogs, and even cats – served. It couldn't be any other way, could it?

The herd of mustang grew nearer. The Judas Horse wondered if things had always been this way, or if they needed to always be the way they were now. Certainly, men were smarter than horses and were able to use machinery, but there were still advantages to being a horse. A horse was faster and stronger. It had a more acute sense of smell and better hearing. Horses could live off the land far better than men could. Was it therefore necessary that men ruled horses? Could not horses rule men? Why should the larger, stronger species constantly be under the yolk of the smaller, weaker one?

The mustang grew so close that the Judas Horse could almost make out their eyes. Then there was no more time for deep thoughts and reflection. He turned, putting his tail to the front of the fleeing, terrified animals, and began to canter. From a canter, he quickly moved to a gallop, periodically glancing over his shoulder. Their minds overcome by fear the mustang fell back and began following him on instinct. As he knew they would. Their lead horses immediately lined up with him, in effect making him the lead horse. The Judas Horse was an instant alpha male leading a mob of frightened, panting betas into captivity.

He led them through an open gate toward the northeastern corner of the valley. The men on horses and machines lagged behind, letting him do his job without interference. They hung back like a pack of coyotes, looking for stragglers. He led the mustang herd through another fence and then burst across a field at top speed, daring its exhausted leaders to keep up with him. Driven by instinct and seeing their pursuers falling far behind they gleefully followed, pouring on the momentum in a last, desperate bid for freedom. The Judas Horse could feel their wild optimism. He could smell their lust for freedom, and see the self-assurance in the way the lead stallions fought to get their breathing back under control. They had outrun their tormentors, and now they were going to be free.

It was then that the Judas Horse led them through the third and final gate into a large corral with wooden fences. When the last wild horse had followed him inside, a cowboy swung the gate shut, trapping all of them inside. The Judas Horse had done his job once more. They were trapped and would never be free again.

Later, when the Judas Horse had been fed, rubbed down, and put into his stall, he had more time to think. The captured mustang had run around the corral for a bit, then stopped, turned, and looked at him through hurt, unbelieving eyes. They didn't *do* anything to him, of course. It simply wasn't in their nature. They could never understand why the Judas Horse did the thing to them he had done – namely, taken away their freedom.

To be honest the Judas Horse didn't know either. He wasn't sure what freedom was. He didn't especially like his human owners. What slave loves his master? He "worked" for something called the BLM. Their brand had been seared into the flesh his left hip. He didn't know what the BLM might be or what it did exactly, except for capture wild horses. For that matter, he had never understood why the BLM wanted to round up wild horses in the first place. It seemed like a very strange way for humans to spend their time.

The Judas Horse understood a decent amount of English: far more than anyone thought he did. He knew that his trainer's name was "Dirk" and that the stable boy's name was "Juan." He knew the individual names of the cowboys he worked with out in the field. He even knew that BLM stood for "Bureau of Land Management," but of those three words he only understood "land," which didn't tell him much of anything.

Dirk walked over to his stall and gave him a carrot. "Good work today Judas." his trainer said while stroking his mane, "Once again you brought it off without a hitch."

The Judas Horse chewed on his carrot. He knew that BLM horses in general led good lives. They were treated with a reasonable amount of affection, fed properly, and nursed back to health if they were injured. He also knew that when he got too old to work, he would be taken to a special ranch where he could spend the remainder of his days in comfort.

Of course, there was the small matter of being a slave.

"How's tricks, Juan?" asked the trainer.

"Well, you know Mr. Dirk, I'm still shoveling horseshit. So I guess that things are going about the same," responded the stable boy.

Both men laughed. It was an old, shared joke.

"Where's Big Dan?" asked Dirk. "I didn't see him come in off the range with the others today." Big Dan was one of the BLM's cowboys.

"Oh, Dan got himself into a fight in Hank's Hualapai Club last night," replied Juan, who was always current on the ranch's gossip. "Sheriff Sal's got him cooling his heels in the jail for a few days until he gets himself together."

"Well, crap." replied the trainer, "That's going to make things tougher. We've got to get this load of mustang fattened up and in good shape before the buyers start to come in a couple of weeks."

"Why so fast?" asked Juan. "There a shortage of dog food or something?"

Both men laughed, and the Judas Horse swiveled his ear to listen more closely.

"Well, basically Juan, if you get right down to it: yes. All that ethanol production the Feds are trying to get going means there's going to be less feed for cows. Less feed for cows, means less cows – and less cows means more call for horses to make dog food out of."

"I thought that shit was illegal now, anyhow," said Juan, scratching his head. "Isn't that a federal law or something?"

"Sure is," replied the trainer, "But there ain't no law like that in Mexico. They send third party buyers up here to snatch them up, and then haul them south the border, slaughter 'em there, and turn 'em into dog food. All perfectly legal."

The stable boy whistled.

"That's some sneaky, devious shit there Mr. Dirk."

The trainer shrugged. "Well, yeah, but what can you do? They're only trash horses, anyhow. Not good for anything much. Not good for training, mostly not good for rodeos, and you can't never put a child on one. Who the hell's gonna miss 'em? They're not even native to the ecosystem. The mustang is just like a rat; only it's bigger and eats more."

He glanced a bit guiltily at the Judas Horse.

"Unlike, say, old Judas here. He's worth his weight in gold."

The Judas Horse flinched almost imperceptibly as his trainer patted him on the neck.

"Well," said Juan with a bit of doubt in his voice, "it still seems a bit cruel."

"Now, nobody loves horses more than me," replied Dirk a bit more reproachfully. "My whole life's been devoted to them. Been riding since I was old enough to walk. But there's just ain't enough land anymore. Your cattlemen, who're getting pushed out by the suburbs, are in turn pushing out the indigenous species. Not enough land to go around between pronghorn antelope, big horn sheep, deer, and cattle. Definitely not enough land for wild packs of trash horses."

The stable hand just looked at him.

"Look, Juan, let's go get some grub." Dirk was obviously eager to change the subject. "You've been working hard, and so have I." He clapped his hand jovially on the smaller man's shoulder, and Juan shrugged. Food was food, after all. The two of them walked out, turning the lights off as they went.

■

Dog food. Dog food? The Judas Horse didn't know what "Mexico" was, and certainly had no idea what a "federal law" might be, but it caught the gist of what the trainer and stable hand had been talking about. Dog food? It had never occurred to him that anything bad would happen to the wild horses. He's always figured that after they were herded up they were paired off with men or put in a pasture somewhere.

Dog food?

From the time he was a foal, the Judas Horse had been trained to behave. This gave him a certain level of self-discipline that many other animals lacked.

Dog food?

He wasn't skittish. He'd been trained to handle himself well in the various dangerous situations his job put him in. It was unusual for him to show any emotion at all, and he knew it. It surprised the Judas Horse when he found himself shaking his head back and forth with violent agitation.

Dog food.

This was where the wild horses had gone. Those proud, beautiful wild horses. The last of his kind free to roam across the face of the earth as their ancestors had. He began pawing at the earth with his huge forelegs. So. Men with their usual factory-like efficiency had turned one of their client races into food for another one of their client races. They had decided to transform those last remnants of his race not under their control – those not enslaved – into food for another that was enslaved.

Dog food!

The Judas Horse was now so angry and agitated now that he was whinnying and banging against the sides of his stall. He'd been complicit in the whole thing. He'd *helped*. He'd guided very the mustang whom he had respected and loved to their doom, not to a field or a cowboy like he had thought. He had been an instrument used to destroy the last of what was good and free in his species. He'd led them to their doom. To become dog food!

Something slipped into the Judas Horse in that instant. Something that had been silently waiting, patiently, out in the desert. Something Other.

In a fury, he began kicking at the back of his stall. Kicking it with all of his might. To his incredible surprise, the old, sun-dried boards exploded on his second blow, blowing out the back of his stall and opening it up to the yard beyond. Unsatisfied with the destruction, he shook his stall some more, rocking from side to side until the boards creaked and cracked under his weight. Shingles began to fall off the roof of the barn. He reared up on his hind legs and smashed out the stall's gate with his front hooves.

The Judas Horse was furious in a way unknown to men, as loaded down with logic and civilization as they are. His intelligent, stoic, and domesticated demeanor had evaporated under an unrelenting onslaught, a crashing red wave of instinct too powerful to be resisted. He had gone mad. He had reached enlightenment. He had been transformed into something new and terrible: the wrath of an entire race. He was Other.

Dog food!

He charged toward the corral where the herd of mustang he had helped to bring in was confined. They looked at him through eyes both surprised and resentful. The Judas Horse reared up on his hind legs, pawing at the empty air with his front hooves and whinnying out his defiance at the men of the world. The wild horses shied back, unused to any display of emotion except those given in heat or in self-defense. The Judas Horse charged toward the edge of the corral, turned, and began kicking at its board with his back legs. Normally he would have injured himself, possibly cracking one of his hooves, but they had been shod with iron shoes for his protection. He beat mercilessly against the boards until they began to break. Finally, they shattered with a sound like a gunshot.

"Judas! Stop!" Jake, the cowboy who also served as an evening watchman at the BLM came running toward him. "What are you doing?"

The Judas Horse turned and struck the cowboy in the skull with one of his front hooves. The man screamed and crumpled to the ground.

It was the last thing he ever did.

The Judas Horse was all over Jake in seconds, stomping him viciously with all four metal shod hooves. The 1,500-pound horse crushed the cowboy's ribs, shattered his limbs, and turned his skull into a bloody, formless mess of flesh, bone, and brain. It was done in less time than it would have taken to saddle up a well-trained mare. Again, the Judas Horse reared up on his hind legs and screamed out his defiance at the natural order of things. Then he reached down with his huge front teeth, grasped a bit of man flesh, and ripped upward, so that an unidentifiable mess of blood, gristle, and meat was left dangling from his mouth. He turned his wild, bloodshot eyes toward the mustang herd, looking intently at each of them in turn. Then he tipped his head back, raised the formless macabre thing into the air, and swallowed it with a single massive gulp.

Dog food.

Without waiting for a response for the herd, the Judas Horse threw himself onto the ground and began wallowing in the gruesome, ragged tatters of the man's corpse until his coat was entirely covered in human blood. He reveled in the sensation of the man's life-juice covering his coat, drank deeply of the scent of his exploded bowels and burst brain, and felt intoxicated by the salty taste of the dead man's flesh. Who was going to "Mexico" now? Who was dog food now?

Who is riding whom, little human?

The Judas Horse stood, feet still firmly planted on the cowboy's remains, and turned to face the mustang once again. Like frightened foals they cowered back from him, their eyes wide and filled with fear. If horses had any concept of Hell, he would have looked like a demon straight from its depths. The Judas Horse had broken the natural order of things, and even the wild horses knew it. He was the Other, the Thing that lay so far outside of their experiences that it literally came from beyond the edge of the world. Only two things ever come from beyond that edge: demons and gods.

The Judas Horse decided to become a god. He gazed into the eyes of his chosen people once more, then turned and trotted away into the night without looking back. He knew that they would follow him. He had transcended so far beyond their concept of alpha male that instinct left them very little choice. He was not surprised when he heard to first few tentative hooves strike the earth behind them, and then more, until a veritable symphony of movement fell into line behind him. In the end, not a single wild horse chose to remain behind.

Without even the tiniest shred of doubt, the Judas Horse led them away from the BLM corral and into the dark desert night.

It was almost dawn when the Judas Horse led his people into an isolated cove along the northern shore of Pyramid Lake. All of them save he rushed to the shore to drink from its slightly alkaline waters. The Judas Horse had no need for drink, or sleep, or food — or anything else for that matter. He had become a vessel of the Other, and would accept no such comforts until his work was complete.

They had passed several settlements and a couple of ranches along the way, but he hadn't stopped to destroy them. He wanted to put as much distance between his people and captivity as he could possibly get before he began doing things like that. Additionally, the Judas Horse knew that the men who lived along the sides of the lake were different from the others. He had heard his trainer speak of them as "Indians" and "Paiute" — whatever those words meant — but the Judas Horse now knew their true name. They were the First Men, and they had been living on this land longer than horses had. Somehow that meant they were not only less deserving of his wrath, but more capable of stopping him as well. He avoided them entirely.

He gave his mustang until sunrise to drink, graze, and rest. Then he set off at a cantor toward the mountains to the north without so much as glancing at any of them. He knew where he would take his people. He knew that they would follow. More importantly, he knew what he would do along the way. He would teach men such a lesson that they would never come after his herd again. He would teach them which species was superior. Man would fear horse before he was through.

It was almost noon before they came to the first ranch. It was a small sheep herding operation tucked into a green elbow between low mountains. Though its hands must have been able to hear the mustang coming from miles away, they did not run. Instead, they came out to meet the advancing mustang herd on horseback and machines, obviously intending to corral them. That was the natural way of things, after all.

Unfortunately for them, the Judas Horse was no longer a natural thing.

The wild horses lined up along a long ridge above the ranch about three deep. The Judas Horse ran back and forth in front of the line like a hell-thing, screaming and pawing the air with his iron hooves. Down below the advancing sheepherder's mounts became uneasy. He continued charging from one side of the line to the other, crying out his defiance at the advancing men, their slave-animals, and their machines. Finally, all of the herder's mounts panicked. Some threw their riders and bolted away into the hills. Several threw their riders and joined the ranks of the Judas Horse's army, lining up with their wild cousins as if it were the most natural thing in the world. Others, piloted by more skillful horsemen, were calmed down, and turned with their masters to face the coming onslaught.

Finally, the Judas Horse charged down toward the men. Within seconds his people where charging behind him in a ragged line, screaming out their defiance as they bore down upon their would-be captors. Most of the men turned and fled on machines, on horses, or on foot. Those that did not were mercilessly trampled down as the frenzied mass of horseflesh passed over them. With that battle won, the Judas Horse directed his herd down upon the ranch itself, where they wrought incredible destruction. They trampled down fences, destroyed small outbuildings, trashed equipment, freed captive livestock, and utterly destroyed a half-acre vegetable garden. Then, brief and hard as a desert rainstorm they were gone, leaving only destruction in their wake.

■

The next ranch was better prepared. The Judas Horse understood dimly that they had been warned of his people's coming, though how this might be he did not know. Its hands were dug in behind a sturdy fence with rifles, and began firing into the herd as it approached in a desperate attempt to drive them away. This merely infuriated the Judas Horse further. Without pausing this time to warn them of his intentions, he charged directly at the firing men with his people in furious pursuit. The first row got it the worst. A stallion to his left collapsed with a scream. The Judas Horse felt a sharp pain as a bullet passed through the flesh of his right flank, but ignored it. Filled with righteous Other, he simply didn't have time to worry about such things. Here and there, horses fell dying from their wounds and were trampled by their own parents or children. Focused on his goal of reaching the line of riflemen, he ignored that as well.

The line of charging horses reached the line of firing men and crashed over it, knocking the wooden fence down upon the men and splintering both beneath their hooves. Those who got away hid in the basement of the ranch house as the mustang wrought an even more terrible destruction on this spread than they had on the last.

Then they were past the few scattered ranches of the Smoke Creek Desert and into the foothills of the Granite Mountains. The Judas Horse allowed his people to forage for a moment while he drank in the scents of the late afternoon. It smelled of dust, alkaline, and sage, with just a slight hint of rain ready to fall, as the Sun prepared to slink cravenly behind the mountains.

They were close. Very close. Only one task left to perform.

The herd emerged from the hills in the late afternoon above the tiny, isolated town of Hualapai. The Judas Horse flared his nose furiously as he looked down upon his final intended victim. *This* would be where he taught men his ultimate, valuable lesson. Once they had experienced his wrath, men would leave him and his tribe alone forever. He would leave the settlement's shattered remains as a monument to horse's superiority over man. For all eternity there would be no mistaking it.

There was no need for the Judas Horse to rally his people with screams and motions. They no longer doubted their mad, equine prophet. As one horse, they charged down at Hualapai, their hooves like thunder upon the earth. Their eyes rolled crazily about in their sockets. Steam blew from their nostrils. Spittle flew from their huge mouths. The immense herd of wild horses reached the edge of town...

And parted around it like a wave striking a boulder.

Confused, the Judas Horse slid to a halt as his people flowed around him, avoiding the town's streets as if they were paved with sharpened nails. What was happening? The air smelled wrong. Like burning sage, hair, and human blood. He tried to take a step forward, but found that he could not move any closer to the settlement. Slowly, the Judas Horse forced his instincts and Other to one side, allowing a more stable and trained mind to emerge from the wrathful chaos of his psyche. For the first time he took a close, critical look at his intended victim.

There was no one in the streets of the town. Every building in town had been painted with bizarre symbols. Some looked like stick figures, others like open eyes, and still others like a crude cross between man and horse. He sniffed the air again, this time letting his instinct – and the Other – analyze things. The figures had been drawn using the blood of two unborn children: a foal and an infant, respectively. The town had been soaked in the life fluids of the innocent of both species. The Other could not pass this way. Those who followed the Other were similarly forbidden.

The Judas Horse reared up on his hind legs and once more screamed his defiance, this time at the unsuspected magic of men. He would not be denied! He *would* teach his lesson to men! His eyes began to glow with a black, unearthly light. Blood flowed from his mouth like spittle. Sparks flew from the ground where his hooves struck it. The man-fluids covering his coat reversed their coagulation, and began flowing as if they were fresh. Yet none of these things mattered. He could not go in.

A man emerged from one of the buildings. He was old, with a fringe of white hair that hung limply from the sides of his balding head. His deeply tanned, pinkish skin bespoke a lifetime spent living out in the desert. The man walked calmly toward the Judas Horse, stopping only a dozen or so feet from where he stood.

"You cannot enter," he said simply. The pink man's mouth was a firm, hard line. "This town has paid the blood price of the blameless. No creature can violate this. Not even you. Because we have paid this price, no being outside of the order of nature can enter. You must go around."

The man pointed toward the edge of the town. "You will find your destiny out there. We will not attempt to help you or stop you, but you cannot bring destruction to this place. Go around."

In answer, the Judas Horse sprayed a shower of blood and phlegm out of his nose into the pink man's face. Calmly, the man withdrew a bandanna from his back pocket and wiped it off. Then his lined face filled with wrath. "Go!" he shouted, "*Mea*! Flesh Eater! *Numu ddukaku*! Evil Spirit! *Tsa'abu*! Go! Go! *Mea*!"

The Judas Horse knew that the pink man shouldn't know those words. They were First Men's words, and he knew the man wasn't one of them. However, the Other in him could no more resist them than he could violate the blood price the town of Hualapai had paid. With a scream of hatred, the Judas Horse turned and followed his tribe around the town.

Past the town lay the Ocean of Sand. It was huge, dead, and waterless, but beyond it lay an uninhabited expanse of canyons, hills, and sandy valleys beyond measure. If he could lead his people into it, they would be safe. Men could do whatever they wished, but finding his herd in that vastness would be practically impossible.

The Judas Horse was frustrated by his inability to destroy the town, but that was inconsequential. He still needed to lead his race to freedom. If he did, he would redeem himself. He could wash away the guilt of his years spent turning them into dog food. He could submerge himself into instinct and Other. He would no longer have to think or remember. He would no longer be a Judas Horse.

The mustang charged across the vast, dead whiteness at a dead gallop. To cross it was freedom, to stay behind certain death. To cross its waterless expanse was also probably death. Yet the wild horses charged with every muscle taut, every bit of sweat pouring from their bodies, every eye turned forward at the distant cliffs of the Black Rock Mountains. A promised land. A place free of men.

The young, elderly, and weak began to collapse, but the rest charged forward with all of their remaining strength. The Judas Horse led them, his eyes burning in the dwindling light as two black lamps lit from within his massive skull. Blood dripped from his nose. His heart felt like it was going to explode. His lungs were filling up with fluid, and he could no longer feel his left rear leg. He charged forward with all of his might, relying on instinct and Other to guide him where intellect surely would have faltered.

Without warning, a flying machine appeared over the horizon. The Judas Horse realized that it had been silently waiting, lurking behind a mountain as they made their desperate rush for freedom. As it came lower and lower, he recognized that it was the machine that belonged to the BLM. A "chopper." Its spinning blades glittered as the last rays of the setting sun struck them, and then it surged forward at a height of only a few hundred feet above the ground. A man holding a strange looking gun hung out of one window. The gun began to fire impossibly fast, each bullet leaving the end of its barrel with an incredible burst of light. All around him mustang began to drop, dying with terrible screams, but the Judas Horse led the rest forward, screaming his unearthly defiance at his human tormenters as the bullets slammed into his flesh.

Freedom and the race! The race and freedom!

The Coals, Waiting To Become Ash

[Posted to midianranchblog.blogspot.com on December 3, 2010]

Yesterday the United States Gypsum Corporation (or USG) announced the January 31st 2011 closing of its mine and plant in Empire, Nevada. Residents of the Empire – the last company town in the West – will have until June 20th 2011 to leave their homes, at which time the mine, plant, and entire town will be "idled." One hundred employees and their families will have to leave the area to search for work and housing.

Those are the bare facts of the story. The reality is, of course, far less sterile and far more terrible. What is actually going to happen is that my community is going to die – and, as I predicted in the introduction to *An Unforgiving Land*, a way of life is going to pass forever from the earth, largely un-mourned save by the few of us that have lived it.

Empire Nevada has been in existence since the 1920s. Many of the people who work for USG there are second or third generation miners and factory workers. I personally have a friend that worked for the company for 42 years. It's a very small but relatively pleasant place whose roads are lined with shade trees and slightly ramshackle duplexes. It has a community center, a small airport, a swimming pool, a golf course, and two churches (Protestant and Catholic), all backstopping the enormous edifice of concrete and steel that is the board plant. All of this is set back a half mile from the road. The first thing most people see when they approach the town, however, is the Empire Store on 447: the only store in northern Washoe County.

But within a matter of weeks the massive chimneys of that factory, which I have watched billow steam since I first came out here fifteen years ago, will go completely still for the first time in 90 years, and the lights of Empire will wink out one by one until they are no more. All of my friends that live there will be gone, scattered outward into a busy, hostile, and strange world in a slow Diaspora of rural, white, and working-class people who are in many cases unaccustomed to the sheer volume of crap that is 21st Century urban life. A way of life – and not the worst one I've seen in my 40 years– will cease to exist outside of footnotes on Wikipedia and the odd story told to children raised somewhere else.

I suppose I should be angry with the USG Corporation. They would make easy villains, especially to someone who distrusts and dislikes urban America as much as myself. They're based in Chicago, are a Fortune 500 company, have annual revenue of 4.61 Billion, and operate 21 gypsum board plants and 14 gypsum mines in the United States, Canada, and Mexico. Yet, as someone who has operated a business, I find it hard to hate a company for simply trying to survive. A quick glance at the facts show that USG's been in and out of bankruptcy for years, mostly as the result of a hostile takeover attempt in 1987 and continuing asbestos legislation. Its stock prices have gone up and down – though mostly down – in an unhealthy manner, and it's now competing unsuccessfully with cheap imported sheetrock from our BFF (Or is that our master?) China. Simply put: the company as a whole is either not profitable or barely so, and this is a corner they've decided to cut in their struggle to meet the conditions of their "Joint Plan of Reorganization," as their most recent bankruptcy is called.

It's simple, unpleasant math, administered as is usual in Nevada by faceless men on the other side of a continent.

Of course, the whole "idle" thing is garbage. The factory will never actually reopen, and the town will never repopulate. How could it? Within two years, this entire region will be dead, and there will be nothing to attract potential workers to it. USG will wait a year for everything to die down, and then a salvage company will come in and strip everything out of the town right down to the copper piping in the walls. Within 20 years, Empire will be little more than foundations, a huge, crumbling industrial structure, a couple of very elderly people who've been somehow forgotten about in their little decaying houses, and dying trees.

In all likelihood, Gerlach will be a variation on this same, melancholy theme.

Those of you who are familiar with the area know that Gerlach and Empire – technically referred to as the Gerlach-Empire Area – is really the same town. Empire is by-and-large the "neighborhood" with the families, churches, and people who work. Gerlach is the place with the hippies, bars, and retirees. Together they have a population of roughly 400, counting the people who live in the scattering of farms and ranches nearby: just enough people to have 75 school-age children between them and support a restaurant, a store, two gas stations, and three bars.

Now, much as the death of a Siamese twin quickly slays her sister, Gerlach is going to die, because a community without children is dead. 68 of our school-age children are going to have to leave, leaving a total of seven. That's right: seven. Of the 30 employees of our school system, no more than two or three will be allowed to stay, and those only to teach kindergarten through eighth grade. All older children will have to be home schooled – an outcome which Washoe County has dreamed of for years in its never-ending, epic quest to defund its northern territory.

Oh, I know some of you reading this work for the county, and probably don't like me saying this sort of thing. Most of you are nice people and mean well enough. However, in the interest of complete honesty (And what's the point of a blog – essentially, a public diary – if it isn't honesty?), during a recent meeting about the closing of our medical clinic, I had some loud, unpleasant, and unfriendly things to say to county representatives. You know the type: the smiling, condescending facemen and power-helmet-women that governments and corporations send out when they have to actually interact with the local rednecks. The kind of people that, when they get back into their white cars with the symbol on the doors, talk about what an ugly place this is and how all the people are old and how they hate driving all the way up here.

These same people have contacted recently about changing what I had to say "for the final record" of the meeting. So let me say this: I only regret that I didn't say more, harsher things to you, because Washoe County is the enemy of everyone who lives north of the Pyramid Lake Reservation.

Need proof? Let's review some facts:

1) We had our own law enforcement under a constable system. Washoe County took that away and replaced it with their deputies. (No offense to our two local deputies: this isn't directed at you personally.)

2) We had our own judge. Washoe County took that away and replaced it with nothing.

3) Washoe County tried to shut our senior center down over a $13,000 budget shortfall, while at the same time approving 1.5 million for an "open area" for the homeless to camp in downtown Reno. (Because, apparently, they're more deserving than Gerlach's elderly.)

4) Washoe County failed to warn us or offer to make up the budget shortfall of $160,000 when Nevada Heath Centers decided to shut down our clinic, while fully knowing they were about to get an additional 3.2 million in tax revenue from our area in 2011 with no outlay, due to the natural gas pipeline being built out here.

(I guess now we know why, don't we? You knew something we didn't: namely, that a ghost town doesn't need a doctor.)

5) Washoe County has always wanted to shut down fully or in part our schools, and has never made any secret of this. After all, we don't want valuable resources being spent on a few scraggly hillbillies in the north when there are real, civilized people down in Reno, now do we? Now they are going to get to do what they have always wanted to do: collect property and sales taxes from us and give us little or nothing in return.

So Merry Christmas Washoe County! I hope that property values continue to plummet, the Ruby Pipeline Corporation gets a property tax exemption from the Feds, and you go bankrupt anyhow.

■

I understand that in Judaism there is a weeklong period of mourning when a beloved family member dies called *Shiva*. Not being Jewish I've never done this, but it strikes me as a good custom. So in the spirit of sitting Shiva for a loved one, I promise as an author to morn Empire using words, as fickle and fleeting as they are. It is the least I can do under the circumstances.

I will remember you as best as I am able with my often-poisonous pen. I promise.

As a father and a husband I have no idea what I'm going to do as Empire dies, pulling Gerlach down into the grave with it. It's not economic. As long as the post office doesn't close and UPS and FedEx don't cancel their routes, we can go on being exactly the same amount of poor and in debt as always. However, most of my wife's friends are going to leave, leaving her with little in the way of a social life. The store will almost undoubtedly close, depriving her of her few little, but highly deserved, spontaneous comforts. The children who would have been my daughter's friends are going to be gone, and I know that Washoe County will fight hard to give my child as little support as possible. I can expect to spend the next 15 years suing them to get the minimum that federal law requires for her.

Come to think of it, all of my carefully laid plans for the precious, wing-plucked angel I call "daughter" are now royally fucked. She will now not be raised around children she can be friends with for the rest of her life, and she will not be educated exclusively by men and women who are friends of mine. For all I know there will be no other children her age for her to play with at all.

All of these things fill me with impotent rage. Whom can I point the stark finger of accusation at? Who can I make myself feel better by hating? The Chinese for making cheap drywall and (rather cleverly) buying up my nation's debt? That's too big of a topic socially and economically for me to even wrap my head around. USG? That's like hating the ocean for being wet. Corporations are not – and cannot be – charities. Washoe County? That's like being angry at the vultures for eating a dead rabbit off the road, even when you're a rabbit. You're beloved mate was dead anyhow, and it's simply the vulture's nature to dine on corpses.

So nobody, really. There's nobody to blame. Maybe things just die sometimes: pets, people, and towns. Even 100-year-old ways of life. Sometimes the life of a thing is like a campfire you build on a cold night. It starts out promisingly with sparks and little flames. Then it roars into its prime, giving off more light and heat than anyone could reasonably expect. Eventually it dies down into coals, which can smolder on for what seems like an eternity. In the end, there is nothing but ash blowing away into the wind.

We who will remain are but the coals, waiting to become ash.

Big Momma

> "All real communities grow out of a shared confrontation with survival. Communities are not produced by settlement or mere goodwill. They grow out of a shared struggle."
> — Larry Harvey, founder of Burning Man

Burning Man. Black Rock City. Sixty thousand artists, hippies, punk rockers, and San Francisco tax accountants going insane in the depths of the Black Rock Desert. Once a year in the heart of that vast, flat, lifeless expanse of baked clay and blowing sand known as the Playa, the third largest city in Nevada springs up for a period of one week. Like many of that state's cities, its purpose is pleasure. Unlike many of Nevada's cities, that pleasure comes from free sex, extensive hallucinogen use, and burning things as opposed to gambling, whoring, and firearms. It is a unique place in a unique place in a unique place. It has its own rules and social structure. It is its own religion. It is not safe. It is not supposed to be safe. Outside of certain rumored celebrations in Central Asia involving kites, razor wire, and boys under eleven, it is the most dangerous art festival in the world.

The inhabitants of the town of Hualapai also attend Burning Man. They have their own camp near the festival's dense, urban heart. It is an easy camp to spot. It is the only camp filled with people who look like they actually belong in the Black Rock Desert. Their well-maintained fifth wheels and RVs are festooned with antennas, solar panels, and extendable windmills. Their sandrails and quads are worn, but well maintained. They dress in light but sturdy tan clothing the same color as the dust that invariably works its way into everything on the Playa. The people themselves are lean and deeply tanned, with hard eyes that both miss nothing and give nothing away.

The locals' camp doesn't get many visitors.

Most of the Burners figure that the locals came to the festival to freak watch. Which is true. They just don't watch the freaks that outsiders assumed they watch.

Hippie, Two Crows, and Uncle Hank sat on comfortable lawn chairs on the side of the camp that faced the road. From there they had an excellent vantage point from which to view the comings and goings of the festival. In the local slang, this is known as "titty watching." And, indeed, there were a lot of topless young women walking past, covered in mud, painted, tattooed up, or all three depending on their personal taste and general level of pharmacological contamination. To the casual observer it would appear that the three weathered men were peering at them with a disturbing intensity. A less casual, more alert observer might notice that that the three men weren't so much staring *at* passersby as *into* them. This, to any sane person, is much more disturbing.

The lilting sound of Ozzy Osborne's voice filled the air as the Scarred Girl opened the door of Hippie's camper and stepped gingerly out onto a set of folding metal steps warmed by the sun. Completely filthy, incredibly pregnant, and totally serene, she selected a pair of mismatched flip-flops from the chaotic pile of footwear Hippie left heaped up to one side of the door, and waddled over to where the three older men sat peering into the crowd of anonymously individualistic San Francisco freaks. She pushed aside Hippie's long, scraggly gray hair and placed her hand tenderly upon his shoulder. He patted it affectionately, but continued staring intently into the crowd.

No one knew where the Scarred Girl had come from and no one had asked. Whether Hippie had gotten her pregnant or she had arrived pregnant was nobody's business. Although she had once obviously been beautiful, her face was now a ruin of scars and gashes. She seldom spoke.

"Look over that way," Hippie said after a few minutes. "That's one of them over there, isn't it? One of those happy devils you been talking about."

The other two men followed his finger in the direction of a young man about ten yards away. He was walking slowly and serenely through the crowd of Burners, his facial muscles completely slack and his hands moving gracefully back and forth in a motion that wouldn't have been out of place on sea creature. It took considerable attention to detail to notice that his feet weren't touching the ground. He walked calmly along atop a half-inch cushion of air, as if he were a slow motion track on some DVD.

Two Crows nodded his head yes, then no. "Yes. That's one of them, but not any sort of devil. That's an Ancestor. It just likes to walk around and observe. It won't use its host too hard. He'll wake up in a few days thinking with a mild hangover."

"An ancestor? Is it one of your forefathers?" asked Hippie.

"No."

"Then whose?"

The big man shrugged.

"I still say that they're devils..."

"There's a fine fucking piece of work," interrupted Uncle Hank. He pointed to a filthy man scuttling along in an almost canine gait. "That's a *Koosebu Etza'a*. A Dust Coyote."

"That's not how you say it," Two Crows muttered reproachfully.

"Doesn't matter how I say it," he shot back. "I know what *it* is. Now that thing's gonna ride *its* host hard. Assuming the poor bastard doesn't die of dehydration or sunstroke in the next couple of days, he's gonna come out of it thinking that he's been on the worst crack bender of his life. Every inch of his body's going to be covered in road rash, he'll have dirt ground into places he never knew you could get dirty, and probably a nasty case of the clap to boot."

The old man stood up.

"Hey! Hey you!" he shouted at the Dust Coyote. "*Pea Sakwa'eta'a!*"

"'Your mother is a very fat and dirty man,'" Two Crows sighed. "You know, there are classes you can take at the reservation—"

"Will that help improve my cursing?" the old man interrupted.

The man turned, cocking his head sidewise as he did. Though obviously tall, he was bent so far forward that his spindly arms swung close to the ground, causing handfuls of long, filthy nails to scrape against the earth. It was difficult to make out his features. Dust seemed to hover around like naked body like some sort of brown force field, obscuring any attempt to make out the particulars of his person. Then the obscuring cloud around his face wavered for a moment, allowing a distinctively canine muzzle to emerge as if from a pool of stagnant, brown water. It opened its jaws, revealing a row of jagged, yellow teeth.

"*Nemaggooma tabebo'o!*" the man-thing hissed back through its inhuman maw. "You lie, white man!"

Two Crows chuckled.

"No," he said in reply to Uncle Hank's question, "but you'll be able to pronounce the words properly. His Paiute really is a lot better than yours, Hank."

Uncle Hank threw his beer bottle at him. It bounced off the Dust Coyote's head.

"*Tubbea!*" he shouted as the possessed man scampered away with an inhuman squeal.

"'Scatter like dirt,'" Two Crows grunted. "Well, that's at least funny. Even if you did use the word wrong."

"That'll teach him to talk better than me." Hippie gave Uncle Hank a bemused look, but the old man took it the wrong way. He was oblivious to his own bad grammar.

"Hey, it's not like the actual guy knows how to speak Paiute, for Chrissake. That's the spirit thing talking through him. How am I supposed to compete with that? It's not even supposed to exist, let alone be bilingual."

Hippie nodded gravely. "You're right. That hardly seems fair."

The Scarred Girl tapped lightly on Two Crows shoulder. She pointed out into the Playa where a large dust devil was making its way purposefully toward the festival. As they watched, it struck the outer perimeter of Black Rock City, causing a flurry of poorly secured pup tents, random trash, and badly stored picnic items to spray into the air amidst a symphony of screams, laughter, and curses. It was moving directly toward them, its howl becoming louder and louder as it approached.

"Oh Shit!" muttered all three old men at once as the Dust Devil shot past the local's camp to crash into a nearby cluster of tents. It hung there for a moment as if caught on something, then began to spin even more furiously. Like a trout on a line, it thrashed about, sending a geyser of newly purchased Big 5 Sporting Goods camping gear in every direction. The three old men clung to their sun hats and covered their eyes as a spray of fine dust crashed over them, following by a burst of wind that knocked them over backwards in their lawn chairs. The Scarred Girl was saved from a nasty fall only by deliberately lying on the ground, where she wrapped herself about her unborn child in a gesture of protection. The sky grew black. Small stones began to fall on them like rain; not hard enough to cause genuine injury, but painful and shocking in their suddenness. A brief downpour of sticky, rancid mud that stung when it met the eyes followed this unexpected onslaught. It left everything within 500 yards of the dust devil smelling like a beached whale for days afterward.

Then all was quiet.

Two Crows wiped the reeking crud from his face with a look of utter disgust. He quickly rose to his feet, pulling a cursing Uncle

Hank up with him. Hippie helped his woman stand. The dust devil had vanished, leaving only destruction and a perfect circle of stench to indicate that it had ever existed.

"Do we run now?" asked Hippie. "Or do we wait for Her to show up first?"

Uncle Hank and Two Crows glanced at each other, and then broke into a mad dash for Hippie's trailer. All around them locals were bailing out: driving away on quads, slamming and locking the doors of their fifth wheels, or simply picking a random direction and running toward it. The two old men didn't even bother to try to get inside of the beaten up old Airstream Overlander. They slid under it like Babe Ruth hitting home plate. Their longhaired friend wasn't far behind. The Scarred Girl was forced to worm her way after them, huffing and puffing as she shoved her pregnant bulk underneath an axle.

"What?" she asked the three of them angrily.

Uncle Hank pointed in the direction of the smashed campsite where the miniature tornado had just touched down.

"Her."

A figure rose slowly, phoenix-like from the remains of a shattered dome tent. She was tall, but not unnaturally so, with a waifish figure and long blond hair that hung down in casual tangles. As they watched, she tore away the remnants of a tie-dyed sundress to reveal a pair of small, perfect breasts and a pubic region devoid of hair. Unlike everyone else within several blocks of Black Rock City, she was impeccably clean. The Scarred Girl imagined that she smelled like sweat mixed some kind of expensive cologne – probably an Ambery or Fougere. She pictured how intoxicating the woman would smell, how smooth her skin must be to the touch, what her mouth must taste like...

The Scarred Girl shook her head violently, forcing the visions out. Uncle Hank chuckled evilly.

"Turning you dyke already, is she? Imagine how we feel."

Without even the slightest hesitation the slim woman walked directly into the confused, malingering crowd of Burners still wiping sour mud off their bodies. They were helping one another up, and being a bit touchy-feely about it even by their own admittedly libertine standards, the Scarred Girl thought. The slight woman walked directly up to a large, handsome black man in a sarong and whispered something in to his ear. He looked at her in surprise and then, after taking a sudden deep breath, nodded his assent. The two of them vanished into the crowd.

"Who was that?" she asked in bewilderment.

"The Devil," commented her man with complete sincerity.

"One of the old gods," Two Crows answered with a slight hint of reverence in his voice.

"Some bitch that shows up once a year to fuck people to death." Uncle Hank rolled over onto his back, straightening his trousers without standing up. "Big Momma. Thank God she doesn't come around any other time of the year or Hualapai would be a ghost town. It's not like there's enough women to go around in the first place…"

A sandaled foot cut off the old man's words by tapping him lightly on the head. Next to it was another foot, similarly attired in $120-a-pair Birkenstock *mocha suede*. These were flanked on either side by pairs of very large hiking boots. Uncle Hank scrambled out from under the Airstream with a particularly complex and vile curse. His companions chose to stay where they were.

"My mother? Really?" commented the owner of the expensive sandals in a slightly amused tone of voice. "Well, possibly she may have in college. I'm pretty sure that my father wouldn't have asked her to do any such thing. He was uniquely unimaginative in that department."

"What the hell do you want Oberon?" snarled Uncle Hank as he futilely wiped dirt from his filthy clothing. "Can't you see I'm busy trying not to get killed?"

Harlan "Oberon" O'Brien was the founder and spiritual leader of Burning Man. He wasn't a tall man, but he radiated a kind of cool, aloof confidence that caused a lot of tough men to call him "boss" from pure instinct. This was particularly remarkable when one considered the fact that he wore white dashikis, sandals, and a fanny pack everywhere he went. He looked kind of like a cross between George Carlin and Zeus, only not as imposing as either one. The colorless dashiki was his "thing," kind of like pajamas are Hugh Hefner's "thing," only not as cool. Oberon wasn't sexy to anyone who wasn't flying on three hits of X or getting paid. This was all right with him. He was a millionaire constantly surrounded by sexy things flying on *at least* six hits of X. With evil old Anton "the Black Pope" La Vey in the ground, Uncle Hank figured that he got his dick sucked by more teenagers than any cult leader currently alive.

Enormous hairy and bearded Black Rock Rangers flanked Oberon on either side. Dressed in their official khaki Steve Irwin uniforms, they looked like grizzly bears that had been shoved into Boy Scout outfits two sizes too small for them. Their massive thighs and barrel chests threatened to burst out of the restrictive confines of their clothing at any moment. Hank knew that they had no real authority. They were "non-confrontational community mediators." Being the size and shape of primordial giant sloths didn't hurt their non-confrontational mediating skills any.

"I don't care if you get killed or not," snapped Oberon. "What I care about is my people getting wasted by that supernatural bitch each year."

"Don't bring them out here then. Shit, Harlan, my first wife left me too. You don't see me dragging 50,000 hippies out into the desert each year, do you? Get over it."

Oberon's face became a snarl. It had been a particularly rotten thing to say, but old Hank had had a bad morning and he didn't really care. Harlan O'Brien's wife had left him 20 years before, taking their infant son with her. A couple of days later a hit-and-run driver on Highway One killed both of them down near Aptos. Crushed with grief, Oberon had burned an effigy of the anonymous man who had slain his family on the beach with the help of a dozen of his friends. They got drunk and threw her belongings into the fire. That was the first Burning Man. It had grown exponentially until even Santa Cruz County couldn't tolerate it anymore. This was how it ended up being held on the Playa.

Oberon's two ursine companions clenched and unclenched their meaty fists as if anticipating what it would be like to rip Uncle Hank into bloody little chunks. The old man held his ground, returning their boss's snarl with an imperious shit-eating grin that would have made old mad Doug Macarthur squirm in his kimono. Finally, Oberon relented with a sigh and a wave of his hand.

"Okay, Uncle Hank, I admit it: you're a bigger asshole than I am. See? Are you happy now?"

The old man chuckled.

"Great. Outstanding." Oberon continued, "Now that you've won a major moral victory over The Man, can we talk about what you're going to do about the inhuman homicidal nymphomaniac that, even as we speak, is killing innocent people?"

"Do?" Uncle Hank scratched his ass through his pants absentmindedly. "Do? Why, I'm not going to DO anything. Screwing people to death is her gig. It's what she does – and she's been doing it since the Paiute showed up. Probably longer. My people know better than to go anywhere near her, and you only lose a half dozen or so to her each year. You probably get more ODs than that. Anyhow, most likely by the time you're ready to burn your three-story wicker man, she'll already have vanished. Melted into the earth, turned back into a tornado, or whatever it is she does. Then she won't be either of our problems for another twelve months."

"And it doesn't bother you that she's murdering innocent people?"

"Not really, no," the old man answered flatly. "None of them are all that 'innocent' anyhow. And she was here first. The fact that she's killing Californians seems like more of a public service to me. What are there, what, like 30 million of you people? Seems to me you can spare a few annually."

"Do you really hate us that much, Hank?"

"Yes! Well, no..." He shook his head as if trying to clear it, finally settling on a shrug to express his thoughts. It was a tough call for most Nevadans when dealing with their overbearing neighbors to the west. They despised them, but at the same time relied upon them for fiscal survival. Without tourism Nevada's economy would die. Many Nevadans were expatriate Californians who had fled the more populous state for one reason or another. All of these factors worked together to create a sort of confused animosity that was difficult to express in words.

"Well," Uncle Hank concluded with a sigh, "if you're so damned worried about it, why don't you take your freak show somewhere else?"

Oberon nodded.

"I've been considering that. I've gotten a good offer from the folks out at Bonneville, but Flat Creek, Texas is already hosting one of our regional events. Everything we need is already in place there. I've been scouting out in Nevada too, some other locations. Goldfield maybe. Possibly Shurtz."

Uncle Hank looked incredulous, but Oberon stared straight into his eyes with such intensity that the old man knew was he on the level. Oberon's voice was steady, resolute, and totally devoid of bullshit.

"One third of your town works for me full or part time. Another third works for them in some capacity or the other. The final bunch is all people over 65. I'll pack up my 'freak show' and leave, but then what? What's going to be left in ten years? Do you honestly think that dirt bikers, hunters, and the odd lost tourist are going to keep your little town alive?"

Oberon shook his head.

"This state isn't as 'silver' as it used to be. Gambling's getting to where it's legal everywhere. The mines are either gone or going. The cattle business is a shadow of what it used to be. The Chinese have flooded so much garlic into the market that farming is dead in northwestern Nevada. It's about the only thing you can grow up here with the limited water you've got."

"That leaves you with us. Take us or leave us, but I'm sick of my kids being murdered. You can stop that psychotic, slaughtering... whatever-she-is from killing any more of my people, and thus extend the artificial economic lifespan of your town. Or you can keep pissing me off, in which case I'm going to take my multimillion-dollar ball and play elsewhere. It's your choice old man. I don't entirely understand what goes on in this place – and I don't want to – but I've got a pretty good idea that you, your idiot friends, and that sheriff who pretends to be dumber than he is have a handle on it."

He jabbed his finger into Uncle Hank's chest.

"Kill that bitch. I don't care what you have to do to put her down for good, but do it. If you do we'll stay and your ramshackle little town gets to live a while longer. If you don't, we'll leave and it will be just one more Nevada ghost town in the middle of nowhere."

With that, the founder of Burning Man turned and stalked off into the crowd, his two enormous retainers dutifully following along behind him like a pair of humanoid Great Danes. Uncle Hank sighed, then turned and dropped down on one knee so that he was eyelevel with Two Crows and Hippie.

"You heard?" he asked. They both nodded, and after a moment of silence both Uncle Hank and Two Crows starred directly at Hippie.

"What?" Hippie squeaked. The longhaired man seemed both confused and a little afraid. His friends chuckled evilly.

"I guess we're going to find out whether or not Big Mamma is a devil after all," replied Two Crows. "I hope for your sake that she is."

■

Hippie lived his life in the shadow of fear. At first, it had been fear of his father, the meanest backwoods preacher that ever thumped a Bible. That was replaced by a fear of the vast moral and spiritual vacuum that is San Francisco. It began sucking him into its depths roughly ten seconds after he began his short-lived Tenderloin ministry there. In the end, that particular fear was replaced by his terror of the Devil. *That* was his big fear, and it had chased him all the way out here.

Like the Devil, Hippie too had fallen. His journey made up in sordidness what it lacked in substance. From the seminary, to the bottle, to dope, to Grateful Dead shows, to the Black Rock. The experience had definitely been more Syd Barrett than Dante, but the results were pretty much the same. Hippie had tumbled away from divinity like a rock. He no longer truly believed in God. The Almighty stopped speaking to him so long ago that, like a childhood memory, which might have been nothing more than a poorly remembered TV show, he couldn't decipher real memories from imaginary ones. He moved to the center of the Black Rock in the hope that, like some kind of Old Testament prophet communing in the wilderness, God and he could get back onto speaking terms. It never happened. The conversation remained strictly one way.

Hippie may have lost his faith in God, but he'd never lost his fear of the Devil. The Adversary remained terrifyingly real. It would have been hard enough to face Him when he was young, filled with the fires of conviction, and too stupid to be afraid. Back then, he could have pretended he believed in the Almighty's superiority to Satan and taken comfort from that. Now he knew the cold, hard truth. God had fled the earth leaving the Devil in charge of things. That Big Mamma was Satan (or some aspect of Him) Hippie never doubted for a moment.

He clutched his tattered Good News Translation Bible like a weapon. He had to clutch it. The binding had gone prematurely bad. The dozen or so glossy inserts of Jesus cuddling lambs, healing the lame, and preaching to blond, cherubic children on green hilltops had separated from the onionskin text. He was afraid that merely holding it would cause the pages to fall out. Still, it felt strange in his hands. He hadn't needed to actually read it. He knew his Scripture – oh, boy, did he know it – but it had been years since he had done anything with it. Now he had to fight the Devil using a faith he no longer had. To make matters worse, exorcisms weren't one of the Southern Baptist Convention's theological strong points. They hadn't exactly offered classes in it at the Seminary. He wasn't even sure if what he was about to do qualified as an exorcism. It was kind of adlibbing, which was embarrassing. Of course, scripturally knowledgeable spontaneity in the face of evil was supposed to be one of a Baptist minister's selling points. He was supposed to be "wordy," as his mother would have called it. But, for better or for worse, Hippie was no Jerry Falwell.

His old man would have known what to say to the Devil. He'd have known exactly what words to use, which scriptures to quote, and how to bellow so effectively that Big Mamma probably would have fled back to whatever elemental demi-plane of lust and grit she came from. But Hippie's dad was long dead. He'd keeled over from a heart attack while delivering a sermon about the Book of Job. One last "The Lord alone gives and takes," and he was off to find out all about that.

Hippie lacked faith. This left words: frail and fickle things at best, unreliable and deceptive things at worst. And, since he was left with nothing but words, they had to be chosen very carefully. He considered them as he plodded through the festival, carefully stepping over tent stakes and politely ignoring the sounds of lust in a manner that was familiar to any veteran of Burning Man. He didn't know precisely where Big Mamma had gotten to, but finding her wouldn't be hard. All he had to do was follow the trail of corpses.

He found the first one in a lawn chair with a beer in his dead hand. Like most of her victims the young man wore an expression triangulated between ecstasy, horror, and longing. He also sported an erection that would last until it rotted off. Hippie patted the corpse's head gently and then closed its eyes with his left hand.

"Our terrible sins oppress us, but You forgive us, Lord. Please take this poor son into your bosom," he muttered a bit absently.

The next corpse lay spread eagled on a sleeping bag spread out on the ground below a pagoda of billowing white satin. She wore the same expression of almost whimsical agony and delight as the other victim, and was so young and beautiful that Hippie couldn't bear to look at her. He passed by without stopping.

The screams finally led him to her. They were distinctly audible through the incredible cacophony of the festival if one knew how to listen. The low, almost baritone groans of Big Mamma and the enraptured cries of her victim were singular and carried over long distances. Weaving through a crowd of drunken, naked men clustered around a makeshift bar, Hippie tracked the cries to an enormous dome constructed from lengths of PVC and festooned with hundreds of multicolored ribbons. He pushed his way through the streamers. The inside of the dome was filled with hundreds of filthy, tattered stuffed animals of every conceivable sort. Teddy bears, monkeys made out of socks, rag dolls, and dozens of other creatures lay piled atop one another like dead Englishmen in a battlefield trench, a hideous graveyard of childhood dreams.

Big Mamma straddled a young, tattooed woman with red dreadlocks among the fallen furry bodies. Her face was a mask of pleasure as she began an ascent to orgasm so profound that it would literally shoot her soul out of her body through her cunt – where the demon hungrily awaited it. Hippie wasn't sure how she did it. Biologically she shouldn't have been able to, at least not with women. Not that there is anything wrong with that.

The demon had grown in size. When Hippie had first seen her, she was a teenage Kate Moss. Now she was a thirty-nine-year-old Anna Nichole Smith, fully transformed from desert aesthetic to high-end porn star. That was the ultimate horror, the true blasphemy of Big Mamma. She turned the act of love into a gluttony that consumed the soul, eventually transforming that part of us that is God into so much hip, tit, and (he imagined) eventually demon shit. It was what made her truly evil, as opposed to merely predatory.

Hippie pinned a tarnished gold cross onto the collar of his tie-dyed Ratdog shirt, held his threadbare Bible before him, and cleared his throat.

She rose: terrible and beautiful, as old as the world when the Creator breathed life into the clay. The dreadlocked girl fell away beneath her, screaming in frustration and clutching at herself. She began to masturbate furiously as the demon strode slowly and seductively toward Hippie.

"Jesus said: When an evil spirit leaves a person, it travels through the desert, looking for a place to rest. But when a demon doesn't find a place..."

He stammered to a halt. Big Mamma's pheromones pushed out before her in a cloud, intoxicating him. His mind grew foggy. His movements slowed. The world began shrinking around him as she grew with every step, a massive fecund sun hovering over his grey and wrinkled desert.

"Your slaughtered god's words mean nothing to me," she murmured, her voice like silk and damp earth, rich and filled with animal sweat. "I was here before. I am here now. I will be here after. Once I gave birth. Now I devour. I will help you fulfill your animal self."

Hippie felt the hard, strong, and unwanted erection of a fourteen-year-old swell inside of his baggy shorts. He had no control over it. He had no control over himself. He couldn't budge. She was on him, all over him like every woman he had ever wanted, reaching down toward his penis. Then he thought of her...

He hit the demon on the side of the head with his Bible in a spray of pages. Hard. Once. She paused for a moment, as if lost in thought, and he tried to scramble away. But his senses had been too dulled by her presence and he was old. She swung out a fist and struck him. It felt like the baseball bat a couple of shitkickers had used to work him over one night in Bakersfield. Very solid. Something broke, and he felt himself flying through the air into a rotting pile of stuffed animals. Purple spots swam before his eyes, but he could still make things out. The woman with the red dreadlocks squirmed along the ground, moaning and desperately clutching at Big Momma's legs. The demon stroked her head as if she were a house pet.

"*Was* here before," she said with more emphasis. "*Will* be here after. I hunger. I devour. *Now!*"

She took a step toward him, but then halted as the Scarred Girl stepped through the ribbons to stand between her and Hippie. His woman's broken features were a mask of rage. She placed her hands on her hips and glared at Big Momma, her vast pregnant belly jutting forward like an ice rigger's prow. The demon hesitated, seemingly more confused than anything else. She tried to look around the pregnancy as if it were a vast, impenetrable object hovering in the air before her. Then with an angry shrug, she tore herself away from the supplicant woman and walked away through the ribbons, vanishing from sight.

The woman howled but the Scarred Girl ignored her. She leaned down and clasped Hippie's head in her hands. The longhaired man's eyes were crossed and he was breathing shallowly. A thin trickle of blood dripped from one of his ears.

She was holding his still body to her breast and weeping softly when Uncle Hank and Two Crows found them.

"Well," said the big Paiute after a moment's silence, "that didn't work out very well."

"No," agreed Uncle Hank in a grim voice. "It didn't."

Two Crows Fremont had nothing to prove. He belonged here. His people (the First Men) had lived on this land since it had been born. Furthermore, his great, great, great grandfather General James Fremont was the first white man ever to walk across it. He was thick and strong and had spent eight years in the Navy back when he was a kid. Now he was Hualapai High School's gym coach, which was good. Two Crows liked working with children, and the town's kids needed more coaching than most. Special things had to be taught when you were raised in the Black Rock Desert, and he didn't trust anyone else to teach them to the next generation.

Two Crows spoke very sparingly. When he did speak, he packed a lot of punch into his words. In his opinion, white people tended to babble a lot without managing to say much. The ones that lived out here were a bit better; but they still talked too much. English didn't do a very good job of getting to the point. Well, okay, sometimes it did.

"Fuck no," he told Uncle Hank. "I won't do it."

The old man sighed.

"Look Two Crows, you know that your Paiute is a hundred times better than mine. If it's going to work, you have to do it. Christianity sure as hell didn't work. I still can't figure out why she didn't kill Hippie and his woman. They should be deader than coyote scat."

The ex-preacher had a nasty concussion but was otherwise unhurt. Uncle Hank had locked him and the Scarred Girl in their trailer under the watchful eye of Sheriff Sal, more to keep the girl under control than anything else. Hank didn't want her stalking the festival in search of vengeance.

Two Crows shook his head. "She's pregnant. Big Mamma can't touch her."

"Hummmm." Uncle Hank looked thoughtful. "So there are certain people that she can't touch, huh? Why?"

The big man shrugged. "Big Mamma is a whore. She works through fucking. If she can't screw you, she can't... see you, I guess. Certain people are immune. The unborn. Children. Some old people."

"I'm old. Does that mean I'm immune?"

Two Crows thought about Uncle Hank's frequent visits to the Wild Horse Cabaret and Spa just outside of Sparks, and then shook his head. "No."

The old man sighed. "So, do you think you can do it?"

The two men stood at the center of the festival enjoying the sliver of shade thrown down on the ground by the Man himself. The huge, explosives-filled wooden figure towered ten stories above them, a pagan god tossed through time and space like a cultural lawn dart destined to land in the heart of the Playa. It didn't belong there, yet it did. They were alone. That is to say that the two men were surrounded by thousands of others. Two Crows always felt alone when surrounded by thousands.

"No." he replied. "I think that I will have the time of my life and then die. But I will try. Help me get ready."

Uncle Hank unfolded the lawn chair that he had slung across his back. The big man dropped the duffle bag he was carrying onto the dust and settled into the chair with a sigh. He wasn't as young as he used to be, and waking around the festival made his feet hurt. He removed his shirt while the old man began pulling various items out of the bag. Hank began painting the contents of various small vials onto Two Crows, turning his face into a skull of clay and ash and his chest into a grotesquery of long, red "scars." The effect was gruesome. The big man looked like a walking corpse. Uncle Hank then lit a tightly woven bundle of sage, tobacco, marijuana, and other herbs, stubbed its flaming end out over Two Crow's heart, and began to "wash" the Paiute with its smoke in a specific, very ritualized manner. The big man began to murmur, rocking back and forth to some inaudible, hidden rhythm.

Occasionally a group of Burners paused to watch the two men working at their ritual, but they quickly moved on. Most were San Franciscans whose jaded attentions could only be held for any measurable length of time by colorful explosions, bloodshed, or extraordinarily deviant sexual acts. It was difficult for them to even notice an old man waving burning weeds around a chanting, painted native unless the two of them were either murdering or buggering one another.

Two Crows stopped chanting and stood. His eyes were rolled far back into his head, leaving only their whites clearly visible. Even though it was 90-degrees in the shade, he shivered slightly as if he were cold.

<I can see all of them.> he spoke in a strange dialect of Paiute that was hard for Uncle Hank to follow. <There are many of them.>

"Just stay out of the way once you get the whole thing started," the old man replied. "We don't want to go looking for a new basketball coach."

The big Indian turned without answering and walked silently into the crowd. He felt liberated, invisible in his death-trance. All around him thousands of Burners celebrated in a riot of colors, dust, paint, and naked skin. They were mostly young, fine looking, and filled with that sort of buoyant enthusiasm that one only finds in people who've managed to avoid learning just how much life sucks. They rode past on bicycles and scooters, drove past on art cars modified to resemble every sort of animal or monster, or simply walked together in multi-colored groups, laughing at in-jokes stoked by psychedelic fires. There was an air of primitivism to the entire festival that Two Crows liked. There was also an air of desperation that he didn't enjoy nearly as much. It seemed to him that city dwellers needed to learn to relax and take more pleasure in their daily lives, rather than compressing all of their recreation into a couple of frenzied weeks each year. It took all of the fun out of fun.

Yet as vivacious as the Burners were, they appeared nearly transparent to Two Crows. His eyes were attuned to another spectrum entirely, one that could not be seen through the retina. It could only be viewed from the bottom of the eye, and only then by people who understood the true nature of the world. Here and there, the spirit creatures of the Black Rock Desert frolicked and fed among the unsuspecting revelers, catering to the needs of their kind. Murder Crows casting about for juicy souls filled with pain. Pronghorn Men on the hunt for willing females. Walking Scorpions on the lookout for prey. But he was not interested in any of these spirit tribes. He was looking for a Dust Coyote.

It took almost half an hour, but Two Crows found one of the filthy, spirit-possessed men rampaging his way through an empty campsite near the edge of Black Rock City. The thing had used its ragged jaws to tear through the unlucky Burner's provisions. Cans of Spam, baked beans, Budweiser, and tins of sardines littered the ground around their encampment like a blast radius of garbage. When he arrived, its face was buried obliviously inside of a bag of potato chips.

Two Crows looked about for a weapon. An empty forty-ounce bottle of malt liquor caught his eye. Picking it up, he realized that the brand was none other than Crazy Horse. The back of the bottle read "The Black Hills of Dakota, steeped in the history of the

American West, home of Proud Indian Nation. A land where imagination conjures up images of blue clad Pony Soldiers and magnificent Native American Warriors. A land still rutted with wagon tracks of intrepid pioneers. A land where wistful winds whisper of Sitting Bull, Crazy Horse, and Custer. A land of character, of bravery, of tradition. A land that truly speaks of the spirit that is America."

"What a bunch of shit," thought Two Crows. Old chief Crazy Horse had hated alcohol. Naming a brand of beer after him pissed off the Lakota so bad that they had sued the brewery. It was pulled off the market years ago. How a bottle of the stuff had ended up out here was far more mysterious to Two Crows than coyote spirits, horny goddesses, or any other such thing. He wondered how the Burners in this camp had come up with it. They must have found it moldering away on the back shelf of a liquor store somewhere in Oakland or San Francisco. It amazed him that it was still drinkable after all of these years.

He shrugged. Life was mysterious. The bottle still made a good club though, and he began to systematically beat the hell out of the Dust Coyote with it. With the first blow to the back of its head, the creature fell to the ground, curling into a fetal position in an attempt to protect its vital parts. A second blow to its spine caused it to begin crying – a strange, completely inhuman sound designed to summon assistance. Six more blows later, it took the hint and stopped doing even that.

Two Crows continued to beat the Dust Coyote until the bottle actually shattered in his hand, spraying shards of glass and bits of rancid malt liquor all over both of them. Too frightened to rise, the filthy man continued to cower on the ground beneath him. Two Crows yanked free a length of rope from a nearby tent, tying it securely around the sobbing creature's neck so that he could strangle it at a moment's notice. He nudged the battered creature to its feet with his toe.

<Take me to your king,> he said simply. <Otherwise, there will be a lot more of that.>

The Dust Coyote bobbed its head up and down in a pathetic attempt to please the big Indian, than scuttled off into the desert away from the festival with his captor in tow. Two Crows rolled his eyes down from inside of his head and looked up at the sky. A dust storm was blowing in from the west. It bore down upon him and his captive like a massive brown curtain being pulled across a vast stage hemmed in only by distant mountain ranges. He shivered again. The storm was like a huge knife slashing across the face of the desert. Two Crows knew that once its veil had passed across him he would be hidden to the inhabitants of Black Rock City, just as they would be hidden to one another. The storm would reduce visibility down to yards or even possibly feet. Being inside of a Playa dust storm was what he had always imagined being on the bottom of an ocean was like back when he was in the Navy: dark, heavy, and final. It was like that, only without the possibility of fantastical phosphorescent fish as entertainment. There were creatures with teeth in that storm though. Oh, yes! Spiritual krakens and soul draining leviathans the likes of which that Jules Verne cat could never have imagined dwelt therein.

The storm engulfed them. The Dust Coyote was naturally enough unafraid of it, and seemed to grow a bit stronger in its embrace. He began to strain against his leash, pulling in random directions like an excited dog and seemingly immune to the effects of strangulation. Two Crows delivered a swift kick to its ribs. The creature whimpered, then began to head in a single, determined direction once again.

A huge, indistinct shape loomed ahead in the storm. It seemed almost organic, with vast, undulating curves that reminded Two Crows of a stranded whale he had once seen on a beach in the Philippines. The Dust Coyote towed him straight toward it, and as they grew nearer the shape, he could see that it was one of the enormous canvas and steel structures that Burning Man allowed particularly resourceful and perverse groups of artists to build outside of their city's limits. These temporary buildings were invariably abstract, obscene, and phantasmagoric creations. Pairs of naked breasts the size of circus tents, enormous erect phalluses like office buildings, spread-legged fat women the size of a bus, and the like. This structure was no exception. A naked and obese man the size of a suburban house emerged from the storm before him, pink and horrible. It lay half buried in the sand face down, its fingers grasping at nothing and its massive ass thrust into the air in a vulgar, piggish gesture of sexual submission. Its gaping mouth lay hungrily open, and it was through this orifice that the dust coyote dragged Two Crows.

The scene within was part Hieronymus Bosch, part Oscar the Grouch. Hundreds of plastic gallon bottles that once contained cheap vodka lay strewn about a "floor" comprised of bright polyester carpet of the sort low-end casinos in Reno throw out when they've been puked on too many times by drunken 70-year-old Chinese women. A disco ball of projectors suspended from the center of the fat man's spine hurled a dozen random, disorienting images around the inside of the structure. They flittered across the floor, walls, and ceilings like desperate cinematic ghosts attempting to flee the scene of an aesthetic crime. Sex change operations, swarming insects, grainy 80's pornography, music videos, and what looked like an episode of the Bob Newhart show swam into Two Crow's field of vision, then quickly darted away. This grotesque apparition was backlit by a throbbing Rave music so bland and repetitive that it came close to shaking the big Indian out of his mystical trance. Perhaps it would have if it weren't shut off seconds after he entered the building.

A group of Dust Coyotes emerged from a corner where they had been humping something pale and bloody that whimpered. It rolled under a pink canvas wall and was gone before Two Crows could get a good look at it. Others emerged from beneath rancid piles of empty bottles. They moved toward him threateningly, scuttling quickly out of his reach whenever he turned to face one of them, then moving back into position when he turned away to face another. He released his captive, who immediately joined his fellows in this bizarre kabuki of intimidation and terror. They behaved like what they were: a pack of dogs.

Two Crows was not afraid of dogs.

He hunkered down, drawing his arms close to his body and staring downward to create an impression of small size and humility. The dog-men scampered forward, waving their arms menacingly and snarling, then scampering back, then coming forward in a dance of nervous aggression. Two Crows neither moved nor made a sound. Emboldened, they came ever closer, almost touching him with their filthy clawed hands. Closer, closer, closer...

He sprang to his feet with a roar. The pupil-less whites of his eyes blazed against the deathly mask painted on his face. Grabbing the nearest Dust Coyote by the neck, he flung him against two of his fellows, and then kicked another in the jaw. The possessed men scattered screaming in every direction, their instincts seizing them in the overpowering grip of fear. With a chuckle, Two Crows strode forward toward their monarch.

The king of the Dust Coyotes had been watching the entire proceeding with an air of distracted, lazy disinterest. He lay sprawled atop a throne of Stolichnaya bottles, his long legs dangling over one of its reeking glass "arms." He clutched a blue bottle of Gilbey's Sapphire Gin in one hand and a long plastic bong in the other. Though his facial features were indistinct, Two Crows imagined that the king looked bored.

<What do you want First Man?> His voice was a deep base rumble that didn't match his body, and his Paiute was so good that Two Crows briefly wondered if Hippie had been right. Maybe certain spirits were his ancestors.

<Your help.> For a moment Two Crows imagined that the Dust Coyote King raised an eyebrow. It was impossible to tell. He took a deep breath and continued. <Oberon demands the death of Big Momma. I want you and your tribe to help me kill her, O Lord of Indulgence.>

The Dust Coyote King laughed.

<Assuming that such a thing is possible, why should we? Big Mamma does not bother us, and we *never* bother her. Flies and scat on Oberon. For that matter, why do you and yours care what the chieftain of Burners thinks, First Man? We have always enjoyed the fruits of this festival together without rancor alike, whether spirit, god, or native mortal.>

While this was not strictly true and they both knew it, Two Crows let the comment pass.

<Her hunger grows. She kills more each year. Oberon is tired of his people being killed, and has threatened to move the festival away if we do not destroy her. Without the festival, our town will slowly die. Without the festival, your tribe can never don the clothing of mortal flesh. Not all at once, in any case.>

<He won't do it,> the king replied flatly. <The Black Rock gives his tribe strength. It grows larger every year. There is no other place like this one.>

<I think he does mean it. He speaks of faraway places, of towns that have made offers to him. He will go, and you will no longer have pleasures like...>

Two Crows gestured widely about the structure to the empty bottles, gnawed bones, and torn, bloody clothing that lay strewn about it. The Dust Coyote king sat silently for a moment, absentmindedly tapping his bong against his throne. Then he set down the symbols of his office and rose. He spread his arms wide, leaned his head back on its long neck, and howled across the spectrum of sound and blood. Two Crows could feel the reverberation in his bowels and hear it in the bottom of his soul. When the Lord of Indulgence finished, distant calls broke through the rush of the storm to answer.

<All right First Man; you have convinced us. We hunt the Goddess of Pleasure. By all that is decadent, I hope it is worth it.>

It didn't take long for the Dust Coyotes to track down Big Momma. She was holding court in Cynthia's Smut Shack, a camp in Black Rock City's "red light district" – an area entirely given over to sexual pleasure. The "shack" was actually comprised of a series of interconnected geodesic PVC domes covered in old parachutes. Red and pink lights pulsated within, betraying dozens of hazy forms writhing just out of sight beyond the shack's thin nylon walls.

When Two Crows and the king arrived, the entire Dust Coyote tribe had silently surrounded the building. The storm made them all but invisible; there was little chance that anyone inside could tell that they had been encircled. After quickly assessing the situation, the Lord of Indulgence gave his orders. Two Crows wasn't certain how he did it. There was no sound, nor any motions of the tall man's arms. Yet all at once, the possessed men used their sharp fingernails to sever the myriad ropes holding the shack's linked structures to the ground. The storm took the parachutes away in an instant. Seconds later the PVC structure beneath them moaned and collapsed. Screaming, naked figures ran screaming in every direction at once. A moment afterward, Big Mamma emerged angrily from the ruins.

She was even larger now, and angrier to boot: a hulking blond Chyna Laurer looking for an opponent to sexually smack down. *Or simply kill*, Two Crows thought. Even through the dust storm, he could feel the wave of her mystically enhanced pheromones wash over him, drawing him toward her. The Dust Coyotes howled and moved in, forming a compact circle around the hulking woman. They linked arms, clinging to one another like frightened shipwreck survivors floating together on a shark-infested sea. Only rather than keeping killers out, they were trying to keep one in.

She paced frantically around the inside of the circle, seemingly unable to escape from the confines of nature's most basic, womblike shape. The dog-men cringed as she stalked past but held their ground. Two Crows and the king pulled four-foot iron cement spikes loose from the ground. These were common items at Burning Man, used by nearly everyone as ultra-heavy-duty tent stakes. Grasping them with two hands like swords, they slipped between the linked arms of the possessed men and wordlessly rushed her.

Lust ran riot through Two Crow's mind and boiled through his veins, but he bent his instinct to his will. He let it draw him toward Big Momma, let it animate his arms into motion. He screamed as he brought it down upon her back, staggering her. The desert goddess responded with a blow that could have floored a horse. He felt the warm, sickening sensation of his arm snapping as he hit the ground, his impromptu weapon flying away. The sudden pain shocked him out of his trance. He began screaming in agony.

She turned to finish the job, her enormous eyes filled with vengeance. That was when the Lord of Indulgence struck, driving the pointed end of his weapon into her side with all of his might. It bit into her perfect flesh like a sin. Now it was the goddess's turn to scream, and even through the blinding red curtain of his pain, Two Crows felt the sort of commanding sympathy for her that one might feel for an outraged lover. In spite of himself, he felt his body ineffectually try to get to its feet in an attempt to come to her aid.

With a four-foot piece of iron still protruding from her side, Big Mamma grabbed the Dust Coyote king by his neck with one hand, lifting him into the air with less effort than it took Two Crows to raise a bottle of beer to his lips. She drew the spike from her side and tossed it to the ground. Blood spattered from her wound onto the earth, and Two Crows felt the horrifying, inexplicable urge to lick her bodily fluids out of the sand. She drew the struggling dog monarch to her breast and placed her mouth over his in an involuntary parody of love. He continued to thrash about, his screams muffled by the hungry presence of her mouth, but his struggles became weaker with every passing moment. As Two Crows watched the obscuring, dusty cloud that was the spirit substance of the Dust Coyote slowly dissipated, drawn into Big Mamma through the hungry vacuum of her lips. Beneath this vanishing mist lay a lanky, confused looking man whose surprised eyes rolled desperately in their sockets. They looked pleadingly at Two Crows, and then finally rolled upward as the man went limp.

This double helping of souls seemed to reinvigorate Big Momma. The gaping wound in her side knitted itself together, leaving barely a scar to mark where it had been. She grew slightly, looking calm and composed as, still clutching a corpse in one hand, she strode over to where Two Crows lay squirming in the sand.

"I do not care about the white man's cattle-god," she purred in English, "and I do not care about what you think you know either, First Man. Tell the other mortals to leave me alone. I have a *right* to feed in this place!"

To punctuate her statement she drove her foot into the big Indian's side. He felt several of his ribs break nauseatingly as her perfect toes bit into his flesh. Then she hurled the corpse of the Dust Coyote king into his followers, who broke from their formation to run screaming and weeping into the refuge of the storm.

Someone in town had to do the things that had to be done, even if it damned them. Uncle Hank was that someone. When the town needed someone to do something distasteful, illegal, or immoral so that everyone else could go to sleep at night and look at themselves in the mirror in the morning, he was that someone. Along with making crude sexual comments and running the bar, it was part of his role as the town's "Uncle." Another uncle named Hank had owned Hank's Hualapai Club when he was a young man. When he was gone, another Uncle would take his place. It had been this way for almost 140 years.

Some people thought the Uncles were sadists. That they did the things they did because they enjoyed doing them. Others believed that, since very few men were strong enough to carry certain burdens alone, Uncles ought to be the ones that bore them. Very few understood what it meant to be an Uncle. Uncle Hank had paid a heavy price for carrying Hualapai's burdens. Sometimes it seemed to him that his entire life was nothing more than a bizarre series of horrifying images projected like a slide show in the back of his mind, visible only when he slept. The body of a rapist hanging upside-down in a deer tent. A severed head being gnawed on by wild dogs in a canyon. A part human, part antelope creature being tortured with jumper cables. A stillborn baby placed in a propane freezer. The last thing he wanted was another ghastly image slid into the carousel of his horrifically cluttered subconscious.

Still, Uncle Hank dutifully went in search of his son.

The boy's mother had been a whore, drawn to Nevada by the promise of safe and legal prostitution. This hadn't saved her when a drunk driver had cut across 447 in the middle of the night, totaling her car. Uncle Hank had been left to raise the boy alone. As much as he was capable of love, he loved that boy. Besides the club and the town, he'd been the center of the old man's life: a friendly, precocious, miniature version of himself with all of the exhaustion and bitterness left out. That was why it pained him so greatly when he realized that his son was a faggot.

In retrospect, he guessed that the signs had been there all along. A lack of interest in girls. A longing for the wider world. A certain instinctive distance between him and the town's other boys. Still, the old man hadn't put two and two together until the boy bolted straight for San Francisco's Castro District after graduating from high school. He'd visited him there once. It hadn't been as terrible an experience as Uncle Hank had expected, but he had never repeated it. His son had remained polite and deferential as the years past, but they were no longer close.

Hank knew he would be here though. Most of San Francisco was here.

His son relaxed casually on a folding recliner. He was a dark and incredibly muscular young man, with the sort of chiseled body that can only be obtained through a strict regimen of diet and exercise combined with a favorable genetic disposition. His handsome face was partially hidden beneath a pair of large, slightly effeminate sunglasses. He wore a martini glass, a jet black Speedo, and nothing else. A man who could have been his twin except for his tanned pink skin and white-blond hair lay on a blanket next to him. They looked like a pair of Greek gods on vacation.

"Hello, son."

The muscular young man lifted his sunglasses to peer up at his father. A surprised expression flickered briefly across his face, but was quickly replaced with the good-natured, slightly mocking look that Uncle Hank had long ago come to associate with his son.

"Hello, Pops. What can I do for you?" His voice was slightly languid. The old man guessed that he was a little drunk.

"I need to speak with you." he glanced at the other young man, "Privately. It's town business."

Uncle Hank's son shot his companion an unfathomable look. The blond haired man shrugged, then stood up and walked away without saying a word. His son sighed.

"Okay, Pops, we're alone. What's up?"

Uncle Hank sat down on the recently vacated towel with a thud. It was warm and smelled slightly of suntan lotion. He looked up at his son. How in the hell did someone that good looking spring from his loins, anyhow? Though he had never met any of them, he suspected that the boy looked a great deal like the men on his mother's side of the family. He could easily picture him making war on Cortez's hard-ass soldiers armed only with an obsidian-tipped club and a leopard pelt.

Uncle Hand pushed that image out of his mind and got right to the point.

"Boy, you ever fucked a woman?"

His son blinked a few times before answering. "Uh, yeah Dad. A couple of times, actually."

Uncle Hank nodded. "So you like girls, just not as much as you like boys?"

"Well... yes. Something like that." He looked distinctively uncomfortable, but Uncle Hank barely noticed. It wasn't his way.

"So, if your libido was a pie, how would you split it up? Fifty percent queer, fifty percent not? Or is it more like seventy-thirty?"

"Look, Pops, I don't know what this has to do..."

"Just answer the damn question boy!" his voice softened a bit. "Please. It's important."

The boy looked bewildered, but nodded. The entire conversation was bizarre but, then again, this was the Black Rock. Bizarre things were the norm here.

"Honestly, it's more like ninety-ten. Women just aren't my thing," he hesitated. "I tried a few times just to make sure."

"So you find them a tiny bit attractive, but nothing more than that."

"That's pretty much it."

The old man paused to think. It could work. The boy had the right combination of traits. He was strong, almost ridiculously handsome, and a fruitcake; but not one hundred percent. If his son was tough enough it might just work.

"Son, there's something we need you to do." Hank's voice softened to almost a whisper. "We've got no right to ask anything from you, but if you do this for the town and for me we would be in your debt. If you ever wanted to you could come home, and nobody would ever say a word about you being a queer."

The boy gave him a lopsided smile. He reached over and gently patted his old man on the cheek.

"Dad, nobody but you ever has."

Uncle Hank blinked rapidly several times, but otherwise froze like a jackrabbit caught in a pair of speeding headlights. His son sighed deeply. It was a world-weary sound.

"Whatever you need, Pops. I'm your man."

Some 40,000 people gathered to watch the Man burn that year. They stood in a vast, filthy sea of humanity around the inanimate wooden statue that was simultaneously their god, their demon, and everything they had come to hate about the modern world. They adored it. They despised it. And more. Every worshiper had his or her opinion about the object of his or her devotion. The faith was a very ecumenical one. Like an ancient Mediterranean mystery cult, it was primarily civic rather than doctrinal, practiced annually rather than continually. Anyone – Christian, Jew, Buddhist, or what have you – could also be a Burner. They need merely to be crazy enough to travel to the Black Rock Desert to participate in the yearly circumambulation of a burning effigy to belong.

This ocean of worshipers was held back from the object of their mixed emotion by a tiny but determined group of firemen, Nevada sheriffs, and Black Rock rangers, whose only desire was to keep particularly stoned and idiotic teenagers from unnecessarily incinerating themselves. For this, they were widely reviled but generally respected. Thousands of Burners chanted lusty, good-natured insults at their would-be protectors as they called for the destruction of the towering, anthropomorphic monolith they had come so far to worship.

"Burn him! Burn the Man!" Thousands shouted through cupped hands, bullhorns, and art car mounted speaker systems that would be the envy of any downtown nightclub anywhere in America. "Burn him! Burn the fucker!"

Uncle Hank, Oberon, the Scarred Girl, Hippie, and Two Crows hung suspended via bucket truck hundreds of feet above the maddening crowd. Thanks to the hydraulic arm of its massive cherry picker, they had literally a bird's eye view of the insanity that lay spread out below them. Hippie's long, grey hair poked out erratically from between white bandages, while Two Crow's arm hung limply in a sling next to his bandaged ribs. Yet it was Oberon who seemed the most irritated of the five of them. The burning of the Man was the culmination of a year's worth of effort and planning. Incalculable amounts of work went into putting on Burning Man, and this single event was the climax of the entire festival. Screwing it up was among Oberon's worst nightmares. If there had been room to pace around the bucket he would have been pacing. Instead, he fidgeted and bitched.

"This plan of yours had better work," he snarled at Uncle Hank for the tenth time.

"So long as your people have put everything in place – and do what we've told them – it will work fine," he replied calmly.

Oberon motioned with his chin toward the old man's two injured friends. "Hasn't worked too well so far, has it?"

"Minor setbacks only," Uncle Hank shrugged. "Hippie's faith didn't work. Two Crows' wisdom didn't work. That leaves treachery, and I've forgotten more about *that* than you will ever learn."

"No doubt," Oberon responded dryly, but he turned his attentions back to the crowd below as a cheer rang out. A naked man carrying a torch burst through the mob, running at full speed toward the six-story figure at the very center of their world. He was naked, deeply tanned, and muscled like an athlete. The expression on his face was once of rapture.

"Jesus!" exclaimed Hippie. A moment later, he added "Uh, sorry Jesus."

"What he said," agreed Oberon. "It's like something out of the 1936 Nazi Olympics. Where the hell did you find a specimen of humanity that perfect?"

"I spawned him," answered Hank, puffing out his chest. "What, you don't recognize the resemblance? It's pretty obvious."

His four companions snorted at once.

A moment after Hank's son emerged from the crowd a larger figure came out of the circle of humanity, shoving aside Burners or simply trampling them as she went. She was fully seven feet tall now, with filthy blond hair that flew out behind her as she ran: a colossal Mae West in pursuit of a tiny Cary Grant. Her long legs carried her along in tremendous strides as she pounded after Hank's son, arms outstretched and her face a mask of desire. But the object of her pursuit had too much of a lead on her. He hit the base of the Man and kept of going, nimbly scaling a ladder to the effigy's torso in spite of the burning torch in his hand. With a scream of frustration, Big Mamma followed after.

"You're a cruel man Uncle Hank," commented the Scarred Girl with a chuckle.

"Ain't I just?" he sneered back. "What, are you feeling all kinds of feminine sympathy for her?"

"Not a drop," she replied, and he knew that she meant it.

Moments later, Big Mamma began a desperate ascent of the Man. There was a mighty rushing sound, quickly followed by a cheer from the crowd. A perfect circle of flame erupted around his base as hundreds of gallons of diesel fuel hidden in a trench ignited at once, bathing the massive wooden sculpture in light. To the crowd below this was a sure sign that The Burn was about to occur. To the luminaries above, it was the beginning of something entirely different.

"Come on bitch. Come on." Uncle Hank snarled. "Be stupid now. Keep on being stupid..."

If Big Mamma noticed the circle of flame surrounding her she gave no sign. She just kept climbing, a lusty female King Kong ascending a wooden Empire State Building. Only her masculine Ann Darrow had no intention of waiting around for the biplanes to show up. He ducked inside of the Man through a door located right at crotch level. A second later he emerged, torch still in hand, out of another door at its buttocks and began descending a latter along the back of its right leg. Oberon held his breath and raised a radio to his mouth. Big Mamma followed her prey inside.

"Do it!"

Down below his two bearlike minions shoved a seven-foot lever downward with all of their might. A four thousand pound hardwood log broke loose from where it was suspended vertically in the center of the Man's chest, slamming straight down into the tiny compartment in his crotch with a sickening crunch that was followed by an inhuman scream heard as far away as Spanish Springs. The mob cheered, thinking it all part of the show.

Hank's son reached the base of the Man. With a dramatic flourish, he turned and tossed his torch into the god's leg. It began to burn.

Roadside Crosses

[First published in the February 2005 edition of City Bike: California's Motorcycling Newspaper. Volume XXII, Issue 1. San Francisco]

Life is full of shocking reminders. They leap out at us in unwelcome bursts from time to time, often around metaphorical corners or, sometimes, from around literal ones. So I suppose that your average San Francisco motorcyclist shouldn't be surprised when he exits a financial district off-ramp only to find himself face to face with that ultimate (yet all too familiar) horror: a two-step MUNI bus stopped suddenly in the middle of an intersection, the battered remains of a once proud sports bike crunched beneath it like a broken child's toy, and the inevitable crowd of puzzled pedestrians surrounding a crumpled, unmoving figure in battered leathers. Often this crowd of would-be good Samaritans emit a low chatter to one another as they weigh the pros (helping out a fellow human being) against the cons (being sued out of everything they will ever have by an ambitious California tort lawyer) of moving the poor bastard out of the street. Invariably inaction rules the occasion. Whenever I come upon this sort of scene my response is without exception a) horror at something that easily could have happened to me and b) relief that it wasn't me that it happened to (well, not so much horror that it could happen to *me* you understand, as my Moto Guzzi 1100 Sport).

This, as any ancient Greek could tell you, is a classically human response to tragedy of any sort. The unfortunate nameless biker I saw lying broken on the street is far from unique. People on two wheels have been getting flattened by MUNI since God first made tiny apples. My poor easygoing friend Thomas Meredith, a downtown bicycle messenger with an unusually sweet disposition, was run over from behind at Second and Market by an orange MUNI behemoth, then dragged screaming for two blocks to his ragged death. I vividly remember looking up at the grease-soaked belly of one of these transportation whales seconds before hearing the distinctive "pop" of one of my Dr. Marten's patented air cushioned soles exploding beneath its rear left wheel.

Yet it's important to point out that these accidents were back in San Francisco's salad days before the city instituted mandatory drug testing for its drivers, back when you could still catch a proverbial gaggle of them blocking the intersection of 10th and Howard with their safety-colored death semis so they could belly up to the bar for a quick drink (or four) before barreling down to 3rd and Williams for a soothing toot of crack purchased from a street side vendor. Back when taking the half-lane highway on your bad motor scooter was a *truly* life threatening proposition.

To be completely honest many people in the 415 area code were, on average, considerably less safe and sober a decade ago than they are today. It is at best bland, beige, safety padded, no-sharp-corners 21st Century Bethlehem we are slouching off into. An age of sex so safe it no longer includes actual women; an age without massive gun stores in the heart of the financial district (yes, children, there was one not so long ago), an age without motorcycle messengers running their businesses (and tabs) out of bars on California Street, or every fifth financial district security guard doubling as a drug dealer to the businessmen who worked in the building. I'm not entirely certain that our taxi drivers even know where the hookers are anymore. Shamefully, I'm almost certain our current mayor doesn't.

Shorn of any somewhat easily accessed frontier or conquerable victim, this mauve-toned Californian century has thus far failed to impress; except for the traffic safety thing. *That* does seem to have gotten better. How do I know? It's easy: roadside crosses. To be more specific, the lesser number of them. When poor Thomas died, the city's messengers turned the traffic isle across from Border's Books on Market Street into a massive funerary pyre like some kind of floral Viking longboat about to embark upon a voyage on the sea of eternity. While not *per se* a cross (Thomas practiced some sort of Native American religion whose name I can't pronounce) it served the same purpose, one, which all motorcyclists should become familiar with, based on the likelihood that they too will someday inspire one. Growing up in the Florida Panhandle where every third person was a drink driver, I had many opportunities to observe this uniquely American religious phenomenon, which, while having overtones of eastern heathenism, can only be considered a final, passionate farewell to those we love.

AN UNFORGIVING LAND, RELOADED

The roadside cross is a temporary shrine to some dearly beloved son, daughter, brother, or husband whose transportation of choice – be it bicycle, motorcycle, or automobile – has inadvertently become his chariot into the next life. Being that most municipalities frown upon half-burying a blood spattered KTM Duke 2 or Chevy Nova along a country lane as a semi-permanent marker to mortality, we proletarians must do with planting simple white wooden crosses at the particular spot we feel that our beloved friend or relation left the windy roads of man for the straighter ones of immortality. In general these are inscribed with the name (or, even more sadly, names) of the deceased and surrounded with wilting flowers placed at their feet like dying supplicants.

In urban America where memories are short, emotions are fleeting, and love is a word often exclaimed too quickly only to be withheld all to cruelly, we tend to begin with huge heaping flowerbeds of angiosperm ornamentation in memory of our beloved friends, only to forget about them within several weeks as we become distracted by the newest shiny object to cross our optical nerves. Out in rural America where people live slower, love harder, and forget only begrudgingly, roadside crosses are often maintained for years by friends, relations, and neighbors. Here in the West this is partly due to the influence in our more sparsely inhabited environs of those three dreaded horsemen of Red Statedness: Catholicism, Mormonism, and Evangelism. No matter how you slice it, in those cultures where the mention of death is regarded as an acceptable topic of conversation rather than an unspeakable sin against a pleasant cocktail hour, it's easier to organize the maintenance of personal shrines. (I've been in Ireland on a Cemetery Sunday so you can trust me on this.) Say what you will about our more devout countrymen, but in those places where the dead are known by all to be in a better place rather than simply in the ground, it pays to keep up appearances for the sake of those you expect to see shortly in that land beyond the veil of tears. To put it another way for my fellow San Franciscans, a little action today may very well spare you a lot of explaining later.

Tweaker Creek

> In the majority of Slasher films, the killer is an ordinary person who has suffered some terrible – and sometimes not so terrible – trauma (humiliation, the death of a loved one, rape, psychological abuse). It is because of this past injustice that he (or in a few cases, she) seeks vengeance – and the bloodier the better.
> — Adam Rockoff, *Going To Pieces*

Iverson sat alone at the bar. In and of itself this wasn't unusual. Iverson was a man of few words and select friendships. He often sat silently by himself when he drank. It was quieter that way. The very picture of a northern Nevada cowboy, he was tall, stoop-shouldered, and good-looking with a handlebar mustache, and a slightly distracted manner. On those rare occasions that he did talk, he was soft-spoken, whispering out tiny handfuls of words with an almost regretful expression on his thin, handsome face.

Women liked Iverson, though he seemed politely indifferent to them. This only made women like him that much more. He had that distinctive Hualapai dark skin and haunted look which marked him as a Basque-O: a descendant of the Basque settlers that had immigrated to Nevada's high country in the 1920s and '30s. There wasn't any particular onus placed on being a Basque-O. Over a third of the area's population was descended from the same settlers. He'd just gotten a heavier dose of the look than most. With a change of clothing and personal interests, he could easily have been a 19th Century Spanish poet/adventurer of the type Lord Byron spent his career mooning over.

Again, women liked him. Actually, everybody liked him, which was why none of the bar's other patrons said anything about the fact he was covered from head to toe in blood, brains, and bits of flesh. He still wore his yellow helmet, and his firefighter's gasmask hung forgotten around his neck, but probably the most shocking thing about Iverson's appearance was the bloody axe that he clung to with one hand. It had left a smear of red across the floor when he'd dragged it to his barstool.

Iverson had staggered into Hank's Hualapai Club about an hour before, dragging his bloody axe behind him. He'd dropped onto his usual seat, and begun wordlessly drinking gin and tonics. The half-dozen other desert rats that sat at the bar scrupulously avoided looking at him. Partially this was because he looked as though he had just walked through an abattoir. But it was also because they were rigorously mindful of their own business. They were painfully curious, of course, but when Iverson felt like explaining what had happened, he undoubtedly would, and not before. Still, they were interested, and all felt a sense of relief when Hippie entered the bar.

Hippie was a newcomer. He'd only lived in the Black Rock Desert for about a decade, and still had an outsider's tendency to ask direct questions. After a single glance at Iverson, the longhaired man's eyes practically popped out of his head, and all the desert rats leaned in a little closer.

"Jesus Christ, dude! What in the hell happened to you?"

The lanky, dark-skinned cowboy motioned for him to take a seat.

Iverson had been peacefully playing Xbox 360 in his trailer when his radio squawked to life.

"Boy, are you there?"

It was his father. Iverson paused the game, grabbing his old, boxy Motorola radio.

"Yeah, Pa, it's me," he replied.

"Son, we've got a fire. Come on over to the House and load up."

With a sigh, Iverson grabbed his heavy fireproof jacket, donned his helmet, and began jogging toward the firehouse. Hualapai wasn't large enough to have a professional fire department, so it had to make do with an incredibly good volunteer one. Iverson took great pride in being a Hualapai volunteer fireman. They were well trained, with new equipment, boasting a professional, if small, station built into the side of the town's community center.

Since nearly everyone in Hualapai carried some kind of GMRS (General Mobile Radio Service) radio everywhere they went, whoever was on call in the station used them to summon the firemen to do their duty. Cell phone service was notoriously unreliable in the Black Rock Desert. Even landlines had a tendency to get blown down by high winds; so most townspeople between 8 and 80 owned a radio. By general agreement, Channel One was set aside for day-to-day adult communication, which meant anything from wives calling husbands at work to gossip to ranches calling one another for assistance. Two was set-aside for children and teenagers, who mainly used it to gab back and forth at one another. Three belonged to the dusty men who worked for NDOT (the Nevada Department of Transportation) while Channel Four was the exclusive domain of Burners – the people who worked for The Burning Man, the town's ubiquitous annual counterculture festival.

Five was exclusively for emergencies. His father had called him on five.

Iverson didn't bother to get into his truck and drive over. Nothing in Hualapai was really that far apart, and he only lived a few blocks from the station in any case. When he arrived, his father and three other firemen were wordlessly pulling on their flame retardant coveralls and grabbing their fire axes. He followed suit.

"So, where are we going, Pa?" he asked as he pulled one leg of his coveralls on.

"Smoke Creek."

Iverson paused. He slowly blew air out through his mustache.

"Sal coming?" he asked after a moment.

"Nope," replied his father. "The sheriff and his deputy are up looking for a lost hunting party or something in the Limbos. They won't be back for a few days."

Iverson hesitated.

"Did anyone... bring a gun?" he asked.

His father patted his hip.

"Yep – your grandpa's .44 Dragoon. I loaded it with alternating snake shot and solid."

He looked at his father dubiously.

"Don't worry, boy," the old man added reassuringly, "*they* won't bother us."

The younger man nodded respectfully, but in his heart, he didn't believe his father. *They* were beyond the old man's control. You might as well promise to keep away a dust storm. All five men clamored into the giant "king cab" of the fire truck. It was a beautiful machine, bright green and chrome with all manner of hoses and fixtures attached to it. It was four-wheel-drive, and could carry 2,000 gallons of water or fire retardant spray over nearly any surface. Iverson was very proud of Hualapai's lone fire truck. It was one of his jobs to maintain it, and this he did meticulously. He changed its oil and other fluids every three months whether the truck had been taken out or not. He kept its chrome polished to a lustrous shine, and had vacuumed and scrubbed its interior so thoroughly that the seats showed no sign of the rugged treatment they'd received over the years. He was obsessive about it, and so good at it that he had received a county citation in recognition of the work he'd done. He kept it framed in his living room above the flat screen TV he used for his Xbox.

The men turned on the lights, fired up the siren, and barreled out of the stationhouse as fast as they could. They smiled nervously at one another as they drove southwest out of town toward Highway 447. A few moments later, they swung left off the comforting paved highway to become the vanguard of fast-moving cloud of dust as they bounced down a barely maintained gravel road into the heart of the Smoke Creek Desert.

Iverson sunk down into his seat, not bothering to look out of the windows at the desolate landscape they were passing through. To an outsider it looked just like the surface of the Black Rock Desert: but not to him. The Black Rock was home. The Smoke Creek was another kind of place entirely, a big, empty stretch of dead that formed a kind of "Bermuda Triangle" between Susanville, Hualapai, and the Paiute town of Sutcliff. Locals from all three towns generally avoided it, and even some smarter city people knew not to drive through it. It had its... people... but there was only one inhabitant of Smoke Creek that Iverson knew and liked. Wolfman Walker. He was too smart to ever have a fire at his place, so that obviously wasn't where they were headed.

The road into the heart of Smoke Creek was a bizarre conglomeration of switchbacks, decreasing radius turns, and hairpin corners seemingly designed to force any vehicle larger than a motorcycle to flip over into a ditch. The wheelman cursed and fought with the fire truck, causing Iverson to wince every time his beloved vehicle nearly went off the road. Still, he knew that they had to hurry. It has been a bad year for fires in northern Nevada and, not to be outdone, California, Oregon, and Washington were burning as well. Smoke choked the skies during the day and hills glowed devilishly during the night as far north as Humboldt. Lightning hitting hilltops during rainless storms caused most of these fires, but there were other reasons for fires in the Smoke Creek. Rather specific ones.

Against his better judgment, Iverson looked out of the window. He could see a plume of greasy, black smoke hovering over the alien landscape up ahead like a strangulated mushroom cloud. For a brief instant, he imagined that the bloom at the top of the cloud was a screaming, emaciated skull – but then the image was gone. It must have been in his head. He glanced at his companions but none of them said anything. Yes, it must have been in his head. The Smoke Creek did things like that to you if you weren't careful.

Then, rather sooner than he would have liked, they were there.

"Boy, get out and have a look around," commanded his father. "We're going to deploy the hoses, and I don't want none of Them sneaking up on us while we're putting that shit out."

Iverson sighed inwardly, but nodded, grabbed his fire axe, and leaped from the truck. Keeping low, he scuttled around its side, and then leaped behind a nearby boulder. Peering around the rock's side, he examined the source of the oily smoke. An old car lay burning along the side of the road. It looked like an '80s model Lincoln Continental from the shape. The air was filled with a distinctive acrid smell of hydrochloric acid and phosphorous – not to mention burning rubber and gasoline – but it was the first two that he had come to expect when putting out fires in Smoke Creek. If he could have inspected the car before it exploded, he was certain that the trunk would have been filled with cough medicine, rechargeable batteries, allergy pills, ammonia, and any number of other household products fresh from the Wal-Mart in Spanish Springs. Obviously, one of Them had been coming back from a supply run when (rather predictably) something had gone terribly wrong. Not just for the driver, but also for the whole universe, really. No plants would ever grow on the spot where the car burned. It was eternally chemically cursed.

He quickly pulled on his gasmask.

Speed. Crank. Gank. Tweak. Bump. Tina. Iverson had done a bit of research after he'd put out his first burning meth lab – along with its thoroughly roasted inhabitant. Of course, that hadn't been here – *here* was different – but the principles were still the same. Besides learning a lot of chemistry, he'd discovered that the Nazis had loved the stuff. They'd actually issued it to their soldiers, and old Hitler himself got shot up with it every day. Which rather explained a lot as far as Iverson was concerned. He'd also discovered that "Meth" is the Hebrew word meaning "dead." This also explained a lot.

Everybody who lived in the desert knew about speed, largely because everybody who lived in the desert had done it. Iverson had done it a few times, but he really wasn't an "upper" kind of person. He liked mellow downs, which meant that he liked drinking. Even if he had liked the shit, reading the list of what went into methamphetamine would have been enough to convince him never to stick it into his nose again. Battery acid? Ammonia? Up the nose? Uh-uh.

Suddenly Iverson heard a shout. Looking over his shoulder, he saw his father making a "shooing" motion at him. The other firemen were deploying lengths of hose along the ground and getting ready to douse the burning car with fire retardant foam. He would rather have been helping them. Still, his father was right. You could never be too careful out here. Things happened. Moving fast and low, Iverson sprinted toward a series of squat hills that overlooked the spot where the Lincoln slowly smoldered. He'd nearly made it to the top when gunfire began.

He spun and looked down the hill. His father was shooting at something in the brush that he couldn't quite make out, but the flashes of muzzle fire that answered it told him everything he needed to know. Just then, his father clutched his side and crumpled to the ground, dropping his gun. Iverson cried out and began racing down the hill, only to be forced to the ground when a hail of bullets whizzed past his left ear. As he scrambled to his feet, Iverson saw the other firemen bundling his father into the fire truck as bullets ricocheted off its solid metal sides. Suddenly there was a "Whump!" from over his shoulder, and a geyser of dirt blasted high into the air near the front of the vehicle. Idiotically someone flicked the lights on, drawing even more fire from the brush nearby. One-by-one its flashing red lights burst under the impact of gunfire as the truck careened away down the dirt road, explosions flanking it on all sides as it staggered off in the direction of Sutcliff.

"Oh shit!" he thought. Then he was alone.

■

Abandoned in the heart of the Tweaker valley of death, Iverson had few options. He could run down the hill in the face of fierce (though admittedly not terribly accurate) gunfire, or head up the hill toward the source of the explosions. After a brief moment, he decided to head away from the source of gunfire. Always better to head in the direction of "not shooting." Keeping low to the ground, he sprinted up the hill as fast as his long legs could carry him. Bullets bounded off the rocks around him as he wove his way upward, zigzagging, careful not to move in a straight line. The lenses in his gas mask fogged up, making it difficult to see as he scrambled over a final boulder and flung himself onto the top of the hill.

He tumbled farther than expected. The top of the hill had been hollowed out and filled with sandbags to create a kind of circular foxhole that he fell several feet into. Fortunately, the four inhabitants of the hilltop didn't seem to notice him. Two were busy laboring over a Rube Goldberg machine of rusty pipes, springs, gears, levers, and air compressors, while the third peered over the side of the foxhole through a battered pair of pink plastic children's binoculars. The final man was in charge of a pile of "shells" that seemed to have been manufactured out of mason jars. The four men had long, yellowed hair, scraggly bears, and were dressed in the ragged remains of old naval uniforms. They wore filthy hardhats and aviator glasses.

"Grid seven!" shouted the tweaker with the binoculars. "Forty seven degrees!" The two men manning the machine cackled hideously, and then began adjusting the machine's levers and wheels so that its many barrels began to point upward. The fourth man opened one of the jars and began snorting some of the purple material inside through a long, candy cane colored straw.

"Load!" screamed one of the "gunners," and the fourth man dropped his mason jar in surprise, spilling the contents all over the ground. With a curse, he fell on all fours and began snorting the "shell's" contents straight off the sand, scuttling along the ground like a hideous parody of a fiddler crab as he desperately attempted to inhale it away from the dirt. The two "gunners" clucked at him with disgust and then, with an almost comically synchronized pair of shrugs, fell to the ground and began snorting up the powder themselves.

Iverson had had enough. His father been shot and his beloved fire truck damaged; he was in no mood for Their hijinks. Slowly he rose to his feet, casting a shadow over the three men crouched on the ground. Noticing him for the first time, their horrified gazes followed him upward as he stood. He was still having a hard time seeing through his gasmask, but the fire axe felt good in his hands. It was solid, reliable: a thing to be trusted when you had serious work to do.

"The Fireman! The Fireman!" one of them gibbered, right before Iverson put him down with a blow from his boot. Then he swung the blunt end of the axe upward, catching the two other tweakers' heads in a lazy arc of cast iron. They went limp in a spray of blood, teeth, and explosive methamphetamine. Then he advanced on the group's "spotter," who was busily attempting to pull a rusty revolver out of his pants. Iverson drove the handle of his axe into the man's stomach, and then brought the blunt end of its head down on top of his skull. The man's eyes rolled up into their sockets before he collapsed limply into the dust.

"Explosive meth," he thought to himself. "I wonder if it's all explosive? Maybe nobody ever tried using it as gunpowder before."

Then Iverson's attentions then turned to the bizarre tweaker-engineered "mortar." He had no idea how to check to see whether it contained a shell. He could tell the thing had 75% more parts than it actually needed, and there was no telling what it would do when met with an angry axe head. Explode, probably. All the same, it needed destroying. With methodical precision he brought his axe down upon the contraption again and again. Metal bent, valves shattered, air escaped with violent hissing sounds, and green fluids sprayed here and there from severed hoses; but nothing exploded. He reduced it back to the scraps and second hand garbage from which hit had arisen.

When his work was done, Iverson stood exhausted and panting among the fallen men and smashed machinery, his axe still clutched desperately in his right hand. With his left one he pulled up his gasmask for a moment and sampled the unfiltered air of Smoke Creek. It smelled like burning plastic, so he hastily pulled the mask back on again. He heard shouts from the valley, followed by the sound of a few haphazard rounds hitting the sandbags around him. With another sigh, he launched himself over the opposite side of the hill, half-sliding, half-running down the steep sandy embankment. He hit the ground moving fast, and headed toward a small grove of scrub pine that sprouted incongruously from the desert floor roughly half a mile away.

■

As he ran, Iverson realized that he didn't have a plan. The fire truck was gone, hopefully to take his father to the tribal medical clinic in Sutcliff. Hualapai was impossibly far away. It would take days to walk there. He was without water in a desert in summer, so it was unlikely he would survive the walk there in any case. Getting out of Smoke Creek under his own power wasn't even in the realm of possibility. Still, he wasn't without options. He had one friend in this alien place: Wolfman Walker. The reclusive soldier-turned-cowboy lived on a private spread near its northern edge less than a day's walk away. He could make it that far even without water.

Iverson glanced up at the sky, which had begun shifting from natural baby blue to sickly, chemical yellow. Then he stopped looking at it. Here and there, creatures shot away in alarm as he pounded through the salt brush: jackrabbits with fangs and three ears, oversized lizards sprinting along on six legs, ground squirrels clutching tiny primitive spears in their paws. He ignored them, too. He knew that he was in a foreign place, a "not home" in which the rules were unfathomable and the regulations unreadable. The only thing that was completely familiar was the sun that beat relentlessly down upon the heavy clothing he wore, driving sweat through his pores and cooking him like a roast in an oven. It was hellish, but a familiar kind of hellish all the same. He took considerable comfort from that.

As he ran, Iverson began taking stock of his equipment. He had his trusty axe, his gas mask, a helmet, sturdy boots, fireproof yellow-and-black trench coat, and a radio. His radio! In the excitement, he had forgotten all about it! He dug it out of his pants as he slid to a halt in the meager shade of a scrub pine.

"This is Iverson to Wolf's Lodge! Iverson to Wolf's Lodge! Do you copy?" he'd had to lift up his gas mask to use the radio, so he held his breath when not speaking. The air in the tiny grove of stunted trees was thick with the scent of burning plastic, aluminum, and rotting meat. Not exactly an appealing combination. "This is a 10-1! I repeat, a 10-1! I need help, man!"

In northern Nevada, everybody still uses ten-codes on the radio. Homeland Security hated the things and was actively attempting to at least convince the state's the police, fire departments, and emergency services to stop using them, but old habits die hard. It was part of the culture. Your average rural Nevadan toddler knew half a dozen ten-codes before she could walk. Of course, the specific meaning of a ten-code varied from place to place, but that was part of the fun... and why the federal government hated the things. Their meanings were far too regional.

Iverson waited a few moments, and then repeated his cry for help. He was using Channel One, which was a bit dangerous – They could be using Channel One – but it was most likely the frequency Walker used at his place. Although he lived alone... sort of... odds were good that the reclusive rancher would have a radio with him in case of emergencies. A moment later, an answer crackled through, barely audible behind the static. Iverson must have been at the very edge of the little 2-watt unit's range.

"....can't... 10-9?" It was Walker's gravelly voice all right.

"This is Iverson! 10-1! 10-1! I'm in the Smoke Creek somewhere north of Sutcliff. I need help! The tweakers are after me. I need help!" Desperate to reach his friend, he took in a solid lungful of the nearby air, which almost reduced him to a choking fit.

"...specify... 10-20?" Walker wanted to know where he was. The only problem was that he didn't know where he was!

"I don't know!" he cried desperately. "Somewhere west of the road north of Sutcliff! Can't stay where I am. I'm heading in the direction of your place..." It was then that Iverson realized that he wasn't at the edge of his radio's range. The battery had gone dead. He was certain that he'd charged it overnight, but it was dead all the same. All of its little lights had gone out. Cursing, he shoved the useless device back into his pocket and pushed his way into the grove in the desperate hope it contained water. Almost every copse of trees that sprang up in the desert had a tiny trickle of the precious liquid at its center. This one was no exception. After shoving his way through a dozen or so tough, thorny branches, he came to a tiny clearing containing a muddy stream. Falling to his knees, he pulled off his gasmask, desperately cupped water between his fingers, and brought it up to his lips... only to realize that the water itself was the source of the choking rotten meat/burning plastic smell that permeated the area. He let it flow through his fingers with a curse.

The sound of a branch breaking. Iverson realized he was not alone.

He rose slowly to his feet. Coyotes stood around him on three sides, their yellow fangs bared. Their intelligent black eyes were crazed with hunger... and something else. They were starved and sickly looking, with motley coats of patchy fur punctuated by weeping sores. He could see their ribs through the sides of their long bodies.

"Been drinking the water, haven't you?" he muttered. Then they attacked.

Iverson caught the first one in midair with his axe as it went for his throat. With a scream, the coyote flew through the air, leaving a perfect arc of blood behind it before slamming limply against a tree. The second one viciously fastened its fangs around his left foot, but couldn't penetrate the heavy firefighter's boot. He ignored it as the third one flung itself against his right arm in a snarling frenzy – but the rugged material of his trench coat blocked its fangs as well. It just hung there, ineffectually chewing on his arm. He found himself hopping comically on his right foot, a demented coyote dangling from one leg and another attached to his arm, yelling while desperately attempting to shake them both free. He bumped against a tree, nearly falling over before he managed to steady himself with his free hand. That brought him to his senses.

Iverson wasn't happy about what he had to do. As a general rule, he liked coyotes. They were smart, handsome animals with a penchant for trickery, and he really had no desire to hurt one. But these weren't exactly normal coyotes... and he wasn't exactly being given a choice, even if he did feel a little sorry for them. With some reluctance he slammed the head of the coyote fixed to his arm against a tree, again and again until it shuddered, its jaws went slack, and it fell lifelessly to the ground. Then he placed his boot on the neck of the second animal, raised his axe up high, and then brought it down with the same sort of determination he used when splitting wood. There was a canine scream followed by nothing.

Exhausted and dehydrated, Iverson sat down on a log and put his head in his hands. He should have turned off his radio this morning and kept on playing Xbox 360. He would probably have broken his record of 50,000 points by now. Then his father would still have been shot, and maybe against all odds the four old tweakers with the homemade artillery piece would have nailed the truck, finishing the job. So maybe there was a reason he was out here. He liked to think there were reasons why things happened. What had that old scientist with the crazy white hair said? "I am convinced that He does not play dice?" Most of the time Iverson was pretty sure that He did play dice. At least He did in Nevada.

A shout roused the fireman from his thoughts. If it hadn't, the bullet that slammed into a nearby tree certainly would have. *Don't They ever give up?* he thought to himself. Of course, They never do give up. Or sleep, for that matter. He stumbled out of the far side of the grove, and dashed into a nearby ravine from which the putrid yellow stream originated. Safely inside, he paused for a moment. The ravine was the sort of deep, narrow gully that tiny springs can gouge into the face of the desert given several thousand years of uninterrupted trickling. Only a few feet across, its bottom was covered in a jumble of rocks, mostly granite with a vast assortment of onyx, flint, iron-bearing ore, and quartz thrown into the mix. He bent down and picked up a fist-sized chunk of quartz. It was flat on one side, which meant that it has been cut free with a tool at some point. Most likely there was a long abandoned gold or silver mine up ahead, which could explain the toxic state of the stream. The chemicals used in the mining process may have contaminated it – though, in his heart, Iverson doubted it. That would be too *normal* for the Smoke Creek.

Still, he had to keep moving. Standing still would get him shot. Standing still would get him killed. Iverson moved forward up the ravine. Perhaps he could hide in the mine. Maybe it was still semi-active, in which case there might be a working phone or a utility vehicle he could borrow. The ravine got deeper and deeper. Its walls became sheerer and rockier, shifting from the dusty tan typical of Nevada to that distinctive shade of earthy, clay red you always saw on the cover of the state's tourist brochures. Maybe the ravine went on for a long ways, in which case it might emerge somewhere outside of the Smoke Creek up in the Black Mountains near Susanville. They wouldn't want to stray too far outside of their territory, and the inhabitants of Susanville had little patience for Them. Then the earthy red color began to give way to a more alarming shade of yellow flecked with veins of sparkling bruise-purple that had no place in any desert, and he doubted that he would emerge anywhere near Susanville. Iverson didn't look at the strange mineral closely. He just kept moving.

A rock bounced off his helmet. He looked up. High above him on the edge of the ravine stood a child. She was emaciated, with limbs like sticks and wilted, yellow hair that wouldn't have been out of place on an old man. Dressed in shapeless brown rags, she clutched a legless Barbie Doll limply in one of her hands. Soon other children emerged onto the edge of the gorge to look down at him. There were dozens of them, all withered and ragged. Some were missing important facial features such as noses, eyes, or mouths. Others had far too many. The all stared wordlessly down at him. After a few uncomfortable moments, he waved awkwardly.

"The Fireman!" shouted the girl with the dismembered doll as if in reply. At least he thought it was a doll. "The Fireman! The Fireman!" she said with increasing excitement.

The other children repeated her chant with voices far from childish. "The Fireman! The Fireman!" He began to get uneasy, but was unsure what to do. Were these mutated, pitiful, obviously abandoned kids asking him for help? Where they pointing out his position to their parents? Or was it something else entirely?

"The Fireman! The Fireman!"

Another rock bounced off his helmet. He turned to see that all of the children on one side of the ravine had picked up rocks in their tiny fists. Then he spun back around. The children on the other side had also picked up various projectiles.

"The Fireman! The Fireman!"

Iverson ran. Rocks fell upon him like rain as he splashed up the decaying creek, leaping over small boulders and dodging fallen logs as he went. He could see the children mirroring his every movement high above, running along in pace with him and pausing only to pick up fresh rocks where they could find them. Iverson ran up the canyon, his long legs pumping furiously in an attempt to escape the pursuing mutant children. A hailstorm of fist-sized rocks fell around him. Occasionally one would find its mark, striking his head, shoulders, or back; but his helmet and heavy clothing protected him from any serious harm.

The canyon weaved back and forth like a desperate rattler trying to squirm away from an angry farmer with a shovel, switching direction every twenty or thirty yards. Iverson was forced to scramble around corners in a desperate effort to avoid the falling projectiles and keep ahead of his monstrous pursuers, who continued chanting "The Fireman! The Fireman! The Fireman!"

More terrified of what the deformed children meant than what they actually were, he splashed through the putrid puddles or slid on the slippery rocks that lay along the canyon floor, trying not to fall as he ran. Then, as suddenly as it had begun, the hail of rocks ceased. Without slowing down, Iverson looked up. The children had vanished.

He slowed to a halt, nervously looking in every direction and expecting the hail to stones to return at any time. He could feel the places on his back and shoulders where bruises were beginning to bloom like large purple flowers. Cautiously he rotated his shoulder blades. Nothing seemed to be broken or fractured, but it still hurt like hell. His heavy black and yellow trench coat must have absorbed most of the force of the falling rocks.

It was then that he realized the air had turned a slightly yellow color. He was of course safe in his gasmask, but that would probably explain why the tweaker children had given up their pursuit. He looked down between his legs. The poisoned water that flowed through the center of the gully was an even more unnatural shade of yellow here – almost the color of Mountain Dew. He allowed himself a cautious, sidelong glance at the abnormal purple veins of mineral that ran along the side of the gully, shooting through the clay like an old woman's veins running beneath her parchment skin. However, they weren't right, so he didn't look at them for very long.

With no way to go back, Iverson reluctantly walked deeper into the billowing, yellow fog.

■

There's an old saying out in the desert: "That's a mistake you only make once – one way or the other." Iverson knew that he was about to explore the wisdom behind that axiom. He didn't have much of a choice. To turn around was to walk straight into the arms of not only the dangerous children, but also Those people who had been doggedly pursuing him with rifles. To go forward was dubious – and almost certainly bad – but he was reasonably certain that no one without a gasmask could follow him in. He would be safe from the known, even if the unknown hid worse monstrosities still.

The mist grew thicker, more yellow and pus colored. It became difficult to see where he was walking. Several times he bumped into the walls of the canyon, and soon learned to keep his axe extended horizontally in front of him in a bizarre parody of a blind man's cane. The air began to grow hot and sticky. A rushing sound came from up ahead. Slowly but surely, moving forward became more difficult. Iverson could feel the yellow mist pushing against him like something organic trying to force him back. The rushing became a roar. The heat became an oven. If he hadn't been wearing protective clothing he could never have come this far.

Then suddenly he was through it. He found himself standing next to a section of two-inch rusty pipe from which the yellow smoke billowed forth with all the force of a cannon. He quickly backed away from it. The gully broadened at this point, forming a small valley that was nestled into the side of a low mountain. The stream ran through the center of it, but was not nearly as polluted at this point... though he certainly wasn't going to take a drink from it, in spite of his overwhelming thirst.

It was then that Iverson realized he was once again not alone.

The valley had obviously been an old gold mine at some point in the distant past, probably in the 1880s or '90s. Its walls had been blasted and hacked apart in a frenzy of dermatological surgery into the face of the earth. It was still filled with old mining equipment: pick axes, shovels, separating pans, and other less easily identifiable pieces of rusting professional paraphernalia. There was even a tiny railroad of oar carts leading up to a large, decrepit, and weathered building constructed from tin sheeting at the far side of the valley.

Around him stood dozens of sunburned, naked women. They were filthy, with their hair in dreadlocks and their eyes wild. Each of them held a pickaxe or shovel in her hands, and was obviously mining away at the unearthly purple ore that Iverson would only look at through nervous canine glances. A single, rusty iron band attached to the left ankle shackled all of the women. Like some sort of 1950s prison gang, all of the shackles were in turn linked together by a single rusty iron chain than ran the entire length of the valley. It was anchored into a cement block in front of the battered building.

The women were bruised, gory, and raw. Many of them had lash marks across their backs or bloody leavings that ran down the inside of their thighs. Their eyes held Iverson. They contained such a profound look of misery, hopelessness, and hunger that he found himself frozen in place by their stare.

"A fireman," one said simply, and they all picked up the chant. "A fireman! A fireman! A fireman!"

They strained at their ankle braces. They waved their arms at him bonelessly, like anemones on the bottom of a vast, filthy sea. The women seemed to be overcome by the unfamiliar emotions of both longing and hope: "Save us, Fireman! Save us! Rescue us, Fireman!" Iverson knew that he would. However, there was other business to attend to first.

He strode purposefully across the valley toward the dilapidated building. The pipe also led straight into that building, so he knew that within its walls lay the cancer that swelled within the heart of this place. The smug rotting worm coiled at the bottom of this rotten, hallucinatory bottle of tequila.

The building was old. It had been constructed during an era when using an entire redwood tree to create a couple of eight-by-eight beams was considered a perfectly acceptable expenditure of resources. It was covered in rust, filth, bloody handprints, and unintelligible graffiti written in excrement. It was a wasteful bit of urban industrial pollution thrust straight into the heart of a pristine wilderness, violating it and changing it forever. Iverson hated the place at first sight.

He kicked the front door open. Inside it looked as though every high school chemistry department that ever existed had run feral into the desert, been corralled like mustang, and then shoved into one location like so many mangy cattle. Test tubes and beakers, Bunsen burners and centrifuges, huge vats and textbooks lay sprawled out in every direction. Work benches whose Formica or wood surfaces had been nearly melted down to their wooden frames by constant exposure to corrosive chemicals held a mad-scientist's array of forgotten or neglected experiments. Everything was covered in a thick layer of industrial grime.

Cautiously Iverson walked in, moving between the rows of chemicals and equipment as delicately as he possibly could. It was chaos. Yet he felt that there was a pattern to the chaos and, because there was a pattern, it had to have a center. So he moved toward that center, careful as a praying mantis tiptoeing its way to the center of a spider's web. There, in the very center of this rusted, hellish place of torment, Iverson found who he was looking for. It. The lord arachnid. The king Them. The Devil. The Cook.

The Cook looked about like what Iverson thought the Cook would look like. He was almost impossibly tall and thin, with long spidery arms that ended in claw-like fingers. He wore the filthy remnants of what once may have been a lab coat and a sturdy leather apron that hung down to his knobby knees. His face was a skull-like ruin whose features had long ago been burned away by some explosion or the other. What hair he had – and his hairline began on the top of his head, presumably where the last explosion ended – hung filthy, yellow, and dreadlocked past his shoulders in tangled disarray. As Iverson neared him, he could see that the Cook clutched a syringe in one hand and a desperately struggling jackrabbit in the other.

The Devil turned to regard him. Then, with a shrug, he casually broke the animal's neck, threw it to the ground, and set the syringe down on a table. It was filled with a strange, shimmering purple liquid exactly the same color as the unearthly ore that was being mined outside of the building. He regarded Iverson with what might have been a smile. It was impossible to tell. Then he spoke in a raspy, bizarre voice.

"You are from Hualapai, yes? You know not to come here. This place is not for you."

Figuring that it was probably safe to breathe here, Iverson pulled down his mask so that he could speak. The stench of chlorine, acid, and rotting flesh nearly made him gag, but he looked into the Cook's eyes and held them with steady glare.

"When you burn things, I have to come. You know that." Iverson nodded over his shoulder. "And the women? Who are they?"

"Captives," he replied. "Wives. Slaves. Family. Food. What's the difference?"

He pointed at the syringe.

"The rock," the Cook continued almost whimsically, "it draws them here. Reno. Las Vegas. Salt Lake City. San Francisco. It doesn't matter: one taste and they must have more. Have more, and they are pulled here to my domain. They leave their world for my world. They abandon their desires for mine. Their organic dreams dissolve into a chemical subservience."

"Your domain is a disease.,." replied Iverson. He struggled to express his profound disgust with the unnatural place he found himself trapped in, but he was simple man of few words. "These things... should not be. That mineral you're mining out there – that should not be. This whole place should not be!"

"But it is," the Cook sounded almost coy. "It is, because I worked hard to make it this way. All men of worth labor to tame frontiers. Being more human in my desires than most, I toil to tame the worlds of flesh and science even as I transform the landscape around me. Those women outside are a frontier. What I discover in my laboratory – that is a frontier! The land beneath us is another; and I have found something unique here, something that drove generations of less worthy men away from this place. The rock. They did not understand its power. Their wives sickened and their children were born monsters. A hundred years ago, they abandoned this mine and left. Some even moved to your precious town of Hualapai. But they were fools! I lust after sickened women. Deformed children are the fruits of my lust. Their hell is my Eden."

He jabbed a bony digit at Iverson.

"I am but a fingernail, a growth thrust outward before progress. I am what comes to the wild when cities grow. I am a child of the suburb, a scion of the sprawl: inevitable, contaminated, irresistible, and hungry. Always hungry, because I am always increasing! My domain will grow and spread – up into the Sierras, north toward the Black Rock, east toward the reservation. The sprawl will come behind even as I move forward. That world has no choice but to grow and spread, just as yours has no choice but to fade and be enveloped."

He grinned through his burnt skull face. Or maybe he didn't.

"And you!" he concluded. "You who have seen far too much must either join me, or die!"

The Cook reached down to the table. He snatched up the syringe with one hand, and then grabbed a propane torch with another. A white-hot flame burst from its spout. Iverson lowered his mask and hefted his axe.

"When I am through with you – all of you – you will be just like me!" The Cook held the burning torch menacingly in front of his skeletal face. Then he lunged at Iverson with surprising speed, his whip-like arm shooting out with the syringe gripped between its long, bony fingers. An arrow pointed directly at the Fireman's heart, he drove it straight into his chest. But the syringe proved unable to penetrate the thick, fireproof folds of his trench coat. It became lodged there, sticking straight out.

With a curse, the Cook drew his arm back, but he was too slow. Iverson struck it with the blunt end of his axe, and felt the satisfying crunch of bone as it slammed against his opponent's slender digits. Iverson smiled beneath his mask as the skeletal man howled. With a snarl the Cook brought the torch around, swinging it in a wild arc upward that left a trail of blue light in the air as it shot toward Iverson's face. Yet once again, his fireproof clothing protected him. The white-hot flame sputtered harmlessly off his chest and gasmask.

With a curse, the Cook threw it torch away. It skittered under a table, where it quickly lit some discarded chemistry books on fire. Iverson didn't have time to worry about that. He had a monster to slay. He swung his axe downward in an attempt to decapitate the Cook, who dodged nimbly away. Instead, the axe head buried itself deep into a laboratory bench, spraying glass and chemicals outward in every direction. There was a loud "Whoosh!" as several more things caught fire, but the determined fireman still didn't care. He was too busy struggling to free his axe. At last, he pulled it loose and spun around, but the Cook was gone.

Angrily he pulled the syringe loose from his chest and hurled it to the ground. Fire spread out behind Iverson like the avenging wings of an angel. Cleansing. Purifying. Burning. A cackle echoed through the building. He followed it toward its source.

"Do you think your friends made it out of here?" called the Cook. "Do you think they made it to that Indian town? Do you think they made it another mile before we got them?"

Iverson tightened his grip on the axe. He stalked between rows of mason jars filled with purple powder as the fire continued to spread around him.

"You'll never find out!" the Cook's voice grew shriller. "Did they make it, or are their corpses being chewed on by coyotes right now? What does it matter? Will anyone in your town be there ten years from now? Will your precious desert be there twenty years from now? You'll never find out Fireman, because you're going to die here!"

Iverson thought that he was probably right, but he didn't care. It would be worth dying if he could yank this poisonous weed up from the earth root and all. Of course, more weeds would grow in its place. They always do. But the land would enjoy a respite before the next assault. It would be worth sacrificing himself for that.

More cackling. It came from behind a bizarre apparatus constructed from dozens of oil drums that had been lashed together with copper tubing running from one to the next. He considered stealthily moving around the contraption, but then decided against it. The time for subtlety was over. He took his axe, buried it in the first drum, and then pulled it down like a giant can opener. Purplish foul-smelling liquid poured out, spilling across the floor. It too quickly caught on fire.

The cackling stopped. Iverson walked directly through the flames around the contraption to where the Cook stood. He wore a primitive iron mask that looked as though it has been cut from a rectangular section of boilerplate. Its eyes were upside-down crosses, its mouth a snarl of sharpened teeth. He clutched an enormous chainsaw in his hands.

Iverson stepped around the corner, his feet planted in puddles of flame and the hems of his coat on fire. The Cook pulled the ripcord, firing it up.

"No, we're evenly matched!" the Cook screamed above the roar of the chainsaw. "May the best maniac win!"

Behind his gasmask, Iverson smiled. He wasn't a maniac. He was a fireman.

The Cook charged in, leveling his chainsaw before him like a spear in an attempt to ram it straight through the Fireman's stomach. Iverson dodged to his left, knocking the chainsaw aside with the head of his axe, and then slamming the butt of it into the side of the Cook's head. The Cook swung his weapon toward Iverson's right arm, but the cagey fireman blocked it with the axe's handle. The chainsaw bit into the wood, then slid off in a shower of splinters. Iverson drove the butt of his axe handle into the Cook's chest. He staggered backwards, slamming against the side of the oil drum contraption. With a scream the skull-faced man raised his chainsaw high above his head so that he could bring it down upon his foe with all of his might. But it struck one of the oil barrels. Purple goop poured out, quickly covering the Cook's body with viscous fluid.

"Noooooo!" he screamed as it almost immediately caught fire. He threw the chainsaw aside as flames began to run cruelly up and down his body. Waving his arms about wildly, the Cook ran toward the front of the building, where he flung himself through a filthy window with a high-pitched scream. Iverson calmly walked toward the door. Clouds of purple smoke hovered menacingly in the air around him. Explosions racked the building, shaking the timbers above. The entire structure was on fire now, but burning to death was not a fate that Iverson feared. Not after what he had seen. Not after witnessing the dire alternative to death that Tweaker Creek offered.

He walked out through the door he had kicked in, the building burning and exploding with purple flame as he exited.

Outside, the broken, still smoldering Cook crawled pathetically along the ground, cackling insanely as he struggled away from the burning ruins of his home. Iverson placed a single flaming boot upon his back. Pushing him firmly to the ground, he raised his axe high into the air, and then brought it down in a single, swift motion. The Cook's head fell away, still gibbering crazily. His body continued to squirm, vomiting purple, yellow, and red pus from the stump where its severed head once lay. Finally, it collapsed into a heap and burst into flame.

Iverson reached down and picked up the babbling head under his arm, then put his foot on the cement block that held the enslaved women's chain in place. Gripping the metal-masked skull in one hand and holding his battered axe aloft with the other, he showed the severed head of the Cook to the naked and abused women in the valley around him, and then hurled it down like Moses smashing stone tablets. The head bounced several times, coming to rest by the feet of the first woman who had chanted his name: "Fireman!" The Cook's eyes rolled up into their sockets and his lips grew still. The head fell silent.

Iverson savored a rare moment of triumph, but was not finished. He swung his axe downward, severing the rusty iron chain that bound the women with a single blow. Freed from their bonds, they all staggered forward at once, their eyes fearful and crazed. Each still clutched a pickaxe or shovel in her hands. As a group they walked to where the motionless severed head lay still upon the ground and peered at it silently for a moment. Then almost as one, they looked up at Iverson with eyes both hard and cold.

"Kill him!" one screamed, and they all repeated it. "Kill him! Kill the Fireman!"

Uh-oh, he thought. Then Iverson began to run again.

■

The world is a thankless, lonely place where no good deed goes unpunished. Iverson had plenty of time to reflec t on this fact as he ran across the desert floor, exhausted, dehydrated, famished, and pursued by several dozen naked screaming madwomen.

You'd think that hard labor, slavery, brutality, rape, and exposure might slow them down a bit, he thought, chagrined. *But no. Of course not.* They charged after him like Olympic athletes, pickaxes and shovels in their hands, screaming and babbling with incredible gusto, eager to tear him to pieces and throw the raw, bloody chunks at one another like monkeys hurling shit in a tree. At least that was what Iverson thought they would do. It was hard to tell. He had never been very good with the opposite sex, and was getting a little woozy at this point in any case.

To say that the situation was unfair was an understatement. Iverson couldn't even hallucinate sympathetically. He heard his father's voice booming from the aether, like Obi-Wan Kenobi speaking to Luke Skywalker in Star Wars. "Boy," he said, "life's a bitch and then you die." Which he already knew, but it sounded a lot more profound with the echoes and other special effects. He hoped that didn't mean that his father was dead. He was pretty sure it meant that *he* very soon would be.

With a final burst of energy, Iverson raced up the side of a small hill, leaping over boulders and scrambling up tiny landslides of loose brown dirt as he went. He wanted some water. Hell, he wanted some firewater. He wanted his Xbox. He wanted to take a shower, and lie on the cool, clean threadbare carpet in the living room of his singlewide. Maybe that was what Heaven was like. A clean singlewide, decent gin, and an Xbox with all of the games money could buy. At least that would do for him. The Muslims could keep their fucking garden with a dozen virgins in it or whatever.

Iverson experienced a strange sensation as he reached the top of the hill. It was like when you know your car was about to run out of gas – you just *know* it – and it does. That is that. It drifts to a halt on the side of the road, you get out with your stupid five-gallon plastic "safety" can that always gets gas on your pants, and your start walking. That's just what happened. Only it was his body without even the option of a defective Wal-Mart gas can. He got to the top of the hill, walked about five feet, and fell to his knees with the bloody axe still clutched desperately in one hand. He could go no further. He had no existential can to carry.

The fireman looked up into the cold, gray eyes of Wolfman Walker.

Walker looked down at him, God-As-Marlboro-Man, a tiny brown Backwoods brand cigarillo clutched between his teeth and a scoped rifle in his hands. He was flanked on either side by four massive Siberian wolves. His rig loomed behind him: a huge lifted Ford F-350 diesel painted in brown camouflage. It was festooned with every conceivable desert rat accoutrement known to mankind: spotlights, winches, hitches, gun racks, spare tires, ladders, and other, less easily identifiable but undoubtedly useful contraptions. It was so large, magnificent, and multipurpose that it blotted out the setting sun.

Walker spat out his cigarillo, and then gestured toward Iverson's pursuers with his head. The wolves locked eyes with him for a moment before shooting silently off into the brush in their direction.

"Tweakers." He snarled. "I've always hated god damn tweakers! And I hate naked mutant female tweakers even more!" Then he slowly brought the rifle's scope up to his right eye.

There was silence in Hank's Hualapai Club as Iverson finished his tale. None of regulars moved or said anything, not even Hippie. The fireman finished his drink and slammed the empty glass down on the countertop. It sounded like a gunshot, like a punctuation mark hovering above his head like an icon in an Xbox game. Startled from his momentary silence, Hippie was the first one to speak.

"So, how'd you get here man?"

"Wolfman drove me here." Iverson replied in a voice filled with infinite weariness. "He's waiting outside right now. He doesn't like people enough to come in."

"Nothing personal," he added.

"Has anyone heard from the rest of the fire crew? My dad? Has anyone called from the reservation?"

Everyone shook his or her head. No, they hadn't heard anything. Iverson resignedly struggled to his feet, holding himself up by using the axe like a cane.

"Then I'm going back to find my father and the others."

As he turned to walk toward the door everyone in the bar rose to his or her feet. Iverson stared at them all in weary disbelief.

"Give us all a moment to get some things," said Uncle Hank as he set down his dishrag. He walked out from behind the bar to turn the sign that hung in the tavern's window from "Open" to "Closed."

"Wh... why?" stammered Iverson.

"Because we're all going with you, that's why," answered Shutup Amy, a Burner whose pale skin had been so deeply tanned and weathered by working in the desert that she could have been sculpted out of the center of a medium rare steak "It's time we did something about Them once and for all."

Unloved Dogs. Unloved Children. Unloved Old Men and Women.

[Posted to midianranchblog.blogspot.com on December 8, 2008. This is the essay that led me to write the story *Crippled Stray*.]

Unloved dogs. Unloved children. Unloved old men and women. The world is a messed up place filled with unwanted people. It doesn't have to be that way. It is. All you can do is try to be a little less messed up than the world you live in.

My old friend the Crippled Stray came back to stay for a while: a tragedy in canine form. This time I decided to call him Toulouse, after the lame French artist Toulouse-Lautrec. I've always loved that whore-mongering degenerate. Jeff Barker brought him over, wondering if I knew the owner.

"Yeah." I said. " I know him. He's a mean ass little vaquero who beats his dogs – when he isn't working them to death, that is. Can't say as I like him very much."

"Shit." Replied JB. "This is a nice dog too. I kind of like him."

"Me too."

Toulouse played with my lab/coyote mix Michelle while we talked. Tough old boy. Probably been kicked, beaten, stomped, and trampled more than any other living creature in the Black Rock Desert. Fortunately, a thick scar has grown in where his missing pad used to be, giving him something like 3½ legs. Unfortunately, at some point in the last year something damaged his hips. Toulouse can't sit like a normal dog; he has to sort of lie on his side and stand up with his front legs.

I took Toulouse in again: and decided that his owner and I were going to have a little talk if he came over. I'm not sure I even know what that would have meant. Probably something violent and stupid that couldn't have been "undone" once it was done. This would have been idiotic, of course. I understand all too well the hard reality of ranch life out here. I know that the old dog is a tool, not a pet. But there are things you shouldn't tolerate given the chance. How you treat your dogs is a good measure of how you should be treated in return. At least as good as any other I can think of.

Toulouse was with us for two days before the little bastard showed up. Not that I knew. Sensing that I was about to write a check with my mouth that my ass couldn't cash (in other words, start a feud with the desert's tough-as-hell sheepherders), Tina left me working in my office while he picked Toulouse up.

No matter. Crippled Stray came back the next day.

He didn't stay. Three days later, he simply took off again. Vanished. It's hard to say what goes on in that old, gray-muzzled dog's mind. Did he miss the companionship of the other dogs in his sheep herding pack? The other Border Collies with their intelligent eyes and touchy dispositions? The massive Great Pyrenees with their independent habits and filthy, dreadlocked hair? Maybe sleeping somewhere warm that involved regular meals was too alien for him. Too soft and sissified. Maybe he even missed the little bastard that owns him.

So tonight, I sit on my porch, listening to the coyotes howl. There are hundreds of the bastards down in the valley this winter looking for food. Hungry. Big. They're getting bigger every year too; these aren't the little scavengers most of you reading this have seen poking around the edges of suburbs. These boys are almost the size of wolves.

Toulouse -- enigmatic, crippled bastard – walked right out into them.

Unloved old men and women. Unloved children. Unloved dogs.

Crippled Stray

> Loneliness is and always has been the central and inevitable experience of every man.
> — Thomas Wolfe

    Maude lived way up in the Black Rocks, much farther back than anyone besides hunters ever cared to go. She was old, alone, and beyond giving a damn about most things. Her days were a patchwork of memories, chores, and regrets about things she couldn't change.

    The winter was a hard one: cold, wet, and covered with snow. Abstractly she knew that this was a good thing. Nevada was the driest state in the union, and her home lay in the driest part of that driest state. Water was always scarce; the last summer had been a holocaust of suffocating dust. All the excess snow would hold the topsoil down and, if they were lucky, strong spring rains would follow the harsh winter, cutting the "dust season" down to a month or two. But she didn't expect they would get that lucky. Life generally didn't work out that way in Nevada.

    No, she didn't like the winter much. The cold hurt her joints and bones in a way that the heat simply couldn't, and snow made her life difficult in a way that dust never did. She had plenty of time to reflect on this as she shuffled up the mountainside away from her battered ranch house, ancient snowshoes creaking under her feet as they hit the thick, powdery snow. She needed firewood for her stove, and the only place she could find plentiful, easy to gather wood was in the aspen forests that clung to the gullies of Black Mountain. It was a difficult hike, but she had little choice. The horses were long dead and she hadn't turned over her old, battered jeep in months. So she clumped determinedly up the frozen slope, her hands shoved deep into the pockets of her soiled Carhartt jacket.

    When her husband was alive, they'd had a propane stove. They weren't on any delivery route, however, so he'd rigged a fifty-gallon tank to his flatbed so that every two weeks when they traveled 100 miles to temple in Winnemucca he could refill it at the Pilot truck stop. Joseph had been clever like that. The whole ranch was rigged up with gadgets of various sorts he'd cobbled together to make her life easier: solar pumps, gravity-fed hydroelectric generators, geothermal water heating, and the like. He'd been a clever, sober man. It'd taken a long time for most of his inventions to break down.

It had been a year since Maude had felt like going to Temple. Correspondingly, it had been a year since she'd had any propane. She'd made do with her great, great grandmother's Franklin stove. The tough broad had hauled it all the way to Nevada from upstate New York in the settler days, and it gave her an odd feeling of comfort when she cooked on it. Heated up the house nicely too.

But the big stove took a lot of wood.

Maude was winded when she reached the aspen forest. She sat down on a fallen tree, gathered up some snow in her hands, and ate it for the moisture. The aspens moved about her, rustling as the afternoon wind moved through them. Aspens were the hardest trees that Maude knew of. Ethically hard. They shared a common root structure and, when the whole of them decided that a particular tree wasn't bringing in enough nutrition, they severed its roots. Aspen roots are shallow. The doomed tree blows over in the first storm.

Maude could never have been an aspen. If she were one, she would have moved down to Hualapai when Joe died. But her roots were too deep for that. She was a Russian Olive: ugly and spiky, with a taproot that drove its way down to the center of the Earth. She would fall over on her own terms.

After sitting for a while, she began to get cold. So she began to gather wood. Branches only. Maude wasn't strong enough to move logs down the mountain on her own, but she'd made a special sling that allowed her to carry half a week's worth of tree limbs on her back. It was hard going, but what wasn't?

She was almost done gathering wood when she saw the first one. It was large for a coyote – a little bigger than a border collie, perhaps – and its fine brown and white coat glistened as the light reflected off of the snow. They locked eyes: hers brown and watery, its shocking blue on white. She could feel its sharp predator brain calculating behind those eyes, weighing the pros and cons. Human = dangerous. But old. Weak. Alone.

It made up its mind and howled. A few moments later the second one appeared. It was a little smaller than the first, but otherwise identical, and it looked at the first coyote rather than her. A mate, perhaps? A child? The big coyote continued howling.

Another appeared, then another, and finally a fifth. They began to slowly circle the old woman, who remained motionless with her bundle of wood. She could see that her presence excited them, and that made her a little excited for them in turn. They were handsome, healthy animals, but lean and a bit desperate looking. She felt bad for them. It had obviously been a difficult winter for them too.

The animals circled closer, growling and trying to build up their courage. It's difficult for a coyote to attack a live human being, even an old or crippled one. Men were dangerous; maybe the most dangerous creature they would ever encounter. Every fiber in their canine beings must have been demanding that they run away, urging them to flee from a prey as likely to bring death as nourishment. Maude felt sorry for them, but admired their courage, even as they grew closer, closer...

The coyotes froze. The largest one stopped howling. As if by remote control, they all turned at once to peer at something in the forest. She peered too, but could see nothing besides the winter wind moving through an empty forest of aspens. She looked even harder but still couldn't see anything. This didn't surprise her. Her eyesight wasn't the best – and the coyotes' eyesight probably *was* the best. They froze for an instant like a scene from one of those fancy collector plates you hang on your wall.

How beautiful! she thought. Then the entire pack turned and bolted down the hill away from her without so much as a yelp, vanishing from sight as if they had never been there at all. Maude continued to wait, curious about what had scared them away. A mountain lion, perhaps? Yet nothing came out of the woods and, after a bit, she knew that nothing would.

Damn. Still alive.

Maude and her husband had lived the hard, strict lives of rural western Mormons. It had never occurred to them to do otherwise. Descendants of the original settlers who'd followed Brigham Young to the promised land of Deseret, they'd simply taken up where their parents had left off, and living the lives their kind had always lived. Unfortunately, their four progeny had had other ideas, and moved to either Los Angeles or Salt Lake City, depending on how they felt about that. It was disheartening as it was inevitable.

Then he'd died, leaving her alone for the first time in her long life.

Because she was who she was, Maude couldn't commit suicide. It was a sin – and she'd never been very big on sin. Still, she wanted to die. The melancholy desire had begun to permeate her existence. It whispered to her on the winds that blew down from the snow topped mountains that towered around her. Had she been from somewhere other than the Black Rock Desert she would have known that living all alone in the winter out in the high country wasn't doing her mood any good. But she wasn't from another place, had never been from another place, and would never be from another place. Things simply were what they were.

The various children had come around and tried to convince her to move in with them after Joe had died. The two from Los Angeles she never even gave serious thought to. She knew that their dwellings would be nothing more than bus stops on the way to a retirement home. Of the two from Salt Lake City, her son's visit had been purely perfunctory. He was a good man; but he didn't want her, or she him, and that was perfectly agreeable. He'd done his duty in coming out. Her daughter that lived north of Provo she gave some serious thought to. But, in the end, she couldn't visualize leaving. It was impossible.

Joe had died a particularly pointless death. He'd pulled over on I-80 to help a family from Nebraska who were stranded with a busted radiator and been struck by a careless trucker as he walked around the side of his pickup to get his toolbox. The semi had crushed his skull and ripped off one of his feet. He'd bled to death before the ambulance could get him to the hospital to pronounce him brain dead.

It was typical of Joe. Dying while trying to do the right thing for somebody he didn't even know.

So. Her beloved husband was dead, her quarrelsome children were gone, and she was alone living among the ruins of her life. She reflected on this as she washed her hands in the kitchen sink after lighting a fire. Had she ever lived anywhere else she would have known that the water pressure in her house was terrible, maybe a third of what it was in the city. She hadn't, so she didn't. She'd always figured that the water pressure in the city was extreme and wasteful, and that the city people were deliberately rubbing their aquatic wealth in normal people's faces. In her mind, that would be just like them. She didn't think about that right then. Her loneliness had become as big, epic, and remorseless as the land she lived in. It just went on and on, didn't end, and didn't leave any time for thinking about the sorts of frivolous people who lived in sophisticated places like Lovelock. There was no crutch for her to lean on in the broken leg of loneliness, either. Her faith was a strict one: no alcohol, no drugs, and no cigarettes. Not even a cup of tea after breakfast.

Still, though she couldn't kill herself, she didn't have to duck and weave out of death's way all the time, either. Maude had always figured that, like most extremely elderly people, she would get pneumonia here in her ramshackle little home at some point. She wouldn't tell anyone if they called, and no one would check in time, and she would quietly pass away in the bed she'd slept in her entire adult life. That would be all right.

Maude was a desert rat born and bred. Tough. Death didn't seem to want her. Still, the encounter with the coyotes earlier that day had opened up an entire realm of new and exciting possibilities. She's always known that there were dangerous creatures in the desert. Rattlesnakes, coyotes, mountain lions, and other things that nobody much liked to talk about. She'd coexisted with them for so long that she'd never really thought about being killed by one of them. It would be a fitting death. What would a Frenchman say? Oh, yes: ap-re-po.

She contemplated being eaten alive while she consumed her meager supper. She had to admit it didn't sound very appealing. There would be a certain amount of irony to it, though. She couldn't count the number of desert creatures she had eaten. Now they would eat her right back.

After she was done, she took a small cup of broth from the mulligan stew she kept going on the stove all winter out onto her rickety front porch and sat down to watch the sunset. She wrapped a stained quilt comforter about herself for warmth and waited. She didn't know for what. For the coyote pack from the mountains, perhaps? Would they come if she wished for them too hard enough? She closed her eyes and concentrated hard, causing her wrinkled features to collapse inward toward the center of her face. Maude pictured them: canine. Their behavior almost – but not quite – human. Faces mysterious and unreadable. Their eyes piercing, intelligent, and unfathomable.

A familiar howl broke her concentration. She opened her eyes and looked out onto the snow-covered hillside. They were there, this pack. Her pack. Coming toward her even as the sun sputtered and died behind the distant Granite Mountains. Death's comforting hand. Five claws on five fingers.

Maude didn't go inside of the house to get a rifle, as Joe would have done. For a moment, she felt like she should go inside and get them something to eat. Out of kindness. Then she let out an uncharacteristic, dark chuckle. Why did she need to go inside to get something she'd already brought out?

They were spread out before her home in a line with the largest – the one whom she had first encountered on the mountain – standing on the right side and the smallest standing on the left. They were equally spaced, as if some unforeseen force had placed them carefully before her porch, and they stared at her with the sort of hungry, aggressive good cheer that only a canine can possess.

She rose from her rocking chair, shedding her tattered quilt and indifferently exposing her flesh to the bitter winter air. She drifted toward one of the beams that suspended the porch's low roof, clinging to it as she might the railing of a ship in a storm. As one creature, the coyotes stepped forward, their eyes gleaming in anticipation. She waited. With another cautious step, then another, they moved toward her home, twenty paws crunching in the newly fallen snow. She clenched her eyes shut and waited, a shudder of horrified anticipation running through her body as her broken, yellowed nails dugs into the bare wood of the beam.

Silence followed by more silence. Cautiously she opened her eyes. The pack had stopped only a few feet from the battered front steps of her home. They were breathing heavily as if fatigued, hot air streaming exhaust-like from their black nostrils. Yet they also seemed to be frozen in place. It was as if they'd been carved from the quartz-like ice that lay about them all in clumps on the ground.

The littlest tried to take a cautious step forward, then hesitated in the way that nervous dogs do. Finally, she whined and put her foot back in its place. The largest turned and looked up the boulder and snow strewn slopes of Black Mountain, far and away at something distant and hidden from the eyes of men. He howled in frustration, for an instant defiant. Then with a shudder, the pack turned and fled away from the ranch house, vanishing into the mist and twilight.

The next time she saw the pack Maude was on her hands and knees digging potatoes out of the frozen ground. Because it was the middle of winter, her quarter-acre garden was under two feet of snow and a quarter inch of ice. Portions of it, such as her beloved plot of herbs, were unreachable. She'd used her old rusty pickaxe to get past the ice to the dry, dusty soil of her potato patch. She rooted around in that bitter reminder of summer in search of any elusive, small spuds that had escaped her autumn attentions. There were always two or three hidden in there somewhere.

This time the coyotes didn't even try to approach her. They stood perfectly still at a distance of about a hundred yards, watching her with a bitter hunger in their eyes. She stood and spread her arms wide so that the winter wind blew her ragged Carhartt behind her like the wings of a skeletal bird.

She braced herself for death, but they came no closer.

"What do I have to do?" she screamed. "Pour barbecue sauce all over myself?"

Instead of tearing her to pieces, they turned and strode mournfully away.

It was after a particularly vicious storm of snow, sleet, and dust had lashed her home that Maude awoke one morning to find him on her porch. He was obviously injured, a single long hind leg missing its vital pad. She could see drops blood forming a trail from her house back out into the frozen wilderness from which he had come. Probably lost it to an old bobcat trap, she reflected. He stopped licking his crippled limb to look up at her mournfully as she peered at him through a cracked front window.

She dropped her tattered curtains back into place and pretended he wasn't there.

The next morning she drew her curtain back to find him still in the same spot, shivering and taking shallow breaths of cold

January air. His maimed leg stuck out oddly as if he had simply given up on licking the ghastly would and left it where it was. A thin layer of snow clung to his matted brown coat, giving him a literally "frosted" appearance.

Opening the door a tiny amount, she set a bowl of mulligan stew down by his muzzle. Hot from the stove, it gave off an aromatic steam heavy with jackrabbit, aspen onions, and carrot. She slammed the door shut as soon as he opened his green-on-white eyes.

■

Over the next several days, Maude set out more and more bowls of food, until her front porch was littered with heavy blue glass vessels that had been licked clean by her crippled guest's enormous tongue. He grew visibly stronger, shivering less and taking time out from tending to his wound to examine his surroundings with his large, green eyes. This was good, as she knew that he had to be strong for the work ahead.

In the meantime, Maude was building up her courage. She cleaned herself up as best she could without having reliable running water, donned the pink and white dress she had worn to temple for several years, and finally put on a set of earrings that had been handed down to her by her grandmother. When she felt sufficiently dressed up, she flung the front door of her home wide. Once again, she stood there with her arms outstretched, this time in her Sunday best. Eyes squeezed shut she braced herself for the dreadful, flesh-rending end that was sure to come.

Nothing happened.

She opened one eye and looked down. He rose tentatively, teetering a bit because of his maimed limb. His piercing green eyes looked into hers from a position that was nearly level.

"Eat me," she commanded firmly, using a tone of voice that had once sent dogs, children, and a husband scurrying to do her will. The green eyes just stared at her.

"Eat me," she said more loudly, beginning to get frustrated. She had dressed up nicely for this, after all. He made no motion.

"Eat me!" she screamed, and he started toward her. Maude stiffened, awaiting the coming pain with an intensity that was almost unbearable in its longing. But he brushed pass her gently, ambling into the living room of her home with a rolling gait to collapse like a sack of stones as close to the stove as he could get without singing his fur. He sighed contentedly, and then rolled over to present his stomach.

"Well I'll be damned," said Maude. It was one of the few times in her life she had uttered a profanity.

The two of them settled into a routine of sorts. He slept in a bony pile at the foot of her bed, yawning and stretching when she creakily rose to her feet at six each morning. Then he patiently hobbled after her as she went through the ritual of her morning chores, not actually helping with anything, but always willing to listen to what she had to say. This was a considerable comfort to the old woman. It had been many years since Maude had had anyone around to talk to. There were occasional visitors, of course, but with them, she hoarded her words in a manner peculiar to deep desert folk. It was as if there was a limited supply of words available to a rancher for the duration of his or her life, making their careless use as unthinkable as wasting food, water, or some other valuable resource. Yet around him, words began to flow out of her tight lips like spring melt pouring over the sides of a badly maintained irrigation ditch. There wasn't any need to organize her thoughts into the clipped, careful sentences she was accustomed to allowing through her lips, either. She could speak all she liked in an unthinkable wealth of words, never pausing to worry whether the jumble of verbiage made sense in the context that she uttered it. She could start a sentence one day, continue it the next, or the day after that, or not at all.

The fact that he didn't talk back didn't hurt, either.

"It's when the first and last child leaves that you feel it bad," she told him as she hung her laundry out on the tattered, rectangular clothesline. "The ones in the middle don't matter so much. 'Less they're *special,* of course, like Opal Joe's son. In that case, they don't never leave. That's its own kind of hurt, but I never had one of those."

"When the first one goes it hits you that the others are eventually going to go too. It's like rabbit punches to the gut, one after another, 'til you're all alone. When the last one goes, you know that you're old. Nothing to do then but hope they make you grandchildren and, if they do, that they'll bring them around now and again."

"Some are luckier in that department than others," she added pointedly. The two of them walked back inside through the dry, ankle-deep snow, their feet making soft crunching sounds as they went along. He dropped down by the Franklin stove with a sigh, a pool of water quickly forming around him as the snow that clung to his coat began to melt. She began to wash the dishes, her wrinkled hands seemingly impervious to the effects of the nearly frozen water that came hesitantly from the tap.

"When I was young we didn't move all that far from home, she continued. "My parents ranched over near Sulfur their whole lives. Two of my brothers never did leave home. Never married, either. Just kept working 'til they fell over, too."

She was silent for a while after that. Maude dried her dishes then put them away in her age-cracked cupboards.

"We all believed that this was Deseret: the Promised Land. Or that it *would* be if we worked hard enough, anyhow. None of my children believes it, or at least not strongly enough to stay out here. They couldn't wait to leave."

"I've never understood it." She shook her head. "Why would you want to live some place like Los Angeles? What do they have there that we don't have?"

He made a deep, muffled sound in what might have been agreement.

It was a couple of days later that Maude decided to call him Joe. He reminded her of her dead husband: big, quiet, and willing to listen. He had green eyes too – though they weren't shaped the same as her dead husband's. She announced this to him one evening as they sat beside the Franklin stove, desperately trying to outlast a blizzard that had already driven the thermometer down below freezing. The wind outside blew so hard that it rattled the old, single-pane windows of the ranch house. It was as if God's fist was trying to rip the old stick home from its foundations.

"You don't mind, do you Joseph?" she asked the stained ceiling idly. "You ain't using the name down here no more, and it would be a lot easier if I had something to call him. Giving him a dog name don't seem fitting, all things considered, and it would feel good to say your name each day like we always did. 'Good morning, Joe.' 'The weather sure is cold, isn't it, Joe.' 'Know what I mean, Joe?'"

She looked down at the new Joe.

"So how do you feel about your new name, Joe? Is it to your liking?"

Joe pivoted one ear toward her for a moment, and then let it drop back down to the side of his enormous head. He looked up at her from the floor with his large green eyes, emotions and desires unknowable. Satisfied, she nodded back.

"Glad you approve, Joe."

■

It's the things you trust that always get you killed, thought Rusty Guerrero. The things that are familiar and comforting. Your heart. Booze. Your car. Your pecker. Doing the right thing. That's what'd gotten Big Joe. Being a fucking Good Samaritan for some damn tourists. Killed the best man in the desert. But that wouldn't get him. Never. He was no fucking Mother Teresa.

Rusty sincerely told himself this even as he maneuvered his battered, highly modified Chevy K-10 across the frozen surface of the Playa toward Maude's isolated ranch. He was a small man that was somehow also big. His mother had been short, short-tempered, and very Irish, his father shorter, shorter-tempered, and even more Mexican. Both were from Nevada, and had never visited the nations that gave them their self-proclaimed identities. The resulting genetic brawl left Rusty with carrot red hair (now going gray at the temples), dark features, a prow-like Aztec nose, and the bulky, slope-shouldered physique of a power lifter: which he had been for a while after getting out of the Army for the first time.

The Playa was dangerous as hell in the winter. Screw up and your rig would end up sunken three feet into the ground until the following summer. If it hadn't been frozen into a solid block of ice, he couldn't have attempted the crossing at all. Guerrero cursed wildly in three different languages as he careened about the road – or where he imagined the road to be beneath the ice, in any case. In Rusty's world profanities were magical things, angelic beings with the power to carry a man's terrors and weaknesses far away into the verbal ionosphere. Potent, magical words that plugged up the vulnerable holes in his soul, leaving him stronger than before. A man that didn't swear was a cripple, forever doomed to dwell in the cellar of his emotions alongside his own fears.

Or so he told himself. Big Joe never swore. Had no fears that

Guerrero was aware of, either. The angry little bruiser had respected the fuck out of that man. But he'd never understood him. They were distinct roads leading to the same location. Two very different ways of solving the same problem: always parallel, never intersecting. Big Joe had lived in the very heart of the deep desert with an effortlessness that still baffled a man who had to fight like hell for every amp of off-grid power, every gallon of homemade methane, and every scrawny rabbit he put in his family's stewpot. Without anger, Guerrero was nothing; could do nothing. It was a basic law of nature: nothing could be accomplished in the Black Rock without a supreme, bitter act of will and sacrifice. How gentle Big Joe had escaped this equation was a mystery that puzzled Guerrero to this day.

Fucking tourists.

The old woman's battered house appeared in the distance, a brown speck against an infinite field of white. The squat man had several milk crates of supplies for her. They were mostly dry goods, but included a few luxuries like cookies and a box of colorful candies. Unfortunately, all of the products in his rig were Western Family brand – the fourth worst thing to be forced upon rural Nevadans besides perpetually high fuel prices, the BLM, and political disenfranchisement. Western Family made sure that everything thing they sold was of the lowest quality in the smallest amount at the highest price. They also supplied all of the general stores between the Paiute Reservation and the Oregon border. It was all he could get without going 140 miles to the Spanish Springs Wal-Mart.

"Well, it'll make her happy anyhow," he muttered between profanities. "Old people do love their sweets. Probably helps to make up for the lack of sex, liquor, and violence." It was yet another thing not to look forward to as he got older.

Rusty Guerrero owed Big Joe. Without his help and sage advice, the angry little man and his family would never have made it out in the deep desert. The number of things he had taught him were too numerous to remember: how to fix a Ford 8-N tractor, how to tap a renegade methane well, how to make gunpowder, how to keep rabbits out of a spinach patch, how to align solar panels. The list seemed endless, and since Joe wasn't around to pay back, Guerrero settled for helping out his widow whenever he could. Of course, for all of his profane bluster the angry little man had a long list of people that he "owed" – and helped because he owed. This was only the first stop on a retributive route that included Tyson (gives him good dogs), Opal Joe (makes his wife jewelry), Hippie (advice on growing dope), and his own brother.

Guerrero didn't like to think about his brother all that much.

He veered off down a flat area of snow he thought was probably the old woman's driveway, the rear of his truck swerving back and forth like a pendulum, sending geysers of filthy snow in every direction. Fucking winter. Frozen fucker was even worse than the fucking summer, which was pretty bad too. Dust. Snow. High winds. Oceans of smoke blown in from California forest fires. Flash floods. Sagebrush fires that came seemingly from nowhere, destroyed everything in their path, and vanished before the volunteer fire department could find them. Whiteouts, brownouts, and "smud" storms in which rain, dust, and snow combined into a single foul mixture that blew sideways into your windshield like shit from God's own ass. The Black Rock Desert was pure hell.

Guerrero knew that he would never live anywhere else. He would die here.

The Chevy K-10 slid to a halt in a patch of mud that he sincerely hoped wasn't Maude's front yard. Grass was hard as hell to grow in the desert, and he didn't want to undo any of what was left of Big Joe's lifetime of work. Guerrero unclenched his hands from the battered steering wheel. He exhaled, and then began searching around the cab of his truck for a can of Redman. Pressing a moist clump of the chewing tobacco into his gum, he began to feel a bit better as a comforting rush of nicotine flooded through his system. It was a nasty habit. He knew it was a nasty habit. There was no way he couldn't know. His wife was fond of reminding him of how nasty it was on a daily basis. It was part of the accepted, established rhythm of their marriage. But he couldn't swear very well with a mouth full of dip, so in her opinion his bad habit had its advantages too.

Guerrero grumbled his way out of the car, went to the back seat, and plucked out Maude's two milk cartons of supplies. He stomped his way through the snow onto her porch and, with his standard lack of tact, threw open the front door and strode in. Maude sat on her usual spot on the scruffy couch that dominated her small living room. Something else lay sprawled out across her feet.

He dropped the groceries, which hit the ground with a resounding thud, sending cans rolling across the floor in every direction.

"Jesus-H-Fucking-Christ's-Half-Brother-Harold!" shouted

Guerrero. Right before he swallowed his chew. It stung as it slid unnaturally down his throat, but the little man barely noticed. He sprinted back across the room to where Joe's ancient lever action rifle lay slung over the doorway. Chambered for forty-five Long Colt, it spat out low velocity slugs of lead guaranteed to reduce anything's pulse to zero over zero.

"Rusty, please don't swear in my home." The thing at her feet began to growl. He fumbled with the firearm, clumsily chambering a round and bringing it to bear. The growling grew louder as the thing began to rise...

"Rusty, for goodness' sake put that rifle down. Joe, you sit down too. I don't want any violence in my home." Her tone was stern and brooked no disagreement. Guerrero lowered the rifle. The thing dropped back to the floor grumbling, one large green eye still focused on the unwelcome intruder.

"You're calling it *Joe?*" he choked incredulously. "Maude, how could you do such a thing? This... thing isn't Joe. It isn't anything like him!"

"Well, I don't know," she replied thoughtfully. "My husband was a big fellow, and Joe's a pretty big example of what he is. A wolf or something..."

"Maude, that's not a wolf. That's not any sort of fucking dog."

"Mind the swearing, Rusty," she replied sternly. "In any case, I liked my husband a lot. He was a good listener. Didn't talk much. Joe here is a good listener, too. He doesn't talk at all. He just follows me around and sighs in that way that big dogs sigh."

"Maude, that ain't no—"

"We're getting along pretty well." She interrupted. Maude walked around to where her supplies had spilled and began gathering them up. She favored him with a gap-toothed smile upon finding the bag of cheap candies, and then rose unsteadily to her feet.

"I don't feel so abandoned no more since he came around." She lied. "The loneliness ain't eating at me like it used to. Maybe in the Spring I'll even go visit my daughter in Salt Lake City."

Guerrero grunted. He placed the old rifle back onto its hooks, and then turned to stare angrily down at "Joe" – who glared maliciously back. Neither the bulky, red-haired man nor the creature liked what he saw. Yet Guerrero was wise in both the ways of the Black Rock, and what it did over time to people. He was shrewd about what it did to everything else over time, too. There were a couple of different explanations for "Joe."

"Maude, I'm not real sure about 'Joe' here," he began slowly.

"He might be sick. Or worse. Maybe I should bring Tyson around to have a look at him – or my brother. Either one of them should be able to…"

It began to growl again. Maude shook her head.

"I don't want either of those two mountain men in my home. Tyson is a monster. Your kin's worse than a monster. No. Joe and me are fine."

"What do I owe you, Rusty?" she changed the subject. "They do that direct deposit thing with my social security. I could write you a check."

Guerrero shook his head. It was an old routine between the two of them.

"Didn't cost much, Maude. Don't worry about it."

"Well, then say hello to your wife for me. Tell her thank you for those blackberry preserves she sent over last time. I'll gather some aspen onions for her next time I'm up in the mountains. They're best eaten fresh, but they'll keep until next time you come up."

Rusty was being dismissed – and he knew it. A gnawing feeling in the pit of his stomach told him that he should snatch the rifle back off of the wall, brain the thing looking fiercely up at him from the floor with the stock, and then finish it off with a couple of well-placed rounds to the head. He was reasonably certain that he could accomplish this before the lamed beast could even get to its feet.

Yet he took no action. It wasn't fear that stayed his hand. Guerrero was too tough, too fast, and too irritable by nature to be scared. Aggravated by everything, he wasn't frightened by much. But he had the odd feeling looking at the old woman and her unnatural pet that he'd stumbled into a story not his own. He'd slipped into this bizarre, unfolding tragedy by accident; he wasn't destined to participate in whatever horror that was about to unfold. (He knew for certain it *would* be a tragedy and a horror. It could hardly be anything else.) This drama had to play out however it played out without his interference. Wordlessly, Guerrero turned and walked out the door.

He knew that he would never see the old woman alive again.

The winter continued as if there had never been anything but winter. Life was an equal mixture of gray skies, powdery snow, mud, and cold. Maude waited to catch pneumonia – or at the very least to fall down, break a hip, and *then* catch pneumonia. It just didn't happen. A lifetime spent on a ranch had made her tough even in the twilight of her years. She was old, but not actually frail. When she fell down, it just hurt. Nothing ever broke.

Maude had always wondered why rural Nevada had the highest rate of suicide in the country. Now she knew. If you survived to midlife out in the American Outback, unclaimed by alcohol or traffic accidents or cigarettes or uranium tainted water or violence or anything else, odds were good that you were hard to kill. It was possible to linger on, to continue far beyond your expiration date into a sort of half-death in which your dreams were gone and the people you loved were gone and the world you knew was gone, but somehow you were still there. You and the big empty land, the snow and yourself… and yourself… and yourself: an exclamation point standing in the center of an unforgiving land, waiting for God to strike you down as He had everything else in your world, closing the Genesis of your youth out with the Revelation of your death.

Only He doesn't.

She sighed to herself. Those other folks had it easy. They weren't Mormon – or at least they weren't *really* Mormon – and she was. A shotgun in the mouth, a ten-cent birdshot shell, the taste of gun oil, a finger gripping a trigger, and then it was done with. The Gentiles had it easy. Maude would have to find another way.

She had all but given up on the idea of Joe eating her. He seemed offended at the very idea; even though she explained he would be doing her a very big favor.

"I bet I don't taste all that bad," she insisted. "Maybe like jerked pork or something. You could make it quick." He only sighed and hobbled out of the room, shaking his massive head and muttering to himself in that way all dogs do. Well, she came to think of it, in the way she always imagined they did. Only he actually did that.

She began to have a recurring dirty dream at night. To be honest it wasn't actually that dirty, but they made her feel quite randy, which at her age was pretty much the same thing. It was a very simple dream, really. She would emerge from the dark cavern of slumber to find that someone was lying on top of her. At first she would think it was Big Joe, quietly sexing her in the middle of the night the way he used to do right up until the day he died. Then she would remember that he was dead, and the masculine-smelling figure mounting her would become the new Joe, all hairy, panting, and possessive in that way big dogs get when they love you. But that didn't seem right either – even in winter it was too hot for him to sleep on the bed – so it went back to being her dead husband Joe, then new Joe, and so forth until it became very confusing – but also quite pleasant.

She would wake up panting, hoping she was having a heart attack or that Joe had changed his mind and was killing her, but to no avail. It was just a damn orgasm.

■

Finally, Maude had had enough. She'd made sense of the dream. Joe was calling to her from heaven through the most intimate bond possible. What other explanation could there be? She was just stalling because she worried that the new Joe still needed her and because she was frightened of dying, but that was a sad excuse. He would be fine, and she had killed so many chickens and rabbits with her bare hands that being anxious about her own death seemed cowardly to her. She wouldn't even have to do anything but call up the Hand of Death. They would take care of it. If Joe hadn't kept interfering, she would happily be little more than frozen coyote scat and a gnawed skull under the sagebrush somewhere. They had come before. They would come again.

Maude knew that Joe would never let her go. It was obvious that he didn't want to be alone. Why else had he stayed after his foot had healed? He was just another poor crippled stray that the ocean of life had washed up on the endless beach of the Black Rock Desert. That fact that he wasn't human didn't make any difference. He was one more reverse-castaway, marooning himself away from the rhythm of life and time and change onto an eternal island of snow, sand, and huge open skies as so many others had.

Maude knew and understood these things, if a bit unconsciously. What she *did* know is that she wanted to go to the Celestial Kingdom and be with her dead husband for eternity. To a Deseret more glorious than any that could be envisioned on Earth. She had one foot in the doorway to that heaven and only the anchor of her body was holding her back. That night she got a footstool and went into the cupboard above the stove where she kept her herbal remedies in a series of antique crystal cookie jars.

Removing her entire supply of valerian root, she ground it into a fine mash using a cheese grater and mixed it in his with evening stew. He wasn't a fussy eater; sure enough, he consumed his entire portion: valerian root and all. He paced about the room a few times in his usual fashion, wandered back to the bedroom, and collapsed at the foot of her bed. The big creature was soon snoring – a lusty, odd, comfortable sound. Maude sat up thinking for a while, and then she too retired. She wanted to have that peculiar dream one more time and to sleep next to her friend. The last, only, and final one she would have.

When Maude awoke, it was snowing. Grey sunlight shone feebly through the curtain of white. Joe slumbered peacefully on the floor in his spot, the slits on the sides of his nostrils flaring and un-flaring as he snored softly. She smiled tenderly at him. It was hard to imagine a better friend to have when the credits finally, inevitably rolled on the end of her life. Before things finally went to black and the curtains tumbled. Quietly she left the room, latching the door behind her as she went.

Without dressing, she walked out onto her rickety porch and from there out into the ankle-deep snow. The cold dug into her withered flesh but she didn't care. She kept walking and, as she did so, used her mind to call out to the Hand of Death: summoning it from beyond, pulling it in from the hidden reaches of the Playa, and the Granites, and the Calicos. Summoning her end as surely as the final shovel of dirt falling upon the surface of a newly buried grave.

They came.

There was no howling this time. The coyotes weren't so healthy and handsome looking now, either. In fact, they had grown so thin that it seemed almost impossible they could still be alive at all. They were like concentration camp survivors in canine form, and she felt a twinge of pity for them. Determined to have their prey, they surrounded her on all sides, the smallest before her and the largest behind. They whined, glancing nervously back at her home, as if asking permission from their lame god to begin the sacrifice.

Only it wasn't his permission to give. It was hers. "Go ahead," she whispered at them. "Bring me home. Take me to Deseret."

They closed in. From within the house she heard a cry of

alarm, followed by the sound of a large body slamming against a door. She spread her arms wide and closed her eyes. The smallest Death closed her anvil-like jaws about Maude's ankle, snapping it like a twig. The howls from within the house became more desperate as she tumbled to the ground. Then they were atop her, ripping at her ancient breasts, biting into her flesh, laying open her jugular. She smiled, and blood poured from her mouth.

With a scream, Joe exploded through the pine board wall of the ranch house, crashing through the railing of the porch and flying into the gray twilight of the snowstorm. Then he was among them, laying out death to Death. He flung the smallest coyote against a fencepost, her backbone breaking with an audible "Snap!" before her limp body collapsed into the snow. He stood upright, grabbed the largest one with his enormous forepaws, and ripped its massive head from its shoulders in a spray of blood and gore that painted the snow red in an enormous radius around the fray. Flinging the lifeless hunks to the ground with a snarl, he sank his massive fangs into another. It struggled and screamed as the grinding of its jaws turned the coyote's flesh and bones into so much bloody pulp. When it stopped struggling, he spat its lifeless corpse to the ground.

With three fingers of the hand amputated, the two remaining fingers fled into the obscurity of the snow.

Joe gathered Maude up into his arms. She was cold, and her blood spilled onto the snow as he stood to his full height. She reached upward with a single, shaking hand to stroke the side of his muzzle.

"Joe," she said softly. "Take me... take me to Deseret."

The huge creature turned his muzzle to the sky and howled. A terrible, mournful, and desperate sound echoed to the farthest corners of the Black Rock Desert in defiance of all natural law. On the other size of High Rock Canyon, Tyson's mutant pack picked up his inhuman cry, one after the other until the renegade breeder emerged from his shack, clutching his rifle in his hands and blinking dazedly at the snow-obscured dawn. In the saddle formed where the Granite Mountains meet the much lower Banjo, the Guerrero family paused from their hastily consumed breakfast to stare in horror at the fearsome head of their clan. Rusty Guerrero cursed instinctively, then sighed, shook his head, and sadly returned to drinking his coffee. High atop the Granites themselves, a massive bear of a man in a bloodstained lab coat paused at his dissection table. Pulling a surgical facemask away from his mouth, he cocked his head curiously toward the mouth of his cave and listened intently, an inexplicable smile slowly crossing his bearded countenance. In the puzzling town of Hualapai, Uncle Hank awoke with a start on his couch, sending a priceless copy of Kit Carson's *Hidden Diaries and Western Observations* flying into a pile of half-consumed bottles of expensive Czech absinthe. On his flat screen, Marylyn Monroe's beautiful frozen face stared back at him from where he had paused *The Misfits* the night before.

Lowering his massive head to his breast, the monster known as Joe finally fell silent. Clutching Maude tightly to his breast, he staggered forward on two unsteady legs and vanished into the storm.

Out Here In The Freezing Fog

[Posted to midianranchblog.blogspot.com on December 24, 2009]

Frozen pipes. Broken generators. A septic system that froze, then backed up through every drain in the house. Debt. Massive propane bills. More debt. Unreliable Internet. Days in which there is no sun for the solar panels and no wind for the windmills. Leaks in the office roof. A battery bank rendered inefficient by freezing cold. Illness. A right hand for a time rendered useless by infection. A child that needs surgery.

And, oddly, a sense of peace. None of these things matters beyond its station. Somehow, I have found something close to happiness here amidst the distracting clutter of ranch life. We Walters came here to be modern day settlers, and to live upon this hard land in the manner of our ancestors: free, independent, and answerable to no one. Those tough, hard people of a century and a half ago suffered like saints and martyrs for the right to be here. They suffered and endured things none of us have had to, tough old birds that they were. Some, like Kit Carson, became legends. Many didn't make it past their first two years, retreating to civilization or dying anonymously in the dry, desolate mountains.

We have endured.

To be honest, I'm not sure how much of an accomplishment it is to simply hold on in the face of adversity. It does certainly feel like an accomplishment, especially in this harsh, barren, and beautiful place. Yesterday a freezing fog rolled into the desert whose impenetrability rivaled any you would find in San Francisco or London: cold, thick, and mysterious. It stayed throughout the day, reducing sunlight to a dim twilight and visibility to a few car lengths. It left white frozen tendrils clinging to every available surface: trees, homes, and even the salt brush, transforming the Black Rock from somber brown to glistening white.

Is this what it might be like to be a settler on Mars? The Moon? One of the moons of Jupiter? Endless mighty vistas, shocking weather, hard work, isolation, and the small pleasures of life shaped into razors by the threat of death hovering in the background like an unmentioned party guest? In another future time, living another life, could that have been our life? Is it possible that, whether through the gentle hand of God or some miracle of modern medicine, this could be Cassidy's future still? To be a pioneer out among the stars: free, independent, and answerable to no one?

I pray for this, but only dreams answer me.

I was driving through that frozen fog when I stumbled upon a photographer, standing by his car at the edge of the Playa, looking out into the white nothing. As is my habit, I pulled over to see if he was all right. Having been stranded in the Black Rock before myself, I've developed a sort of "leave no man behind" attitude about this sort of thing. I always pull over. I hopped out of my pickup truck and strode over to where the man stood with his camera, taking pictures of the snowy infinity.

We spoke. In retrospect, he to me as one might handle an escaped lunatic or an overly affectionate drunken stranger: delicately, carefully. I can see why. I was dressed in snow boots, a filthy surplus industrial jumpsuit, and a battered black fedora. Beard, earrings, hair uncut for years – all moving toward him in the fog in the middle of a (nearly) uninhabited wasteland.

A mutant. A Crazy. Somebody Mad Mel shot in Road Warrior.

Many of us get like that out here, given enough time and an initial disposition toward craziness. Our day-to-day appearance rather... unravels, turning us into weird, dusty cartoon characters. Many don't, too. There are cowboys out here, real ones, whose clothing outside of their ranch is so crisp and sharp you can set your watch to them. Then there are the Burning Man DPW people, who often look like the road warrior has already killed them, and they've been reanimated for a sequel that involves flesh-eating zombies. They make me look like a Montgomery Street bank manager.

However, then again, they're seasonal and not out here in the freezing fog.

Mexican Cowboy

> Good actions ennoble us, and we are the sons of our deeds.
> — Cervantes

Unloved dogs. Unloved children. Unloved old men and women. The world is a fucked up place filled with unwanted people. It doesn't have to be that way. But it is. All you can do is try to be a little less messed up than the world you live in.

That was the unspoken slogan of Lupe Maldonado's life. He was a little less fucked up than the world he lived in. When his amigos were falling down drunk, Lupe made of point of being able to stand up. When one of his fellow *vaqueros* beat on one of the numerous dogs that helped them in their work, he made a point of giving the animal a bit of his dinner. While most of the younger inhabitants of the Black Rock Desert ignored the mass of wizened widows that were the backdrop of town life, he was always polite to them, making a point of performing helpful little chores for the most elderly of their number. When his fellow Mexican cowboys blew their entire paychecks drinking in Hank's Hualapai Club, Lupe always made certain to send a portion home to his mother in Jalisco.

Because of these facts, many of Lupe's friends thought that he was soft, crazy, or both. However, his malady of sympathy had its advantages. Not many of the Hispanic expatriates who toiled on the ranches and farms near Hualapai had women. Fewer still had white girlfriends. Lupe's girlfriend was not only white; she was also one of the sexy, crazy, sunburned hippies that work for Burning Man.

As far as his friends were concerned – and, for that matter, as far as many of the local Anglos were concerned – Lupe might as well have been screwing a Martian.

The little vaquero held on for dear life. Shutup Amy cursed extensively, in the process using up about half of Lupe's repertoire of English words. The battered green Ford Courier swung wildly to the left, failing to hit the house-sized beach ball it was aiming for but successfully slamming his head through the side window in a shower of glass. Fortunately, both he and the driver wore battered football helmets. He wasn't injured.

The small truck emerged from the enormous cloud of playa dust it had kicked up, narrowly missing a blue K-Car in hot pursuit of the massive sphere. It was on the other team, so Amy did her best to ram it. Cursing, she missed her competitor by a matter of inches. That was how Playa Pool was played – an occasionally deadly combination of amateur crash up derby, team billiards, and profanity. This month's game was between the Freaks, whose rigs were painted bright green, and the Shitkickers, whose rigs were painted dark blue. Lupe technically should have been in a shitkicker vehicle, as the team was mostly comprised of cowboys and vaqueros, but chose instead to brave the questionable driving of his ladylove and ride in a Freak rig. Though shit-scared out of his mind, Lupe stoically bore the terror, his face showing all the emotion of a stone.

Shutup Amy was an entirely different matter. Tattooed and topless in the blistering summer heat, glass-flecked blond dreadlocks sticking wildly through a hole cut through the top of the helmet, she was a demonic caricature of feminine emotionalism. This was nothing new. Amy's expressions typically moved across the spectrum of human passions, even when she wasn't high.

Amy pulled up the emergency break, effortlessly executing a barrelhouse reverse on the loose, dusty surface of the desert. The vehicle swung sideways 90-degrees like a pendulum. Then she released the break, slingshotting it forward in the opposite direction without losing noticeable momentum. It was a maneuver that, on normal pavement, would have required a stuntman's level of expertise. On the Playa, all it required was a willful disregard for one's own personal safety.

They charged back into the cloud of blinding, choking dust. Lupe could vaguely make out shapes that he assumed to be other cars desperately attempting to kill them both, but they shot past without incident. Then they were through the cloud with the massive ball directly in front of them – and, beyond that, the blue, half-buried railroad tie that was the opposing team's goalpost.

Amy grinned wickedly, jabbing the accelerator to the floor with a sudden jerk of her leg. Lupe braced himself as the little pickup jumped forward, slamming into the ball with all the force its underpowered four-cylinder engine could muster. There was a crunch as the truck's grill collapsed inward, then the sphere bounced forward, striking the tie before shooting off into the distance at a right angle.

Amy turned her truck in a slow arc to the right. She began a victory lap around the "field" (though, really, the field was the entire desert) that ended when it slid into a halt before the two yellow school buses upon which the entire population of Hualapai stood in relative safety, watching the insanity below through binoculars. She stepped out of the truck, removed her football helmet, and bowed with a flourish, sweeping the battered helmet before her as if it were a French cavalier's feathered fedora.

Amy's reward was a shower of hoots, insults, and half-empty beer cans.

"Put some clothes on you fucking crazy whore!"

"Baby, if my tits were that small, I'd keep my shirt on!"

"Ever heard of a bra?"

"Fuck a bra – ever head of a comb, Moldy Locks?"

Amy slowly reversed her bow, flinging her helmet harmlessly at the crowd as she slowly extended the middle finger of her suddenly empty hand. The townspeople repaid her with more derision. Turning her back to them, she bent forward, wiggling and slapping her buttocks in an obvious gesture of "kiss my ass." Amid peals of laughter she walked back over to where Lupe was standing by the little truck, a bemused, half-comprehending smile spread across his handsome, swarthy features. She threw him the keys.

"Take me back to my place and fuck me."

He only understood two of the words that came out of her mouth. They were enough.

■

Later that night, Lupe sat upright in bed, naked except for a single stained satin sheet that covered his legs. He smoked a cigarillo with his right hand while he lazily ran his left through Amy's hair. She was dead to the world; one shapely leg sprawled out over the side of the bed, her head lying gently on his lap. The light of the moon fell through a dirty window. A dog barked in the distance. The town of Hualapai was asleep.

He wasn't sure how old she was. His best guess was that she was slightly younger than his mother was, though it was hard to say. The desert sun did funny things to Anglos' skin. She could be any age, really. He didn't care. Lupe Maldonado loved the woman they called *Callate* Amy. It was true that she did talk all of the time, but he wasn't particularly concerned.

After all, Lupe had almost no idea what she was saying.

Yet he *knew* her. They were familiar in a way few people ever could be. She was a confusing mix of good, evil, and other things that weren't so easy to define. Like most people, he mused, only extreme. Lupe liked extremes. They were like the goalposts at the edge of the Playa Pool field. Intertwined extremes defined his life, as they did that of every desert dweller: gentle and cruel, violent and peaceful, wise and ignorant, hardworking and lazy. These were reflections of the land upon which they lived: alternately blisteringly hot and freezing cold; breathtakingly mountainous and monotonously flat, and unusually safe – except when it was extraordinarily dangerous.

He knew that he was a good lover, filled with seemingly endless reservoirs of passion. Lupe knew how to please a woman. He also knew how to please himself, which was an integral portion of pleasing one. Women could instinctually sense dissatisfaction: in the bedroom, in the kitchen, anywhere at all. It was as if they possessed a supernatural power for seeing such things. Fortunately, Lupe was a natural man who found happiness in the simple pleasures of life. Amy never sensed dissatisfaction from her boyfriend because he was simply never dissatisfied.

Not these days, in any case.

Lupe thought back to his childhood in Jalisco. His mother: so quiet and careworn. His father: a hard-drinking, tough-as-leather *charro*. A horseman. A Mexican cowboy, just like his son. In the rest of Mexico and in *Los Estados Unidos*, people called them vaqueros. Not back home. There weren't any "cow-boys" back there. Only "horse-men."

Lupe had always thought it was better that way.

He remembered the cinderblock home in which he was raised. His father and uncles had left tall lengths of rebar extending out of the roof every couple of feet so that the construction remained officially unfinished... and thus exempt from property taxes. They had whimsically tied lengths of colored ribbon to the tips so that when the dry desert wind blew down upon the town the roof of their home appeared to be a shifting, shimmering piñata. This is why everyone in town called it "casa piñata."

He remembered the smell of dust in his parent's home: different yet similar to the smell of dust here. He wasn't certain he missed the smells of home anymore. Lupe was no longer positive, exactly, were home was. Or what it was. That bothered him. Like most cowboys, Mexican or not, he was a quietly philosophical soul, and the concept of "belonging" mattered deeply to him. However, it was a hard concept to measure. Did it mean having ties to a people? To a culture? To the land itself?

He felt adrift, between two worlds.

Lupe knew that he was supposed to miss his family: his stern, eccentric father, martyred mother, bullying brothers, and *punta* sister. He did... in a distant, melancholy kind of way. He was always careful to send home money, after all. But it wasn't a knife in his gut the way the sad mariachi songs said it was supposed to be. Mexicans were culturally required to be sentimental about their families, home states, and nation in precisely that order. Most genuinely were. Lupe wasn't. When the recruiter had stopped by the ranchero where he had worked with his father and uncles, the young charro had leaped at the chance to go to Los Estados Unidos... and to get the hell out of Jalisco.

He'd wanted adventure and opportunity, which for a poor Mexican meant one of three things: Mexico City, the army, or a voyage to El Norte, legal or not. He hated the army, which given his nation's history was understandable. The Mexican army was as likely to fuck you over as protect you. He didn't like cities very much, either. They were noisy, dirty, and claustrophobic, filled with men whose only profession was taking advantage of *nacos* like him. So, given the chance to travel legally – and at another's expense – to El Norte, Lupe had quietly climbed off his horse, set down his lariat, and gotten into the back of the recruiter's van. He didn't even go back home to get his clothing.

Now he was here. He had worked hard to be here. But was this home?

Were the people of Hualapai his friends? Certainly the other vaqueros were. Lupe was famously easygoing, possessing a peculiar sense of humor that only made sense to his own kind. He had always gotten along well with the Guerrero family, even if they were crazy and their Spanish was terrible. He knew they saw him as a fellow eccentric desert rat, though that wasn't how he thought of himself. His employers the Gladwells had always been kind to him, though they expected a lot of work from their ranch hands; which they always got from him, at least. It had never occurred to Lupe they would expect anything else. His entire life had been an unbroken paragraph of hard labor punctuated by frenzied exclamation points of sex, drinking, and general craziness.

He worked well with the Anglo cowboys, mostly by just doing what they told him without comment. This didn't mean that Lupe was naturally subservient. Far from it. But most of the white cowboys were foremen of one sort or another – their various titles and stations didn't mean much to him – so he simply rolled with it. He was at work to *work*, after all, and he really didn't care who gave the orders so long as the myriad tasks on the Gladwell Ranch were completed. It was an attitude that was appreciated by all concerned, though it might have drawn a certain amount of scorn from his fellow vaqueros if he weren't so likable.

Mostly, though, Anglos were unfathomable to Lupe. He had never thought much about them back in Jalisco: though, to be honest, the only whites he saw there were fat, old men journeying south in search of small brown natives to hump. It wasn't a situation designed to ingratiate one race to another, so nobody even tried; but at least it was easy to understand.

Not so in Hualapai.

Uncle Hank. Hippie. The PH. Oberon. Iverson. The Scarred Girl. Even his own beloved Shutup Amy. These weren't easy people to get to know. Their motivations remained obscure to him, as if he were trying to put together a puzzle that was missing half of its pieces. Complicating matters was the fact that the non-whites like Two Crows and Tyson were even stranger than the sunburned, light haired foreigners who so baffled him. He had begun to suspect that there was something about being an American that drove people entirely crazy, though what it was he had yet to discover. The bad food, maybe? Too much wealth? It was hard to say.

Regardless, Lupe Maldonado had come to a decision. Propping himself up on one elbow, he leaned over and shook Amy's shoulder. She groaned. She shook her again, until finally her eyes fluttered open and she looked up at him.

"What, you're ready again?" she asked a bit groggily. "Good Lord! Are all the men where you come from like you? If so, I'm fucking moving there!"

He shrugged helplessly. He's understood the word "fucking," but he knew the word had two or three meanings. Probably she wasn't asking for sex. He petted her sunburned cheek and looked deeply into her blue eyes.

"I've been up all night thinking about this, Amy," he said as eloquently as he could in Spanish. "I love you. I want to take care of you. I would like for us to get married and have a family. I know it would be tough at first, but if we work at it for enough years, we could probably buy a ranch of our own. We could live our lives out here among our friends. That would be nice, wouldn't it?"

Now it was Amy's turn to stare at Lupe helplessly. Then she was silent for what seemed to him like a very long time.

"Lupe, you know my Spanish sucks," she replied at last, speaking very slowly as if to a child. "I caught a few words: love, friends, family, and ranch. *Amore. Amigos. Familia. Rancho.* Those I know, but I don't understand. *No comprende.*"

He smiled at her. Reaching down, he picked up her left hand. Then he made the unmistakable motion of sliding a ring down onto one of her finger. He pointed to her, then to himself, and then stood. Picking up a sweat-stained pillow, he cradled it in his arms, rocking it back and forth and making little cooing sounds at it. Then he looked back at her, perhaps a bit shyly.

Lupe didn't get the response he expected.

Amy had turned a shade of deep, deep purple. Her eyes were open and staring. Her mouth opened and closed like a fish's, as if it was trying to form words it was unable to utter. Finally she rose, pointing a single finger toward the door.

"Get out!" she shouted. "Get the fuck out of here!"

Lupe didn't understand. He shrugged sheepishly, and then smiled once again.

"Get out! Get out! Get out!" She reached down, grabbed the lamp on her bed stand, and threw it at his head. It was an old, heavy thing made out of cast iron that could have seriously hurt him had it struck; but he nimbly jumped out of the way, allowing the lamp to sail past him into the wall. The large blond woman had thrown it with such force that it went straight through the paper-thin wall of her singlewide's bedroom and into the bathroom. Lupe heard something shatter on the other side.

He took the hint.

With what he imagined to be curses and insults – and what he knew to be more flying objects – following close behind him, Lupe sprinted out of the bedroom, scooping up his boots and clothing from the floor in one smooth motion as he went. A moment later, he burst through the front door and found himself standing naked and thoroughly confused on the street in the middle of Hank's Hualapai Trailer Park.

"Evening, Lupe." The little vaquero turned to find that Iverson had emerged from his own singlewide and was standing on the tiny, crude porch that was built around its doorway. The tall fireman's brown, haunted eyes looked down on him with knowing sympathy. "Love's a goddamn delight, ain't it?"

Lupe nodded, more at the tone than the words. Then with as much dignity as a naked man could muster, he turned to walk toward his battered Mazda pickup truck.

███

He looked up at the ceiling. Lupe's bunkroom was a tiny ten-by-ten closet barely big enough for his bed, a nightstand, and the battered footlocker that he kept his meager possessions in. His leather chaps and jacket hung on a hook on the wall. His good clothing – a worn, western wear style black suit – hung on a hook next to them.

The little cowboy lived with relatively minimal adornment. A picture of his mother hung on the wall. As if equivalent, an icon of the Virgin of Guadalupe hung next to it. The two of them were separated from one another by a slender, wooden crucifix from which a particularly miserable – and Mexican – Christ hung, glaring pleadingly outward through oversized eyes. Lupe seldom contemplated this odd trinity. He preferred to stare up the two posters he'd stapled to the crude wooden planks above his bed the day he'd arrived at the Gladwell Ranch. They stared down at him: distant, unobtainable, and manly, like demigods calling from the afterworld.

Rodolfo Guzman Huerta. El Santo – the greatest of all masked Mexican wrestlers. A real life superhero, athlete, and movie star. To many lower-class Mexicans he was the personification of all that was awesome. It was as if Superman, John Wayne, and Frank Sinatra had been compressed into a single man. For nearly five decades he'd not only wrestled villainous *rudos* in the ring, but werewolves, vampires, and blonde Martians on the silver screen as well. El Santo was a living folk hero and symbol of justice to the common man.

He also had an extremely well developed and manly chest. Not unlike Lupe's... or so he fancied.

John Simon Ritchie. Sid Vicious – the greatest of all punk rockers. A living, pus-filled wound overflowing with impotent rage, drugs, noise, and nihilism. The bassist of the Sex Pistols, the first and possibly greatest of all punk rock bands, Sid Vicious rebelled against everything. His life was completely – and tragically – unsuccessful in every way. He accidentally killed his great love. His friends abandoned him. He never learned to play his instrument properly. He squandered away any money he made.

In short, Sid Vicious was a complete fuckup.

Yet in death he had achieved immortality as a sort of iconic supervillain. An anti-Buddha who smashed everything he touched, injured everyone he loved, and indulged in every conceivable vice. He was what every man wished they could be at some point in their lives, if they only had the courage to be truly, grossly masculine. Sid Vicious was a real life Incredible Hulk, only scrawny with acne and scars.

He also had black, spiky hair. Not unlike Lupe's... or so he fancied.

These two ionic men would seem to be irreconcilably opposed. Hero and villain. Traditionalist and rebel. Athlete and junkie. Yet in Lupe's mind, they were somehow one and the same: twin sides of a coin tumbling through eternity. It was a great mystery. Maybe all men contained El Santo and Sid Vicious in their souls, battling to drive them either toward self-sacrifice or self-indulgence, valor or villainy. He felt them struggling within him every day. Sid Vicious was overmatched. El Santo usually won. Lupe was responsible, thrifty, honorable, family-oriented, and hardworking. On a few occasions, he had even been brave, charging into a stampede to rescue a fellow vaquero from beneath trampling hooves and placing himself between a drunken coworker and an enraged trucker in Hank's Hualapai Club. Yet deep down much of his strength came from the long-dead father of punk. Lupe nursed a burning coal of senseless rebellion that kept him strong in a way that something as explicable as virtue never could. He knew that Amy – tattooed, wild haired, pierced, crazy, and sunburned – had been Sid Vicious' gift to him. Things had only gotten messed up when his inner El Santo had taken over.

It made perfect sense if you only understood.

Very few people knew of Lupe Maldonado's love for classic punk rock. He had only ever confided it to Sol Guerrero, because the son of the fearsome Rusty Guerrero was a musician and would understand such things. Amy has puzzled it out after she'd listened to his iPod while he was sleeping. The expression on her face when he'd exclaimed names like "The Germs" and "Dead Kennedys" among an incongruous flow of Spanish had been priceless. Lupe liked the old stuff from the '70s and '80s: The Clash, Fear, Los Circle Jerks, and the like. He'd heard plenty of Mexican punk, as well as some of the newer stuff from places like Berkeley. Those bands didn't cut it. They just didn't have the power of the old stuff. Punk had become institutional. Robbed of its own revolutionary spirit, like the Institutional Revolutionary Party that had wielded power over his homeland for 70 years.

Of course, as any Mexican can tell you, institutional revolution is never a pretty thing.

Lupe wasn't surprised that Amy avoided him for few days. He guessed that the proposal had thrown her off balance. He knew that he'd upset her, so he went about his daily life, giving her some time to calm down. Along with the other vaqueros, he gathered in cattle from the Gladwell's easements on the side of the Calicos. This took several days. He repaired the roof of an outbuilding. It was hot, unforgiving work: but less so than rounding up cows. He accepted a load of methane from Hugo Guerrero, Sol's hulking, taciturn older brother. The two of them first pumped 1,000 gallons of the foul-smelling gas into the ranch's massive tanks, and then spent the rest of the day shoveling truckload after truckload of manure onto the Guerrero's 26-foot flatbed. The day after that he spent repairing the fencing around Mrs. Gladwell's large vegetable garden. This was tricky, as the wind had damaged the garden's high wooden fencing, exposing it to potential predations by deer and antelope. Lupe was careful to fix it in such a way that more high winds wouldn't easily tear it back down again.

Finally, it was Friday night. All the Gladwells' vaqueros piled into Lupe's battered, rusty Mazda pickup truck and he drove them into Hualapai for the weekend. Mostly they would go to Hank's Hualapai Club. There they would drink tequila and Tecates, flirt with Anglo women as best they were able, shoot pool, gamble at Uncle Hank's few, aging slot machines – the cool kind that spat out coins, not tickets – and generally cut loose in a way that outsiders coming in from places like San Francisco and Reno found intimidating, but the locals found amusing. Upon occasion, they'd get in a fight, usually with each other, or more rarely with one of the cowboys they worked with. Other patrons of the bar usually broke up these skirmishes, though Uncle Hank had a unique method for dealing with anyone getting extremely drunk and belligerent in his establishment. He kept a filthy, foul old toilet plunger below the bar and whenever anyone crossed the line with him – say, became rude or violent and then refused to leave when he asked them to – he'd whip it out in a sudden, fluid motion and stick it straight into their face. Invariably the startled drunk would fall backward off his barstool at the site of the horrid thing, causing all of his friends to laugh at him.

With men, humiliation works a lot better than violence.

Lupe dropped his friends at the club. He ducked his head in for a moment and, noticing that she wasn't at her usual barstool, went to Amy's house. The sun was setting behind the Granites, causing the other trailers in the park to cast long shadows as he walked up onto her porch to bang on the flimsy, battered door. There was no answer. He beat on it again. There was still no answer. He walked around to the other side of her trailer and noticed that her much-abused, often-crashed Suzuki Samurai wasn't there. He walked to Burning Man's office on the main street. The lady behind the counter – a bizarre apparition with a Frankenstein bride's halo of blue hair, cheek piercings, and horn-rimmed glasses studded with what Lupe thought were probably real gemstones – knew who he was. After some gesturing and the use of a few simple words, she seemed to figure out what he wanted, but didn't have the Spanish to explain anything to him. She gestured down the street in the direction of the home of a frightening character that Lupe knew only as the PH.

Lupe knew the PH was something like British. He had always wanted to ask him if he'd known Sid Vicious, but the tall, gray man with the dead eyes emitted such strong twin auras of menace and authority that Lupe never felt comfortable around him. Not that the PH was anyone's boss, as far as he knew; but so much authority radiating out of one man pushed away at Lupe's rebellious soul like two magnets of opposite polarity being forced together.

Lupe dreaded trying to have a long conversation with the tall man, whom as far as he knew didn't speak Spanish either. Yet he dutifully walked a block down and stepped onto his front porch. Fortunately, the PH wasn't on his front porch, though several other people were. Lupe quickly figured out why the lady with the crazy glasses had sent him there. Sol Guerrero lay sprawled across a wooden chair, his lanky body somehow simultaneously leaning against the porch's wooden railing and sitting down. He strummed something slow, sad, and romantic on a battered wooden guitar for two blond girls that sat on a swing nearby. They looked so much alike that they could have been sisters, though Lupe thought that they probably weren't. Sol was crooning some sort of ballad in English. Lupe thought he had a good voice, though he could only make out the words "cherry" and "chicken" from the lyrics. Whatever the song was, it certainly impressed his audience.

Lupe politely removed his cowboy hat and smiled at the three of them. Sol stopped playing.

"*Hola Lupe!*" he said. "*Como esta?*"

"*Asi-asi*" he responded, and then continued in Spanish. "Sol, have you seen Amy around?"

The youngest Guerrero was of mixed ancestry. He had long, light brown hair and hazel eyes, but was just Hispanic enough to be tan rather than sunburned and freckled. Lupe thought he looked like a country singer, or maybe a rock star. *Someday he probably would be one, too, if his current audience is any indication*, Lupe thought with a little envy.

Those striking hazel eyes looked very seriously at him just then. Knowing that something was wrong, the little vaquero felt his heart drop to the bottom of his stomach.

"Listen, Lupe," he said. "After you left last week, Amy announced to everybody in town that she needed some time alone and that she was going to go up into the Granites to camp for a while. Everybody told her that was a bad idea, too, but she wouldn't listen. She also didn't say when she'd be back."

"And nobody stopped her?" Lupe exclaimed angrily.

Sol shrugged.

"None of us *liked* it Lupe. But Amy's an adult: we couldn't very well stop her. And, frankly, after that incident in Smoke Creek... well, it's not like she can't handle herself."

Lupe didn't know what Sol was referring to by "that incident in Smoke Creek." Even the idea of his beloved Callate Amy going into *that* place sent shivers up his spine.

"This is all my fault," replied Lupe.

"What are you talking about?"

"It's all my fault she went up there," he responded despairingly. "I asked her to marry me."

Sol's mouth formed an "O" very slowly. Then he said his guitar down and leaned over toward the two girls with blond hair. He said some things very softly to them in English. They laughed, got up, smiled at Lupe a little shyly, and then left.

The little cowboy looked at his friend with a slightly irritated expression, causing Sol to raise his hands up defensively with the palms facing outward.

"I wasn't making fun of you," he said. "I just made a little joke to get rid of them. Okay?"

He nodded, but at that moment, a lever went down in Lupe's head.

"I'm going after her," he said firmly. "I'm going after her. Right. Now."

"Whoa, whoa – easy hombre. We don't even know where she went. The Granites are huge. She could have gone in any number of ways. She could be anywhere."

"Your family knows that range," replied Lupe. "In fact, your family knows that range better than *anybody*."

"I don't," replied Sol.

"Your uncle lives up there," said Lupe, placing a lot of stress on the word "uncle." The two young men locked eyes for a moment. Then Sol looked away.

"Okay, okay," the younger man gave in. "But I want you to talk to Uncle Hank and my dad before you go. Come with me."

The two men walked over to Hank's Hualapai Club and went inside. It was Friday night. The jukebox was blaring out country songs from the '70s. Tall, thin, sunburned men with flamboyant moustaches drank Bud Light alongside short, brown ones with even more flamboyant moustaches. They drank Coronas. Women in their middle age whose features still contained hints of past beauty danced with these men – or sometimes with one another. Eccentric bottles crafted to look like miners, cowboys, old west prostitutes, and every other conceivable shape lined racks all over the walls, as did yellowing posters advertising goods that had vanished well before either of the young men was born.

Uncle Hank – old, sunburned, and bald, with whips of white hair clinging to the sides of his skull – raised an eyebrow as Sol Guerrero came in. By local custom teenagers and children *were* allowed in the club, but usually only with their parents and then only briefly.

The young man walked straight over to the barkeep. He began speaking rapidly and quietly in English. Hank listened, raised his eyebrow once more, looked at Lupe, and then answered back.

Sol turned to Lupe. "Wait here for a minute. Have a beer or something. We'll be back."

Dutifully the vaquero sat down at the bar, slapped a couple of dollars on the table, and, leaning over, got himself a Corona from behind the counter. Self-service was far from uncommon at Hank's. Some time passed. Two Crows, the big Paiute Indian who served as the town's gym coach, sat down next to him. He smiled down at Lupe, but didn't say anything. Not that the big *indio* ever said much.

Sol reemerged from the doorway in back and motioned Lupe in. Two Crows followed. Uncle Hank sat on a beer keg in the backroom, which was filled the sort of paraphernalia you needed to run a club: cases of wine and beer, boxes of candy bars, an old, broken jukebox, and the like. He held an ornate box in his lap and, as Lupe entered, the old man motioned him over.

Sol stood by Uncle Hank, acting as an interpreter, while Two Crows leaned curiously against the doorway. The old man opened the box and began unwrapping two objects that were inside of two purple Crown Royal bags.

"These," he said through Sol, "are armbands that once belonged to the great Sid Vicious." This was said extremely solemnly as he removed the two large, black leather bracers with multiple buckles running down the side. They were plain, yet somehow at the same time ornate, with a pattern of little studs along their interior rims. They were two of the most beautiful things Lupe Maldonado had ever seen.

"When I was a young man," Uncle Hank continued, "I worked at a nightclub in San Francisco that he used to play at. He left these behind one night after a gig. For many years I've looked for the right man to give them to."

He turned his pale blue eyes on Lupe.

"You are that man. And this is that time."

The Mexican cowboy took them delicately in his hands with the reverence one might reserve for a holy artifact. He rolled up the sleeves of his shirt and buckled them on, one after the other. As soon as he was done, he glanced at his right shoulder and noticed a tiny Sid Vicious sitting there. He was perched casually, as if he were on the front stoop of a London flat. He was shirtless and wore battered black leather pants. The word "hate" had been etched crudely across his chest with a razor. The father of all punk was playing a base guitar and he glared up, annoyed, as Lupe looked down at him.

"Oy!" he snarled distinctively. "Geezer's gotta practice, don't he?" He said this in extremely oddly accented Spanish, which Lupe didn't find at all alarming or unusual. He simply nodded.

"Of course," he said aloud, still looking at his shoulder. The other three men eyed him very curiously. A long, very awkward silence followed.

"Umm, okay, Lupe," Sol said at last. "Let's go see my dad. I think he might also have something you can use."

Still staring at his fantastic armbands Lupe nodded absently. He followed Sol out of the doorway and then out of the front door of Hank's Hualapai Club.

Two Crows watched them go.

"You gave him the armbands your queer-ass son accidentally left behind after Burning Man last year, didn't you?" he asked.

"Shut the fuck up," replied Uncle Hank.

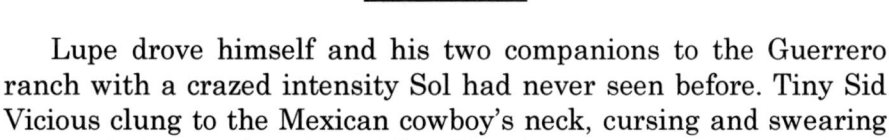

■

Lupe drove himself and his two companions to the Guerrero ranch with a crazed intensity Sol had never seen before. Tiny Sid Vicious clung to the Mexican cowboy's neck, cursing and swearing as he held on for dear life. The little man's combat boots periodically slipped off the collar of his shirt as he struggled for purchase.

"Oy, mate, be careful!" he shouted. "I don't want to die all over again!"

Lupe tore down the gravel roads as if the hounds of hell itself were hot on his tailpipe, sliding around corners and kicking up a cloud of dust that wouldn't have been out of place behind the space shuttle. Finally, he slid sideways to a halt inside of the gates of the Guerrero compound. A visibly rattled Sol opened the door and stepped out, gingerly holding onto the edge of the car like a man who'd been at sea to long.

"Wait here," he croaked hoarsely. "Let me go get dad. I'll be... right back."

Lupe sat in silence, listening to the sound of chickens in a coop nearby. Sid Vicious reached into the aether to produce a bottle of Bombay Sapphire Gin, which he promptly began guzzling.

"Have to steel my bloody nerves after that bit o' helter skelter," he grumbled. Then he drank more.

Finally, Sol emerged and walked back to where the two of them were sitting.

"Dad will talk to you now."

Without further comment, Sol turned and walked back to the

house. Lupe got out of the car and followed him into the large complex of linked doublewides and shipping containers that the Guerreros called home.

"Jesus Fucking Christ!" exclaimed Sid Vicious. "It's like a bloody cross between Mad Max and Deliverance, idn't it?"

Lupe nodded. However, once within the structure he found himself inside of an 800-square foot sitting room. It was surprisingly nice: sheet rocked with an improbably high ceiling. There were comfortable looking old couches of various sorts. La-z-boys. Coffee tables. A large flat screen TV. What looked like an old, scarred up dining room table with one leg that had been replaced with a length of 2 by 4. There were several small desks along one wall. At one of them, a tall, rather slim blonde woman whose hair was just beginning to turn grey worked feverishly on a laptop. Lupe guessed that she was in her late 40s. She smiled at him as he walked in. He smiled nervously in response.

"*Buena noche, Senora Guerrero,*" he said politely.

"Good evening, Lupe," she replied in English, and then turned back to her work.

The patriarch of the Guerrero family sat at the jury-rigged table. Its surface was covered in old newspapers. He appeared to be bluing pieces of an old handgun, though Lupe was no expert in such things. He glowered at the vaquero as he entered. That was hardly surprising. Rusty Guerrero glowered at everyone.

"Sit," he said in oddly accented Spanish, motioning at one of the la-z-boys. Lupe dutifully sat. Guerrero continued his work for a few moments: painting chemicals onto the bits of metal and then washing them off with other chemicals. Finally, after several long minutes had passed, he got up and wiped his hands on a rag.

"Wait here," he said simply and walked out of the room. Lupe waited. Sol had vanished and Mrs. Guerrero was silent save for the sounds of her fingers tapping on the keyboard. He wasn't certain what he would have said to her, anyhow.

Rusty Guerrero intimidated him. It wasn't that the man was physically large. They were about the same height – though Rusty was much wider than Lupe was. There was just a certain aura about the man. If he were a video game character Lupe was certain an icon symbolizing "dangerous motherfucker" would hover above his head.

"Caw! He's a scary bugger, ain't he?" said Sid. Lupe nodded.

Two minutes later the oldest Guerrero returned with a Cuban cigar box in his hands. Lupe was impressed by that alone.

Guerrero walked over to where a wooden chair lay propped against the wall, dragged it directly in front of Lupe, sat down, and glared at him. The much younger man met his eyes evenly.

"This," said Guerrero, tapping the box with one meaty finger, "was given to me by my uncle. I've been saving it for just the right occasion." He opened the box away from himself so that its contents were directly below Lupe's eyes: which promptly bugged out in disbelief. The contents of the box cast a silvery light upon his startled features. It was as if they contained some mysterious, inner luminescence.

"Yes," Rusty Guerrero nodded, "it's real. It belonged to Him. He wore it in the Arena Mexico, battling *rudos* and all other sorts of evil. His blood, sweat, and tears are soaked into its fabric. Take it out."

Gingerly, as if holding a relic, Lupe Maldonado removed the Santo mask.

"You see," continued Guerrero, closing the box, "my uncle was none other than Gory Guerrero, the great El Santo's tag team partner for many years. The great Champ gave it to him as a present after they'd won a particularly vicious mask vs. hair match. Therefore, it passed from the hands of the Guzman family to the hands of the Guerrero family. Now it passes from my hands to yours, Lupe Maldonado."

Lupe began to remove his shirt. Guerrero looked startled for a moment, then grunted and nodded as the younger man removed the garment entirely, revealing a tan, muscular, highly developed chest. Then, with great ceremony, he put his face into the mask, pulled the drawstrings tight, and tied it snugly in place. There was a bust of surf guitar music. Lupe looked down at his right shoulder just in time to see a tiny El Santo materialize right on the tip of his shoulder blade. The Man in the Silver Mask was dressed immaculately in a 1970s-style business suit – with, of course, his signature mask.

The surf music continued. With perfect balance, the tiny El Santo leaned around Lupe's Adams apple. On the other shoulder, Sid was doing a fair imitation of Dick Dale using a classic Fender Stratocaster.

"Thank you," said El Santo. "That will be quite sufficient."

"No problem, mate," replied the miniature punk rocker, tossing his guitar outward to vanish into the aether, "just trying to keep up appearances for the lad."

El Santo nodded and adjusted his powder blue tie. "Well Lupe, what are you waiting for? Thank the man and go rescue the girl!"

Lupe nodded at the tiny El Santo, and then looked up to see Rusty Guerrero staring at him with the same bemused expression that Uncle Hank had worn.

"*Gracias, Senor Guerrero,*" he said, not realizing that his normally soft and mild voice had suddenly become a deep, rumbling base, "you will not be disappointed that you've entrusted this holy artifact to me. I go now to rescue the woman I love."

With that, Lupe leaped dramatically up and sprang from the room. He ran out of the door, flew off the porch, and ran to his pickup truck, where he proceeded to leap through an open window like a character from the *Dukes of Hazzard*. A moment later, the battered Mazda was little more than a plume of dust in the distance.

Rusty Guerrero shook his head.

"Dad," said Sol, stepping from the shadows, "you didn't have any uncles; well, not any that were Mexican, anyhow. We're not related to Gory Guerrero."

"So?" said Rusty.

"So? So that's not one of El Santo's real masks!" he exclaimed, switching to English. "You bought that in an open air market in Tijuana!"

"Maybe," replied his father.

"Maybe? You went down there two years ago after you and Iverson bet Uncle Hank that there was no such thing as a donkey show!"

"Doesn't matter."

"Of course it matters!" The youngest Guerrero looked extremely exasperated. "Shouldn't we have told him about—"

"No."

Sol got even more exasperated.

"Then shouldn't we tell Uncle Al that Lupe—"

"No."

"It's your brother we're talking about!"

"So?"

"So what if somebody gets hurt?"

"What if somebody's already hurt?" Rusty replied.

"Dad," Sol tried again, "Loopy Lupe is my friend. He's a damn nut, but he's my friend. It's a tossup which one is crazier, him or Uncle Al, but I *definitely* know which one is more dangerous. And—"

The older Guerrero cut his son off by putting a meaty paw on his shoulder. "Boy, these things have a way of fucking working themselves out. And *this*," he spread his arms expansively, "is the Black-Fucking-Rock Desert. Who are we to say what a magical artifact is and what it isn't? And if you didn't want things to go this way, you shouldn't have started this shit back in town with Uncle Hank and his magical fucking Village People bracelets!"

Sol began to open his mouth.

"Shut up!" barked his father, cutting him off again. "It's done. Now go shovel some chicken shit into the compost pile."

▄▄▄

Lupe Maldonado saddled his horse. He'd just returned to the Gladwell Ranch from the Guerrero place moments before. Rushing into his small room in the bunkhouse, he'd looked about quickly for items he would need on his trip. He couldn't take his truck into the Granites. He couldn't get further in than the foothills with it. The only practical thing to do was to ride. He threw on his battered brown leather chaps and stuffed his iPod into a pants pocket after making sure it was fully charged.

"You might want to consider bringing some hooch," said tiny Sid Vicious. Tiny El Santo looked reproachfully at him from below Lupe's chin.

"Ah, for strictly medicinal reasons, of course," he added. El Santo punctuated his remark with a barely audible "harrumph!"

Lupe went to the stable.

His horse was named Sancho. He was an appaloosa: brown, white, and very obedient. He was also surefooted, which was an advantage where Lupe was taking him.

He was also a small horse: a mustang that the Gladwells had purchased the BLM corral at the edge of Spanish Springs. Generally, they bought a few each year and broke them using the old-fashioned ways... of which less is said, the better. They were effective, though. Sancho obeyed.

Lupe knew that last year there had been a stampede in which one wall of the corral collapsed. A cowboy had been killed as the mustang came running out into the desert, never to be recovered. The BLM had stopped selling mustang after that. Lupe knew where the renegade horses had gone, but he'd never told anyone. It wasn't anybody's business but theirs.

He wouldn't be able to take Sancho all the way into mountains, of course. There was no way anything besides a man, a goat, or a mountain lion could do that. He made sure that the saddle was securely strapped. Lupe always made sure of that. Un-strapping your buddy's saddle so that he hopped on and promptly flipped over was one of the oldest cowboy practical jokes in the book, north or south of the border. He climbed on, rode out of the Gladwells' barn, and headed toward the Granites at a trot.

The sun was rising behind him as he came around the edge of the low mountain known as the Banjo and into a valley containing an old Mormon homestead. The nameless vale separated the northern and southern portions of the Granites. In the past, inhabitants of the Black Rock Desert used it as a pass to travel back and forth to the Smoke Creek Desert. Vice versa for the people that lived there. Though in recent years the traffic dwindled as the age of settlers passed... and the new inhabitants of the areas found one another not to their liking.

Lupe was masked, shirtless, and dressed in chaps. He'd been revving himself up for the confrontation ahead by listening to Discharge's *Free Speech for the Dumb*. Not that he knew what the lyrics meant.

"Bloody good choice, though." commented Sid from his shoulder.

Lupe knew of a spot in the nameless valley where there was a small spring – barely a trickle, really – but enough for Sancho to be able to drink. The horse wouldn't be able to go any further. The juniper trees grew too thick and the earth rose too steeply, until eventually the trees trailed away entirely and the ground became almost too rocky even for a normal man to climb. He hobbled the small horse in a field next to the stream, then removed his saddle, blanket, and bit, hanging them from the branches of a nearby juniper. When he was done, he brushed the little horse down, speaking soothing words to him as he ran the bristles through his mane and coat.

There were dozens of different ways up into the Granites. He had no way of knowing which one she had taken. But, though there many ways in, there weren't actually that many places to go to. Most of the ways in led to the southern section of the Granites. These were the ones most commonly frequented by hunters, cowboys, and backpackers... as much as the Granites were commonly frequented by anyone. The northern section of the mountain range was infrequently traveled. *Very* infrequently traveled. Like the nearby Calicos, the remoteness of the northern Granites made them useful for certain people, though Lupe could be reasonably certain that Amy hadn't gone there. She was a desert rat, and thus had a fair idea of where *not* to go... though, technically speaking, all of the Granites were an excellent place not to go in his opinion.

The limiting factor in camping on the southern Granites was the lack of flat land upon which to pitch a tent, make a fire, or even to spread a sleeping bag out on. It was almost all steep hills and sheer cliffs with no level places – and of those places where one could set up camp, very few of them were near water. Amy's choices for camping were quite limited. He personally would have ascended at a point south and east of his current position. Amy was a skillful "off-roader," and there was a well-maintained dirt road there. It led through what had been the Barker place and straight up into the mountains. If Lupe left Sancho here and ascended through the steep and treacherous north-south passage nearby, he would emerge at one of the high points in the Granites, right below a peak that towered some 10,000 feet above sea level. From there he could actually look down into the Black Rock Desert and, with any luck, spot where her little red jeep was parked, somewhere on the mountain's eastern slope. Lupe's eyes were very good. The day was bright and clear, enabling him to see clearly for many miles.

It wasn't a great plan. But it wasn't a great situation, and Lupe felt it was the best shot he had at finding his ladylove. He ascended. It was slow going. The slope was incredibly steep and covered by juniper trees that grew thickly side-by-side. The only way to climb up it was to go hand over hand, pulling yourself up using branches while digging your toes into the loose, sandy soil. It was a treacherous, difficult process in which almost as much time was spent sliding backward as climbing forward. But Lupe was familiar with this country. He knew its awesome sterile beauty and its lurking dangers. Which was why, rather than heading straight through a pass that would have easily taken him out of the valley and into the steep, rolling mountains beneath the lower most of the Granite Peaks, he chose to make his way to the sheer granite cliff face to its west. Moving as stealthily as possible and cursing underneath his mask as his inevitable slips sent cascades of tiny pebbles down the hillside below him, he made his way toward the imposing edifice and began to slowly ascend it, hand over hand.

Life was simple for the pronghorn man. Most of the year, he guarded the Granite's northern pass. He was well suited for this task. He had enormous, sharp horns, a muscular torso, and a penis that would have made a porn star envious – though the pronghorn man naturally had no idea what a porn star was.

Guarding the pass was not a difficult job. Very few visitors came up it. The valley below wasn't accessible by machine, only by foot or horseback; and by horseback only in its lower reaches. The cowboys and sheepherders who used the valley in the spring never came up to the pass. Every so often, certain women from Hualapai or the surrounding area would come and visit him, which was fine. That was good for everyone concerned. Every once in a while a backpacker or someone working for the Bureau of Land Management would stumble across him, in which case he threw them over a cliff to their death below when he was done with them. This was also fine.

Once a year, the pronghorn man got to take a sort of vacation. He descended the mountain quickly as only his kind could do and entered the Burning Man Festival during the night. In the dark and – under the influence of any number of hallucinogens – the festival's participants couldn't really tell the difference between him and a man in a costume, which allowed him to frolic freely with the women who attended the event. Then, an hour or so before dawn, he slipped easily past the festival's security and ran back up the mountain to his pass. He got to repeat this each night for a week. No one seemed to notice or care. Even He didn't seem to care.

The pronghorn man spent most of his time sitting on a boulder looking thoughtful, one elbow propped up on his knee and the other clenched into a fist beneath his handsome, inhuman chin. He looked as though he were deep in thought, though in fact he really didn't do a lot of thinking. It was simply a comfortable position from which to scan the pass for intruders: though, to be fair, the creature was extremely patient, if not particularly intelligent. His inhuman senses could detect most interlopers a mile before they got to his position.

Which was why he couldn't have been more surprised when something small but very strong plummeted off of the cliff beside him, tackled him, and sent them both tumbling down the pass.

A few moments before, Lupe had concluded his ascent of the cliff face and laid flat on his stomach, peering down at the silent apparition seated below. Miniature Sid and Santo lay prone on either side of his masked head, peering over the cliff along with him.

"Kaw," commented Sid, "would you look at that thing! It looks like it otta be back where I came from."

"In London?" whispered Lupe, confused.

Sid smiled grimly.

"In Hell," Santo answered for him. Then he politely changed the subject. "In any case, I think you should use a Flying Plancha on that thing."

Lupe nodded in agreement.

"Naw," disagreed Sid in a stage whisper, "use an Inverted Surfboard Suicida!"

"You stick to playing the guitar. I'll give out the wrestling advice," replied Santo sharply. Then he turned his attention back to the Mexican cowboy. "Lupe, avoid those horns! Be very careful. However, as dangerous as those things are, they are also his weak point. This creature is not balanced like a human being. If you can knock him down, and keep him down, he will not get back up again."

Lupe nodded. Then he leaped – man and monster plunging down the slope together in a tangle of limbs and a whirlwind of curses. Trying desperately not to get impaled, Lupe held on for dear life to the creature's massive antlers. Taken completely by surprise, the pronghorn man attempted desperately to grab onto juniper tree after juniper tree as they tumbled past. But the branches ripped free from his meaty hands even as he grasped them. Finally, the two combatants' descent was halted when they slammed into the trunk of a large tree together.

The creature tried to get up, but its impressive antlers had become caught in the tree's lower branches. Lupe had no such problem. Struggling to his feet and regaining his wits, he flung himself into the air, executing an elbow drop on the muscular monster even as it began to free itself from its entanglements. It returned to the ground with a grunt, still struggling to free itself. Lupe leapt onto its back, wrapped a muscular arm around its neck, and began to strangle the creature using an elbow triangle hold.

The creature was incredibly strong. It freed its horns from their entrapment and, with a muffled growl that came from deep within its chest, ran backwards with Lupe still clinging to it, slamming its attacker against another tree. Lupe refused to let go. Again and again he slammed the masked man painfully against the tree, desperate to free himself from his grasp. Lupe would not let go. The creature fell to its knees, then onto its face. Finally, it lay still.

■

It took Lupe quite some time to climb back to where he had tackled the pronghorn man. He was bruised and sore from the ordeal, but he knew that he could not stop. His ladylove awaited him and, with her, his destiny. But it was still slow going. The "foothills" leading to the Granites southern peaks were more like mountains hidden beneath disguises of green, flowering meadow. They were steep and difficult to navigate, requiring an enormous expenditure of energy to ascend. He was covered in sweat by the time he reached the summit and was able to gaze down the eastern side of the range.

Both tiny Santo and Sid remained oddly silent during the ascent. Perhaps they'd been shocked by his violent encounter with the pronghorn man, thought Lupe, though that seemed unlikely. Hadn't both of their lives been dominated by violence of one sort or another?

He enjoyed the quiet while it lasted.

Peering down the eastern ridge, Lupe was able to spot Amy's jeep roughly a quarter of a mile below. Something was wrong. The vehicle was on its side, a crumpled wreck broken on the rocks fifteen feet below the dirt road that lead upward toward Granite Peak.

"Shit!" exclaimed Sid. Santo looked as though he was about to add something when Lupe flung himself over the side and began a rapid, blood-curdling slide down the side of the mountain.

■

Most men could not have made such a descent. However, the Mexican cowboy was not most men. He combined the conflicting acts of running, falling, and sliding on his ass with surprising grace. He hit the flat surface of the road solidly with both feet and kept going. His legs pumping in a brisk run, he leaped over the side of the road and slid another 15 feet, coming to a halt amidst a cloud of dust next to the crumpled vehicle.

Lupe sat in a dazed huddle, panting with his masked face between his knees. Santo and Sid leaped from his shoulders and ran to the vehicle, their tiny forms vanishing around the side of the wreck. The little vaquero kept staring downward, his face pressed between the tattered remains of his chaps. He realized suddenly that he was very frightened. That he didn't want to see what lay inside of Amy's jeep.

His two companions emerged a moment later, moving as quickly as their tiny legs could carry them.

"She ain't there," panted Sid, his pale hands clasping his leather-clad legs. "There's some blood, but not a whole lot."

"There *are* some very odd footprints," added Santo, looking considerably less winded, "Some small. Some larger. None human. They lead up toward Granite Peak itself. They must have taken the girl with them."

Relieved, Lupe motioned for the tiny men to climb back onto his shoulders. When they were safely aboard, he began following the strange tracks straight up to the summit.

■

Lupe realized that if he'd thought his first two ascents arduous, then he had been mistaken. His climb redefined the entire concept of "arduous." In some places, he was forced to climb hand over hand up sheer rock faces, risking death or crippling injury should he fall. The rest of the ascent was merely a next-to-impossible exaggeration of what had come before: a slippery, dusty scramble up 70-degree hillsides. These were even more exhausting than the sheer ascents, though without them he would never have been able to follow the creatures' trail. They'd left deep footprints in the loose soil wherever their inhuman feet had fallen.

Finally, after what seemed like an eternity of struggling up vertical and near-vertical surfaces, Lupe climbed over the side of an outcropping of rock and fell onto his face before the yawning mouth of a cavern. He lay there for a moment, feeling the late afternoon sun beat down upon his back as he gulped lungful after lungful of dusty air. While he recovered, his companions once again leaped from his shoulders and went to investigate.

Lupe rolled onto his back and stared up at the sky. He was exhausted. His thirst was intense, causing his vision to blur around the edges and dull his wits. Yet he knew that he had to stay focused if he was to save Amy from whatever fate had befallen her. He had to continue.

His helpful little hallucinations returned.

"About ten feet within this cavern there is a barrier constructed of sandbags," Santo informed him. "It has what appear to be several different doors in its surface. One is man sized. The other two are much smaller. I do not think they are locked."

Lupe drew himself to his feet. His legs quivered slightly and his sight swam distressingly, but he pulled himself together with a single, resigned breath. The air was hot beneath his mask. He could smell his own sweat and the dust that was mixed with it. He turned his iPod back on. The Dead Kennedys: *Holiday in Cambodia*.

Right. Good. Ready.

He leaned down, extending his arms like two brown ramps of muscle so that Sid and Santo could run to their positions on his shoulders. Then he strode forward, the fringe of his dusty chaps swooshing rhythmically against his thighs, and kicked the largest of the three doors into splinters with a single booted foot.

Lupe knew that no matter what lay beyond the threshold of that door he would be best served by surprise. So he charged down the dark corridor at top speed, the mysterious screaming of Jell-O Biafra blaring in his ears as he emerged into a dimly lit cavern roughly 2,000 square feet in size.

What it held came straight out of a nightmare.

No, Lupe corrected himself, it came straight out of an old Mexican wrestling film. *Santo in the Wax Museum* or *Against All Monsters,* maybe. Computers and scientific equipment of various sorts, incongruously drawn from different decades of development, dominated the walls of the room. Flat screens hung next to old reel-to-reel Univacs that were cheerfully spewing out 1970s-era punch cards. Jacobs' ladders shot arcs of electricity into the air that ended in showers of sparks. There were racks of chemistry equipment and industrial shelving containing bins of vacuum tubes, computer cards, and old plastic milk jugs containing powders of various sorts.

Yet it wasn't the inanimate contents of the room that drew Lupe's eyes. Alcoves and side rooms that were barely visible amid the clutter held row after row of cages, tanks, and pens. Their inhabitants sprang to life as he barreled into the room, greeting his arrival with squawks, screams, and howls of surprise that were audible even through his headphones. Some of the inhuman inmates threw themselves violently against the walls of their prisons. Others skulked indolently in the shadows of their pens just out of sight. Some were recognizable as creatures of the desert.

Others weren't recognizable at all.

At the far end of the room, an enormous bear of a man turned away from a chalkboard in surprise. It was covered with multicolored notes and diagrams that Lupe did not understand, though they had obviously been drawn with considerable skill. The man had a bushy brown beard streaked with white. He was dressed in what obviously had been a lab coat, though the garment was tattered, patched, and stained almost beyond recognition. On either side of the man stood two... well, it was hard to say what they were. *Some kind of badger, perhaps*, thought Lupe. They wore tool belts and seemed equally as surprised as their master.

In an alcove past the three figures lay a rolling hospital bed. On it lay Shutup Amy. She was unconscious. Bandages covered much of her body. One of her arms was in a cast. Some sort of fluid dripped into her body from a large, complex-looking machine. These images came at Lupe Maldonado as if they were slow motion shards of broken glass flung at his consciousness by a shattering windscreen at the moment of impact. They were unreal, like something on a movie screen.

It was bad. Then he looked down. That made it worse.

He stood in a sea of tiny figures. Humanoid, they nonetheless resembled large field mice and were engaged in a myriad number of tasks. Some worked together, carrying dishes of food between them. Others lugged spools of wire, bottles of chemicals, or computer parts like miniature longshoremen. Yet others were armed with tiny spears or miniature crossbows. Lupe felt pinned down by countless eyes and held in place in a single, seemingly endless moment of silence that began the second *Holiday in Cambodia* ended.

The huge man yelled something at him in English as he began to lumber forward, a single meaty hand outstretched before his body. Lupe stood frozen with indecision, the weight of all those tiny little mouse eyes pressing downward on him, holding him in an infinite sliver of time.

"He's bloody Charles Laughton from *Island of Lost Souls!*" screamed Sid, breaking the silence. "He's going to turn her into an animal or something!"

"I would say he is more like Claudio Brook from *Me in the Wax Museum*," replied the tiny superhero from the other shoulder, "but the result is the same. Save the girl, Lupe! We will hold them as long as we can." With that, both icons flung themselves from his shoulders, plummeting down into the crowd of startled mice-men below.

The Cro Mags' *Show You No Mercy* cycled onto his iPod, blaring a war cry of raw hate into his ears. All hell broke loose.

Lupe dashed into the alcove where Amy lay still and silent on stained sheets, scattering dozens of tiny figures as he went. He pulled the needles and wires that attached her to the strange machine free with a single violent jerk, then gathered her limp form up in his arms. Sprinting back to the cavern, he paused for a moment to take in the bizarre spectacle spread before him. Miniature El Santo and Sid Vicious battled dozens of mouse-men, their fists and feet flailing in a desperate attempt to clear an escape path for him. The bearded man stared, slack-jawed with fascination at the spectacle spread before him. It was like a convulsing playroom of toy soldiers being tossed about by excited children. His two belted companions waved their arms desperately at Lupe, as if they were trying to get his attention. Their inhuman mouths opened and closed, as though they were trying to tell him something.

Unfortunately, Lupe didn't speak raccoon English.

The music stopped. Still clutching Amy in his arms, Lupe shook his ear buds loose.

"Run!" screamed Santo, "Run!"

Lupe ran, bounding through the swirling tide of tiny struggling figures and back up the tunnel. He burst into the daylight just as the setting western sun descended behind the mountains, covering them in a rapidly advancing blanket of shadow. For the first time in months, he felt cold.

He would not be able to descend the cliff face with her in his arms.

"Amy!" he cried, "Wake up! We must flee!"

He shook her desperately, but she remained lifeless; a limp rag of bandaged flesh in his arms. Her head lolled lifelessly to one side, eyes closed. He could not tell if she was breathing.

He thought not.

There was a commotion behind him out of sight down the tunnel: dozens of tiny clangs as cage doors were thrown open. Roars and inhuman screams drifted up out of the darkness to where he stood on the tiny rock outcropping. They were followed closely by the pitter-patter of countless numbers of tiny running feet.

Everything horrible in the world was coming toward them at once.

The Mexican cowboy ran one hand through the tangled mass of his ladylove's hair. Then he kissed her forehead gently, once. It tasked like home.

"Come, my wife," he whispered, "We will make our escape from this place."

He walked toward the cliff.

Ironic Antipathy: The Relationship Between Gerlach Locals and the BLM

[Published on the Friends of Black Rock/ High Rock website at www.blackrockdesert.org on 04/01/2010]

To the right person with the right set of ascetic tastes, the Black Rock Desert is one of the most beautiful places on earth. The towering mountains, the vast, dusty flatlands, and the scattered green oasis of life: there's no place like it. Living here is like living on another planet. Each morning I can walk out of my front door and look out across the Hualapai Valley at the mighty Granites to the west, the desolate, imposing Calicos to the north, and the Playa itself to the east. A vast, unconquered landscape which is... almost completely owned by the Bureau of Land Management, headquartered on the other side of the continent in Washington D.C.

Bastards.

That's not a rational reaction, of course. I'd probably say the same thing if the same land was owned by a holding company based in Los Angeles or a ranching outfit from Arizona. I'm always looking for a reason to bitch. Reactions generally aren't rational. It's not rational for city people to distrust police officers tasked with protecting them from... well, other city people. Many of them do. It's the basic American disposition to distrust authority. In fact, it could be argued that the only reasonable attitude to have toward authority is a mixture of cynicism and curiosity. Any other reaction smacks of naiveté, and even a lack of civic responsibility.

Those of us who live out here approach the doings (or, more often, alleged doings) of the BLM with a mixture of dread and morbid fascination. What areas are being closed off to quads this year? Where are they letting that coal power plant be built? Which cabins did they tear down, again? Often the things we imagine the Bureau of Land Management is planning to do are more frightening than anything it actually ends up doing, but the psychological effects are the same: fear, dread, and a certain sense of melancholy. When you consider that it owns 87 percent of our state, a bit of paranoia doesn't seem unwarranted.

Few of us locals view the National Conservation Area – the act of Congress which the BLM and its subsidiary organization the Friends of the Black Rock are sworn to help implement – as anything other than meddlesome and baffling. To be perfectly honest, we're not big picture thinkers. We just want to be left alone to live our little lives. Why do people in Los Angeles, Reno, and San Francisco care where we drive our quads or hunt deer? Why do they care where and how we camp, or what hot springs we use? It's not like they come out here except for Burning Man, anyhow. It's no different from a San Franciscan wondering why people in Texas might object to the city legalizing gay marriage. What business is it of theirs, anyhow?

Life is seldom simple, and people are eternally meddlesome. This, in a democracy, means that the government is eternally meddlesome. Hence the BLM and the NCA. It wasn't always this way. The two component organizations from which the BLM was formed – the Grazing Service and General Land Office – were probably the best friends rural westerners ever had. Even after the creation of the BLM 1946, its duties mostly consisted of managing grazing, water, and mining easements for people like us. In 1976 (re: Carter Administration) Congress decided that these lands would remain in "public ownership" *in perpetuum* to "meet the present and future needs of the American people." The Bureau was given the mandate of eternally managing these lands and any resources they contained.

In other words, the BLM administers the greatest non-military land grab in human history.

I don't mean to make the Bureau of Land Management out to be some kind of ogre. It does many fine things that we Gerlach types appreciate. It puts out fires and controls the mustang population. (Not that the locals didn't do a better job of that before it took over, but that's a whole other topic for another time.) It reintroduced big horn sheep into Nevada and works to protect other legitimately endangered desert species. Overall, it's mostly a neutral, understaffed organization charged with managing millions of acres of barren land according to the shifting policies of whatever barely-interested administration is in power on the other side of a continent. As part of its mandate the BLM has to listen to all sorts of cranks from all sides of the spectrum complain about every action it takes... or doesn't take. At least from the outside, it seems like a thankless job.

This brings us back to Gerlach, where we aren't particularly thankful. We're a cantankerous, individualistic, reclusive bunch, happy to ignore the rest of the world and be ignored by it in return. For better or worse, the NCA has put an end to that. It's a little like being a tenant farmer whose absentee landlord hasn't come around for a century. When he finally shows up and starts making rules, it's only natural to respond with ambivalence, whether his rules are fair or not. It just doesn't feel right.

Of course, the irony of this ambivalence is that the BLM and we locals need one another. Without us rustics, there would be no one to clean hotel rooms, pump gas, serve beer, fix cars, repair roads, and perform the many other minor tasks that make 99% of tourists feel comfortable enough to come to a National Conservation Area. Without those crucial tourists, the billions of dollars allocated to the BLM each year would end up as a "bridge to nowhere" piece on the O'Reilly Factor. Without the BLM, the Black Rock Desert would probably be a massive strip mine punctuated with coal power plants.

Well, that and high paying union jobs with benefits. But that too is a topic for another time.

Crucified Coyote

"What sane person could live in this world and not be crazy?"
—Ursula K. Le Guin

The whole world is made of dust. The ground is just dust and worm shit held down by gravity. The sky is filled with dust, invisible unless illuminated by whimsical sunlight. The sea is dust suspended, moving in currents of slow motion. It is in our skin. It is our skin. We are dust, animated by the hand of God for a time, and then cast back into the brown firmament from which we arose when time is done with us.

Dust is holy substance: the undivided atom at the core of all mysteries. It is very real: the baseline of substance. The core element. This is why the Black Rock Desert is so very real and so very holy. It is nothing but dust revealed: on the earth, in the air, and more often than not, covering the sky. It is a place of extremes. Of prophesy. Of death.

None of which the woman known as Shutup Amy gave a fuck about as she drove her battered Suzuki Samurai hell bent for leather across its khaki heart. She had other concerns, other questions. Big ones. Tough ones. Her emotions were like an overwound watch waiting to burst out of her chest in a spray of gears and tiny bits of shrapnel at any moment. They were always like that – had always *been* like that. Tight. Contained. But it had been worse lately. And she had to get away.

He'd proposed. She'd fled.

Maybe being alone would help her. Maybe sleeping beneath the juniper trees would help. Maybe nothing would help. Maybe a mountain lion would eat her. Maybe she would fall over the invisible edge of the world.

Most terrifyingly, maybe afterward nothing would be different at all.

The jeep bucked suddenly, sending the tiny blob of mercury in the Tilt-O-Meter screwed into the dashboard swinging in an arc from "one" to "three" in either direction. Three was bad. Six was worse: horizontal. Crash. Broken bones. Fatality. Amy didn't care. She never paid attention to the Tilt-O-Meter. She took pride in it, actually.

Bravado. Machisma. Death wish.

The transition from Playa to rutted and battered jeep trails was jarring. One moment her vehicle was gliding along as if it were on pavement. The next it was bouncing up and down as if it had four flat tires, its tired, two-decade-old suspension actually helping the ruts and rocks toss her around. Not that she slowed down. She almost never slowed down. Instead, Amy pounded down a series of unidentified almost-roads that zigzagged toward the Granite Mountains, goggles dug into her forehead, her hand shifting crazily, and an unlit cigarette clenched between her teeth, the filter nearly bit in two.

It was at that crossing from glass to gravity where she saw the crucified coyote.

Nothing says "old-school Nevada rancher" like a dead coyote crucified on a barbed wire fence. It sounds cruel to outsiders. It *is* cruel. But it is also no one's fault. Its martyrdom is the inevitable result of a collision of opposite natures. The coyote behaves according to its nature. It knows no laws, only opportunities. It will eat anything it can grab: cats, dogs, chickens, and even small children, given the chance. In the spring it attacks newly born calves. Sometimes it works alone. At other times it works in groups of three or four.

It is very smart, even tactical in how it behaves. For example, six coyote approach a ranch. There are the usual dangers. Dogs. Guns. Traps. Three approach from one side, making as much noise as possible, drawing danger toward them. Meanwhile three come in silently from the other side, like Indians in an old John Wayne movie. They grab what they can get.

The next night everyone switches places. Coyote. Rancher. Everyone.

Or two coyote wait behind a ridge near a ranch. The third – a big male or a bitch in heat – comes into the ranch, looking for its fertile opposite. It looks like a dog, smells like a dog, behaves like a dog. It flirts. It licks backs. It sniffs butts. However, it is not a dog.

It lures its prey out into the brush with promises of pleasure. Then the coyote kill it and eat it. Because they are not dogs and this is there nature.

A Nevada rancher is much like the coyote. He also behaves according to his nature. For much of his life he knows no laws but his own. He knows even fewer opportunities. He is lord of dogs and sheep and cows and dirt and dung. Sometimes he works alone. He *likes* working alone. At other times he works with small, taciturn men from Mexico and Peru. He is very tough, and very careful.

He is very smart, even tactical in how he behaves. He guards his water rights with the fervor of a mountain lion protecting her cubs. His water is his life. In a very real way, it *is* life. For without water there can be no cattle, no sheep. Therefore, he donates to local politicians. He attends long and boring Bureau of Land Management Sub Rack meetings 100 miles away. He makes friends in the county building department so that he will know when other ranchers are filing water rights. He watches his neighbors and the BLM closely, very closely.

He is serious about this. He is serious about what is his. He will kill over it.

There can be little quarter between the coyote in the rancher. Each exists to bring death what the other holds dear. One day the coyote will win: the desert will be devoid of men, sheep, and cattle, but he will remain, living off rabbits, mice, and kit fox cubs. Until then the rancher will win, and to win he must set examples. Other coyote must see clearly what happens when the invisible line between nature and civilization is crossed. More importantly than seeing it, he must *smell* it. The rotten warning. The head on a stake. The decaying bandit hung from a tree branch. *Infelix lignum.*

Most ranchers are content to crucify a single coyote somewhere. Others get all "I Love You Spartacus" and make their own Appian Way somewhere out in the light, stone, and sagebrush. Others are whimsical in a Tertullian kind of way. They crucify coyote upside down, like Saint Peter. The results are always the same. The lesson teaches what it needs to teach: coyote stays away. For a time.

Amy stopped her jeep. She got out and stood there, all nipple rings, sunburn, dirt, and frustration, staring at the dog messiah. It didn't mean anything, really. There were probably a dozen coyotes dead and creatively mutilated in the Black Rock at any given time. She peered at the thing. Flies buzzed around the empty sockets of its eyes. The rotting remnants of a tongue hung loosely between its leering, monster teeth. It reeked of death. It *was* death, manifest into our world through the apotheosis of an angry rancher with a rifle.

Was she like it? Like the corpse-god-dog-thing? Joseph Fucking H Campbell Shutup Amy was not. What she knew about mythological symbols you could fit into a dime bag and still have room for your cheap, Mexican dope. Yet she felt an odd kinship with it. The crucified coyote was like Shutup Amy herself: a poorly understood conundrum. A broken patchwork of opposites left to its fate in an unlikely land. Dead/Alive. Victim/Victimizer. Man/Animal. Free/Prisoner. She supposed the list was endless. She also imagined that she should get back to the task at hand.

But she couldn't. Or at least she couldn't just yet.

Was it was a warning? It was obviously not intended as a warning for her. Or was it? Was God warning her? Did God warn people anymore? She didn't know. She had a hard time imagining that He could care about her, though. Had He warned her before at some point in her miserable, confused, meth-addled wreck of a life? No. Maybe. If so, why didn't she listen? Was it not loud enough? Or had she simply ignored the subtle whisperings of divine advice?

He'd proposed. She'd fled.

After a time her shoulders slumped, and she returned resignedly to her jeep. It was too big for her. There were no easy answers here. Maybe there were no easy answers anywhere.

■

The Granites. They were one of those places that everyone could see (you could hardly miss them), but few knew how to get up into. Maps did you little good, and GPS was worse than useless. The Granites weren't so much a series of mountains as a thousand contrary hills leaning uncomfortably together: a vertical maze of brown, green, and steepness threaded by almost forgotten roads. There was more than a little risk in visiting it alone. There was more than a little risk visiting anything in the Black Rock alone.

So much the better, thought Amy, tightening her grip on the steering wheel. Her jeep was a testament to how much punishment an inexpensive Japanese car could take and still function. Its taillights were patchworks of transparent red tape. Its paint, which had been a cherry red at some point in the 80s, had faded down to a sort of dull gray flecked with rust. It had no uncracked windows. The bulb at the end of its stick shift had been replaced with the wooden top of a corkscrew. It had no second gear. It was a bucket.

The drive gave Shutup Amy – once, though less accurately, known as Shasta Amy O'Hanlan – a rare moment to reflect. Perhaps more accurately, it forced her to reflect. She wasn't a naturally introspective person. If she had been, the brutal tragedy that was her life might have played out differently. Be she wasn't, and it hadn't.

She knew that introspection was the enemy. It assaulted her with a kaleidoscope of "self" in the past tense. All her "was" kept bubbling up to the surfaced of her "is" in a mélange of memory. A dirty little girl with a black eye sitting in the dust near a singlewide in Bakersfield. A terrified teenager sitting in an LA abortion clinic where everyone else spoke Spanish. Arguing her way into a club in San Francisco's SOMA district. Working as a bike messenger deep in the cement canyons of the city, alternately dodging and screaming at cars. Cooking meth in a warehouse in San Leandro. *Doing* meth until the normally hard lines between real and unreal, possible and impossible, and good and bad became blurry and hard to recognize. The arrest. Bending over a metal laundry table for a fat, sweating guard in Chowchilla. Waiting tables at a rundown restaurant in the no-man's-land between Berkeley and Oakland, the days turning into months as she waited for... for what?

For her messiah. For her religion. For Oberon.

Harlan "Oberon" O'Brien was a frequent customer at the café Amy worked at. One of his several homes was located within walking distance of the establishment and, when he wasn't speaking at the Commonwealth Club, giving seminars on the Gift Economy online, or performing some other such Oberonish function, the founder of Burning Man liked to hang with the

California hoi polloi. A first she'd ignored him: an old, bearded white man in a dashiki wearing a fanny pack. In other words, another Berkeley freak. Then she began to notice things. Laughing young hipster girls coming in with him in the morning. Middle aged hippies asking for his autograph. The $120-a-pair Birkenstock mocha suede sandals on his manicured feet.

The old man was someone. Some kind of Timothy Leary or something. She was no one – less than no one. A damaged negative zero. If she could get close... Shasta Amy O'Hanlan didn't remember what her reasoning was, exactly. Some security? A chance to be close to meaning in the hope that some would rub off? A way to remove the negative before the zero? She started talking to the old man. He talked about Burning Man. He talked about community. He talked about fire. He talked about death.

Before too long Amy was the laughing hipster girl coming in with him in the morning. Only not so young.

Old broads don't get to hang onto the arms of Christ for very long. Virgin mothers? Naturally. Hot, reformed ex-prostitutes? Absolutely. But not the used bitches. Amy's time spent blowing the Mohammed of the Black Rock Desert was necessarily brief. She knew from the beginning it would be. But for all of his decadence and delusion, Oberon wasn't actually a *false* messiah. He performed his miracles. For example, he administered the rite of rebirth. A new name. A purpose. A place. A holy land. The cleansing act of burning. A movement and a rest.

Then there was the festival itself: an annual overload of everything. Lights. Art. Dust. Drugs. Booze. Tits. Explosions. Cars. Music. Dancing. Costumes. Fire. Fire. Fire.

And so she found herself a resident of that burning land: a holy inhabitant of Mecca rather than a pilgrim, charged with handing out seven stones to toss at the Devil. Well, in charge of stones in any case: she'd ended up as Burning Man's Nevada property manager. Which mostly meant host sand, rocks, sagebrush, and special use permits.

And Lupe Maldonado.

In the end, it all boiled down to a question of identity: *her* identity. Shasta O'Hanlan hadn't had one. Less than one, if it was possible to have your sense of identity scoured out by life while still remaining above ground. Shutup Amy did. It wasn't much of an identity: an aging loudmouth tweaker tasked with monitoring empty fields of sagebrush and crumbling buildings on a dying main street. A late, satisfying adolescence defined by minimal pay and maximum debauchery, all performed in front of a Greek chorus of dust, fire, and desolation.

It wasn't much to ask out of life. It wasn't even much of a life. But Lupe was threatening even that, with his offer of yet another identity. Lupe Fucking Maldonado. Loopy Lupe: her Mexican cowboyfriend. Short. Dark. Handsome. Strong. Insanely virile. Beautifully non-English speaking. For that matter none-too-talky even in Spanish. Liked to listen to Punk, even though he couldn't understand the words. Oddly gentle. Generous. A tough, little exclamation point of a man, noteworthy even in a place known for its noteworthy characters.

He'd proposed. She'd fled.

He only wanted the things that any good man wanted. In her heart she knew that. A wife. Children. His own ranch. His own life, really. It wasn't unreasonable. But could she even do those things? Be a mother? It was biologically possible, though she doubted her ability to actually mother with a capital M. Wife? That implied loyalty and monogamy – or at least not sleeping with other men – and she wasn't particularly good at those, either. Or at keeping a house that didn't look like a pit. Or at cooking. Or...

Was it another chance at redemption? (How many chances did one get, anyhow?) Or was it a temptation to regress, to lose what she had become and revert to less than zero once again? An opportunity to become a normal person (whatever and whomever that might be), or an opportunity to lose the tiny, painful handholds that she'd clawed out for herself over a lifetime?

She shivered in the 90-degree heat. She almost went off the road.

■

Amy knew that scaling a mountain to confront your problems was a quintessentially male thing to do: the hero-with-a-thousand-faces lone quest for meaning and all that masculine crap. If she's been a normal woman — hell, if she'd been anything even *resembling* a normal woman — she'd be talking it over with her friends while drinking herbal tea, or tearfully calling her mother for hours at a time. Maybe even driving a convertible off a cliff with Susan Sarandon.

I should be more reasonable, she thought as she brought the Samurai too quickly around a sharp turn, ignoring the Tilt-O-Meter. A shower of small pebbles cascaded down the mountain nearby. But she was not reasonable. Could not be reasonable. Years of tweaking had left the line between real and unreal permanently blurred. Amy knew this intellectually, but that knowledge did her little good. Gack had permanently modified her. Even though she didn't do it anymore, it didn't matter. She was already perma-fried. Now all Amy could do was hold on for the ride.

She didn't like being assaulted by visions of her past selves, either. They were unwelcome strangers intruding into the protective layer of fire and bullshit she'd spent years building around her soul. Those women were not *her*. They were ghosts, banshees exiled to the basement of her Celtic memory. She did not want to confront them. She did not want to absorb her shadow self. She did not want to come to terms. She was not a fucking Ursula Le Guinn character. She did not want to heal and forgive and be a natural woman and be made whole. She was fractured; but she held onto her crazed, splintered self because it was that all she had. All she could do was hold on.

Maybe I'll fight a lion at the top of the mountain, she thought, *like in a movie.* What other standard did she have, really? Nothing really dramatic happens in books. The mountain was steep at this point, the road almost non-existent. Amy deliberately didn't look behind her, didn't look back at the brown depths falling away, leading downward, downward to the valley below. She would go out to gather wood or some shit and it would attack her. Wounded, she'd make a spear and fight it in some climactic battle near a cave. Maybe an old Paiute medicine man lived in a cabin in some hidden valley nearby. She'd sprain her ankle hiking and he would rescue her. Unable to drive back down with her injury, she would spend weeks taking peyote and learning the secrets of the wilderness. Maybe she'd be stalked by an axe-wielding, serial killing maniac straight out of a Tobe Hooper film. He'd chase her around the mountains in a series of tense cutaway scenes, until finally Lupe showed up. Then they'd kill the maniac by tricking him into running off a cliff, or...

Back to Lupe. Tears weld up in her eyes. He'd proposed. She'd fled. More tears. She'd behaved according to her nature, just like a crucified coyote.

She didn't pay attention to the Tilt-O-Meter.

She didn't pay attention to the Tilt-O-Meter.

She didn't pay attention to the Tilt-O-Meter.

She didn't pay attention to the Tilt-O-Meter.

She didn't pay attention to the Tilt-O-Meter.

She didn't pay attention to the Tilt-O-Meter.

Geppetto's Bench

[Posted to www.midianranchblog.blogspot.com on May 15, 2010]

A strange thing happened two or three months ago: I stopped being the father of a Poor Retarded Daughter, and simply became a father. It was a complete transition, like the sudden, shocking passage from desert storm to sunlight one often encounters out here. I'm not completely certain when the transition happened, either – though I can speculate about why. I also won't pretend that I fully understand my own emotions. My own heart can be as obscure to me as, surely, yours can be to you; filled one minute with raging waters, another will calm, beautiful sunrises. But I will wade through the foggy murk of my feelings in that hopes that, should anyone reading this find himself or herself in the same situation as me, it might serve as a humble beacon, leading you from ocean to shore.

One reason for this transition was almost certainly Cassidy herself. It simply became impossible to feel sorry on a deep, emotional level for such a friendly, good-natured, loving, and quixotic child. Of course, people upon occasion say extremely strange things to me. Recently, while I was at the wake of a well-liked Gerlach resident, a very nice lady came up to me and asked if my daughter was Cassidy. When I responded that she was, the lady said to me "I had six children, the last when I was 40. She turned out fine – there was nothing wrong with her. If I knew then when I know now, I would have been too scared to have her." When I replied that Cassidy makes an extremely good Cassidy and that we loved her very much, the lady became embarrassed and excused herself.

She needn't have. I wasn't upset with her. It's no crime to not be able to express yourself well under unfamiliar circumstances – and she really is a very nice lady. What I told her was no platitude. Cassidy does make a very good Cassidy, and we do love her very much. That is part of the unseen transition that happened when I wasn't looking. Not the love (I've always loved her) but the emotional understanding that having Down syndrome doesn't somehow make her invalid as an individual, any more than being blind or deaf makes one less of a person. Though I intellectually understood that early on, the knowledge simply hadn't made its way to my heart until a few months ago.

The second reason was my beloved (and, at least to me, enigmatic) wife Tina, who has never worried about what Cassidy *wasn't*, instead always concerning herself with what our daughter *was*. Tina's one and only cryptic comment on the matter: this kid's alright, and this kid's going to be all right. So, while I busied myself reading Down syndrome-specific books like Groneberg's *Road Map To Holland* and Pueschel's *A Parent's Guide to Down Syndrome: Toward A Brighter Future* (both excellent books), Tina was reading general baby books like Murkoff's *What To Expect: The First Year*. While I spent my time looking at the Down syndrome child development chart, Tina was looking at the standard child development chart. A funny thing happened. It became apparent that, like nearly every other child, Cassidy was ahead on some things, behind on other things, and pretty much the same on most things.

Like nearly every other child. Don't get me wrong: I'm not deluding myself. Cassidy's emotional and intellectual development may – no, most likely will – in many ways freeze when she is four, eight, or twelve. They also might not. She may have serious health problems beyond her current heart issues. She might not. For months, these facts ate away at my soul; the soul of an idealist, a worrier, a *preparer* obsessed with his family's complete independence from a society he had personally declared irredeemably corrupt... and that he now desperately needed for his daughter's sake. Having a child with Down syndrome seemed like an unbearably cruel joke played upon me personally by God, one of those awful "teachable moments" college professors and politicians are always banging on about. Everything was lost. Everything I had worked toward, pointless. My dreams, empty. I was filled with dread at having a child that could never live up to my ideals, and terrible guilt at even conceptualizing such a cruel thought. My idols shattered, I became as I told my friend Elizabeth Jackson, "ideologically up for grabs." It was for me an extreme admission of hopelessness.

Then, like a quiet voice in the darkness, the transition. *Reasons* why God had done this that were not at all cruel, but loving (Though not easy. No, never that. It isn't the desert way.) Was I not raised alongside of a disabled brother? Who better to raise a child with Down syndrome but a father obsessed with personal independence? What better way to the test a man who had always claimed to be a champion of the individual, than by giving him a child whose individuality is predetermined? (As are all men's, but you surely know what I mean.) What better place for such a child to grow than a small, odd community more accustomed to eccentricity than normalcy?

These things made sense to me. By suddenly clicking together, I found myself more at peace.

Finally, two or three months ago, I got over the tragic death of a daughter that never was, but whose non-existence I felt as bitterly as anything I had ever felt in my life. Let us call her Elisa, after my real daughter's middle name. I had big plans for Elisa. I spent endless hours at the intellectual equivalent of Geppetto's bench, carving out my imaginary Pinocchio daughter. She would naturally be highly intelligent (as I flatter myself into thinking I am), extremely naturally healthy (as I have fortunately always been), and extremely energetic (as I am annoyingly so). Elisa was going to continue my intellectual legacy after I died, creating works that celebrated rural self-sufficiently and decried urban duplicity. She was going to get the college degree I never got, and then become the young traveling adventurer that I, perpetually at my small-business workbench, never was. She would continue the epic struggle to build a multigenerational Jerusalem from sand and rock that is Midian Ranch. Only she'd do it better than I ever could have, because she would be better. She would also have all of the children that I, an autumn father, was too foolish to have when I was younger and stronger.

Elisa... no, *Cassidy* was going to be a cross between Lara Croft, Ayn Rand, and Wonder Woman. I was certain of it; as I'm sure all men who father a beloved child are certain of such things when they hold that child in their arms for the first time. These dreams were all dashed to pieces 30 minutes later with two words: Down syndrome. So was I.

In my defense, I didn't get even an hour to enjoy being A Father before I became A Father Of A Poor Retarded Child. It was terribly... abrupt. Subsequently discovering that my daydreams were those of a self-centered idiot didn't help, either. There are only so many unpleasant revelations that a sane, solid, and rational man can have about his own character, life, and worldview in a very brief period of time and remain stable. And I've never claimed to be entirely sane, solid, or rational. For a time, the traumatic "death" of Elisa hovered in the background of my love for Cassidy, though I did not consciously know it. It took some time for me to sort the whole thing out. To quote Wordsworth:

Was the worst pang that sorrow ever bore,
Save one, one only, when I stood forlorn,
Knowing my heart's best treasure was no more

Only, unlike poor William, I was quietly mourning the death of a daughter that never was outside of my own mind, rather than a real one (a horror I recoil from conceptualizing). In mourning phantasm Elisa, I was doing Cassidy the worst disservice possible. I was discounting the possibility that she *actually was* Elisa: in her own unique way, better than me. Purer, and less intellectually weighed down with philosophical and ideological baggage. Lighter, freer, and perhaps even continuing a legacy that I haven't even fully grasped yet.

That was the final part of the transition: grief for what-wasn't passing away, to be replaced by love and quiet optimism. I'm sure that this a normal experience for thoughtful parents of children with Down syndrome. (And I pray that we all are just that about our children: thoughtful). In fact, award-winning *Sesame Street* writer Emily Perl Kingsley said it much better than I ever could:

I am often asked to describe the experience of raising a child with a disability – to try to help people who have not shared that unique experience to understand it, to imagine how it would feel. It's like this...

When you're going to have a baby, it's like planning a fabulous vacation trip – to Italy. You buy a bunch of guidebooks and make your wonderful plans. The Coliseum. The Michelangelo David. The gondolas in Venice. You may learn some handy phrases in Italian. It's all very exciting.

After months of eager anticipation, the day finally arrives. You pack your bags and off you go. Several hours later, the plane lands. The stewardess comes in and says ,"Welcome to Holland."

"Holland?!?" *you say. "What do you mean Holland?? I signed up*

for Italy! I'm supposed to be in Italy. All my life I've dreamed of going to Italy."

But there's been a change in the flight plan. They've landed in Holland and there you must stay.

The important thing is that they haven't taken you to a horrible, disgusting, filthy place, full of pestilence, famine and disease. It's just a different place.

So you must go out and buy new guide books. And you must learn a whole new language. And you will meet a whole new group of people you would never have met.

It's just a different place. It's slower-paced than Italy, less flashy than Italy. But after you've been there for a while and you catch your breath, you look around... and you begin to notice that Holland has windmills... and Holland has tulips. Holland even has Rembrandts.

But everyone you know is busy coming and going from Italy... and they're all bragging about what a wonderful time they had there. And for the rest of your life, you will say "Yes, that's where I was supposed to go. That's what I had planned."

And the pain of that will never, ever, ever, ever go away... because the loss of that dream is a very, very significant loss.

But... if you spend your life mourning the fact that you didn't get to Italy, you may never be free to enjoy the very special, the very lovely things... about Holland.

Guerrero's War

"I have a problem," Kenner said, "with other people deciding what is in my best interest when they don't live where I do, when they don't know the local conditions or the local problems that I face, when they don't even live in the same country I do. But they still feel, in some far off western city at a desk in some glass skyscraper in Brussels or Berlin or New York, they still feel that they know the solutions to all my problems and how I should live my life. I have a problem with that."

"What's your problem?" Bradley said. "I mean look: you don't seriously believe that everybody on the planet should do whatever they want, do you? That would be terrible."

— Michael Crichton, *State of Fear*

It was one of those slow, brutal, grinding August days when Sheriff Sal drove his cruiser down the mile of unmarked dusty gravel road that separated State Route 34 from the Guerrero Place. It wasn't something he enjoyed doing. Guerrero liked his privacy and, under most circumstances, Sal was more than happy to give it to him. Few of Hualapai's scattered population of outliers lived the way they did because they relished company, especially the company of law enforcement. But he didn't have a choice. If he were going to keep on living in the community he'd chosen to live his life in, then Sal would have to tell Rusty Guerrero that he'd just arrested his best friend for murder.

The two made unlikely friends. Hippie: un-aggressive, sunburned, and slight, with a tendency to talk too much when he got nervous. Rusty: belligerent, dark-skinned, and thick. He seldom spoke, but when he did, it was usually to curse blackly and with a creativity that would have shocked Sal's father, who'd been no amateur himself when it came to profanity.

It was an unlikely friendship with uncertain roots. Both men had hacked their rough kingdoms from the stone and sagebrush of the desert without the benefit of easy money. But that in and of itself was no guarantor of friendship; plenty of the desert's inhabitants passed the empty years cultivating intricate animosities with neighbors like themselves in nearly every respect. Nor was it their profession that drew them together. A secretive and suspicious lot under the best of circumstances, pot growers are more likely to hate their colleagues than nearly anybody else. No, it was an abstract friendship in the Asian style: a marriage of light and darkness, yin and yang.

Not that any of these thoughts rushed through Sal's mind as his lifted cruiser ambled down the rutted lane that led inexorably to the gate of the Guerrero family's compound. The Sheriff didn't waste a lot of time thinking about such things. He was just worried. There was no way to know how Guerrero would react to his friend's arrest. That it would be tragic, violent, unpredictable, or some horrifying combination of the three, he had little doubt.

And he was right. But even he had no idea at the time of how right he was.

The gate was closed. Sal got out of his car, walked over to it, and leaned against the hot metal bars framed on all sides by signs that read things like "Keep Out!", "Protected by Smith & Wesson," or some other variation on that theme. He waited, knowing that it would be a short wait. The Guerreros always seemed to know when someone was at the edge of their property.

Sure enough, less than five minutes had passed when Rusty Guerrero rolled to a halt astride a battered ArcticCat ATV.

"Morning, Sheriff. Anything I can do for you?"

Sal got right to it.

"I had to arrest Hippie last night. Thought you should know about it."

The stocky man scowled.

"What the fuck for?"

"Murder."

He was silent for a moment.

"Anybody we know?"

"I don't think so," replied Sal. "But I've only got a head to work with, so I'm keeping an open mind."

Rusty ignored the morbid joke.

"If it ain't one of us, why are we even having this conversation?"

Silence.

"What are you trying to say, Guerrero?" Sal snarled back after a moment, a little more sharply than he'd intended. The shorter man responded with a dismissive wave of his hand.

"Like you've never shown some out-of-control motherfucker from L.A. or S.F. a hole before."

It was a statement, not a question. Sal bristled but didn't respond. A few more moments of silence followed.

"It was one of those freak things, Rusty," the Sheriff continued after a bit, "That rat-bastard Senator Henry Willow showed up on my doorstep yesterday, demanding a tour of the area…"

Guerrero made an extremely rude comment about his elected representative. Sal continued, once again ignoring him.

"…so I spent the day driving him, his bodyguard, and his two assistants around the Black Rock. They wanted to see some mountain lions, so around dusk I grabbed some night vision equipment and drove them up to the Calicos. Didn't see any, but we did get a flat tire. By the time I'd fixed it and driven back out of the mountains it was ten at night."

"Willow was starting to bitch, so I decided to take a shortcut around the edge of the mountains. I was surprised to find Hippie's truck way the fuck out in the ass end of nowhere. I was even more surprised to find him burying a human head."

Guerrero scratched his beard thoughtfully.

"Well, shit."

The two men were again silent for several very long minutes. Too long, thought the Sheriff.

"Let him go, Sal," Guerrero said at last. "Whatever he did it must have been in self-defense. Hippie doesn't even own a gun. Just say he escaped or something."

"Can't do it. Too many witnesses. Plus, there's the matter of that head I have back at home in my fridge. The crime lab in Reno is sending a guy up for it tomorrow afternoon. Sheriff's Department is sending one for him, too."

"Let him go Sal." Guerrero said grimly, his mouth set in a hard, straight line. He was pleading now in his own way. "An old desert rat like Hippie will never get a fair trial in Reno. They don't think much about us down there – but when they do, they don't think much *of* us, either. We might as well live in different countries."

Inwardly the lawman nodded. Washoe County was one of the largest counties in the United States, stretching from Reno to the Oregon border. However, 99% of its population lived either in Reno or one of its bedroom communities. The majority of its inhabitants thought of themselves as modern, urbane people whose values were increasingly in line with those of the inhabitants of places like Los Angeles and San Francisco. They had little use for the sort of people who lived in little towns like Hualapai. Hippie probably wouldn't get a fair trial at that.

Outwardly, Sal shook his head.

"I can't do it. Wouldn't be right. Even if I wanted to, I can't with Willow and his flunkies hanging around. But I do think that you and your wife – especially your wife – should see him before I ship him out. She still a member of the bar?"

Guerrero nodded, and then scowled.

"Good. She's a smart lady – and I have a feeling he'll need a good lawyer."

Sal tipped his hat to the still scowling rancher, walked back to his cruiser, and drove away without another word.

Washoe County is a long, arrogant middle finger of land thrust up against California's northeastern border. The vast majority of its population lives in its southernmost tip: the Reno-Sparks area along I-80. The remainder is scattered northward along a vast expanse of mountains, dry valleys, and sagebrush larger than 175 recognized countries and three U.S. States. They are a motley bunch: ranchers, miners, farmers, Paiute Indians, hippies, survivalists, and mountain men spread thinly across the land, save for where they congregated into communities such as Wadsworth, Nixon, and Hualapai.

In as much as he could be considered typical of anything, Rusty Guerrero was typical of northern Washoe County. He was stubborn, plain spoken, and contemptuous of authority – though not necessary of police officers individually. He swore a lot and when he drank, he drank hard. A born Californian urbanite, he despised city dwellers and "those fuckers from over the border" in equal measure.

Guerrero was both a pessimist and an optimist at the same time. He was pessimistic enough about the fate of mainstream society to abandon it, but optimistic enough about life in general to build his own world from the ground up. His contempt for government in all its myriad forms would be difficult to overstate. This wasn't a philosophical issue. Simply put, Rusty didn't like to be told what to do (though he had far less of a problem with telling others what to do), and acted according to a moral compass that was sometimes difficult for others to understand. As a member of the public, he felt entitled to any public property that he came across. Guerrero would rather have died than stolen from one of his neighbors. But taking things from the government was something of a sport to him. His ranch was partially powered by solar panels sawed off poles along I-80 in the dead of night. His roads were covered in gravel pilfered from NDOT depots. This, in turn, had been spread by a grader stolen from a BLM work site.

In the autumn months, Guerrero took a week off, gathered his family together, and went "camping" over the border into Lassen County. Camping consisted of logging the national forest there for the coming winter's firewood, plus any timber as might be useful for fence posts, outbuildings, and the like. At the same time, certain associates of Guerrero's drove up from Berkeley in a van. Transactions were made: some in cash, some in dry goods or ammunition, and yet others in laboratory equipment. The Guerrero family then retreated to their home, confident in their ability to ignore the outside world for another year, if they chose to do so: and assuming, of course, that the outside world was willing to ignore them in return.

■

Rusty sat thoughtfully on his quad for several minutes after watching Sal vanish down the gravel road. All was silent. Large beetles hummed about his head, occasionally bumping against him in their eagerness to arrive at their unfathomable destinations. Somewhere nearby a coyote chased a rabbit, yipping wildly as it went by. Yet he sat silent, frozen like a stone in a moment that seemed to stretch on forever.

Below him lay his entire world: the Guerrero Place, built by him and his family using every ounce of strength, determination, intelligence, guile, and even ruthlessness they could muster over 20 long years. He could see the row of old railroad tanker cars that he and his wife had converted into massive methane collectors, so efficient that they not only powered most of his equipment, but also even produced a surplus for barter and trade. He could see the entire acre of pygmy apple, peach, and plum trees he had carefully tended for a decade, nursing them through freezing winters and blazing summers until they at last yielded acres and acres of ripe, delicious fruit. He could see the distant, black blur of the blades of his windmills, humming as they recharged the batteries that powered his home. He watched as the sun glinted off the surface of a catfish pond, dug by his own hands, stocked with fry netted in the American River, and ingeniously fed with ground table scraps and offal until he'd created a stable population of edible fish. He looked at his home itself: 3,200 square feet of almost free space. Doublewides he'd bought for next to nothing, hauled 130 miles up from Reno, gutted, painted, skirted, and arranged into a rectangle with a garden in the center.

It was more living space than anyone in his family had ever had – more than he had ever expected to have – purchased for less than some people spent on a new car. And that space didn't include the Place's other buildings: its Quonset huts, barns, shipping containers, sheds, and the singlewide in which his oldest Son lived with his wife and baby. All of them surrounded by dozens and dozens of carefully drip-fed Russian olives, salt cedars, poplar hybrids, and willows: an oasis of green, vivid life in the heart of the brown, suppressed un-life that is the Black Rock Desert. A lifetime of work crafted by a man capable of having a work of a lifetime. His life. His work.

So why fuck it all up?

"Shit," he said to the silence. Then he answered his own unspoken question with "fuck."

Guerrero remembered his friend. The fucking slacker. The hot August nights spent alternately drinking moonshine on Hippie's dilapidated front porch, or smoking pot on his own expertly crafted one. He thought of his friend's unselfconscious bravery in risking Tyson's wrath to rescue the Scarred Girl. He remembered the tenderness with which Hippie had counseled his oldest son and daughter-in-law when their first child was stillborn, revealing the compassionate minister he once had been. Then he recalled the unqualified affection his friend always showed a child that may or may not have been his own: that smiling, chubby-faced little girl that called the odd, old man "daddy."

Guerrero cursed again, this time wordlessly. He knew what he had to do.

That week Cassidy Guerrero had the unenviable job of shoveling chicken shit, manure, and human waste into the Place's massive composter. It was a surprisingly complicated undertaking, as operating and maintaining her father's methane-capturing contraption involved a tedious amount of adjusting valves, reading dials, and recording data onto a clipboard. Cassidy was unusually meticulous and patient for a 14-year-old girl, hardworking and mindful of her many responsibilities. Thus, she was so deeply involved in the process of taking a pressure reading off tank three that she didn't hear her father come up behind her.

"How does it look, daughter?" he asked.

Startled, Cassidy looked up. Her father stood solemnly behind her, observing her work with an uncharacteristically serious expression.

"Tank one is two thirds full. Tanks two and three are at a quarter, while four is almost a hundred percent. I'd say that we're doing pretty well, Dad. I'm going to pump number four into the generators' holding tanks. Should last almost 'til the end of the year."

"Don't. Vent them all."

Cassidy blinked. It was perhaps the most shocking thing she'd ever heard him say.

"Huh?"

"Don't argue: just do it. Vent them. Let it all out."

Then her father turned and walked away.

Guerrero's next stop was the 20-acre pasture where his family kept their cattle and horses. He found his middle son Hugo there, hay bucking inside of their small lean-to style barn. A carbon copy of Rusty's own heavyset, dark-haired Mexican father, Hugo sweated in his chaps and he wielded his hay hook with expert precision, tossing 150-pound bales onto the top of the rig with a practiced swing. He was a powerful young man, and Guerrero paused for a moment to admire his progeny's thick muscles straining beneath his shirt.

"Son," he said at last, "stop that and come over here."

Hugo obeyed silently. Also like his grandfather, the young rancher was a man of extremely few words. "Wouldn't say shit if his mouth was full of it," was the charming expression Rusty's mother had used, but it was true enough.

"Don't bother with that anymore. Instead, throw open the gates and drive all of the horses and cows out into the desert. All of them except for Soren and Rand. Saddle them up and get them ready."

Hugo looked at his father oddly, and then nodded. That was all it took with him. Then Rusty walked out into the field to speak with the horses.

———

Guerrero walked out into a seemingly untouched field of saltbush and sage, weaving between waist-high brush until he came to a hatch, almost perfectly camouflaged under a layer of tan paint and dirt. Opening it with one hand, he descended a ladder of welded rebar covered in grip tape ten feet to the floor. Then he closed the hatch shut using a rope, once again concealing the presence of his pot-growing lair.

The strong scent of high-grade marijuana filled his nostrils. Guerrero's preferred crop was a strain of Afghan White Widow that he had been breeding for decades, even before he moved to the Black Rock. He used to grow it in a closet in San Francisco. It produced a strong, mellow high with very little paranoia. It was good for working, which was why his customers were mostly UC graduate students and Silicon Valley programmers. In contrast, Hippie grew a variety of Panama Red that was popular with the older hippie crowd. It produced hallucinations and a whole lot of paranoia, so Guerrero almost never smoked the stuff. "What's the point of pot without paranoia?" Hippie always chided him. "It's like decaffeinated coffee."

The facility consisted of three 400 square foot shipping containers that had been buried side by side six feet down. They were linked by a series of welded doorways and lit by thousands of dollars of high intensity metal halide lamps powered by the Place's innocent looking field of stolen solar panels. Everything was watered hydroponically via a drip-feed system whose water was gravity-fed into the containers directly from the Place's spring. It was an incredibly efficient and organized system.

Oskar looked like his mother. He was tall, blond, and had a whimsical sense of humor that Guerrero found annoying. But he was a good pot farmer, and his work kept the family financially afloat. He was listening to some insufferable noise that Guerrero knew was called Tool; which made sense, as his oldest son was something of a fucking tool.

The oldest Guerrero boy was humming to himself as he moved between the waist high rows of plants, checking on each plant with practiced care.

Oskar looked up when his father turned off the music.

"What the fuck, Pops?" he demanded. "I'm busy here. You're breaking my flow."

"I'll break your fucking neck is what I'll do. Stop that shit and get over here."

With obvious reluctance Oskar obeyed, which made Guerrero relax a little. Obedience was never a given with his oldest son.

"Right. Good. Listen, this is what I want you to do: harvest everything right now. Whatever you can't harvest, I want you to destroy. Burn all that shit in the incinerator. Then, take all of our fucking seed stock and bury it somewhere good and far from the Place. Don't even tell me where it is – just do it."

Oskar started to open his mouth but his father stopped him with a dismissive wave of his hand.

"Then I want you to bag and bury every damn thing on our property that even hints at dope. Books, DVDs, pipes, bongs, whatever – make it go away. I want us to look like we've been living Christian out here.

"Empty out every damn pot and tray in this place in a third location somewhere in the outback. Then spray everything down with fucking bleach until it smells like a Florida swimming pool in here. Got it?"

"But Pops!" Oskar finally blurted out. "The plants aren't ready yet. We're not going to get a third of what it's worth from Trey and Dillon!"

"Doesn't matter," his father replied matter-of-factly. Then he thought about his contacts in Berkeley. "Start right now. Get it all bagged up, even if you have to work through the night. When you're done with everything I've said, load it all up in the van with the California plates. Go to the usual place and meet them. Don't worry – I'll contact them today. Take your wife and my grandson too. When they've paid, you keep the money. Dump the van in Susanville, buy some junker, and make yourselves scarce for a while. I'll email you when it's safe to come back."

Guerrero turned and walked back toward the ladder. In a rare moment of insight, Oskar thought that he looked like the most tired man in the universe.

"Dad, what the fuck is going on? What are you doing?"

His father turned once again, looking him squarely in the eyes. "Destroying our world."

With a heavy heart, Guerrero trudged toward his home. He'd done many hard, unpleasant, and even dangerous things in his lifetime, but none of them had inspired in him the dread of facing his wife at this moment. She would understand – she was strong – but he wasn't certain that things would ever be the same between them after what he intended to do. After all, the Place was as much her Matrimony as it was his Patrimony.

Solstice Guerrero sat idly on the porch of their home, strumming his guitar. Of all of Guerrero's children he was by far the most useless; a indolent, slight, 15-year-old charmer who spent most of his time singing, playing music, and trying to lift up the skirts of the local girls. He was also Rusty's favorite child. Hell, he was *everybody's* favorite child. The boy really could do no wrong. *Hierba mala nunca muere*, Rusty's father would have said: the Devil looks after his own.

The older Guerrero folded his arms across his broad chest.

"Don't you have something to do?"

"Yes," responded Sol without even looking up, "practice."

Guerrero grunted and sat down on a rickety chair near his son.

"I should practice breaking that damn thing over your head, that's what I should do."

Sol chuckled.

"Like you're really going to break grandpa's Santos Hernandez. It's older than you are, pop. Better preserved, too."

Rusty snorted. His father's Flamenco guitar was indeed a classic, manufactured by one of Spain's great *luthiers*. It was the only thing that the old man had left him besides an old Chevy truck on blocks, debt on paper, and a shoebox filled with gold Krugerrands. The latter more than made up for the former.

"Too bad you haven't spent more time with it, Pops," his son continued, "you and I could do duets at Hank's Club on Saturday night."

"Problem isn't that I can't play it," Guerrero answered truthfully, "it's that I've got no voice – and *no tender duende*. Got no soul."

"But you do, son. Play something for me. My heart is heavy right now."

Sol nodded. He began playing with long, dramatic sweeps of his hands, followed by the strong, melodic tenor of his voice. Guerrero soon recognized the song: *La Vuelta* by *El Nino de Ronda*. The Turning Page. It was one of the most mournful flamenco songs ever written, which was saying something. The sheer melancholy of the music made him feel oddly better.

When Sol concluded his song, Guerrero leaned over and patted him on the knee; a rare gesture of affection from a man who preferred to keep his distance from others, even his own children.

"Thank you, son. But, as much as I enjoy hearing you play, I have a task for you."

Solstice Guerrero sighed.

"I thought it was Cassidy's week to shovel chicken shit."

Rusty chuckled sadly.

"No, not that kind of task: something important. Perhaps a little dangerous. Here's what I want you to do..."

Guerrero's wife was silent during their drive to the tiny building that served as Hualapai's police station and jail. She'd been silent for over 12 hours as far as he knew. After explaining his plan to her, he'd taken a bottle of Tequila out of the liquor cabinet and wandered out into the desert to be alone. Guerrero woke up a few hours before dawn beneath a large sagebrush, filthy and hung over. He wasn't feeling particularly talkative, either.

The Sheriff was sitting at his desk, busily scribbling away at the mountain of paperwork when they entered. Hippie sat in the cell behind him, reading the tattered copy of the Book of Mormon that Sal kept in there. It was completely quiet except for the rattling whir of an air conditioner, making Guerrero feel as though he was intruding on some kind of domestic scene. Both looked up as they opened the door.

"Sheriff Sal," nodded Karlotte Harbach Guerrero.

"Mrs. Guerrero," he replied politely, setting down his pen.

"I think it would be best if I could talk to my client in private. Would you mind going somewhere for an hour or so?"

The big man nodded. He rose from his chair, grabbed his hat, and left the building without another word. Karlotte sighed, then grabbed the Sheriff's extremely tattered rolling chair and wheeled it squeaking over to the edge of the cell.

"Well, Hippie, what happened?" she asked bluntly.

The small man shifted uncomfortably on his cot, then set down the book. He looked at his hands for a few seconds, as if they were something alien.

"I've never killed anyone before. Never wanted to, either. Didn't mean to this time."

"What happened?" she asked, more gently this time.

"Well, you know I've never been as good at the generator thing as you guys or the Gladwells. Mine tend to shut down at weird times. Probably a loose connection in the joiner box. Anyhow, at about ten 'night before last my generators shut down right when the Girl was watching *America's Got Talent*. She loves that show. Says she might have tried to get on it if her face hadn't been scarred up so bad. Well, anyhow, my battery bank's getting old. Works fine when the sun's out and the solar panels are feeding juice into it, but doesn't work so well at night. Didn't think she'd get all the way through the show.

"So I walked out to the shed to tinker with the damn joiner box. There the fucker was! Um, sorry Karlotte..."

Guerrero's wife waved her hand dismissively.

"So, anyhow, this fellah," Hippie recovered himself, "had picked up my gas cans and was pouring them out all over my generators, my woodpile, and the side of one of my outbuildings. Didn't take a genius to figure out what he intended to do. I picked up the old shovel I use to put dirt over my compost and hit him over the back of the head with it as hard as I could. He went down like a sack of potatoes.

"Figured I would tie him up and call Sal, but when I turned him over I realized he was gone. His eyes were wide and staring, the way dead people's are."

Hippie looked at his hands again.

"I kind of... I kind of freaked out, I guess. Like I said, I didn't know what to do and I ain't never killed anyone before. But I knew deep in my soul that I would have to get rid of him. He had to go. So I hauled him into my deer tent and began processing him.

"Never much liked shooting animals. Never really much liked guns, for that matter. But remember when I used to work for that traveling taxidermist that comes up during hunting season? I learned a lot from that guy. Been doing it on my own the last few seasons for whatever hunters ask me. I do it in trade for meat: the Girl, the Child, and I eat well during the winter."

Hippie's voice became a little distant at this point.

"The guts came out okay, just like with a deer or pronghorn. I put those into a couple of buckets. To be honest the liver was bigger than expected, but everything else seemed about normal. Then I took the arms and legs off. Again, that wasn't a big problem. Used a dressing saw for that."

"Quartering the torso was a bitch, though. That took some time, though not as much as you might think. That just left the head. Wasn't going to put it up on my wall or anything, like a deer's head. That would just be creepy."

Nervously he returned to looking at his hands.

"Who the fuck are you, Lady Macbeth?" snarled Guerrero. "You caught some bastard trying to torch your place. You tried to stop him, and accidentally killed him while you we're doing it. You had to get rid of the body. No problem there. My question is this: how the hell did you get caught?"

Hippie shrugged.

"Bad luck I guess. When I was done with... well, with what I was doing, I decided to get as far away from my place as I could and scatter the remains out for the coyotes. Not much chance of there being any evidence left when they're done. I drove out to the base of the Calicos. Only problem was the head. Had to bury it. I *was* burying it when Sal showed up!"

"Jasper," Karlotte Guerrero never called Hippie "Hippie," "why didn't you just call Sal in the first place? You weren't guilty of anything until you disposed of the body. Feelings in your gut aside, you were clearly defending your home. Defending you would have been easy, city jury or not."

Hippie nodded.

"That's exactly what I was going to do – at first. Then I checked his wallet." He shrugged. "Like I said, I never killed anybody. I was curious who he was. When I found out, I decided to do what I did."

Rusty and his wife looked at one another.

"So?" she replied bluntly. "Who was he?"

Without another word, Hippie reached into his back pocket, removed a small piece of plastic, and handed it through the bars to her. It was an identification card, roughly the size and format of a driver's license. It read "Joseph R. Carson, Bureau of Land Management."

The Bureau of Land Management owns 87 percent of Nevada, 68 percent of Utah, 50 percent of California, and large portions of nine other western states. Administered from far away Washington DC, it is by design a largely faceless and anonymous branch of the federal government. Formed in 1946 when the Grazing Service was merged with the General Land Office, it was given the responsibility of administering vast territories originally intended to supply western settlers and newly emigrated citizens with homesteading allotments. For its first 20 years its duties mostly consisted of managing grazing, water, and mining easements for the West's rural population. But in 1976, Congress decided that these lands would remain in "public ownership" *in perpetuum* to "meet the present and future needs of the American people." The Bureau was given the mandate of eternally managing these lands and any resources they contained.

In other words, the BLM administers the greatest non-martial land grab in human history.

Perhaps the grab was not precisely "non-martial" after all. The BLM fields a force of approximately 200 Law Enforcement Rangers (uniformed officers) and 70 Special Agents (criminal investigators). The agents are notoriously aggressive toward rural populations, sometimes to the point that local law enforcement has been forced into armed confrontations with them over the "SWAT team mentality" and hardcore tactics they employ against ranchers and miners.

To make matters worse, in 2007 *Wilkie v. Robbins* arrived on the desks of America's dubiously competent Supreme Court justices. The facts of the case were straightforward: the BLM acquired an easement on a ranch, but neglected to record it. Wyoming rancher Harvey Frank Robbins subsequently purchased the ranch and, due to the BLMs's mistake, acquired the property *sans* easement. BLM officials demanded that he sign it over anyway and, when Robbins refused, the government officials sought to give him a "hardball education" and retaliated by, among other things, harassing Robbins and his guests and filing trumped up charges against him. Enforcement Rangers promised that his refusal to allow the government to use his land would "come to war" and that they would "bury him."

The rancher sued the BLM and the case made its way through the federal court system. The Solicitor General argued on behalf of the government "there is no Fifth Amendment Right against retaliation for the exercise of property rights." Ever eager to expand the federal government's powers, the Supreme Court agreed, legally removing any protections rural westerners had against the BLM's abuses... and doing more harm to private property rights in two weeks than had been done in 200 years. The federal government has subsequently maintained in court that it owns *all* of the rights to BLM land regardless of existing filings, century old habit and custom, adverse possession, and improvements, with the "plenary" right to kick anybody off it, any time they choose to do so.

For the most part, however, the BLM is the greatest absentee landlord in the world, content to ignore the people who dwell on the fringes of its vast empire. It seldom consults those whose lives and communities are impacted by its actions – after all, they represent a negligible seven percent of the West's population – and even affects an air of hurt surprise when called to the carpet for its indifference. Its policies are an odd and inconsistent mix of, on the one hand, supporting whatever ill-informed ecological views are embraced by the average suburban housewife or urban sophisticate at any given moment, and on the other bending over backwards to facilitate enormous corporate undertakings such as gas pipelines, water resource transfers, and high-end housing developments. One thing unites the odd ends of this seemingly incongruous Ouroboros of conflicting interests: they are always in the interests of the urban population and utterly apathetic to the interest of the rural.

Woe unto the man who gets in their way.

■

There is very little of value to most people in the Black Rock Desert. The drying of the land had strangled off most of the region's few farms generations ago. Slowly, over the last 40 years, the BLM had choked its once-mighty family owned cattle and sheep operations down to a few thousand head as well, replacing them with Wilderness Areas and Wilderness Study Areas to service tourists who never came. There was still plenty of mineral wealth in the area. Prospectors working in teams of two or three using equipment that could fit in the back of four-wheel drive pickup trucks scratched a precarious, semi-legal living from claims here and there; but most of its mineral wealth had been placed off limits by the federal government as well.

There is water, though. Not very much by the standards of most places. The Black Rock is in the driest region of the driest state in America, after all. But there is some. Here and there, streams trickle down from the tops of mountains or springs bubble out of the desert floor. Carefully husbanded and managed using storage and drip feeding, one meager spring or trickle of a stream can provide enough water for a small ranch's needs, plus a little left over for gardens. These sources of water are carefully, even jealously guarded, both in court and, upon rare occasions, with acts of violence outsiders found shocking and baffling.

It becomes more understandable when one realizes that the people of the Black Rock manage to run entire agricultural operations and feed their families using about the same amount of water that comes out of the end of a suburban garden hose.

***

It's a basic law of human nature that anything of value one man has, another will try to take. It's a second, equally basic law that the government will help him to take it, especially if it benefits some politician's constituency or some bureaucrat's resume. Thus, it had happened that even the modest water resources of the Black Rock Desert fell under the greedy eye of faraway developers in Spanish Springs, a sprawling bedroom community to the north of Reno. Nevada's laws require that the developers of new suburbs be able to supply the homes they construct with water. And there is no more water in Reno; not if the recent wave of immigrants from places like San Francisco and Los Angeles wish to live in the manner in which they are accustomed, that is.

There *are* more voters in a single Spanish Springs suburb than there are in all of northwestern Nevada, however. These voters want their homes to have beautiful quarter-acre lawns, Olympic swimming pools, and water heaters the size of World War II Japanese mini submarines. The profits to be made from these homes both for the developer in sales and for the county government in property taxes are irresistibly large. Additionally, the two state political machines rely on the county-level machines to deliver votes, and the national political machines rely upon the state ones, so on and so on up the food chain until the BLM found itself in the unenviable position of legally facilitating the construction of a 130-mile-long pipeline between the Black Rock Desert and Happy Ranch, an ambitious and beautiful "planned living community" on the northern tip of Spanish Springs.

At first, only the usual sorts of things happened. The Happy Ranch people hired a team of pet experts to draw up reports showing that the acre-feet of water that they would pull from various water easements would amount to its evaporative rate if used for irrigation. The various ecological groups countered with their pet experts, who argued the opposite: namely, that the proposed pumping would kill the desert's ecology. The BLM dutifully agreed to conduct a two-year study, though everyone involved knew that the fix was in on this one on the side of the developers. The local people stayed mostly neutral, as the "greenies" had been a notorious pain in their collective asses for years and, at a price tag of 80 million dollars, it seemed likely that the economy would tank before the pipeline ever was built.

Then two things happened. The first was that the Washoe County Water Engineer, in a state of career ending madness, made his report public. It showed that the effects of the pumping would be even *worse* than the greens had said it would be; drying up most of the wells, springs, and streams to the west and north of Hualapai and endangering the towns own water supply. The second was that Senator Henry Willow, the "Green Senator," suddenly and unexpectedly put the weight and the finances of the federal government behind the Happy Ranch project.

No one knew the exact reasons why the Green Senator decided to support the development. It was pretty much an open secret in Nevada that Willow was mixed up in dozens of shady land deals throughout the state. These were all conducted through proxies: friends, lawyers, and family members. It wasn't *illegal* exactly, and nobody was in a position to question him, so in the end nobody did. Some thought that was it. Others reasoned that he was just doing his part as the head of the state's Democratic machine to secure some more votes and, along with them, a shot at some currently Republican seats in the assembly and state senate. A few – mostly Republicans, to be honest – muttered darkly to one another that the developers had simply bribed Willow to get his support.

The real reason was far darker and more complex. The Senator hated rednecks.

These revelations galvanized the inhabitants of the Hualapai area in a way that hadn't been seen since the Paiute Indian War of the 1860s. Happy Ranch, the BLM, and Senator Willow realized to their shock that the Black Rock had a surprisingly large number of alphabet organizations representing its tiny population. HCAB – the Hualapai Community Advisory Board – demanded an explanation from a sullenly evasive BLM, while the HCID – the Hualapai Community Improvement District – promptly sued Happy Ranch, Incorporated. The NNRA – the Northwestern Nevada Rancher's Association – sued to prevent the water transfer in state court. The Sierra Club and the Great Basin Water Network soon joined their lawsuit, followed shortly thereafter by Ducks Unlimited and several other hunters organizations.

In the end, the needs of 7% are always outweighed by the wants of 93%, and the whole thing lumbered forward like a slow motion train wreck. The BLM ended up as the conductor of that train, charged via Willow's influence with the administration to arrange the easements necessary to move the pipeline forward. For most of the 130-mile-length of the pipeline this wasn't a problem, as the BLM held most of that land in "trust for the American people," and could thus use it in any way they damn well pleased. However, to the south of Hualapai, there was a ring of ranches, farms, and privately owned land blocking the pipeline; and the BLM had no actual claim to easements across these lands. However, *Wilkie v. Robbins* meant that there were no longer any rules constraining their behavior when there was something they really wanted. All they had to do was find the "weakest link" in the chain of property owners blocking their progress southward and pressure it until it broke.

Hippie looked like that link. Only he wasn't. The sunburned old preacher had inner reserves the bureaucrats in Winnemucca hadn't counted on. They started by politely requesting a construction easement across his land. He refused. They threatened to simply build it whether he gave permission or not. He refused again, replying that he could "unbuild" anything they constructed as soon as they left and that they didn't have the right to do it anyhow. The BLM responded by demanding that the Washoe County Commission exercise eminent domain to expropriate a section of his ranch for their use on the grounds that the water pipe was a "civic improvement" for Spanish Springs. By now, however, the county commissioners were wary of getting involved in any way with the increasingly unpopular – and, worse yet, very public – boondoggle in the northwestern part of their county. They declined.

By this point the BLM had gotten to know their quarry well enough to learn that it was an open secret that he was a pot grower. They convinced the Drug Enforcement Agency to raid his ranch, resulting in a net gain of... nothing. They didn't find so much as a bong on his property. Unlike Guerrero, Hippie grew dope in hidden fields up in the Granites rather than on his ranch and, reasonably certain he would get raided at some point during this process, had given his personal stash away to Iverson. The result of this fiasco was a front-page story in the Reno Gazette Journal and an editorial in the Sparks Tribune critical of the DEA. This, in turn, resulted in some extremely angry words exchanged between the head of the DEA MET (Mobile Enforcement Team) and one Joseph R. Carson, the BLM Special Agent in charge of the Washoe County Groundwater Development and Utility Right-of-Way Project (as the pipeline project was now known) that culminated with Mr. Carson getting a bloody nose.

The BLM man had had no idea how vicious 5'2" Agent Esperanza Gomez's right hook could be.

In the meantime, Hippie's ordeal managed to make the pages of *High Times*, *Reason Magazine*, and *Range Magazine*, drawing even more attention to the Happy Ranch pipeline controversy. He began haunting Washoe County Commission meetings, using his legally allowed two minutes of public access television time to criticize the Winnemucca office of the BLM. He wrote rambling editorials for any blog, online magazine, or small circulation magazine that would publish them. He crashed HCAB meetings, yelling at the BLM's timid PR representative until Sheriff Sal had to forcibly eject him. In other words, he made a very public, very loud nuisance of himself in that uniquely rural and western way that had sparked every unspeakable, idiotic tragedy from the Johnson County War to Ruby Ridge.

All the while pressure on Special Agent Joseph R. Carson, whom had never even met Hippie, grew and grew and grew from every direction until he did something incredibly stupid. He lit the spark.

No one spoke for some time on the way home to the Place. She drove. He glowered. The seemingly endless brown hills rolled by, one very much like the other to the untrained eye, until finally Karlotte Guerrero took a deep breath and broke the silence.

"You don't have to do this."

Time passed. Her husband remained silent.

"We can win this in court. I *can* beat this. Jasper is guilty of involuntary manslaughter at most, plus maybe some obstruction of justice charges. I—"

"No," her husband interrupted, and then fell silent again, brooding.

"Damn it, Guerrero!" she snapped back at him, "You can't win a war with them. You just can't. You're a big man in many ways, but there are things beyond you. You—"

"Turn left at the dirt road before Hippie's place," he interrupted her a second time. "I've got a hunch that there's something up there I want."

"Stop interrupting me, Rusty!" she paused, barely controlling her temper. "I moved to this country for you, gave you four good children, and helped you build the Place…"

"Two good children," he said gravely. "Oskar's a jerk and Solstice is useless."

"What do you think they're going to do?" She ground her teeth together in frustration, gripping the wheel with both hands. "Just forget about him? Don't you think they're going to figure it out? Figure *everything* out?"

Rusty Guerrero shrugged.

"They're not that smart – or that good. Oskar and his family are gone by now. Alan and his people will take Hippie into the mountain. They already have the Girl and her child. You, Sol, Cassidy, and I will… make ourselves scarce in the desert for a while. They will search, find nothing, give up, and go home. Things will go back to normal, except that there will be one less BLM man around."

Karlotte grunted, obviously unconvinced.

"Turn over there," Guerrero pointed, infuriatingly as if their conversation had never even occurred. The Chevy K-10 turned sharply, and then headed down an unmarked dirt road in a cloud of summer dust.

It was exactly where Rusty thought it would be. The brand new Ford F-350 with BLM tags was parked at the end of one of the Black Rock Desert's many roads to nowhere, directly behind a hill a quarter mile from Hippie's home. It would have had to be somewhere like that, and Guerrero had guessed that the government man wouldn't have wanted to walk any further than he had to.

He slithered out of the passenger side door, dropping several feet onto the earth below. Then he searched the ground for a few moments, obviously looking for something. His wife leaned against the side of the K-10, shading her face with a Wal-Mart straw hat and wishing that she still smoked. It had been 20 years since she'd had a cigarette. She wanted one now.

Finally, her husband found what he was looking for. He hefted a shoebox-sized piece of granite into the air appreciatively for a moment, and then threw it straight through the driver's side window of the big Ford. He reached inside, popped the hood, and walked around to the front of the truck. A few moments later, the engine roared to life.

Rusty sauntered back over to his wife, wiping grease onto his shirt and obviously pleased with himself. He reached into the K-10 and pulled out his radio.

"Guerrero to the Place," he said, oblivious to whoever else might be listening. A moment later, his daughter's voice crackled back.

"This is the Place. Go ahead, Guerrero."

The redheaded man smiled.

"Tell Hugo to get the welding gear out. We have some work to do."

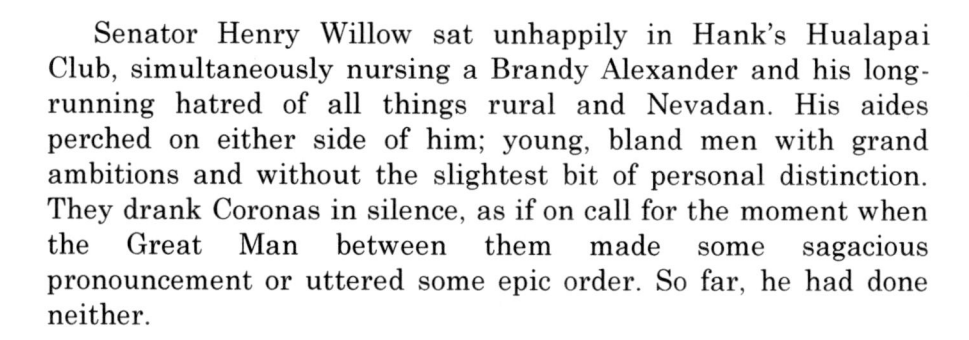

■

Senator Henry Willow sat unhappily in Hank's Hualapai Club, simultaneously nursing a Brandy Alexander and his long-running hatred of all things rural and Nevadan. His aides perched on either side of him; young, bland men with grand ambitions and without the slightest bit of personal distinction. They drank Coronas in silence, as if on call for the moment when the Great Man between them made some sagacious pronouncement or uttered some epic order. So far, he had done neither.

Off in a corner stood one Jefferson Q. Harrison, silently watching the three with an air of personal detachment. He lacked the grand ambitions of the men in his charge, though he made up for this fact by possessing quite a bit of personal distinction. One could even say that he was trying to be inconspicuous – if it were possible for a six-and-a-half foot tall, bald, jet black man in a business suit wearing a gun could be inconspicuous in Hank's. Fortunately, the other patrons seemed inclined to pretend that such a thing was indeed possible; a courtesy that Harrison appreciated.

Willow didn't like Hank's Club. He didn't like Hualapai and, for that matter, he didn't like the Black Rock Desert. To be brutally honest, he didn't like Nevada; which was inconvenient, as he was one of its two United States Senators. When forced to return home from Washington – a situation he avoided as often as possible – he liked to restrict his activities to Las Vegas and Incline Village; the former because it was where all of his supporters lived, the latter because it was where his mansion on Lake Tahoe was. *And* because that location was as close to a truly civilized state as he could live while still enjoying a certain amount of urbane luxury.

Willow's political detractors called him Dusty Henry, which was genuinely unfair. He hated dust. In fact, his political ambitions were partially motivated by a strong desire to stay indoors as much as possible. Henry had been born in the tiny of community of Jackpot on the Idaho border. His father was a tough-as-nails third-generation Mormon potato farmer, determined to "turn-and-burn" his 240 acres of land into some kind of semi-mythical fertility. The smallest and smartest of five brothers, from an early age Henry had been the target of bullying and idiocy from every direction. He longed to escape from the torturous clutches of his environment, even as he was shaped by it. He knew that to break out he would need money. Later, he came to understand that to get even he would need power.

By the time he was 22 Henry, hardworking and clever, had become manager of a farm equipment dealership. By 30, he owned it, and had become a politically active member of the chamber of commerce. By 40 he was an Elko County Commissioner, and from there it was a fairly straightforward climb to State Senator, Nevada Democratic Party Chairman, Lieutenant Governor, and, finally, Senator. Along the way, he developed a simple political philosophy that had served him well over the years. One, always stand for what 51% of the population believe in at any given moment. Two, always refer to yourself as an "independent." Nevadans like independence, so it was a logical thing to splash all over your reelection material, regardless of your actual voting record.

That wasn't what concerned the Senator right then. The next election was a long way off and he would win it in any case. What concerned him was that he had just seen an opportunity and was unsure of how to use it. Willow didn't care that some hillbilly had killed what he assumed to be another hillbilly. These desert rat hicks did that sort of thing all the time, and it just meant there would be one less of them when they did. What *was* important was that this particular hillbilly had been a pain in his backside for months, stirring up all sorts of trouble over the Happy Ranch pipeline project. Not particularly effective trouble – the BLM had kept the damn thing slowly moving forward no matter what – but every little bit hurt. Now he had an opportunity to pay the little bastard back. If he could just figure out the right way to spin the whole thing, he could turn all the bad PR of the last year around.

But how, exactly? The most obvious way was to try to tarnish everyone opposed to the project with this bastard's crime. That wouldn't be easy, even with constituents as stupid as his. Moreover, there were probably all sorts of extenuating circumstances that would come out in the wash. The whole thing might backfire, garnering more sympathy for the little rat. And there was always the possibility that people might get confused and somehow associate the murder with the actual project, rather than those who opposed it. It was illogical, but he'd seen that sort of thing happen before.

So, rather than calling his contacts at the various news outlets and papers, Willow sighed, ordered his fourth drink from the weathered old barman, and watched the sun set behind the Granites through the dust-etched windows of the tavern. He would have to give it some thought, but he understood even through a haze of brandy and chocolate liquor that it was going to be a long night.

■

Hippie had been asleep for hours when something hit him on the head with a splash of pain. He gasped and sat up just in time for another rock to hit him, this time squarely on the forehead.

"Ouch!" he exclaimed.

"Shut the fuck up," growled a voice from behind the cell's single barred window. Hippie peered into the darkness outside of the Hualapai jail, but couldn't see anything.

"Rusty? That you?" he whispered.

"No: it's Garth Fucking Brooks. Of course it's me!" Rusty staged whispered back at him. "You want out of here? Cause if so, now's your one chance."

The thin little man was silent for a few, long moments. Then he sighed.

"Yeah. Yeah, I want out of here Rusty. If I don't get out now, I'll probably be looking at cement walls for the rest of my life."

"Then get as far away from the window as you can. Pull the cot over you or some shit to protect yourself."

Hippie did just that as he heard the sound of what he assumed to be a heavy chain being linked about the windows of the cell. Outside Rusty Guerrero finished linking the chain to the bars of the window and walked back to the F-350. He had to crawl up onto the bed and through the hole he'd cut in the cab to get in, but once inside he fired up the powerful V8 Diesel Engine. He listened with some satisfaction to its low, 390 cubic inch grumble, and then slammed it into gear, ripping the back wall of the jailhouse apart with an astoundingly loud crash.

It would have made for an impressive television commercial... if Ford were in the habit of advertising that its trucks were "Jailbreak Equipped!" To be fair, the jail *was* over 60 years old. Its cinderblocks were cracked and desert worn, with gaps where the mortar had long ago crumbled out of them. Guerrero probably could have done the deed with his wife's Subaru BRAT.

But that wouldn't have made the point he wanted to make.

Hippie scurried through the opening where the back of the cell used to be and looked about, dazed by the odd turn his normally predictable life had taken once again. He was covered in dust, bits of mortar, and a bit of his own blood.

"Get in, you nitwit!" screamed Guerrero. "Through the bed of the truck!"

Hippie did as he was told, diving into the bed of the truck. On either side of him 4 by 4s had been crudely bolted to the truck's bed, forming a sort of armor. He scrambled forward to where a low metal opening had been cut into the cab and went inside. Another piece of metal shut behind him with a loud bang!

He clambered into the passenger seat. Guerrero grinned at him with an expression that would have made one of the desert's old cowboy outlaws proud.

"Didn't think I was going to leave you for the fucking vultures, did you?"

Hippie shook his head, and then laughed.

"Sal's gonna be really pissed," he warned.

"He'll get over it."

Then Guerrero floored it.

The bartender, Willow, his two assistants, Harrison, and all of the bar's other patrons came rushing out into the night, running straight into Sheriff Sal and his deputy, both half-dressed and blurry-eyed from sleep. As they watched, *something* that used to be a pickup truck came tearing around the side of the jailhouse, dragging a chain attached to what had been the bars of his one cell. Old boilerplate had been welded over the windows, the hood, and most of the side doors, except for one small portion where the BLM's distinctive inverted triangle-and-tree was located. Someone had thoughtfully added red horns and a devil's tail to it.

In a shockingly fast and fluid motion, Harrison removed his sidearm and took a shot. It glanced off the side of the truck with a clanging sound before the Sheriff's arm shot up, grabbing the bodyguard.

"Not in town!" he exclaimed. "Things could get out of hand quickly. People could get hurt."

Harrison nodded, lowering his gun as the pickup truck gathered speed and vanished around the corner of a nearby house. Shouts of alarm and the startled cries of children woken up from deep slumber sounded around the town, and people began running into the street, many of them clutching rifles.

"What the fuck just happened?" snapped the Senator, who much to his amazement suddenly discovered that he was stone cold sober.

"My guess would be," answered the bartender, who Willow had come to understand was the almost legendary local Uncle Hank, "that Guerrero just happened."

Sal groaned.

Later, seated back at the bar next to the Sheriff, Willow asked the obvious question:

"Who in the hell is this Rusty Guerrero?"

Sal sighed, nursing a triple shot of Wiser's Deluxe on the rocks.

"Hippie's – er, Jasper Herndon's – friend. Another rancher," the Sheriff replied after a moment. He didn't normally drink. Then again, people didn't normally break out of his jail. He didn't really want to tell the Senator any more than that. He still harbored a distant hope that he could get the whole thing back under control.

"Very popular around here," added Uncle Hank unhelpfully. "He and his whole family. A real desert rat's desert rat: independent, works hard, generous, takes care of his own." He placed heavy emphasis on the last part.

"Don't forget to add short-tempered, foulmouthed, opinionated, heavily armed, and suspicious," Sal added, glaring at Uncle Hank. What the fuck was the old man trying to do?

"Why don't we just go get this Guerrero and your prisoner?" asked Harrison thoughtfully in a deep, baritone voice that would have done Levi Stubbs proud. "For that matter, why haven't we gone after them already? Surely you know where he lives."

"He won't be there. And we won't be able to track him in the desert until daybreak. Oh, don't get me wrong," answered the Sheriff, waving his hand in the air. "He'll be there in the morning. Rusty has some sort of jackass plan in motion right now."

"It'll be fiendishly clever and stupid as shit at the same time." Sal realized that the booze was getting to him. Just then he didn't care all that much. "And his wife is a lawyer, so I want to handle this properly. First thing tomorrow morning I'll call the judge in Wadsworth and get a warrant to search the Guerrero Place. I doubt I'll find anything, but I'll arrest Rusty for destruction of public property, being an accomplice to a crime, and whatever else I can think of. Maybe I can scare him into telling me where he's hid Hippie."

Uncle Hank snorted.

"And I want to avoid some sort of armed standoff between us and the Guerrero family... or any other weird crap." Sal eyed Uncle Hank meaningfully. "No Waco shit: I have to goddamn live here. I go in alone, arrest Rusty, and leave. We'll let the system handle it from there, for better or worse."

But it was too late. Senator Henry Willow had gotten an idea: a big one. When news of the severed head's owner came in the form of a frantic phone call at 6:00 AM the following morning, the possibility that he could turn the entire situation to his advantage became even more self-evident.

■

"Area Four clear."
"Roger that. Johnson?"
"Area Three clear."
"Understood. Trihn, Stevens, and I are going into Area One. All other agents hold position. Understood?"

Cries of "Yes Ma'am!" filled the ears of DEA Agent Esperanza Gomez. She sighed. Gomez had been woken from a deep sleep at 2:00 AM by the obviously agitated division head of the Reno field office and told to assemble her team for action. Which, in and of itself, didn't surprise her. She and her team had been living in crummy Reno hotels since the abortive raid on Jasper Herndon's "ranch" (if that's what you wanted to call it), left in a sort of administrative limbo while some decisions that clearly had nothing to do with drug interdiction took place. Obviously, they were being kept around for a reason.

Nor did it surprise her that they had been sent back to the Black Rock Desert to raid an isolated ranch reputedly owned by a heavily armed pot grower. She was a highly intelligent and motivated woman who made a point of keeping track of what was going on in local politics, especially in situations like this. She knew all about the Washoe County Groundwater Development and Utility Right-of-Way Project: not to mention the resulting clusterfuck the BLM had gotten itself into because of it. Furthermore, she was certain that, despite the lack of evidence, Herndon was indeed a dope grower, as was this Guerrero character. Esperanza had a sixth sense for such things.

What had surprised her was the alphabet soup of agencies represented at the mobile command center – basically, a trailer filled with communications equipment – that had been set up two miles down the road from the Guerrero place by the time she'd arrived. Gomez was used to working with local law enforcement. Her MET's main job was to provide some "muscle" in rural and small urban areas where the police simply didn't have the manpower to deal with an organized drug gang. She'd worked with the local sheriff on the last raid and, despite the fact that it was a fiasco, found him to be a likable, competent man. He wasn't at the command center. Instead, crowded into the trailer or huddled outside of it smoking and drinking coffee, were two BLM Special Agents, a lone ATF Agent, a couple of guys in Level One HAZMAT suits (the kind that had breathing apparatus built in), a Washoe County health inspector and a building inspector, and what appeared to be a State of Nevada manufactured housing inspector. She could tell by reading the inscriptions on the sides of their vehicles. All of them looked as pissed off and tired as she was.

There was also a tall black man in a suit who screamed ex-military from every pore of his body. He seemed to be in charge, though whom he worked for exactly was unclear until she'd demanded to know.

"My name is Harrison and I'm a special assistant to Senator Willow, who has taken a personal interest in this operation. You would be Agent Gomez, correct?"

She nodded.

"This Guerrero character is ex-military," he handed her a folder, "a medic, then a sniper-spotter in Desert Storm. Wounded, then sent to Germany to recover, which is where he met his wife Karlotte. They have four children and a grandchild, all of whom we believe live on the ranch."

"Sounds like he could be dangerous," she replied noncommittally.

"He hasn't filed his taxes in ten years. Has a history of making extremist anti-government statements and is known gun nut. He and his family have no visible means of support."

"So... pretty much like everyone else out here, huh?"

Harrison ignored her. He was all business, though she could tell he wasn't particularly enjoying himself.

"Satellite images taken of the area show at least three rectangular structures buried on the northwestern corner of his property, probably beneath a grove of trees. We believe that he is growing marijuana in them, probably for export across state lines into California. This is where your MET team comes in."

"You will find that we have already helpfully divided up the property into zones on the map in your folder. Your team is to go in, secure the property, and then radio back so that we can move supporting units in. Guerrero is suspected of having broken Jasper

Herndon out of jail last night, where he was being held for the murder of one Joe Carson."

"Whom I believe you know," he added with a bit of irony. Gomez grimaced at the memory of the annoying BLM Agent. Hearing that he was dead made her feel oddly guilty, though punching him in the face had seemed appropriate at the time. She shook her head, bringing herself back into the moment. All areas of the property had been secured without resistance, save for Area One: the main house.

It was an odd structure that appeared to be four old doublewides joined together to form a square and ringed on all sides by a well-constructed porch. The front door was wide open. They stood silently behind the wall of what looked like a shed, observing it.

"Boss, you ever get the feeling someone is watching you?' whispered Trihn. The small man scratched the back of his head nervously.

"I can practically *feel* the scope of the back of my neck," she replied quietly. "Somebody is watching us from the bush; probably from one of those hills."

"It's not just that. There's something..." he hesitated, and then fixed her with his brown, inquisitive eyes. "Wrong. Wrong with this place. I felt it last time, too. My grandfather was a sorcerer back in Vietnam. He taught me all sorts of stuff. This whole desert is just *wrong*."

"Shut up, Ba!" hissed Stevens. "You're freaking me out."

"Both of you shut up," Gomez said evenly. Then she motioned with her left hand. "Trihn, you go to the left of the door. Steven, you go to the right. I'm going straight through. If I yell 'clear,' come in with your guns down. Anything else, come in shooting."

The men nodded, moving forward. The sun was coming up and Gomez was hot in her bulletproof vest and blue DEA jumpsuit. Leveling her Glock directly in front of her, she sprinted directly for the door, taking the steps to the porch in a single stride. Then she stepped through the door, leveled her gun, and screamed, "Hands in the air! Hands where I can see them!"

Guerrero looked up from his breakfast, a fork halfway to his mouth.

"We're having *huevos motulenos*," he said levelly. "Would you and your men like some? There's plenty."

Karlotte Guerrero emerged from what Gomez assumed to be the kitchen, a wok in her hand.

"Ma'am, could you please put your hands in the air?" Gomez said, a bit more politely. Karlotte set the skillet down on the kitchen table and put her hands slowly into the air. A moment passed before Guerrero set his fork down and did the same.

"There," he said. "Our hands are in the air. Could you please stop pointing that gun at my wife? She's not armed, and neither am I."

She lowered her gun. "Clear!" she shouted, and Trihn and Stevens entered, their AR-15s at half-mast. Guerrero smiled at her, which she found oddly unnerving. Trihn may have had a point about this place.

"Mr. Guerrero," she began, reverting to the familiar territory of DEA procedure, "you are suspected of the cultivation and sale across state lines of Marijuana, as well as destruction of public property, being an accomplice to a crime, and probably a dozen other things I don't even know about. I've been sent to arrest you."

"Sure." He replied amiably. "Consider me arrested. Care to have some breakfast with me before we go? I'm betting the food is terrible at county lockup, so I thought I'd eat now."

Gomez ignored him.

"Johnson?" she spoke into her headset.

"Ma'am?"

"Have you searched buried shipping containers in Area Three?"

"Yes ma'am." Johnson had a heavy Alabama/Georgia southern accent. "They're completely empty. No dope. I can see where the water and power are supposed to come in, but there ain't no hydroponics equipment or nothing. Smells like bleach too. Bet they just cleaned the place out."

She sighed. It was a long, resigned sound that she was beginning to associate with this godforsaken place.

"Keep searching, Johnson."

"Yes, ma'am."

"Mr. Guerrero, why do you have three 40-foot shipping containers buried on your property?" she asked wearily.

"I like to grow tomatoes," he replied innocently.

"There are no tomatoes in those containers, Mr. Guerrero."

"It isn't tomato season."

"Actually, it *is* tomato season."

"These are very special tomatoes. They only like to grow when there aren't feds poking around my ranch."

Gomez sat down across from Guerrero with a thud.

"What the hell. I'm still going to arrest you, but I'll have some of those *huevos motulenos* now, if you don't mind."

"I don't mind, dear," replied Karlotte, vanishing back into the kitchen.

Gomez stapled her fingers beneath her chin thoughtfully, staring straight at her quarry.

"So, old man, what the hell is your deal?" she asked slowly.

"What do you mean?"

"Well, here you are way the fuck out in the middle of nowhere, living in a compound made out of old shitty '70s doublewides, trailers, and shipping containers. Generally speaking, being a white supremacist requires that you have to be white..."

"You do know there aren't actually any of those fuckers out here, don't you?" Guerrero interrupted. "That's an urban myth made up by city people to make themselves feel righteous."

"...and you're too organized and sane to be cooking meth." she continued. "You don't seem particularly religious to me, so that's out too. With all those years in the Army you're no granola eating hippie, even if you are growing dope."

Karlotte reappeared and began shoveling steaming eggs, tortillas, and black beans onto a plate. She poured Gomez some coffee, and then offered some to her men. The lead agent accepted, as did Stevens. Trihn declined, glancing about nervously. Guerrero munched contemplatively before answering.

"Where are you from really, agent? They don't just keep a team like yours hanging around Reno: specialized training, equipment, and the like."

"New Jersey."

"What part?"

"Camden."

"Nice place?"

"No. It's a shit hole."

Guerrero nodded.

"Got any kids?"

"No."

"Why not?"

She didn't answer. Guerrero leaned back in his chair. It was old, and creaked under his weight. He pointed at her with his fork.

"I'll tell you why not: because it's even odds they'd turn out to be pieces of shit too, that's why. You know it. I know it. My kids were raised out here on the... what did you call it? Oh, yeah 'compound made out of old shitty '70s doublewides.' They're hardworking, polite, and fun to be around. And they'd die for their parents, each other, and their neighbors."

She didn't respond. He waved his fork around expansively, indicating the land around them.

"I like this desert. It's no shit hole. You want to know the truth? It's not that Camden is a shit hole. It's that all cities are shit holes. *All* of them. I've lived in enough of them to know: San Francisco, Las Angeles, and Oakland. *All* of them. Cities do something to people deep in their souls that can almost never be undone. They make them *wrong*, unable to think for themselves or fend for themselves without a bunch of complicated, entangling shit to back them up—"

"Hey!" interrupted Trihn suddenly. "I'm from San Francisco. It's a beautiful city."

Guerrero glared at him.

"You look at my folder?"

Trihn shook his head.

"I was an EMT in San Francisco for five years," Guerrero said flatly. "Teenage boy selling his ass on Polk Street? I've seen that. Girl dead on Haight Street, sitting in a recliner with a needle in her arm? Seen that too. Bike messenger with her head bashed in by some crack-head who knocked her off her bike with a two by four? Bum dead in his own puke and piss in an alley in the Financial District? There's your beautiful city."

"But that's not all a city is! That's not all San Francisco is," protested Trihn.

"It sure as fuck is," Guerrero growled.

"That's all very interesting," Gomez interrupted the two men before their discussion could get heated. "But that still doesn't answer my question: what the hell is your deal?"

"Freedom. That's my deal."

"Sure, sure," it was her turn to wave a fork around. "That's *everybody's* deal. Everybody wants to do whatever they want to do, right?"

Guerrero glowered at her.

"Doesn't matter what they want," he replied after a moment. "They don't know how to do what they want. They don't know how to be free. Here's what freedom is and how you get it: first, move to a place with as few people as possible: the fewer the people, the greater the freedom. When you press a bunch of assholes together, they immediately get into each other's business. They fear each other, and why not? They're all competing for the same few square feet of space. So they make up all sorts of rules, hoping they can use them to hold each other down. If they can hold their neighbor down, then they're less afraid.

"Once you get the hell out of that shit," he continued, "you got to learn how to sever ties to things so that nobody can hold the basics you need over your head: power, water, and food. They will use the very power lines that tie you to the grid to tie you down. If you have to get it from the store, they can take it out of the store. You have to get it from them, then ultimately they have control over you. You will never be free."

"Who are 'they' Guerrero?" asked Gomez, suppressing a sigh. Another paranoid. "The government? The corporations? The Masons? The Jews?" She threw those last two in for fun.

"Whoever is trying to keep me from getting whatever it is I want on my own damn terms," he said bluntly. "I don't know nothing about Masons or Jews. Don't mind buying things from corporations, so long as the deal is fair. Otherwise, fuck 'em. Worked for the government long enough to not trust it. And that's that."

"That's all very noble and whatnot," interjected Stevens, "except that your little nitwit friend murdered Joe Carson. Then you broke him out of jail. He murdered a freaking park ranger, man. Come on!"

"Park ranger? *Flashwichser!* Do you really think the BLM are harmless? That they're our friends?" responded Karlotte, joining the conversation for the first time. She tended slip into German when she got truly pissed off. "*Verdammte Scheibe!* They're trying to facilitate this whole water project down to Spanish Springs. It'll pump more acre-feet out of this place than we've actually got! Kill every damn ranch out here."

"You know what the BLM's main job is in Nevada?" added Rusty. "Its keeping the rural population poor, that's what. Keeping ranchers, farmers, and miners from using 87 percent of their own state – or making it so difficult that they don't even try."

"The BLM," responded Esperanza Gomez evenly, "is a thousand under-funded, marginally competent bureaucrats charged with managing an area the size of Western Europe. Oh, and they put out fires every year so that your ranches don't burn to the ground."

"Bureaucrats don't carry guns," Karlotte responded hotly. "Neither do firemen."

"Speaking of which," Gomez set her fork down and leveled her gaze at Rusty Guerrero. It was a hard, impressive gaze had actually caused Mexican drug smugglers and tattooed bikers to piss themselves. Guerrero looked blandly back at her. "Do you have any guns on the property Mr. Guerrero?"

"On the property? No."

"Are any other members of your family on the property? I don't want anyone getting hurt."

"On the property? No."

"That's what I thought," she responded dryly. "I suspect that some of them are just outside – along with your guns. But no matter."

She sighed. She was sick of sighing at people in the Black Rock Desert.

"Man, you have no freaking idea what you unleashed when you busted Jasper Herndon out of jail. When I take you out of this place, you're never coming back to it. Never."

Guerrero smirked.

"No, I mean it. There's a shit-storm of bureaucracy just outside of your gate waiting to flood in the second I take you out. BLM. County property inspectors. State housing inspectors. I couple of guys in HAZMAT suits I think are from the health department. They're going to nail you to the wall for anything and everything about this place. Whomever you pissed off – and I have a pretty good idea of who it is – is going to make this a teachable fucking moment. By the time they're done with you and your family, your neighbors will be digging that pipeline themselves to avoid sharing your fate."

His smirk turned into a snarl. He leaned forward angrily, gripping the edges of the table.

"Then let me tell you something, lady. You – all of you – are screwing with people you don't understand. *Things* you don't understand; that you can't control or even fight. One of the most important of them is this: nobody is going to separate me and my family from our home. Nobody."

"I'm afraid they are. Right now." Gomez motioned to Trihn and Stevens, each of whom placed a firm hand on the arm on one of the Guerreros. "This isn't personal, Mr. and Mrs. Guerrero. I find you both quite likable, even if you are paranoid dope farmers. If it's any consolation, I don't think any of the drug charges we're going to make will stick in the long run."

"I'm not kidding, Gomez!" shouted Guerrero. "This land doesn't love you. It doesn't love anyone. We've learned to get along with it. You can't. Get the hell out before it kills you and your men!"

"Read them their rights," she replied evenly. "Then march them to the command center. I'm going to turn this place upside-down."

▬

Gravel crunched beneath boots as Trihn and Stevens walked Rusty and Karlotte Guerrero out of the front gates of the Place and toward the mobile command center. Both had their hands cuffed behind their backs. A dark cloud passed in front of the sun, shutting down the bright morning light as if God had suddenly slammed a window shut. Then, seemingly from nowhere, the wind picked up, rustling as it passed through the sagebrush.

Trihn shivered. It was over 90 degrees out.

As the wind continued to play through the thick brush around him, the small man imagined that he saw all kinds of things moving within which had been invisible but moments before. The muzzles of oddly mutated looking dogs. Strange horses with blazing eyes and sharp fangs. An oddly humanoid coyote. He shook his head, trying to clear the fog that had obviously accumulated there.

Rusty chuckled darkly. Maybe sadly.

"I lied a bit," he said to Trihn. "*You* might be able to understand what's out here some, little witch man. You have enough old country in your veins to *see*. Unfortunately, that means it can see you, too."

Something moved in the corner of his vision. He spun around, leveling his M16 at the brush. But there was nothing there. Instinctively his companion turned as well, pointing his rifle at exactly the same spot.

"What the hell, Ba?" he complained. "Didn't I tell you not..."

It was then that Ba Trihn did see. So did Stevens. It rose out of the brush, black and horrible, all fangs, spines, and dripping blood. It glared at them malevolently through one red eye. Three times the size of a lion, it opened its shark's mouth and howled: an unearthly, terrible thing. Ba Trihn howled too, opening up on the unnatural creature in a spray of .223 rounds that should have torn the thing in half.

But didn't.

▬

By the time Gomez, the rest of her team, and the men from the command post reached the spot, all the screaming and shooting had stopped. Bits and pieces of Stevens were sprayed in an arc outward from his vivisected corpse, which lay broken in the sand. Of Trihn and the Guerreros there was no sign, though the agent's rifle was discarded on the ground nearby. Spent shell casings lay everywhere: tiny metal shells on a vast seashore of sage.

Holy shit, she thought to herself, *the sonofabitch was telling me the truth.*

■

It could not be said that Henry Willow was good for much. He was neither strong nor brave, either physically or by temperament. He was corrupt and hypocritical and knew it and didn't care. What he *did* excel at was creating appearances, at projecting subtle, persuasive impressions outward onto the voting public in a manner that benefited himself and his friends. That these projections were often falsehoods concerned him not in the least. That they often harmed his constituents and his country was beneath consideration.

He felt purely in his element at the morning's hastily assembled press conference in Reno. All of the proper elements were in place. His favorite members of the fourth estate – the ones who acted as his cat's-paws in return for special access – had been called the moment after he'd had his epiphany in that shitty redneck bar. The rest had been contacted via their respective networks at the last possible moment. They stood around uncertainly, eyes still blurry with sleep and minds filled with the uncomfortable pre-coffee fog of Starbucks not being open yet.

He cleared his throat to get their attention.

"Ladies and gentlemen, thank you for coming her on such short notice," he began. "As you already know, the Washoe County Groundwater Development and Utility Right of Way Project is an intricate part of Nevada's emerging green utility Smart Grid, which will supply not only clean power that will improve the quality of life for all Nevadans, but will supply badly needed jobs to boost our economy."

There. He managed to fit "green," "smart," and "jobs" into one sentence. That would pay well in Vegas and Incline Village.

"As you also know, there has been a certain amount of opposition to this project. Some of it from well-meaning but ill-informed people, but most of the opposition has been funded by greedy special interest groups: agro-business corporations who are unwilling to share resources that don't even legally belong to them with the public."

That bit would play equally well to the trailer park types in Reno, Vegas' poor, and (most importantly) with his supporters in California. Willow had been on an anti-corporation kick lately; which was ironic, considering that he owned controlling stock in several of them. No matter. He didn't practice what he preached because he wasn't the sort of man he was preaching to.

"Up to this point these special interest groups have refrained from violence. Unfortunately, as of yesterday this is no longer the case."

Willow held up a picture of Joe Carson. The dead ranger looked very pleasant and fatherly with his salt-and-pepper beard.

"While in the Black Rock Desert checking on the status of the endangered sage grouse population, BLM Ranger Joseph Carson was brutally murdered by a person or persons associated with the special interest groups. His body was then viciously mutilated."

There was a gasp from the assembled reporters, forcing Willow to suppress a smile. He was wearing his serious face for the press conference. Of course, he had no idea what in the hell Carson had been doing when he got killed, but saying "sage grouse" allowed him to "endangered," which was good. He'd also managed to squeeze in three "special interests." People hated those, even if they didn't know what they were.

"Senator Willow, is there any truth the rumor that this killing is the work of an extremist anti-government hate group?" asked Mary Gannet from the *Gazette-Journal*. She was one of his favorites.

"There is no evidence of that," he replied, adding ominously, "Yet. However, late last night persons unknown attacked the Hualapai jail, freeing the suspect. Local law enforcement has requested the aid of state and federal agencies in apprehending the suspect and his accomplices, who are believed to still be in northern Nevada."

"So Senator, what you're actually saying is that there is a link between the agro-businesses opposed to the pipeline into Spanish Springs and violent extremist groups?" asked Joe Israel of the *Wall Street Journal*; definitely not one of Willow's favorite publications, but too respectable to ignore. "Doesn't that sound a little farfetched?"

"I said no such thing," snapped Willow. Of course, it was exactly what he was saying, but the bastard was forcing his hand. These things needed to be done subtly. "There is no evidence of that at this time. However, it's now a fact that opposition to the Utility Right of Way Project has gone beyond the level of civilized debate to include the murder and mutilation of government employees. Does that sound like the Girl Scouts to you?"

An appreciative chuckle rose from the crowd, and Senator Henry Willow knew that he had them exactly where he wanted them.

"Dad, this is the stupidest idea you've ever had."

"Shut up and hand me another one."

Solstice Guerrero dutifully reached into the massive duffel bag filled with white, five-gallon cans of methane, pulled out one that was orange with rust, and gave it to his father. The older man opened it slightly; with a small *whoosh,* the air between them was filled with the organic reek of the gas. Satisfied, rusty tossed it into the opening in the roof he'd created when he'd used a pry bar to rip off one of the building's swamp coolers.

"No, really Dad: in the great fucking history of bad ideas this one is up at the top. That guy who strapped an old JATO rocket onto his '67 Impala and embedded himself in a hillside in Arizona? A genius compared to us."

"Just shut up give me another one."

Solstice obediently complied. The container hissed as it banged off the sides of the aluminum ventilation shaft, and then disappeared into the depths of Winnemucca BLM Field Office.

"Dad, they have a word for this. It's called terrorism. T-E-double-R-ism. It's a *bad* thing, and definitely won't make me one of the cool kids in school."

"Sure it will," responded Rusty cheerfully. "Plus it isn't terrorism when they attack you first. Then it's called 'war.' Terrorism is evil and immoral. War is justifiable and righteous. So hand me the rest of those, will you?"

Sol did what he was told. He had a bad feeling that there had been many conversations like this in history. Osama Bin Laden had something like ten sons. Had one of them said, "Dad, I don't think this whole 9-11 thing is such a hot idea?" Sol was betting one had.

Guerrero dropped the last of the methane cans through the hole in the roof. With a sigh of satisfaction, he began to unwind the coil of homemade fuse he'd brought with him: fifty feet of flammable rope covered in glue and charcoal. Trailing one end down the hole, he began to crab-walk backward toward the edge of the roof where they had left their ladder.

"Dad, what if there's somebody working late in the building?"

"At 2:00 AM? Son, these are government employees. They leave at five sharp."

"Maybe there's a night watchman or something."

Guerrero snorted. "What would he watch? There isn't one." He tossed the rope over the side of the flat asphalt roof, and then began descending the latter. Solstice followed, sincerely hoping that his father's cockeyed scheme wouldn't work, anyhow. Using cans of methane and a homemade fuse to blow up a building? It couldn't possibly work.

When they reached the ground, Guerrero tossed the ladder into the back of the K-10. He flicked open his lighter and eyed the flame appreciatively.

"Dad, we could just drive away. It will make the news without destroying anything."

"Sure," replied his father. "But then they wouldn't learn nothin', would they?"

He touched the flame to the fuse.

▬

Sheriff Salvatore "Sal" Giovanni knew ass-chewing. As a Reno patrolman, he'd had his chewed by some of the best. As a chief on a destroyer in the Navy before that, he'd gnawed on more than his fair share. Still, the dressing down he'd gotten from his superiors in the Washoe County Sheriff's Office had been epic. Biblical, even.

He'd been woken up at 6:00 AM and ordered to drive straight to the big complex on Parr Boulevard in Reno. He arrived to find himself before a firing squad of captains, lieutenants, and what-have-you, all determined to peg the breakout of the night before squarely on his chest. Forget the fact that nobody had pulled an

Apple Dumpling Gang stunt like that since the days when Kit Carson trapped beaver in the Sierras; Sal should have been on the lookout for it, since he should have known there were "extremist anti-government hate groups" active in the Black Rock Desert.

Anti-government what? Rusty, you fucker. He thought silently. *What have you done to all of us?*

He spent the next few hours in hell, moved from room to room in a sort of demonic cakewalk so that he could be asked the same questions repeatedly by various different angry people. After that, Sal was brusquely seated at a desk and given half a day's worth of paperwork to do. Or so he thought at first. It took longer than that, and by the time he was done, the sun had long before vanished behind the Sierras.

Exhausted and depressed, Sal went over to his brother-in-law Mike's house to spend the night. Mike, his wife, and his three children had a nice place in Spanish Springs, and the two men stayed up 'til early morning drinking Coronas and bitching about their jobs, their family, and the general state of the world.

It was masculine, human, and rejuvenating. The Sheriff woke up in the morning feeling like a new man. He snuck out of the house at 6:00 AM without waking anyone so he could make the two hour drive back to Hualapai in time for work. He drove the first hour in silence, his thoughts alternating between anger at his superiors and fury at Rusty Guerrero: the author of his misfortunes. Friend or not, he was going to make damn sure that that prick cooled his heels in county lockup for a year or so. *That* would calm him down a fucking bit.

Finally, he grew tired of brooding and turned on the radio. The Reno Aces had played the Vegas 51s the night before, and Sal wanted to hear the scores. He wouldn't mind hearing the news, either. Listening to how rotten things were in Iraq or some other shithole would make him feel better in comparison."

"...the blaze that destroyed the Winnemucca BLM station has finally been extinguished," growled the low baritone of Reno's morning AM newsman. "Nearby residents report an explosion at around two in the morning started the blaze. No one was hurt, but the Winnemucca police department has confirmed the rumor that the fire was a result of arson, perhaps related to the murder of a BLM ranger in the Black Rock Desert two days ago."

"The office of Senator Henry Willow issued a statement this morning," he continued. "The Senator once again decries the use of violence by extremist hate groups, and hopes that the individuals involved in the most recent act of terrorism will have the decency to turn themselves in before further incidents lead to more bloodshed."

"In the meantime, to prevent any further loss of life or damage to property, Federal warrants have been issued for at least two individuals, and Homeland Security personnel have been dispatched to northwestern Nevada along with other law enforcement agents, including the FBI, BLM Rangers, DEA agents, and local law enforcement."

"Now, for Aces news, we turn to..."

Sal turned the radio back off again.

His town looked like an anthill that had been kicked over. It was as if there had been some sort of military takeover, and Sal feared that many of his fellow townspeople would view it as exactly that. He didn't see any of them, however: only dozens and dozens of heavily armed men and women dressed in what seemed like a half-dozen different sorts of uniforms. There were at least two distinctively different mobile command posts set up in the parking lot next to Hualapai's small town park, surrounded by what seemed to be an ocean of vehicles with emblems on their doors. A helicopter lifted off the town's medevac helipad as he pulled in.

Sal looked for a friendly face among the crowd of tired-looking police standing around the vehicles: smoking, drinking coffee, and talking among themselves. His eyes finally settled on Esperanza Gomez; which, he had to admit privately to himself, was an easy place for them to settle, after all. He got out of his cruiser and walked over to her.

"Good morning, Agent Gomez," he said pleasantly. "What the fuck has happened to my town?"

Gomez looked up from the cup of coffee she'd been staring into, as if it contained some sort of mystical insight within its brown depths. *Perhaps it does,* thought Sal.

"For the moment, at least, your friend Guerrero has screwed your town," she replied bluntly. "He's brought the wrath of Uncle Sam down on this place, and your *amigos* all seem to know it. Everybody's gone except for the old man that runs the bar."

Sal frowned.

"You're sure it was Rusty that did that thing in Winnemucca?" he asked, already knowing the answer. "I mean, there were witnesses?"

"No, no witnesses," she responded with a shrug. "But, yeah, he did it. You already knew that, though."

"Sure. But I was hoping you would tell me something different."

She frowned, his attempt at a joke falling flat. Another SUV pulled into town, this one with a Department of Homeland Security emblem on it.

"Look, this isn't public knowledge yet," she continued, "but two of my men got killed arresting your friend and his wife yesterday. Well, one of them, anyways. We haven't found poor Trihn's body."

Sal felt his blood run cold.

"Shit, Esperanza! I didn't think he'd do that!"

"I didn't say that he did." she scratched the back of her neck uncomfortably, and then sighed. "In fact, I don't think that he did; which is why you haven't heard about it yet. We found bits and pieces of Stevens all over the place. Someone – or something – tore him apart in seconds and carried off Trihn. I thought it had gotten the Guerreros, too. But with that attack on the BLM last night, I'm guessing not."

She frowned.

"We found some tracks nearby: huge and weird, like nothing anybody's ever seen before. Some blood that hasn'tbeen analyzed yet. Not much else. Oh, and my boys must have pumped thirty, forty .233 rounds into... whatever it was. I don't think much of poodle-shooter as a round. Who does? But thirty rounds of it will drop an elephant in its tracks. So what the fuck were they shooting at, Salvatore?"

The Sheriff opened and closed his mouth a few times silently. *Like a fish when you pull it out of the water,* she thought. *He knows something.* Finally, he stopped and shook his head.

Bastard.

"Damn you desert rats! Damn this place!" she cursed. "You and all your fucking secrets!"

■

The Sheriff found Uncle Hank in his apartment above the bar. The old man was busily shoveling items into a battered leather suitcase. He wasn't certain, but he thought he saw him quickly slide a book inside as he entered. *Secret* something.

"Uncle Hank."

"Sheriff," replied the old man politely, setting his suitcase down.

"Where you going, Hank?"

"Well, Sal, I'm not really going anywhere," he answered. "I'm fleeing."

"Fleeing?" Sal was frustrated. "Fleeing what?"

"Why, death, of course. What else is worth fleeing?"

Sal threw his hands up in exasperation.

"No one wants to kill you Hank! No one's after you or anybody else, except for Rusty and Hippie. Maybe Rusty's wife and one or two of his kids at this point. I don't know. But no one's after you or anybody else!"

"No, not yet," the old man replied. "But that's the thing about witch hunts. They don't usually stay restrained to a couple of people."

Sal fought to keep his temper under control.

"Witch hunts? Look: Hippie killed a man. He killed a BLM Ranger to be exact. Guerrero busted him out of jail, hid him somewhere, and then went and blew up the goddamn BLM office in Winnemucca. There's no witch-hunt. Just stupidity and craziness."

"You forgot the part about the two men getting killed out at Guerrero's ranch."

Sal looked surprised.

"Oh, I know you know about it," said Hank with a sigh. "But we all know about it, too. And you forgot the part where they kicked Rusty off his land. They didn't go out and arrest him for aiding and abetting or anything like that. They went out, did some chickenshit drug bust, and found nothing. All the same, the harm is done: men are dead, things are destroyed, and half the goddamn federal government is here."

He returned to putting things back into his suitcase. Then, after a few uncomfortable moments had passed, he continued.

"Look: Rusty and Hippie and their families and all that lot have vanished into the mountains. Digging them out isn't going to be a small matter – and it's *not* like nobody sympathizes with them and it's *not* like nobody's going to help them. And when all of these assholes start rooting around the Calicos, the Granites, the deep desert, and what-have-you, all sorts of things are going to happen. This 'anti-government extremist' shit is only the beginning. It isn't the half of it. No, fuck that, it isn't even a quarter of it. You *know* what's going to happen. You *know* what's out there."

"Yeah," muttered Sal, "Rusty's fucking brother and his.... people."

"Sure," continued Hank. "Al and his people. *And* Tyson and his. *And* the damn horses. *And* Phat Albert: who, you may remember, you never got. *And* the dust coyotes. *And* every other goddamn thing that lives out there. Plus things you can't really say are alive anyhow. Everything we've kept bottled up here for generations. The government's gonna pull the scab off that wound and it's gonna bleed out into the world. That's what Guerrero's personal war is going to do. Everything that came from everywhere else because it had nowhere else to go is going to get pushed into a corner. And you know what happens when you push shit like that into a corner."

Sal sighed, sitting down heavily on one of the rickety chairs that littered Hank's living room. He took off his hat and wiped his brow with his hand.

"Then why the fuck did you encourage that peckerwood Willow?" he demanded. "What the fuck was that the other night?"

"*That* my friend," replied Hank, "was fate at work. The feds were going to come up here and do something like this at some point in the near future no matter what. It was predestined."

"The fuck it was."

"No, it was. Listen."

Hank sat down on the edge of a battered couch near Sal. He leaned over to speak to him more closely.

"You weren't even born yet," he began, "but you know that back during the 1940s and '50s the Air Force used the Black Rock Desert as a bombing range, right? I mean, you've been out to some of the outliers' ranches and seen how they use unexploded shells as lawn ornaments?"

"Sure," replied the Sheriff. "I know that. Everybody knows that. So what? What's the point?"

"Well, they blasted the shit out of this place. Fifty years before that in 1908, the feds decided to 'improve' Lake Winnemucca and Pyramid Lake by digging a canal between them. The idea was that it would balance out the water level between the two, allowing for a single, giant lake you could use to travel almost from Reno to here. Great idea: only problem is, they didn't do any basic research before they did it. If they had, they would have realized that that one of the lakes was at a much higher elevation than the other. Lake Winnemucca drained straight into Pyramid Lake. Killed one of the biggest lakes in the west; killed its whole ecology and drained it. It was totally gone by the '30s. Now what we got is a big giant desert south of here where the lake used to be."

"Yeah, okay," said Sal, "I knew about that. Kinda."

"Right," Hank replied. "Fifty years before that, some stupid-ass bushwhacking by *somebody* – nobody really knows who to this day – kicked off the Paiute Indian War. The Paiute did all right for a few years, but eventually the feds came in and crushed them. The federal government was simply too big for them to deal with, no matter how tough and clever they were or how well they knew the land."

"Alright, alright," replied Sal, more than a little exasperated. "So what's your point? That every fifty years something like this happens out here?"

"Yep, that's exactly my point. Roughly every fifty years the federal government comes out here like a force of nature and destroys a bunch of stuff. It's predestined. It's gonna happen now, and in fifty more years it's gonna happen again."

"That's a bunch of shit, Hank," Sal replied heatedly. "Those things don't have shit in common with each other."

"Well, except that they were destructive, happened here, and the feds did them all. What more do you want out of prophesy, Sal?"

"Hank, you're assigning meaning where there isn't any. You're like one of those fucking people who see the number 23 everywhere."

Hank shrugged. He got up and resumed putting things into his suitcase.

"Cycles are common in nature," he replied. "Most cultures don't have as big a problem with that as we do. Plus, do you have a better explanation for what's going on here?"

"Yeah," Sal shot back. "Duh: they're all here because Hippie cut off some guy's head! That's why they're here!"

"Sure," replied Hank smoothly, "that's the surface reason. That's the trigger. But look deeper at what's been happening." He put a final pair of socks into his suitcase and zipped it shut with a flourish. The Sheriff just stared at him.

"Alright. Well... whatever." said Sal at last. "Where the hell are you going, anyhow?"

"I'm going to strap this on the back of my quad and I'm going to get out of here."

"Out of here to where?"

Hank shrugged, "Just out."

"Well, where in the hell am I supposed to go?" the Sal complained wearily. "I don't have a town left to protect."

"Nope, at the moment you don't," replied Hank matter-of-factly. "You want my opinion? Had any sick days lately?"

"Ah, no."

"How about your deputy? He had any sick days lately?"

"No."

"Take them. Go to Reno. Get the hell out of here before they make you hunt your friends down."

"But I *should* be hunting them down," he insisted. "Whatever the circumstances are, Hippie killed a man. And Guerrero broke him out of jail, blew up a building, and – I dunno – maybe killed those two DEA agents as well."

"Do you *really* believe that?" asked Hank.

"No," he admitted honestly. "But he sure as shit got them killed somehow."

"Maybe. Maybe not, too. Look," Hank made a motion with one finger in the air, "what's happening here is a spiral." He made another one for good measure.

"Every time it concludes a loop, it touches on the same point; which in this case means that something gets destroyed or someone gets hurt. The circle widens itself as it travels. It all started small: someone wanted to build a pipeline to move water, somebody else didn't want them to. Now it grows from spiral to spiral. It's going to keep on doing that, growing and getting more and more extreme, until finally it gets so broad it dissipates."

"But that time's not going to come for a while yet," Hank continued. "And it's not going to be a good idea to be anywhere near that spiral as it grows. You're a good man, Salvatore. Do yourself a favor: get out of here while you still can."

It wasn't until he saw the muzzle flash that Solstice Guerrero realized he'd made a terrible mistake. But by then it was too late.

He'd grown tired of listening to his father and uncle drink and argue, argue and drink. For days they'd sat in Uncle Alan's cave lair high in the Granites, hiding among this lab equipment and the monstrosities that dwelt within them. Separated from their homestead and comforting routine, his mother had withdrawn into her own silent world: smoking, sleeping, and staring out at the stars when his uncle opened the lair's vault-like doors at night. His sister had busied herself helping Heckle and Jeckle – Uncle Al's annoying humanoid assistants – with their tasks. After examining the contents of the cavern complex, Hugo settled on attempting to finish a long-abandoned cistern and water purification system his uncle had given up on years before.

Solstice practiced on his old Santos Hernandez. There were no girls. It was boring.

"What I want to know," asked Rusty late one night after the two men had consumed the better part of three bottles of pinot noir, "is why you sent Phat Albert. When I sent Hugo up to tell you to create a diversion, I meant 'create a diversion.' Not eat two fucking cops!"

"I didn't send Phat Albert," his brother replied, slurring his words slightly. He'd spilled wine all over his bushy beard, and blood-like droplets of it were spattered across his filthy, often-patched lab coat. "I sent Joe. He was supposed to do it."

"Joe? You sent that fucking thing!" cursed Guerrero. "I should have killed his mangy ass when I had a chance."

"Well," continued Uncle Al, "he's been depressed since Maude died. I thought having something to do would be therapeutic."

"He didn't show up. That other thing did. Why's that?"

Al shrugged. "I dunno. Maybe Joe asked him to do it."

"You can... ask Phat Albert to do something? That fucking monster?"

"I've got no idea."

"Then what kind of mad scientist are you, anyhow? You should know this stuff." Guerrero leaned back in his chair, waving his wine glass in the air profoundly. "That's why dad sent you to mad science school!"

"He sent me to UC Davis," Al responded flatly. "And I'm enough of a scientist to know when I don't understand something, if you can wrap your tiny mind around that, *mi hermano*. And there's a *lot* I still don't understand about this place."

They went on and on like this, around and around in circles. At first it had been fun to listen to the two of them go at it like that, but Sol quickly tired of it. He hadn't volunteered for any of this. He'd just wanted to go to school, chase skirt, and after he graduated, try his hand at being a professional musician. Being a revolutionary or fighting some sort of half-assed guerrilla war against the government had never been one of *his* ambitions, even if the rest of his family had taken leave of their senses.

So late one night, he slung his guitar over his shoulder, left the cave, and began working his way gingerly down the mountain. The full moon provided plenty of illumination for his youthful eyes and he picked his way between the rocks. He easily avoided the monstrous sentries his uncle had posted, all of whom were looking for approaching threats, rather than escaping Guerrero family members in any case. By the time the sun rose violently above the eastern mountains he was on the floor of the valley, walking down a little used dirt road toward the Gladwell Ranch and whistling a happy tune. The youngest Gladwell daughter was pretty in that well-fed blond, Midwestern kind of way that Sol preferred. Her family liked him, too. They would be happy to see him.

Two hours later he found himself seated on their front poach, enjoying a glass of iced tea while he worked his way through his considerable repertoire of Tom T. Hall songs. Solstice knew how to play all sorts of things. Like the great bluesman Robert Johnson, he worked hard at learning whatever he thought an audience might want to hear: Flamenco, Mariachi, Country, Rock. Even Folk. Unsurprisingly, the ranch's oldsters loved old '60s and '70s Country, and Ariel was so generally enamored with the young musician that she would listen to him play *Pop Goes the Weasel* Hendrix style with his guitar on fire without complaint. In fact, he was working his way through *I Care* when three white SUVs with emblems on their doors came tearing up the gravel driveway, ignoring the sign which requested that visitors keep their speed down to protect the family's dogs. They pulled to a halt directly in front of the ranch house, and twelve armed men got out of the vehicles simultaneously.

Somebody's been practicing, thought Sol wryly. Then he set his guitar carefully down, leaning it next to his chair.

Mrs. Gladwell rose to her feet, put her battered white cowboy hat on her head, and walked out to greet them. "Good morning, gentlemen," she said politely, "what can I do for you today?" One of the men produced a badge, held it in front of her face until she nodded, and then placed it back in his pocket.

"Ma'am, my name is Breckenridge, and I'm from the Department of Homeland Security. I'm looking for a number of suspected terrorists we believe are hiding in the area." He was extraordinarily polite. Sol thought he sounded sincere as well, which made him feel oddly guilty. "May I ask you some questions?"

"Of course," she replied. "Though my family and our hands don't leave the ranch very often, so I'm not sure of what help we can be."

Breckenridge nodded. "That's fine, Ma'am, as long as you answer to the best of your abilities." He removed a small notepad from the breast pocket of his jacket. Sol thought it was somewhat cool in an old school, Colombo kind of way. "Have you seen or do you know the whereabouts of a Jasper Herndon?"

She frowned. "I don't think I know a Jasper Herndon."

"He also goes by the name Hippie."

"Oh, yes," she smiled. "I know him. Odd man. But I haven't seen him in weeks."

"How about a man named Rusty Guerrero? Do you know him?"

"Everybody knows Rusty," she replied. "He's what you might call 'colorful.' But I haven't seen him in a few weeks, either."

"Have you seen any members of his family recently? Say, in the last two or three days?"

She shook her head again. "They don't leave their place all that often. We usually see them at dances, town dinners, and that sort of thing."

He nodded, and then peered at the people assembled on her front porch. Sol held his breath. The man's light blue eyes moved from person to person until they finally settled on him. They seemed to bore into his soul, looking for guilt.

Sol gulped.

"How about that kid over there?" he asked after a few, pregnant minutes had passed, "The one with the guitar. He looks a lot like one of Guerrero's sons."

She laughed. Sol began to get the idea that Mrs. Gladwell had lied to the police before. "That's Lupe. He's one of my hands. Grew up on a ranch in Jalisco. He doesn't speak a lot of English, but you can talk to him if you like."

"He seems pretty young to be a ranch hand," offered Breckenridge, "and awful white to be from Jalisco, if you'll pardon the expression."

"What? You think they all look alike?"

"No," he responded. "But how many of them look exactly like the photograph of Solstice Guerrero I was shown this morning?"

Sol realized that all of Breckenridge's companions were staring directly at him now. Several of them had moved their hands to the butts of their pistols, probably subconsciously. It made him extremely nervous.

"Look," replied Mrs. Gladwell evenly, "this man's name is Lupe Maldonado. He's a ranch hand. I have his paperwork around here somewhere, if you'll give me a few moments to look for it…"

Breckenridge was no longer paying any attention to her.

"Solstice Guerrero," he said, looking directly at Sol and speaking slowly. "I want you to put your hands in the air and walk over here. Slowly. We don't want to hurt you, but there are questions we need to ask you. You can help your father a lot by coming with us peacefully."

Again, it sounded to Sol like the man was being sincere. But he wasn't going to go anywhere with him. He was going to run for it. However, he couldn't go anywhere without his beloved Santos Hernandez. Without thinking, he reached down for its battered neck.

"He's going for his gun!" he heard a man shout. Almost in the same instant he heard Breckenridge scream "No!" Sol looked up just in time to see the muzzle flash.

The guitar dropped to the ground with a horrible crunch. Then came darkness.

Shutup Amy ended up delivering the news of his son's death to Rusty Guerrero. She was one of the few people who knew where his brother's lair was. She looked guilty, as if his murder had somehow been her fault. The old man simply listened, emotionless, until she'd finished explaining everything Mrs. Gladwell had told her about his son's murder. Then he walked silently out to the cliff nearby and stared, unmoving, at the Hualapai Valley below.

Karlotte had burst into tears at the news of her son's death – as had, oddly, his normally unflappable brother Hugo. They clung to one another, their tears cascading into the dust. Cassidy simply stood dumfounded, unable to make up her mind how to respond. Finally, she went back inside of the complex, and wordlessly resumed helping Heckle and Jeckle feed the various experimental animals within. Guerrero just stood where he was through the twilight; letting the no-see-ums, mosquitoes, and horseflies feed upon his exposed flesh. He looked confused, as if for the first time in his life he had no idea of what to do. Finally, as the almost-full moon rose huge and intimidating above the eastern horizon, he looked accusingly up at the heavens.

He thought of all the things his beloved son would now never be. All of those limitless possibilities snuffed out in a moment of stupidity. Roads that could never be taken, conversations that would never happen, grandchildren that would never bounce upon his aged knee. It was too much to bear.

"What the fuck!" he screamed, still looking upward, "What kind of fucking God punishes a man through his children? What kind of sick bastard could even think of doing such a thing? Why? WHY?"

He was shaking with fury now. He clenched and unclenched his huge fists, as if they of their own accord were looking for a divine throat to strangle. His hatred, impotence, and self-loathing hung palatably in the air about him, like a cloud of aetheric dust kicked up in the wake of his rage. There was a hint of something, though it was hard to pinpoint what it might be. Perhaps the smell that wafted across the battlefield just before Napoleon met Wellington, or the scent that filled the air when Alexander the Great's Macedonians smashed into Darius' Persians: the faint pressure given off as a storm of doom is about to break.

"You wanna know why?" asked a familiar voice. "Because sometimes it's the only way He can get your attention."

Guerrero spun in surprise, his rage instantly forgotten.

"Sol?" he said softly, hesitantly. "Sol? Son, is that really you?"

"Yes," said the voice sadly, "And, at the same time, no."

A figure stepped from the moonlight shadow cast by a nearby boulder. It was Solstice; or, rather, it had been. The bullet hole was clearly visible on his forehead. His skin was a blue-gray color; his handsome eyes were dead and vacant.

"So," commented Guerrero flatly, disappointment evident in his voice. "They really did kill you."

"Yes," Sol bent forward so that his father could see the ghastly exit wound on the back of his skull. "It was a stupid thing. I reached down to pick up granddad's guitar and one of the cops thought I was reaching for a gun."

He tapped his forehead. It made an unnatural, somehow hollow sound. "Great shot, especially with a nine millimeter handgun. Breckenridge – the guy in charge – tried to stop him, but..."

"That won't save him," his father replied darkly. "He's a dead man all the same."

"Dad," Sol replied gently, "I'm a dead man. Kid. Er, teenager. In any case, you wanted to know why God does what he does?

Because of sonofabitch family patriarchs like you, that's why. Abraham? Noah? Saul? Read your Bible: they were flawed, dangerous men. Like you."

"Without sacrifice You. Will. Not. Listen."

"How about Job?" retorted Guerrero, "He was a blameless man. The Bible says that too. And God fucked him over all the same."

"You ain't him, Pops. You're more like those other guys."

Solstice held out his left hand, palm extended upward. With his right hand he reached into his filthy jeans and pulled out three tiny bits of bloody gristle. He set them on his open palm and tapped them. With a sputter they sprang to life, spinning and throbbing, spraying tiny amounts of flesh and bone outward as they melted and grew, grew and melted. They reshaped themselves repeatedly until, finally, three tiny figures stood where the bits of flesh had once been. Guerrero recognized them: Joe Carson and those two DEA agents. They glared accusingly at him with their miniature zombie eyes. He glared right back, unimpressed by the undead.

"It wasn't easy to find bits of their bodies, let me tell you," Revenant Solstice said conversationally, "especially these two guys."

He tapped the tiny DEA zombie agents on their heads.

"I had to pull them out of Phat Albert's scat. Not very pleasant, even when you're dead."

"How did you get loose, anyhow?" asked Guerrero, trying to change the subject.

"I unzipped the body bag and left. Nobody was paying any attention."

At this Guerrero began to pace angrily about, not looking directly at his son's corpse. *They murdered him, and then didn't bother to keep track of his body?* He thought furiously. *Just another in a long line of reasons to kill them all.*

"Dad, you need to stop this. It's killed us. It will kill more if you don't end it now. Turn yourself in." He smiled; a ghastly, blackened thing. "The feds really screwed the pooch when they shot me down in front of the Gladwells. You haven't killed anyone. They have. It'll balance out in court; if it even goes to court. None of the players involved wants this thing anymore. It'll be okay."

"So, God brought you back from the dead to give me fucking legal advice?"

"His ways *are* pretty mysterious, Pops."

"Can He bring you back to life?" Rusty said bitterly. "No, let me rephrase that: *will* He bring you back to life? I mean, real life? Will He do that?"

"No," Sol replied. "That's done."

"Then no," his father replied angrily, though not at him. "When those fuckers killed you, they killed what was best in me. They murdered all the Love I had inside. Now I am Vengeance."

"Don't do it, dad!" pleaded the shade of Solstice Guerrero. Even the tiny men looked up pleadingly from his blue palm, still outstretched. "Don't call them. Don't ask them."

"It is done," he replied. Guerrero turned and began to walk away. "I didn't have to do anything. It was done the moment I found out you were dead. I felt the desert wind passing through me, taking word away to all of its corners."

"Then stop them!" he pleaded. "Think about mom. Hugo. Cassidy. Your friends."

"I am," he replied, and vanished into the cave. Revenant Solstice looked sadly down at his tiny companions, who looked back at him with equally mournful expressions. Then they all simultaneously shook their heads.

"Yes," he answered their unspoken question. "Even when they see, they do not believe. That's just like in the Bible too."

One storm began to grow before the other even had a chance to form. As he had told the shade of his son, the dark wind that had blown through Rusty Guerrero's soul traveled to the distant corners of the Black Rock Desert. It whistled deep within the sandy gullies of the Smoke Creek, up to the jagged peaks of the Granites, and down across the dry Calicos into the stark Jackson Range. It blew across High Rock Canyon, then down across the flat desolate surface of the Playa. It swirled around the base of the massive granite edifice of the Black Rock itself. It bubbled up through isolated hot springs. It fell down along with isolated, unexpected bursts of rain. It traveled along the icy surface of Pyramid Lake.

Some heard the wind but did not understand: mostly hunters, off-roaders, and the odd tourist, camping in the shade of their $50,000 recreational vehicles. Others heard and understood; just as the desert itself had heard and understood. It was going to war, and those that heard and understood the message were drafted without exception.

Some that were called were men. Others *had been* men, while yet others had never been men. Those that used material objects gathered what they needed. Those that didn't simply stopped grazing, chewing, or rending and began making their way toward the town of Hualapai. They walked, trotted, scurried, and slithered. They burrowed and flew. Some climbed onto mounts, others into sandrails or onto motorcycles.

Many of these newly minted allies didn't like one another. In fact, more than a few of them had tried to kill one another at some point in the last ten years. Yes, as another desert culture in another place at another time once wisely phrased it; I against my brother, my brother and I against my cousin, and my brother, my cousin, and I against the world.

Agent Esperanza Gomez wanted to get drunk. This wasn't normal for her. It wasn't that she never drank. It was more that she seldom drank and, when she did, she liked to drink alone. But there was something about the Nevada desert in summer that made you want to get drunk and stay that way. Maybe it was the heat. Maybe it was the monotonous, unchanging brown of the landscape, or the way the dust got into everything, no matter how many times you washed and cleaned.

No matter: there it was. The desire to get shitfaced.

There were, of course, other reasons. She'd lost two of her team – two of her friends, really – to something she couldn't understand. She was stuck somewhere profoundly depressing on many levels. Deserted by its inhabitants, the town of Hualapai had filled up with a pseudo-population of law enforcement personnel, various sorts of state regulatory agents, and the media. The latter, confronted with tight-lipped public servants and having little else to do, were getting drunk and interviewing one another. They had begun helping themselves to the alcohol in Hank's Hualapai Club and the now abandoned Hualapai General Store the day before.

Among the law enforcement types, the usual game of bullshit one-upmanship had begun, with everyone puffing up their chests and claiming jurisdiction over this-and-that... until Guerrero's kid had been brought in dead by that Homeland Security team a few hours ago, that is. Now the reverse was taking place. Chests had deflated and nobody was in charge of anything anymore. Word had somehow gotten to the press that a teenager had been killed, probably by law enforcement. The lack of any organized and coherent statement by the assembled personnel had lead to a frenzy of speculation, almost certainly inaccurate and damning.

So, she thought wearily, *another Ruby Ridge. What the hell is it about this part of the country that causes these damn things? Does the combination of heat, five-percent humidity, and juniper trees cause the collective IQ to drop 50 points?*

She really had no idea what had happened with Guerrero's kid. But she knew what the result would be. Guerrero would come looking for revenge. She'd looked into the man's eyes, taken his measure, and knew one thing. He. Would. Come. Looking.

And he wouldn't come alone.

She didn't blame him, really. She imagined that she might do the same thing in his shoes. All the same, she did not intend to join that BLM agent, Ba Trihn, Stevens, and his kid on the list of the dead martyred by his personal war. The moment she saw him, he was dead – and that was that. It wasn't personal. It was survival.

■

After a day of fighting it, she finally gave in. She and Johnson, the last surviving member of her MET team, wandered into Hank's Club, went behind the bar, and selected a couple of bottles. A southerner to the core, Johnson found a reasonably priced bottle of premium Rev. Elijah Craig Kentucky bourbon, while she picked a bottle of Don Julio 1942 tequila (which was neither reasonable nor inexpensive). They left a hundred dollar bill under the cash register; a courtesy that few of their fellows had paid the absent owner of the establishment.

They wandered away from their associates toward the edge of town. There, where Hualapai's humble street grid stopped and the sparsely covered dunes of the desert started, they found a singlewide that had been converted into a home. It was freshly painted, though admittedly in a shockingly tacky pastel pink, with new trim in what Johnson referred to as "Barney-ass purple." A front and back porch had been carefully constructed out of stained wood, and it had an immaculate if tiny front yard.

The two of them wandered around back to where the owner had carefully built a chain link fence that contained a series of small flowerbeds, a vegetable garden, and perhaps fifteen feet of carefully maintained sod. They let themselves through the fence and had a seat on a pair of folding chairs that were positioned by the shade cast by the late afternoon sun.

"Well, Ma'am," commented Johnson, taking a plug off his whisky bottle with a wince, "somebody sure put a lot of lipstick on this particular pig."

"Whatcha gonna do?" she shrugged, and then winced in turn as the Don Julio struck her throat. "Stick homes are rare out here. It's just a bitch to build one. Whatever contractor you hire has to come all the way up from Reno – with all that extra pay for travel."

"Yeah, I guess you're right," he replied. "And don't get me wrong. I understand these people pretty well. I don't exactly come from the aristocracy myself."

Gonzales snorted at that. Johnson was, from the top of his sunburned head to the bottom of his big toe, a true redneck.

"I figure there ain't any economy out here besides that Burning Man Festival of theirs," he continued, "plus whatever tourism huntin' and fishin' brings in. Maybe throw a bit of ranching and farming in where you've got the water. Most of these people would be retired, living off their social security and whatever pension they have. The rest live hardscrabble: cowboying, working at one of the two or three little stores, or doing odd jobs for the old people. Not an easy existence."

She nodded slowly, and then frowned.

"Guerrero seemed happy enough with his."

Out on the Playa floor a storm was beginning to form. She'd seen them before out here: massive plumes of dust blown into the air by winds traveling north, focused out onto its desolate surface by the canyons that led in from eastern California. The wind blew down out of the Sierras, traveled around the corner of the Granites, and hit the dry, dusty surface of the old alkaline lakebed head on. In her brief time out here she'd seen storms that, had they been on the ocean, would have sent the most experienced ship's captain fleeing to port in alarm. Except these were all composed of blinding tan sand, not water.

Funny thing, though. The storm looked as though it was coming from the wrong direction.

She took another hit of tequila and peered out into the desert. It was odd, though possible, of course. She'd heard that winds sometimes came down from Siberia via Alaska. However, it couldn't be very common. It was visibly picking up strength too.

"Do you see that, Johnson?"

"Yes Ma'am. Looks as though it's coming right for us."

It did too. The storm of dust was building into a massive wall, hundreds of feet high, like a tidal wave rolling toward an unsuspecting beach.

"I don't..." Johnson hesitated. He took another drink. Then he spoke slowly, carefully. "I don't like the looks of that very much, Ma'am."

"I don't either," she replied. In the distance, she thought she could make out the forms of tiny figures moving in the storm. That had to be an illusion. Who would be out in anything like that?

It grew closer.

"You know, Ma'am," he continued, "I'm not normally one to see danger where there ain't any. But I think I see things moving around at the very front of that storm; maybe just outside the edge of it. Course, that shouldn't be possible, but, ah..."

"Me too," she nodded, peering even harder into the gathering brown chaos. The tequila was starting to make her feel a little light headed. Something nagged at her like an infected hangnail. Something at the edge of her consciousness that wouldn't, possibly shouldn't, materialize. Something was wrong that she couldn't put her finger on.

They sat silently for a moment as the storm continued to move forward toward the tiny town of Hualapai. Now she knew what it felt like to be a fiddler crab, scuttling along a beach in Hawaii right before some tsunami came crashing down on its head. Yet they were both rooted to the spot, drinking and watching the awful spectacle with the certainty of the damned.

Gomez wondered idly how many times the inhabitants of the tiny house sat in precisely this spot on the same chairs, watching the epic weather patterns of the desert stir and spin like something demonic.

How could you bear to live with such a monster right at your back porch? She thought. *How could you live knowing how small you were? How insignificant in the face of such terrible nature?*

Then with a suddenness that shocked her, the storm was upon them.

The wind was incredible, the visibility nonexistent. But their eyes were protected by sunglasses and they sat transfixed as the ability to see what was around them dropped and dropped. Gomez realized that she could no longer see more than ten or fifteen feet in front of her. It was amusing in a ghastly sort of way. She could see what brought all the people out to that festival once a year: the incredible, epic desolation of it all.

Then she saw the first one.

She wasn't certain what it was at first. It loped through the dust at the edge of her vision. It was definitely humanoid, but too large to be a man. Its arms were far too long and its legs bent the wrong way. It turned to look at her, its large eyes green-on-white. Then, before she could make out its features, it turned and vanished into the wall of brown mist.

"Jesus H Fucking Christ," said Johnson with no particular passion. Gomez guessed that he was getting used to being shocked. "What the fuck was that?"

All the same, he fumbled for the pistol at his side.

Next came a herd of horses: fierce and wild with their eyes gleaming. By the dozens they poured around the sides of the house, screaming rage and hatred. Gomez caught a glimpse of yellow fangs where there should have been square, white teeth. Their eyes were wild, rolling around their long heads in an alien manner.

Then they too were gone. That's when the shooting started.

That broke her from her trance. She followed Johnson's example, withdrawing her pistol from the tactical holster on her hip.

"Come on!" she screamed at him, suddenly alert to the danger that surrounded them. She dashed off the porch without waiting to see whether or not he was following her and ran around the side of the house.

All about her blinded men fired into the swirling dust. It was difficult to make out who was who or what was what. There were screams. She ran forward, crouching low to avoid stray bullets with her finger on the trigger. She dashed across the street to another house, and then pressed her back against the wall in an attempt to present a smaller target to... whatever they were.

What she observed was unbelievable. Sanity cracking. Hualapai had become hell on earth and chaos. She could only bear witness to the horror that unfolded around her, as inevitable and unstoppable as a hurricane.

...what looked like a fireman complete with gas mask, helmet, enormous boots, and a black, fireproof jacket staggered out of the dust holding a huge ax in his hand. He was tall and lanky. An ATF agent fired at him: once, twice. The man staggered back as the bullets hit his chest with a sick, wet sound. Then with a grunt, he ran forward and buried the ax in the agent's shoulder. The man screamed as they both fell into the dust outside of her vision...

...a huge mechanical dragon lumbered out of the dust. It was made of light, rusted pig iron, and spray paint. Seated on its back were two girls: one with a red Mohawk, the other with short, spiky white hair. They wore aviator goggles and were covered in dust. Tools dangled from wide leather belts slung provocatively on their hips.

Suddenly, bullets bounced off the metallic hide of the creature. The huge apparatus turned, its blind, Volkswagen-sized head swinging toward the threat. It opened its ragged jaws and an enormous plume of flame shot from its mouth at a target Gonzales could not see. There were screams of agony, followed by a smell that reminded her of bacon. Finally, the terrifying thing lumbered out of her vision back into the dust...

...she stared in disbelief as a tiny army of humanoid mice armed with spears swarmed over a screaming man, stabbing at his exposed skin with their razor sharp tips as he ran blindly about, futilely attempting to dislodge them from his ravaged flesh...

...Breckenridge and his Homeland Security men had formed a square using their cars. They were using it like an old time wagon circle to create a protective barrier between themselves and the blood soaked chaos that swirled around them. They were leaned across the hoods of their vehicles, carefully taking aim at anything that wasn't wearing a windbreaker with letters across the back. So far, it had worked: they were unscathed by the carnage.

Then something impossible walked around the side of Hank's Hualapai Club.

Gomez blinked at the impossible thing. It was *huge,* naked, and female – like a giant Jane Mansfield, or a monstrous Macy's Day Parade Marilyn Monroe balloon. Its breasts were the size of tents; its legs like the cement pylons used to hold up freeway overpasses. Around its feet scampered blurry, feral figures that howled and gibbered with excitement as they neared the trapped men.

Terrified, the Homeland Security men all opened fire at once. The unthinkable female *thing* only laughed, its voice deep and booming, yet somehow oddly sensual at the same time. It made Gomez feel... uncomfortable to listen to that sound. Dirty somehow. It lumbered forward, shoving the men's huge SUVs out of the way with the same level of effort as one might use to shove small pieces of furniture aside. Then, as the creatures that scampered about its feet leaped snarling upon the agents, it picked up Breckenridge under one arm like a naughty child and strode away laughing, its enormous, sexual voice booming like thunder, out into the blinding brown cloud and out of sight...

...she watched as what appeared to be El Santo, the masked Mexican wrestler complete with sequined cape and muscular bare chest, leaped from the roof of a nearby doublewide, tackling a BLM agent. The two men rolled about on the ground, struggling, and then they too tumbled out of her field of vision.

That's impossible! Gomez thought to herself. *Santo's been dead for years.* Then she decided that she really didn't want to know...

...a tall, rugged-looking black man with gray dreadlocks strode out of the storm: fierce looking, with teeth that had been filed down to points. He gestured at something she could not see, and then brought an odd-looking whistle to his lips from a chain that hung around his neck. He blew it silently. Enormous, lanky dogs the size of small ponies came bounding out of the storm: howling, seething, bloodcurdling, suppressed rage and fury boiling out of them in waves. They seemed unstoppable, the living embodiment of everything man had ever feared in his genial, complacent servant Dog.

Then they bounded off out of her vision, once again to the sounds of gunshots and screaming. The man turned and, seeing her for the first time, smiled with his hideous shark's mouth. Then he too strode away into the brown curtain of horror...

...a cowboy on a dappled horse road out of the tan mist, the six guns in his hands firing at targets she could not see. He was dressed in a brown duster, his face covered by a tattered red bandanna that only left his narrowed eyes visible. With a shock, Gomez realized that this was not a man at all, but an elderly woman. Her gray hair streamed out wildly from beneath a weather-beaten hat as she pulled her horse about, causing it to rear up on its hind legs with a scream. For a moment, the two women locked eyes: the old woman's pale and blue, hers dark and brown. Then the cowgirl nodded, turned away, and vanished like the rest...

■

Gomez had been frozen: unable to move, unable to respond to the carnival of horrors around her. Guerrero had told her the truth. They genuinely hadn't known what they were playing with. Sweat poured from her brow, mixing with the dust to form rivulets of mud as it dripped down her delicate features. She could feel her bowels trying to release and the contents of her stomach trying to rise up her throat. She forced them both back under control with effort, stiffened herself, and rose from her crouch. She chambered a round in her Glock, knowing that it was time to join the fray – and knowing with certainly that she would die doing it.

Then, without warning, she felt the touch of something metallic on her neck. Agent Esperanza Gomez looked down in horror to see an enormous hunting knife pressed against her throat. She could feel its razor edge cutting into the flesh above her windpipe.

"Easy now agent," said a familiar voice. "Drop the gun. Slowly."

Gomez did as she was told. The Glock dropped from her hand, hitting the ground with a faint thud.

"Good," said Rusty Guerrero.

"Go ahead Rusty, you monstrous fucker." snarled Gomez. "Go head and cut my throat and be done with it."

To her surprise, she found that she meant what she'd said too. She wasn't sure that she wanted to go on living having seen the horrors that she'd witnessed on this day. Her view of reality wouldn't – couldn't – ever be the same again. She felt broken.

She heard him chuckling darkly behind her. Felt the heat of his breath on her ear.

"Don't tempt me," he said. "After what you people did to my little boy, I could murder the entire world and it wouldn't be enough. I could spill every drop of blood in San Francisco and Los Angeles. I could drown the West in an ocean of clot, bile, and gore and it wouldn't satiate my hatred. It wouldn't even come close."

Then he sighed.

"But that's not what Sol would have wanted." Guerrero continued. "I've had my revenge. And now, if you're interested, I have a plan to end all this."

"I'm listening." Gomez responded through gritted teeth.

"Then all right. You've killed, we've killed. There's no fucking justice in it anywhere. It's like the Tar Baby in that Disney film they won't show anymore: the more we hit each other, the more stuck we get. Now we're all covered in nasty shit and there doesn't seem to be any way to get it off or get loose from it.

"Well," he continued, "I've got a plan to get us all unstuck and make everyone happy: you, your people, Willow, us. Everyone. Now listen..."

Salvatore Giovanni sat on his brother-in-law Mike's living room couch in his underwear. He wore a stained sleeveless T-shirt, smelled bad, and had a five o'clock shadow. Normally he would have been embarrassed; the Sheriff was a fastidious and organized man. Now he just didn't give a damn.

His brother-in-law sat next to him, smoking a cigarette. Empty and partially empty cans of Coors Light lay strewn about the room. They'd already finished their first case and were working on a second one. Sal was so drunk he almost felt sober. For what had seemed like days he'd done nothing but watch the local news. It was mostly the sort of crap you expected in Reno: somebody had died in a motorcycle crash during Street Vibrations, Nevada's prison system was woefully underfunded, the governor had not one but two mistresses and didn't really care who knew, and the Californians weren't coming over the mountains to spend money as they used to. Blah blah blah.

He wanted to go home, but he knew that Uncle Hank had been right. Now was a bad, possibly career-ending, time for him to be there. For all he knew he had no home to go to. His tiny town of 160 souls had been scattered to the winds and was possibly obliterated forever. He knew that eventually he would hear something like the latter on TV. It was as predictable as death and taxes. What he was curious about was the size, shape, and reek of that turd when it appeared in the punchbowl of his life.

Fucking Rusty, he thought with drunken, sloshy anger. *For that matter fucking BLM, fucking water pipeline, and fucking...*

Then PLOP, there it was, right in the punchbowl.

Sal had been switching from news channel to news channel, even forcing himself briefly to watch MSNBC. When Senator Henry Willow's bespectacled face – pale, bald, and solemn as a preacher – appeared on the six o'clock news, he didn't know which station it was, and had no idea whether this was because he was drunk, or because he was so exhausted he didn't care.

"I'm afraid that I have tragic news from Nevada," began Willow, "not only for my fellow citizens in the Silver State, but for the country as well. Tragic not only for the families of the brave law enforcement officers who gave their lives trying to defend those citizens, but for the animals and even the plants of northwestern part of Washoe County."

Sal and his brother-in-law sat up straight.

"Before I continue, I want you to know that you are in no danger. I repeat: there is no danger." He held up a piece of paper. "I will be reading a brief statement. Afterwards I will take questions.

"It is my sad duty to inform you," he continued after a moment, "that violent terrorist extremist elements have managed to create and release a destructive and highly contagious biological weapon in the vicinity of Hualapai, Nevada. This bio-terror device appears to be a weaponized aerosol containing a highly virulent form of rabies. Like normal rabies, it appears to be effective on all mammalian species, including humans. It does, however, not appear to be contagious. I repeat: it is not contagious."

"But didn't he just say that..." began Mike.

"Of course!" he snapped back. "But that's what the asshole does best. Now shut up and let me listen."

"...fast acting." Willow went on. "But it must be inhaled in its aerosol form to be effective. In all observed cases, it kills its host so quickly that it has no chance to incubate and reproduce. We believe the hate group or groups involved in creating this weapon released a large amount into a storm headed in the direction of Hualapai in the hopes that it would kill the agents sent there to apprehend them and shut down their ring before it could murder any more innocent people."

"This disease, which as of yet has no name, appears to drive its victims violently insane before they die. Fortunately, most of the inhabitants of Hualapai were evacuated to safety, as were many law enforcement agents. We also believe that the terrorists themselves were killed by the toxins they released into the air: an ironic but fitting end for such evil men."

"As we speak, Homeland Security in conjunction with the FBI's anti-terrorism division and state and local California, Nevada, and Oregon HAZMAT teams are sealing off all access to the area of the

Black Rock Desert and the town of Hualapai. An indefinite quarantine has been placed on that area until the proper experts can ascertain the nature of the danger contained therein. This may take weeks, months, or possibly even years. We don't have enough data yet to say."

"One thing we do know is that this menace has been contained. Furthermore, as tragic as the loss of any life is, let alone the dozens of lives that have been lost in this preventable and horrifying incident, let this stand as an example of the hardiness and independence of the people of Nevada and America, and to our willingness to stand against those who would spread hate and attack or democratic and free way of life..."

Sal's brother-in-law hit the mute button and then turned to him.

"Well ain't-that-some-shit?" he said slowly, trying to digest the Senator's typically nonsensical speech through a haze of Coors. "What did that fucking *mean*, exactly?"

Sal looked back, his eyes huge. Then he began to laugh. He laughed and laughed, and couldn't stop laughing until it had begun to hurt. Then he coughed instead of laughing.

"What's so damn funny? Your town infected with weaponized aerosolized whatever-it-is. There's nothing funny about that."

"Hualapai ain't infected with shit," Sal managed to croak out between coughs. "Guerrero just won his war."

Then the former sheriff of Hualapai thought about Agent Gomez and wondered if there might be an opening on her MET team.

■

They gathered at the crossroads.

It was 6:00 AM; one of the most pleasant times of the day to be in the desert in any of its three hot seasons. The two unmarked gravel roads met on the far side of the Black Rock in the direction of eastern Oregon over 100 miles north of Hualapai. The HAZMAT teams, backed up by the FBI and National Guard units from each of the three neighboring states, hadn't yet finished sealing off the desert and, in any case, two of the four groups assembled would have been allowed through.

As had been agreed upon, each of the parties involved was represented by only two people, unarmed. Guerrero stood in the western road: his arms folded, his expression grim, yet somehow arrogant. He had won, had he not? Uncle Hank stood behind him.

On the northern road stood Shutup Amy. She'd arrived on a sandrail – a stripped down dune buggy – driven by what appeared to be a Mexican wrestler, who sat in the vehicle with his arms also folded. She too glared at the others with a mixture of annoyance and hostility.

Jefferson Q. Harrison stood in the eastern road, flanked by one of Willow's bland young men. Clad in immaculate black business suits and dark glasses, the wind whipped their ties about their shoulders. Cell phones were slung on their hips like six-guns. They stared blandly back at Guerrero and Amy as if showing emotion, or even faint interest, were beneath them. Alone among the people gathered they did not seem to be covered in fine, tan dust.

Finally, Gomez and Johnson stood in the south road, still wearing their blue DEA windbreakers. Neither indifferent nor angry, they just looked tired.

Uncle Hank began, counting on his fingers.

"Just so there can be no misunderstandings, let's review the terms of our agreement. One: Guerrero and Hippie are legally dead. They will not be pursued or harassed by law enforcement."

"So long as they never come down out of this desert," interjected Harrison. "Furthermore, if they ever get spotted by some hunter, tourist, or Burner hanging out in Hualapai, we hunt them down like dogs and go for the death penalty."

"And no more dope growing for either of them." growled Gomez. "That's over with. They'll have to find some other way of making a living."

"Well," replied Guerrero speculatively, "we could always try gun running."

"Shut up, Rusty," Uncle Hank said firmly. He gave his companion a hard look, "Agreed. Hippie and Guerrero stay out in the high desert for the rest of their lives. They don't go drinking in town, they don't drive to Spanish Springs for supplies, nothing."

After a moment, Guerrero nodded.

"Two," continued Uncle Hank. "Willow will make sure that this place is declared uninhabitable for the next eight months; but, discreetly, any locals that wish to return are allowed back in. That will give us time to clean up and put our house in order, so to speak, but still allow Oberon and his people to get Burning Man ready for next year."

"Speaking of which," interrupted Shutup Amy, "the boss wants you to know how pissed off he is that you didn't include him in any of this before you decided to do it."

"Fuck," spat out Hank. "Guerrero didn't include any of us in this when he decided to do it. Oberon can take a number."

"Do you have any idea how this will affect our ticket sales?" she complained.

Hank shrugged. "It's the best we can do. Plus, people have short memories. A year from now they probably won't even remember this happened."

"Sad, but probably true," she agreed.

"Three," he continued, "we all stick to the story that some unknown terrorist group — whoever they might be — released a bunch of aerosolized super-rabies into that storm, driving everyone violently insane. Nothing any of the survivors saw was real. It was all a hallucination; they simply got a lesser dose, which passed through their system without causing permanent harm or being contagious.

"All of the bullet and... other wounds are either from people accidentally shooting each other in terror, or are due to the terrible actions of now deceased members of a nebulous and unspecified hate group. No coming back up here to 'better investigate' later. No sending some kind of X Files assholes, either. Right, Gomez?"

Both she and her companion nodded wordlessly. Having not been present for the aforementioned storm, Willow's men gave them an odd look.

"Four, and perhaps most importantly," Hank went on. "Nobody's name get associated, whether publicly or in private records, with this now defunct nebulous hate group. Everything remains vague and alleged. The Senator does what he does best — dances around any actual substance — outside of the fact that several dozen people died tragically."

"And after eight months?" asked Jefferson.

"People will be nervous coming out here at first, what with the 'extremists' and mystery disease," answered Hank. "But I think that, within a few years, the hunters, off-roaders, and Burners the like to come out here will be about as nervous as people who go skiing in Idaho are about '80s Nazi skinheads: which is to say, not at all."

They all nodded at this.

"You know," said Gomez, looking directly at Guerrero, "a lot of good people died because one man and his dumbass friend didn't trust the system enough to go to trial over something they would have won."

Guerrero stared blandly back, silent for few moments.

"No," he said at last, "a lot of people died because the system isn't trustworthy enough *not* to convict a man for defending his home."

"Enough," said Uncle Hank. "What's done is done. Now we have to make the best of the situation we're in."

He nodded toward Willow's bodyguard.

"The Senator will come out on top, smelling like a rose like he always does. I give the DEA my word, as does Guerrero and everybody else, that there will be no more dope growing in the Black Rock Desert. There was a terrible price tag, but in the long run the government won that one too."

"The Burning Man Festival will continue," he nodded at Shutup Amy, "even if ticket sales are down for a few years. People's memories are short, and their love of going to North America's most epic parties isn't likely to vanish.

"And, finally," he said, turning to Rusty Guerrero, "you, your Island-Of-Doctor-Moreau-Ass family, and your animal friends can go back to your Manson Family Robinson existence, so long as you don't screw up. Agreed?"

Slowly Rusty nodded.

"Right," said Jefferson. "It's agreed then. We meet here precisely at this time eight months from now to decide whether or not everyone's kept up their end of the deal."

The all nodded at once, then turned and walked back to their vehicles, talking among themselves. Uncle Hank and Guerrero walked away as well, but not back to a vehicle. They walked silently across the seemingly infinite floor of the desert for some time. Finally, they went around the side of a large dune covered with low, scruffy grass. There on the other side sat the corpse of Sol Guerrero, his hands on his knees, looking up at the sky absently for the entire world like a normal teenager.

"So," he said to the two men as they approached, "none of this was exactly what He wanted. But, as the silent partner in this agreement, He understands. He'll be watching in eight months too."

"He's always watching."

Hank stared curiously at the undead teenager. "So what now?" he asked.

"Now?" Sol Guerrero answered. "Now life – the most precious, delicate, and beautiful thing in the entire world – goes on."

With that, he lay down and became dust that was soon blown away into the desert wind.

The Angel and the Saint

[Posted to www.midianranchblog.blogspot.com on December 19, 2010]

An Angel tumbled from heaven and struck the ground with such force that she broke her wings. Fortunately, she fell near the cottage of a Sage, who found her and took her home with him. He put her in his bed, tended her wounds, and cared for her until she awoke one day.

"Thank you for taking care of me Sage," exclaimed the Angel, "Soon my wings will heal, and I'll be able to fly back to Heaven where I belong."

This made the Sage very sad because he could clearly see that her wings were forever broken and could never, ever heal. However, because he was a sage, he was also wise enough to know that he could never tell her this: for if she lost her hope of returning to Heaven, she would surely perish from sorrow. He also could not lie to an angel, as she would surely know. So he thought very carefully before he spoke.

"Angel," he said, "It may be that one day you will fly back to Heaven. Until then you will have to learn to live like a normal person. You shall have to learn to walk, speak, learn, work, and play like the rest of us, so that you can be happy until that day comes."

The Angel agreed to learn to do these things, and he taught them to her. In time, she became a special and loving woman, adored by everyone in the Sage's community for her good cheer and compassion, and was happy even though her wings never healed.

Then one day to the Sage's surprise the Angel unfolded her broken wings and flew away, leaving him to wonder: who was really teaching whom?

About the Author

Jason Walters is an author, editor, and lecturer from Nevada's Black Rock Desert. His works include *The Vast White*, *Scourges of the Galaxy*, and *You Gotta Have Character*.

A recluse, exurban refugee, and survivalist, he lives off-grid with his wife, daughter, and numerous animals on a small spread near the town of Gerlach. When not writing, he spends his time target shooting, gardening, and watching Burning Man blow things up on their nearby ranch.

Also from BlackWyrm...

The VAST WHITE
by Jason Walters

Highdome and his crew of cutthroats, monsters, and mutants don't care. They just want to stay alive. But when sorcery backfires and the fury of the Vast White desert is unleashed, the men of the Red Regiment must look inside of themselves to find the strength to survive.
[Dark Fantasy, ages 14+]

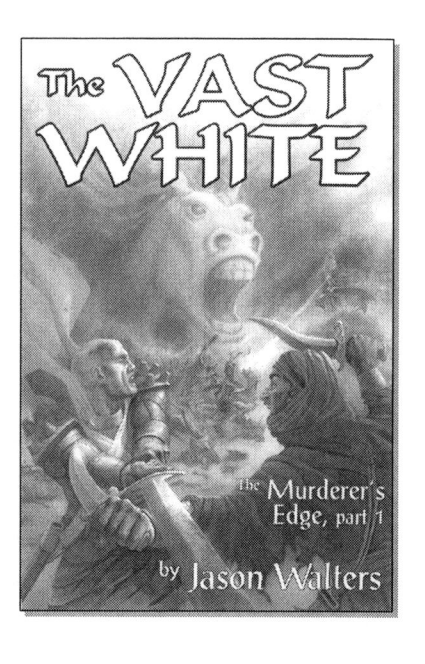

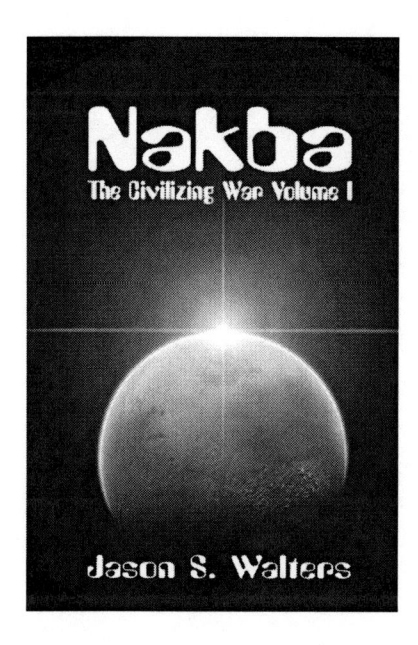

Nakba
The Civilizing War, Volume I
by Jason Walters

All that stands between a newly imperial Earth and the rest of the solar system is a loose coalition of Maasai tribesmen, cloned feminists, shape-shifting humannequins, and vengeful Berbers led by the least likely hero in human history: a young woman with Down syndrome and a bad attitude.
[Science Fiction, ages 14+]

THE RAINBOW CONNECTION
by Ian Harac

One FBI agent
One geekette
One dead munchkin
Parallel worlds galore
An interdimensional conspiracy.

When Matt Anders stumbles across the body of a dead munchkin in a suspect's apartment, a conspiracy begins to unravel that leads him on a reality-jumping adventure to the magical Land of Oz... and beyond!
[Snarky SciFi Thriller, ages 14+]

VINE
an urban legend
by Michael Williams

An amateur theatre director's sensational production starring an eccentric fly-by-night cast and crew draws the attention of ancient and powerful forces. Vine weds Greek tragedy and urban legend with dangerous intoxication, as the drama rushes to its dark and inevitable conclusion.
[Modern Mythic Fiction, ages 14+]